Praise for Catherine Bybee

Wife by Wednesday

"A fun and sizzling romance, great characters that trade verbal spars like fist punches, and the dream of your own royal wedding!"
—Sizzling Hot Book Reviews, 5 Stars

"A good holiday, fireside or bedtime story."
—Manic Reviews, 4½ Stars

"A great story that I hope is the start of a new series."
—The Romance Studio, 4½ Hearts

Married by Monday

"If I hadn't already added Ms. Catherine Bybee to my list of favorite authors, after reading this book I would have been compelled to. This is a book *nobody* should miss, because the magic it contains is awesome."
—Booked Up Reviews, 5 Stars

"Ms. Bybee writes authentic situations and expresses the good and the bad in such an equal way . . . Keeps the reader on the edge of her seat."
—Reading Between the Wines, 5 Stars

"*Married by Monday* was a refreshing read and one I couldn't possibly put down."
—The Romance Studio, 4½ Hearts

FIANCÉ BY FRIDAY

"Bybee knows exactly how to keep readers happy . . . A thrilling pursuit and enough passion to stuff in your back pocket to last for the next few lifetimes . . . The hero and heroine come to life with each flip of the page and will linger long after readers cross the finish line."

—*RT Book Reviews*, 4½ Stars, Top Pick (Hot)

"A tale full of danger and sexual tension . . . the intriguing characters add emotional depth, ensuring readers will race to the perfectly fitting finish."

—*Publishers Weekly*

"Suspense, survival, and chemistry mix in this scintillating read."

—*Booklist*

"Hot romance, a mystery assassin, British royalty, and an alpha Marine . . . this story has it all!"

—*Harlequin Junkie*

SINGLE BY SATURDAY

"Captures readers' hearts and keeps them glued to the pages until the fascinating finish . . . romance lovers will feel the sparks fly . . . almost instantaneously."

—*RT Book Reviews*, 4½ Stars, Top Pick

"[A] wonderfully exciting plot, lots of desire, and some sassy attitude thrown in for good measure!"

—*Harlequin Junkie*

TAKEN BY TUESDAY

"[Bybee] knows exactly how to get bookworms sucked into the perfect storyline; then she casts her spell upon them so they don't escape until they reach the 'Holy Cow!' ending."

—*RT Book Reviews*, 4½ Stars, Top Pick

SEDUCED BY SUNDAY

"You simply can't miss [this novel]. It contains everything a romance reader loves—clever dialogue, three-dimensional characters, and just the right amount of steam to go with that heartwarming love story."

—Brenda Novak, *New York Times* bestselling author

"Bybee hits the mark . . . providing readers with a smart, sophisticated romance between a spirited heroine and a prim hero . . . Passionate and intelligent characters [are] at the heart of this entertaining read."

—*Publishers Weekly*

TREASURED BY THURSDAY

"The Weekday Brides never disappoint and this final installment is by far Bybee's best work to date."

—*RT Book Reviews*, 4½ Stars, Top Pick

"An exquisitely written and complex story brimming with pride, passion, and pulse-pounding danger . . . Readers will gladly make time to savor this winning finale to a wonderful series."

—*Publishers Weekly*, Starred Review

"Bybee concludes her popular Weekday Brides series in a gratifying way with a passionate, troubled couple who may find a happy future if they can just survive and then learn to trust each other. A compelling and entertaining mix of sexy, complicated romance and menacing suspense."

—*Kirkus Reviews*

NOT QUITE DATING

"It's refreshing to read about a man who isn't afraid to fall in love . . . [Jack and Jessie] fit together as a couple and as a family."

—*RT Book Reviews*, 3 Stars (Hot)

"*Not Quite Dating* offers a sweet and satisfying Cinderella fantasy that will keep you smiling long after you've finished reading."

—Kathy Altman, *USA Today*, "Happy Ever After"

"The perfect rags to riches romance . . . The dialogue is inventive and witty, the characters are well drawn out. The storyline is superb and really shines . . . I highly recommend this stand out romance! Catherine Bybee is an automatic buy for me."

—*Harlequin Junkie*, 4½ Hearts

NOT QUITE ENOUGH

"Bybee's gift for creating unforgettable romances cannot be ignored. The third book in the Not Quite series will sweep readers away to a paradise, and they will be intrigued by the thrilling story that accompanies their literary vacation."

—*RT Book Reviews*, 4½ Stars, Top Pick

NOT QUITE FOREVER

"Full of classic Bybee humor, steamy romance, and enough plot twists and turns to keep readers entertained all the way to the very last page."
—Tracy Brogan, bestselling author of the Bell Harbor series

"Magnetic . . . The love scenes are sizzling and the multi-dimensional characters make this a page-turner. Readers will look for earlier installments and eagerly anticipate new ones."
—*Publishers Weekly*

NOT QUITE PERFECT

"This novel flows extremely well and readers will find themselves consuming the witty dialogue and strong imagery in one sitting."
—*RT Book Reviews*

"Don't let the title fool you. *Not Quite Perfect* was actually the perfect story to sweep you away and take you on a pleasant adventure. So sit back, relax, maybe pour a glass of wine, and let Catherine Bybee entertain you with Glen and Mary's playful East Coast–West Coast romance. You won't regret it for a moment."
—*Harlequin Junkie*, 4½ Stars

NOT QUITE CRAZY

"This fast-paced story features credible characters whose appealing relationship is built upon friendship, mutual respect, and sizzling chemistry."
—*Publishers Weekly*

"The plot is filled with twists and turns, but instead of feeling like a never-ending roller coaster, the story maintains a quiet flow. The slow buildup of a romance allows readers to get to know the main characters as individuals and makes the romantic element more organic."

—*RT Book Reviews*

DOING IT OVER

"The romance between fiercely independent Melanie and charming Wyatt heats up even as outsiders threaten to derail their newfound happiness. This novel will hook readers with its warm, inviting characters and the promise for similar future installments."

—*Publishers Weekly*

"This brand-new trilogy, Most Likely To, based on yearbook superlatives, kicks off with a novel that will encourage you to root for the incredibly likable Melanie. Her friends are hilarious and readers will swoon over Wyatt, who is charming and strong. Even Melanie's daughter, Hope, is a hoot! This romance is jam-packed with animated characters, and Bybee displays her creative writing talent wonderfully."

—*RT Book Reviews*, 4 Stars

"With a dialogue full of energy and depth, and a twisting storyline that captured my attention, I would say that *Doing It Over* was a great way to start off a new series. (And look at that gorgeous book cover!) I can't wait to visit River Bend again and see who else gets to find their HEA."

—*Harlequin Junkie*, 4½ Stars

STAYING FOR GOOD

"Bybee's skillfully crafted second Most Likely To contemporary (after *Doing It Over*) brings together former sweethearts who have not forgotten each other in the eleven years since high school. A cast of multidimensional characters brings the story to life and promises enticing future installments."

—*Publishers Weekly*

"Romance fans will be sure to cheer on former high school sweethearts Zoe and Luke right away in *Staying For Good*. Just wait until you see what passion, laughter, reconciliations, and mischief (can you say Vegas?) awaits readers this time around. Highly recommended."

—*Harlequin Junkie*, 4½ Stars

MAKING IT RIGHT

"Intense suspense heightens the scorching romance at the heart of Bybee's outstanding third Most Likely To contemporary (after *Staying For Good*). Sizzling sensual scenes are coupled with scary suspense in this winning novel."

—*Publishers Weekly*, Starred Review

FOOL ME ONCE

"A marvelous portrait of friendship among women who have been bonded by fire."

—*Library Journal*, Best of the Year 2017

"Bybee still delivers a story that her die-hard readers will enjoy."

—*Publishers Weekly*

HALF EMPTY

"Wade and Trina here in *Half Empty* just might be one of my favorite couples Catherine Bybee has gifted us fans with so far. Captivating, engaging, lively and dreamy, I simply could not get enough of this book."

—*Harlequin Junkie*, 5 Stars

"Part rock star romance, part romantic thriller, I really enjoyed this book."

—*Romance Reader*

FAKING FOREVER

"A charming contemporary with surprising depth . . . Bybee perfectly portrays a woman trying to hold out for Mr. Right despite the pressures of time. A pitch-perfect plot and a cast of sympathetic and lovable supporting characters make this book one to add to the keeper shelf."

—*Publishers Weekly*

"Catherine Bybee can do no wrong as far as I'm concerned . . . Passionate, sultry, and filled with genuine emotions that ran the gamut, *Faking Forever* was a journey of self-discovery and of a love that was truly meant to be. Highly recommended."

—*Harlequin Junkie*

SAY IT AGAIN

"Steamy, fast-paced, and consistently surprising, with a large cast of feisty supporting characters, this suspenseful roller-coaster ride will keep both series fans and new readers on the edge of their seats."

—*Publishers Weekly*

MY WAY TO YOU

"A fascinating novel that aptly balances disastrous circumstances."
—*Kirkus Reviews*

"*My Way to You* is an unforgettable book fueled by Catherine Bybee's own life, along with the dynamic cast she created that will capture your heart."
—*Harlequin Junkie*

HOME TO ME

"Bybee skillfully avoids both melodrama and melancholy by grounding her characters in genuine emotion . . . This is Bybee in top form."
—*Publishers Weekly,* Starred Review

EVERYTHING CHANGES

"This sweet, sexy book is just the escapism many people are looking for right now."
—*Kirkus Reviews*

When It
Falls
Apart

OTHER TITLES BY CATHERINE BYBEE

Contemporary Romance

Weekday Brides Series

Wife by Wednesday
Married by Monday
Fiancé by Friday
Single by Saturday
Taken by Tuesday
Seduced by Sunday
Treasured by Thursday

Not Quite Series

Not Quite Dating
Not Quite Mine
Not Quite Enough
Not Quite Forever
Not Quite Perfect
Not Quite Crazy

Most Likely To Series

Doing It Over
Staying For Good
Making It Right

First Wives Series

Fool Me Once
Half Empty
Chasing Shadows
Faking Forever
Say It Again

Creek Canyon Series

My Way to You
Home to Me
Everything Changes

Richter Series

Changing the Rules
A Thin Disguise
An Unexpected Distraction

Paranormal Romance

MacCoinnich Time Travels

Binding Vows
Silent Vows
Redeeming Vows
Highland Shifter
Highland Protector

When It Falls Apart

CATHERINE BYBEE

Text copyright © 2022 by Catherine Kimmer
All rights reserved.

Published by Montlake, Seattle

www.apub.com

Amazon, the Amazon logo, and Montlake are trademarks of Amazon.com, Inc., or its affiliates.

ISBN-13: 9781542034869
ISBN-10: 1542034868

Cover design by Caroline Teagle Johnson

Printed in the United States of America

To Tim,
I couldn't have done it without you.

AUTHOR'S NOTE

Dear Reader,

Thank you for trusting me with your valuable time as you pick up *When It Falls Apart* and settle into the pages that I've created for you. Oftentimes, when I put my fingers on the keyboard and begin a new book, I start with completely made-up people in made-up worlds with made-up drama.

This is not that book.

At least not in its entirety.

For the sake of argument, let's suggest that I have perhaps taken liberties with certain truths pulled out of the pages of my own life and of the people I know. Let's call these portions of *When It Falls Apart* "creative nonfiction" and leave the reader to guess which parts of the story are real.

I have pushed this story a few years into the future from the year it was written, 2021. And have used my creative license as an author with what I feel will become a way of life when it comes to caring for our elderly in group homes. If my assumptions do not stand the test of time, then all I can say is this is, at the heart, fiction.

As many authors will tell you, life is often stranger than fiction. So why do we always strive to fill our books with things greater than life?

Why not simply tell a story that so many will relate to and find the inspiration to overcome within the pages?

This, dear reader, is that book.

Happy Reading.

Catherine

CHAPTER ONE

The wretched shriek of the telephone ripped the deep bliss of sleep instantly from her head and had Brooke shooting up off the pillow. Her heart started to pound as the second ring did in fact prove she wasn't hearing things and the phone *was* ringing. Her palm smacked the lit screen of her cell phone.

"San Antonio Hospital" flashed like a bad omen.

"Not again."

Beside her, Marshall moaned at the interruption and rolled over.

Brooke took a deep breath and answered. "Hello?"

"Miss Turner?"

"This is her."

"I'm calling from San Antonio Hospital's emergency room. We have your father here."

Brooke swung her legs off the side of the bed, turned the light on. "Is he okay? Did he have another stroke?"

"No, no. Not a stroke."

Marshall sat up behind her. "What's going on?"

Brooke placed her hand over the receiver. "It's my dad." She turned her focus back to the conversation on the phone. "What's wrong with him?" she asked.

"He has a bowel obstruction."

Brooke sighed with some relief. That didn't sound too bad. The last time she received a middle-of-the-night call, he was having a stroke. And that had ranked right up there with flirting with death. "Okay."

"I'm going to admit him and see if we can stabilize him before taking him to surgery."

"You're the surgeon?" Brooke thought she was talking to one of the nurses.

"Yes, I'm sorry, I should have said that right away. I'm Dr. Dubois. Your father is really sick, Miss Turner. I understand you're his advance care director for health issues. I'll need your permission for surgery."

"He can't consent?"

"No. The medication we've given him for pain has elevated his confusion . . ."

Brooke pushed off the bed, switched the phone to her other ear.

"Babe?" Marshall questioned.

She lifted the phone from her ear briefly. "Dad needs surgery."

Marshall let out a sigh, and Brooke tiptoed from the bedroom into the kitchen and turned on the lights. Not that she needed to be quiet since they were both wide awake now, but the late hour made her want to walk softly and whisper her words.

She sat at the small dinette set and pulled a pad of paper and pen in front of her to jot down notes as Dr. Dubois spoke. The momentary relief of hearing her father only had an obstruction quickly turned to dread at how deadly his condition could be. The doctor described some rather disturbing scenarios involving blood infections and ICU admissions. Brooke lifted a hand to her lips in an old habit of biting her nails, caught her nervous response, and twisted a lock of hair instead. Her eyes narrowed on the clock. It was just after midnight. Late-night flights were a crapshoot for availability.

By the time she was off the phone, her anxiety was making her twitch. Her mind scrambled with how she was going to rearrange her schedule to accommodate her father . . . again.

Footsteps told her Marshall had walked into the room. He moved around her and crossed to the sink, where he turned on the water and filled a glass. Wearing only a pair of lounge pants, he turned to face her and leaned against the counter. "How bad is it?"

"It doesn't sound good."

She looked up, and he averted his eyes.

Brooke reached for her laptop and opened it. She needed a flight.

"You're leaving." His voice was accusing.

"Of course."

"What about Florida?"

They were scheduled to go to Key West the following week. Marshall made his living creating travel vlogs for YouTube, and he'd been grounded a lot over the past few years. They'd been looking forward to this trip. "You'll have to go without me."

"Again."

The disappointment in his voice snapped her chin up. "My father is sick."

"Your father is always sick."

Why did he do this? Why did he always do this? Marshall's judgment on her relationship with her father came through in his digs, sighs, and shakes of his head. "I'm his only daughter."

"You have a stepsister."

"Who is going through a divorce and has her own ill parents. It's not the same."

Marshall rolled his eyes, drank from the glass. "This is getting old."

They'd argued about this before when she'd returned from California after almost six months of rehabilitating her father. The first couple of weeks had been touch and go. But once it became certain her father would survive, the long haul of rehab took over. A lengthy stay at an in-patient rehabilitation center was followed by daily visits to physical, occupational, and speech therapy when he returned home. He progressed from a wheelchair to a walker to walking on his own, albeit slow and wonky, and if a stranger was watching, they'd think he'd been drinking. His speech suffered, but he managed well enough. And the right side of his body simply didn't speak to the left side very well.

But he'd survived.

"What do you expect me to do?" Brooke asked Marshall.

He ran a hand through his hair. "Is he dying?"

She narrowed her eyes. "I don't know. I hope not."

A flash of something she didn't want to name crossed over his face. "How long will you be gone this time?"

"My dad is in the hospital right now with a possible expiration date on his life and all you want to know is how long I'll be gone? I don't know, Marshall. A week. A month . . . a year?" Three years she'd been with this man. Six months in they both agreed that marriage was a paper that neither of them needed. Both of them from divorced families, hers several times over and his twice . . . they didn't need it. They agreed to keep it honest and faithful. And they'd done that. At least she knew she had. Their base was Seattle, but they traveled often. She worked from home with a creative marketing company, which had made life easier when her father got ill two years prior.

"I don't get it, Brooke. It wasn't like the man was around for you growing up. I don't know why you bother."

Her backbone stiffened. He wasn't wrong. She hated him for pointing that out. "It isn't for you to understand. You either support me and my decisions or you don't."

For several moments they stared at each other. Her expression neutral. His blank.

Finally, Marshall set his glass in the sink and left the kitchen without any further words.

She squeezed her eyes shut, swallowed the hurt that pooled in the back of her throat, and typed in her airline of choice.

~

"I can take you to the airport."

Marshall stood at the door while Brooke rolled both suitcases from the bedroom and hiked her massive purse on her shoulder. "Carmen is picking me up."

Brooke had booked the flight, slept the rest of the night on the couch, and all but ignored Marshall as she packed.

"You're mad."

"I'm hurt. There's a difference."

"Babe . . ." He placed a hand on her shoulder. She shrugged it off.

"No. Don't."

He dropped his hand.

"I'm sorry."

She paused. "For what?"

"That you're mad." He quickly corrected, "Hurt. That I hurt you."

She rolled her eyes and reached for the door.

"Brooke."

"I have to go."

"Those are big suitcases."

She'd packed as much as she could fit in the luggage she had. The last time, she'd been caught unprepared and needed to buy clothes. That wouldn't happen again. "Are you afraid I won't be back?"

"Yes."

The look in his eyes said he wasn't lying.

"Good. I might not."

Marshall's jaw dropped.

"What? Really?"

Her heart raced in her chest and her pulse soared as she spoke. "Last night I needed the man in my life to put his arms around me and ask if I was okay. I needed him to see if there was something he could do to make things better. All I got was a whiny kid that was mad that I was screwing up his vacation."

Marshall recoiled. He was three years her junior, something they'd joked about in the past, yet his lack of maturity seemed to be playing a role now. "I guess I deserve that."

She started past him and he grabbed one of her suitcases. "At least let me help you out."

Without argument, she allowed him.

Carmen had her car parked in the red zone with the engine running.

Her best friend jumped from the driver's seat and rounded to the back of the car. "Perfect timing," Carmen said.

Marshall hoisted both bags into the trunk and closed it before standing back.

He looked at Brooke and she stepped out of his orbit . . . making it clear she wanted nothing to do with any goodbye hugs, kisses, or promises. The restless night on the couch reminded her of those she'd had during her father's rehabilitation. She knew that the days with her dad were likely numbered, and this was only an example of Marshall's behavior around things he didn't approve of. His lack of support before bothered her, now it crushed her.

He pushed his hands in his pockets. "Call me when you get there."

She'd text at most.

Brooke offered a nod and opened the passenger door.

"See ya, Marshall," Carmen said as she slid behind the wheel.

They pulled away from the curb.

Brooke glanced in the side mirror as Marshall watched them drive away.

"What was that all about?" Carmen asked.

"Marshall is a selfish ass."

Carmen started to laugh and continued to until Brooke looked at her. "What?"

"You're just now figuring that out?"

They turned the corner and Marshall disappeared from sight. Brooke focused her attention on the road in front of them. "I'm having second thoughts about him."

Carmen glanced her way, then back to the road. "You're serious."

Not trusting herself to speak, Brooke nodded.

They were silent for a full minute. "Do you want me to say something? I mean . . . I don't want to say 'I never liked the guy' and then have you all in love with him next week and you mad at me. I don't want to say 'He's the best guy for you' and you break up and you hate me."

Brooke closed her eyes, turned her head toward the passing city-scape of Seattle as they made their way onto the freeway en route to the airport. "I won't hate you for being honest with me."

Her friend took a deep breath and let it out slowly.

"Are you sure? I don't want—"

"I'm sure, Carmen. Give me your gut feeling without censoring. Even if I don't want to hear it."

Carmen tightened her grip on the steering wheel, licked her lips . . . and Brooke knew what she was going to say before the words left her mouth.

"He made you happy . . . the first year. Well, the first six to eight months."

Before her father had his stroke.

"You haven't been happy since. He convinced you that you don't need the fairy tale."

"I don't."

Carmen looked over. "Yes. You do."

Her friend was wrong about that, but her heart was in the right place.

"Marshall isn't the guy for you. He's young, selfish, and can't commit to a dog let alone a wife or children." Carmen sucked in a sharp breath. "God, I'm sorry. I didn't mean—"

"It's okay." The loss of that time wasn't something Brooke liked to think about . . . ever.

"No, it's not. I'm sorry, Brooke."

Too much loss . . . too many emotions swam in the back of her throat.

She needed to change the subject. Fast.

Carmen reached out and placed her hand over Brooke's. "You need a man who wouldn't dare let you go to your father alone. He wouldn't question your relationship. He'd simply be there and hold your hand because you needed it. You don't deserve anything less, Brooke. That's all I'm saying. If you think that's Marshall, then fine. I don't think it is. And as long as you have him in your life, the other guy isn't going to show up."

The tears that had threatened all night and all morning finally pooled and started to spill.

Carmen voiced so many things that Brooke had said to herself. Not the stuff about the next guy. She didn't give two thoughts about the next guy . . . At the very least Marshall should have cared about how she felt.

He didn't.

"I can fly down." Carmen's voice was soft.

"Ben?"

"I have a husband . . . he's capable of taking care of our son. If my friend needs me, I'm there. Say the word."

Brooke squeezed Carmen's hand. "I'll pull that card if I need it."

They turned into the departing terminal at Sea-Tac Airport and climbed out of the car. After retrieving her luggage from the trunk, they hugged. "Thank you . . . for the ride. And your honesty."

"Don't hate me tomorrow if you change your mind."

"I won't. Love you."

"Love you, too. Call me when you land."

Brooke kissed her friend's cheek, and walked into the airport.

CHAPTER TWO

Antiseptic and despair. Why was it hospitals always tried to cover up the ugly with the sharpest contrast in the form of bleach, or its second cousin that had a name no one could actually pronounce?

Ever since Brooke's father's stroke two years ago, traveling back and forth to California was a difficult task at best with her life settled so far away. The physical distance between her and her father made helping him challenging to manage.

He insisted he could drive.

She didn't think he could.

"No one has taken my driver's license away."

"That's because the DMV and the hospitals don't talk," she argued.

"I drive better than I walk."

He drove a double cab truck he'd once used to move parts from his machine shop. He only drove three miles to the grocery store, but that didn't stop her from worrying about him . . . and the other guy on the road. She'd shown him how to use Uber. She'd ordered grocery delivery.

No.

Her dad wanted nothing to do with that.

He was fighting the loss of his independence with every breath he had left in him.

And she was gaining gray hair at an early age because of his obstinance.

There was no way to stop him.

Taking away his license to drive became a waiting game. Waiting for the accidents or tickets. Not that her father would tell her about either of those things occurring. Maybe one of his doctors would make the call to the DMV. Even then, there was no telling whether her father would willingly stop driving even if they revoked his license. The whole thing simply sucked.

The middle-of-the-night phone call about a car accident was a predetermined given.

Yet here she was, not because of an accident, but because of a bad gut.

He had the eating habits of a twelve-year-old. The man had been married four times. Great at getting married. Failed at staying married. Even he agreed to that much.

His idea of a decent meal was anything that took less than five minutes in the microwave. God forbid you needed to stop in the middle of the heating cycle to open, poke, or turn the plate around and restart the thing . . . That was *too* much effort.

This wasn't the first time his diet had sent him to the hospital.

As much as Brooke had preached, he didn't listen.

Only when a woman he was sleeping with was in his life and cooking for him did he pay attention. To be fair, he was good when Brooke was there doing just that when he was recovering from the stroke. But he'd gone back to his old ways when she'd left him on his own. Old habits and all that.

Here she was . . . walking through the halls of the hospital after a health screening, with a sticker on her chest so she could enter the floor her father was on. Though the pandemic was behind them, hospitals, doctors' offices, and care centers for the elderly and sick ran by a new set of rules.

She'd come straight from the airport, and her luggage was still in the rental car.

Before walking to her father's room, Brooke stopped to talk to the nurse.

"I'm Joe Turner's daughter, Brooke. How is he doing?" she asked.

The nurse's smile was kind, her words slow and calculated. "He's either in pain or confused from the pain medication. So far, he hasn't tried taking out any of his tubes."

"Tubes?"

The nurse explained what Brooke should expect when she walked into the room. Nasal tubes, IVs . . . bladder tubes. "Surgery is scheduled for the morning."

Brooke signed the paperwork needed and walked down the hall.

Stiffening her spine, she walked into his room. "Knock, knock," she said before pulling back the curtain.

Her jaw dropped.

Her father was sprawled in the bed with one leg dangling off the side. In his hands was one of the IV pumps.

"Hi, Dad."

"Brooke." Her name was muffled. The tube in his nose was attached to the wall. His eyes were glazed, his hospital gown dangling from one shoulder exposing more of his body than it covered. An adult diaper appeared to be falling off. He didn't look like he knew where he was.

"What are you doing?" She dropped her purse in the chair and walked to his side.

"What?" he asked, completely oblivious to how ridiculous he looked half on and half off the bed holding an IV pump.

She pointed to the IV equipment.

Joe shook his head as if she were indicating a fly on the wall. "Someone has to h-hold it."

"Isn't that what this pole is for?" she asked, placing her hand on the rolling pole he'd obviously taken it off of.

"Oh . . . huh."

Yup . . . her father was completely confused.

11

"Let me help you." She took the pump from him and pressed the call button for the nurse.

~

The heat still clung to the day even though the sun had set. That was what it was like in the middle spaces of Southern California.

Brooke pulled into the driveway of her father's condo.

Her condo.

She'd bought the place for him a few months before his stroke. Brooke had been itching to buy a place for herself when Marshall came along. Marshall convinced her that roots for the two of them didn't make sense. Renting would give them the freedom to work around the globe. That didn't stop Brooke from wanting to invest her money in something.

After her father's fourth marriage failed and he was forced to walk away from joint assets—again—the man had been reduced to living in his machine shop. As the years ticked on, however, and his health started to decline, living in a dirty shop became less of an option. When she'd come to him with a proposition to buy a condo that he would live in, he balked at it. She talked about investments and the need to look to her future and eventually he agreed. Knowing he had a home to go to at the end of the day gave her peace of mind, and after the stroke, it had been an absolute necessity.

Although they'd originally talked about him helping financially with the place, that never came to pass. The stroke forced his retirement and stopped his ability to make an income. In addition to helping her father rehabilitate, she took a crash course in how to liquidate a machine shop. At the end of it, she'd managed to make her father close to fifty thousand dollars, which would be his only retirement outside of his social security checks. All he had to do was be frugal, and he'd likely be okay.

Or so she hoped.

Brooke looked at the garage door of the condo before getting out of the rental car.

Déjà vu hit her hard.

She unlocked the front door, took a breath, and walked in. The smell hit her first.

Placing a hand over her nose, Brooke turned on a light.

The acid stench of illness filled the air.

Brooke moved around the living room, opening windows and doors. She put the ceiling fan on high, helping move the air about the room.

Evidence that her father hadn't been well for a while sat in waste containers at the ends of the sofa and dining room table.

And the filth.

The place was filthy.

Dirt in cracks and corners. Dishes in the sink.

She opened the refrigerator and found processed cheese, orange juice, and an assortment of condiments. The freezer met her with her father's normal diet of frozen breakfasts, dinners, and ice cream. The kind with nuts that he wasn't supposed to be eating.

One look in the bathroom and she closed the door . . . disgusted.

Dog tired, Brooke rolled her suitcases into the second bedroom, which was left relatively untouched, and rolled up her sleeves.

The offensive smells needed to be taken to the trash, and the bathroom had to be tackled or she'd need to find a hotel.

For the life of her, she didn't think she knew a hotel within a ten-mile radius that looked any better.

What her father saw in the Inland Empire, Brooke couldn't say. She'd never liked the area. Hot, dry, oppressive in the best of times. And when the Santa Ana winds started to blow, it became unlivable as far as she was concerned. Yet Joe had lived there for over thirty years.

Exhausted as she was, Brooke moved about the condo looking for cleaning supplies to tackle the most unpleasant needs first.

Sadly, she was fairly certain the bottles of disinfectants were the brands that she favored and likely the ones she'd bought the last time she'd been there. Which meant her dad didn't pull them out and use them often enough. As evidenced by the smell and condition of the place.

It ticked her off, much as she hated to admit it.

Maybe he couldn't do the work and was too embarrassed to tell her.

In search of a mop, Brooke opened the door to the garage and flipped on the light.

She stopped dead in her tracks.

There, in bright sparkly blue, was a brand-new, *clean*, four-door Subaru sedan.

Her jaw dropped.

"Son of a bitch."

~

"Where are you?"

"In the parking lot of the hospital." Brooke had her phone on speaker talking to Carmen. The windows of the rental car were cracked just enough to let in some fresh air. "Dr. Dubois said she'd call me when they were out of surgery."

"You sound tired."

"I'm exhausted. The condo was a pigsty. *Is* a pigsty. I was up cleaning until after midnight and only made a dent."

"Oh no. Do you think your dad is losing whatever he has left?"

"That's exactly what I thought, until I saw the car."

"What car?"

"The brand-spanking-new freaking car in the garage." She'd been seething about that ever since.

"Your dad bought a new car?"

Brooke nodded her head, not that Carmen could see her. "What the hell was he thinking? A little sporty Subaru fit for a seventeen-year-old. And it was spotless. Spotless, Carmen. My dad had enough cleaning supplies to keep the car on a showroom floor for the next five years, but he couldn't brush a toilet to save his life. What the actual hell? He's had the car for five months. Did he bother to tell me? No."

"You would have bitched at him."

"Of course I would have bitched at him. The money from liquidating his business is for his retirement. It has to last the rest of his life. He had his truck, it was fine. It was in good condition. It was paid off. What the hell did he need a new car for?"

"Deep breath, girlfriend. Stop pulling your hair out."

Brooke looked at her left hand, which had wrapped around a chunk of hair, and forced it to her lap. "It's so frustrating. I buy him a condo, it's a filthy mess. He buys a car, it's eat-off-the-engine clean. The payment is five hundred a month. Did he offer to help me with the mortgage? No. He bought a car. Ugh!"

"If your father was fiscally responsible, you wouldn't have had to buy him the condo."

"It's maddening. And I'm pissed at myself for being pissed at him. He's in surgery right now, and who knows how it will turn out, and I'm in a parking lot cursing about his life choices."

Carmen's voice of reason came out in her tone. "It's okay, Brooke. Anyone in your shoes would feel the same."

She wanted to scream. "Blah . . . just blah!"

"Have you talked to Marshall?"

"I texted him."

"And?"

"Nothing. Just said I was here. He tried calling; I didn't pick up. I told him I didn't have the energy to fight with him and I'd call when I was ready." Brooke wasn't sure when that would be. If she told Marshall about the condo, the car . . . any of it, he'd only be clamoring about how she shouldn't be doing so much for her dad, and how she should walk away and not care. The fight would circulate again, like it had so many times in the past.

"He'd just be a dick about this anyway."

"Exactly."

"You don't need that," Carmen said.

"I know."

"You need the fairy tale."

Brooke rolled her eyes. "That isn't here." She looked out the windshield at the neighborhood surrounding the hospital. It was quiet enough, but flat and boring. No rivers or lakes, mountains or ocean in sight. "This place is depressing."

"I remember." Carmen had come for a few days after the stroke and left once they knew he was going to make it.

Brooke's phone buzzed with an incoming call. "That's the doctor. I gotta go."

"Go. Call me back."

An hour later she was allowed to go in and visit her father in the ICU. He was sent there after surgery because his blood pressure was low, and the surgeon opted to keep him on the ventilator overnight with the hopes of weaning him off the machine the following day.

Brooke hesitated as she walked into the room and to his bedside, making sure she didn't get in the nurse's way.

She slid her hand into her father's swollen fingers and squeezed. "Hey, Daddy. It's me. You did great. You just need to rest up and get better now."

He didn't move, didn't bat an eyelash.

The soft push and flow of the ventilator and the beeping of the monitor watching his heart rate filled the room with noise.

It was hard to believe that three short years ago, this man was riding his motorcycle and splitting lanes in traffic acting like he was

James Dean. "You pulled a couple of bad cards," she whispered to the room.

Ten minutes later the nurse let her know she'd call if anything changed. It was Brooke's cue to leave.

A kiss to her father's forehead, a promise to see him the next day, and Brooke exited the hospital.

Outside, the temperature had risen. She walked to the rental car and climbed behind the wheel. "Now what?"

~

Her phone rang.

Brooke's eyes shot open, her pulse instantly in her throat. Not bothering to look at who was calling, she answered. "Hello?"

"Miss Turner?"

"Yes?"

"This is Lily . . . your father's nurse tonight. We think you should come to the hospital."

"Oh, God . . . what happened?" Brooke's feet were already on the floor, her hand reaching for the light on the bedside table.

"Your father is alive. Just very sick. He spiked a fever. His blood pressure is low. We have him on medication to support it. His kidneys are failing."

Tears were starting to gather in the back of her eyes. "Is he going to die?"

"Not if we can stop it. But it is a possibility, which is why I'm calling. Can someone drive you here?"

"I'm . . . no. I'm okay. Not far."

"Okay. Take a deep breath. You have time. I've already cleared it with my charge nurse. I have a chair in the room for you."

Brooke grabbed the pants she'd worn during the day and was shoving her legs inside. "Thank you."

"Stay calm."

"I will. I'm okay."

"Okay."

Brooke disconnected the call, threw her clothes on, slipped into a pair of flip-flops, and ran out the door. Once in the car, she realized she'd left her cell phone on the bed. She gripped the steering wheel and took a deep breath.

Back in the condo she retrieved her phone and a power cord. Then, she walked into her father's bedroom and found a rosary he had sitting on his nightstand. The symbol meant nothing to her, but everything to him. The back of her throat filled with emotion so strong she choked. The sound that came out of her resembled a wounded animal.

"Take a deep breath," she told herself.

She retraced her steps to the car and pulled out of the driveway.

Hospitals changed in the middle of the night, and yet the ICU did not. Yes, a few of the lights in rooms were dimmed, but most were on, curtains pulled back so the nurses could see the patients without having to walk inside. Privacy wasn't a priority for the critically ill.

Brooke stood at the open door of her father's room.

Unlike a few hours before, this time her dad had half a dozen more IV bags and pumps and machines hooked up to him. Looking at him, she didn't notice much of a difference. He was still on the ventilator, his eyes closed. His arms were loosely tied to the sides of the bed.

"You must be Joe's daughter," the nurse said when she noticed Brooke standing there.

She didn't trust herself to speak. Instead, she nodded.

"I'm Lily."

"Everything was okay earlier. How did this . . ."

"His blood is infected. Bacteria in the bloodstream is never good." Lily waved her hand at the montage of medication being pumped into her father. "We're doing everything we can to reverse it. The next twenty-four to forty-eight hours will tell."

Brooke approached the bed, reached for her father's hand. The swelling in his fingers seemed to have doubled. "Why is he tied down?"

"We eased up on the sedation since his blood pressure is low. Sometimes he reaches for the tubes."

That wouldn't be good. "Can he hear me?"

Lily offered a smile. "He can. But don't expect much."

Brooke leaned close to her father's ear. "Daddy? Can you hear me? It's Brooke. I'm here."

His head moved, slightly. Even that brought the tears that she wanted so desperately to hold in. "I love you, Daddy. You need to fight, okay." She squeezed his hand, felt a twitch of his fingers.

She brushed away a tear with her shoulder.

"I'm not leaving until you get better, and you know how cranky I get without any sleep."

Her dad didn't budge this time.

Brooke shivered and stood tall.

"I'll get you a blanket and some water. Do you want coffee?" Lily asked.

"You don't have to—"

"It's not a problem. We keep it cool and I'm guessing you left without a sweater."

Brooke nodded.

Lily pointed to a chair. "That reclines. Makes for a crappy night's sleep, but you might manage some."

One look and Brooke shook her head. She'd spent a couple of nights in one of them when her father had his stroke. "I'll take some coffee."

"I'll be right back."

"Thank you."

Lily left the room and Brooke turned back to her father. "C'mon, Dad. You got this."

~

"I'm flying down."

Brooke ran a tired hand through her hair. She needed a shower and a few hours of sleep. "Carmen, no. Please. There's no point. Not yet."

"Brooke—"

"Listen. They're only allowing me in the room and that's where I'm staying until he either gets better or he . . ." She couldn't bring herself to say the word *dies*.

"That's exactly why I need to be there."

"Carmen, please. If you're here, I'll just worry that I'm putting you out. And if it is my father's time, I'm going to need you after. Right now, this is what I need. To pick up the phone and talk to you."

"Damn it, Brooke. You did this the last time."

"And I told you when I needed you and you came and I'm so grateful. This time is no different. Trust me. There is nothing for you to do. You'd be sitting in a parking lot, or at my dad's condo hating it. When he makes it out of this, I really need to talk him into moving somewhere with a better climate." She froze her ass off all night and now she was hot as hell standing outside the hospital taking a breather.

"You're a stubborn bitch, you know that, right?"

"You love me anyway."

"Yeah, I do."

Brooke looked up as a couple walked past where she was leaning against her rental car. "I need to talk to Marshall."

"You haven't done that yet?"

"I keep putting it off. He leaves for Florida day after tomorrow."

"He should be in California with you. If he cared."

Brooke twisted a finger in her hair. "I'm glad he isn't here. Relieved, really. I had a lot of time to think last night. And you know what I didn't think about?"

"No."

"Missing him. Wanting him here. Feeling like a piece of me was empty without him by my side. When Dad had the stroke, those emotions flooded my mind, my heart. Now I'm just relieved I don't have to juggle Marshall's feelings and directions on what *he thinks* I should be doing or not doing. Here I am half expecting my dad to die, and I don't want the man I'm committed to to be by my side. That's saying something pretty loud and clear, don't you think?"

"I think your emotions are really off the charts right now," Carmen said, her voice low.

"You think I'm wrong?"

"That's not what I said. As your best friend, I'm going to suggest you get through this crisis with your dad, at least within the next few days. See what happens, before making any big moves."

Brooke released her hair, forced her hand to her side. "You're right. I'll keep it short and civil. We'll know in the next couple of days if my dad is going to pull through."

"And if he does?"

"I don't know. No one has even addressed that." Which made her believe they didn't expect him to make it.

Brooke was too afraid to ask.

"Okay. I'm texting you every hour. If you change your mind, I'll be on the first flight I can."

"Thank you."

"Love you, girl."

"Love you, too."

Brooke disconnected the call and stared at her phone.

She'd been outside for twenty minutes and felt the pressing need to get back to her father's side. Her rush would be the excuse to get off the phone quickly if Marshall picked up. With her exit in sight, Brooke dialed his cell phone.

Two rings in and she wondered if he was going to pick up.

On the third ring he did.

"Hey. I was wondering if you were going to call."

She squeezed her eyes shut. "Yeah. I can't talk long. Dad's in the ICU. He's really sick."

"Hmm. I'm a . . . sorry. Yeah. Sorry to hear that."

Brooke paused.

Waited.

Swallowed.

The long silence felt like a knife in her side.

Finally, when it became obvious that she wasn't going to fill the empty conversation, Marshall said, "How are—"

"You know what . . . I've got to go. Enjoy Florida, Marshall."

"Brooke?"

"Really. I gotta go." She hung up.

All of the red flags Marshall had been flying slid up her spine and slapped her in the face with his silence over the phone. *I'm sorry.* Not "Oh shit, what can I do? Let me get on the first plane out. I'm coming to be there with you. What happened?" God, any number of questions or concerns. Just *I'm sorry.*

Carmen might have been right in waiting to do anything about her decisions, but Brooke had already made them.

Regardless of what happened with her father, her relationship with Marshall was over.

CHAPTER THREE

Her father was in the ICU for over a week, then moved to a surgical floor where he stabilized enough over three weeks to be transferred to a skilled nursing facility. That didn't mean he was a hundred percent. Sepsis did a number on his body, his recovery. He'd lost a ton of weight, couldn't control his own bodily functions, and his wound wasn't closing.

Brooke was once again on the hamster wheel of caring for her father, as best she could, and attempting to balance her life.

Which she was failing at miserably.

The nursing home wasn't as welcoming with visitors as the hospital was, and their rules made it so her father needed to be kept in isolation for his first week in the facility. Which meant she couldn't visit.

Back at the condo, she pushed open the door and looked at stacked boxes of her life filling the free space between the furniture.

She'd broken things off with Marshall with very little fanfare.

Truth was, he saw it coming.

How could he not?

"So that's it? You're not even going to come home and do this in person?" he asked through the FaceTime call she'd made in an effort to not break up in a regrettable way.

"I waited until you were back from Florida. It's the best I could do. Leaving now isn't an option and I see no need to pretend any further."

Marshall was sitting at the counter in their kitchen, his kitchen, staring into his phone. "I knew your father was going to come between us."

Brooke literally bit her tongue to keep from saying the words that wanted to escape. Her father's illness had been the catalyst, not the cause. The point in arguing now was moot.

It was over.

She'd made up her mind and nothing was going to change it.

"I asked Carmen to help pack up my things."

"I can—"

"Marshall."

"Fine." He leaned back in the chair, narrowed his eyes at the screen. "You hate your father's condo."

"That's no longer your concern."

"You'll go crazy there in six months."

She was already going nuts. But she wasn't about to tell him that.

They ended the conversation with little more than a bitter goodbye.

With the help of FaceTime and Carmen, Brooke's belongings had been packed up and sent down.

The bulkier things she'd brought into the equation with Marshall she told him to keep or sell, or do whatever he wanted with. She didn't own a car. There wasn't a need when living in the heart of Seattle. Now it seemed as if it was all meant to be.

And pathetic.

Her life had been boxed up and shipped off in a matter of two weeks.

Now she'd been plopped down smack in the middle of her father's life.

Yes, the condo was hers . . . technically.

Living there to take care of her father to help him convalesce—again—was the right thing to do.

Yet with her own belongings surrounding her, it felt more like a noose around her neck that threatened to choke the breath from her lungs. Worse, her father wasn't even there. And no one had an end date to his time needed in the nursing home.

There was a question as to what his needs would be when he came home and if she had the capability to manage him.

Brooke covered her face with her hands and tried to steady her breath.

In Seattle, when she felt as if the walls of her life were closing in, she'd make her way to the water's edge. She'd sit on a pier in Puget Sound and listen to the ocean meeting the land. The crisp, wet air would often drive away her thoughts and give her something else to meditate on and release her anxiety.

Here, in an area where water could only be found in backyard swimming pools and man-made rivers forged from concrete, that escape wasn't possible. Even though Brooke didn't miss the constant rain of the Pacific Northwest, she missed the effects of it.

Realizing she'd been standing in the center of the condo staring at boxes for a good twenty minutes, ruminating on her situation, Brooke dropped her purse on the coffee table and moved to the kitchen.

From the refrigerator, she removed a bottle of chardonnay. A few minutes later she found herself on the small back patio with her laptop open. The work project she had to complete sat before her unfinished. A marketing campaign for an organic vegan soap company that normally Brooke could work up something brilliant for in a weekend. Well, at least the ideas, and then the work and effort of putting it together would take a bit more time. While her boss understood the delay, it was time to get on it, and now that there wasn't the possibility of her father stealing her time, she absolutely had to get the work in.

But Brooke stared down at her computer and blinked.

She sipped her wine and rolled her shoulders.

Her computer pinged, telling her she had a text message.

She clicked over.

How's dad?

It was Carmen.

Instead of typing, Brooke pressed FaceTime.

Carmen's smiling face came in view. "Hey, you."

"Hey."

"Oh no."

"No. It's okay. I'm okay." *I'm not okay.*

"Where are you? I thought you'd be with your dad. Didn't they transfer him today?" she asked.

"They did. They won't let me in. Apparently, the nursing homes don't play by the same rules as the hospitals."

"When will that change?"

"At least a week." Brooke reached for her wine.

"What are you doing?"

"I'm trying to work."

"How is that going?"

Brooke looked at the pergola above her that was falling apart. She really should do something about that. "Not well."

"Wait . . . is that wine?"

She glanced at the glass in her hand. "Yeah, why?"

"It's two o'clock . . . on Tuesday."

Brooke rolled her eyes, sipped unapologetically. "My days bleed into each other here."

Carmen was silent for a breath. Then . . . "I think I need to come down before you need an intervention."

Brooke set the glass down, looked away from the screen, and said nothing.

"What? No argument?"

The constant feeling of being out of control rose to the surface once again. "I don't know how to do this, Carmen. Not this time. I'm already drowning, and I've only been here a month."

"I'm booking a ticket."

Brooke looked at her best friend, a single tear rolled down her cheek. "I need you."

~

Carmen sat by Brooke's side during the consultation with the nursing home director.

She'd arrived the night before and they drank too much wine, laughed . . . cried, and ate entirely too many carbs.

"Your father's level of care is rather intense at this time. The wound nurse expects his need for care to be a minimum of two months. The antibiotics he's on will last for the next three weeks and at that time we will reevaluate for his discharge home."

"Wait, I thought his wound care needs were for two to three months."

The director, Kyle, was an older man, salt-and-pepper hair, and looked as if he needed to put on a few pounds to be truly healthy. Brooke felt as if he was annoyed she'd requested an in-person meeting.

"A home health nurse can be requested after he is off the IV antibiotics."

Carmen sat forward. "I understand Mr. Turner is incontinent and confused."

Kyle looked at his notes. "Ah, yes. But he'd had a stroke."

"Which he recovered from enough to not have issues with incontinence. He was independent before this last illness. He had some right-sided weakness, but he managed." Brooke looked between Kyle and Carmen as she spoke.

"Oh, well. Right. He lives with you?"

"No . . . Yes, kind of." Brooke looked at Carmen. "I'm here to get him back on his feet like I did after the stroke."

Kyle nodded a few times, then shook his head. "It's too soon to say how well he'll progress, but in my experience, in cases like your father's . . . as the medical problems stack up, the independence diminishes. I wouldn't expect your father to be what he was before this episode."

Brooke blinked several times. "The doctors said—"

"Doctors tell you that wounds heal, and conditions improve. Here, we see patients lose their ability to feed themselves or use the bathroom . . . take their medications on time. The routine of normal life is completely oppressed by admission into our facility, and the desire to improve sometimes dissolves as well. I'm not saying that is your father, but I am suggesting that you prepare yourself for what his long-term care needs might be."

"And what do you think those are?" Carmen asked.

Kyle looked back at the papers in his lap, flipped through the notes. "Your father lived alone?"

"Yes. Completely independent."

"Did he drive?"

She sighed. "Yes."

Kyle looked up at her. "You don't think he should have."

"No."

"How was the condition of his home?"

Brooke opened her mouth, thought of the mess she'd walked into.

"Has your father made any extravagant purchases lately? Anything out of the ordinary?"

Carmen reached over and took Brooke's hand.

Kyle stopped asking questions and rested his hands in his lap. "Bowel obstructions can happen to anyone, but elderly people who aren't eating a balanced diet or getting enough exercise are more likely to have issues. Your father's independence may not be something he can return to." Kyle tilted his head. "It's not my place to tell people what they should or shouldn't do when it comes to their family members, but

I can tell you after a lifetime of taking care of the elderly, caring for them is a full-time twenty-four-seven job with no weekends or nights off. It's too soon to say if your father will get control of his bodily functions. If he doesn't, you'll need to—"

"I get it!" she cut him off.

"Either way, you might ask yourself if your dad should return to living on his own. Once the antibiotics are no longer needed and home health can be requested and you're willing to change diapers and give baths, he can be discharged home."

Brooke squeezed her eyes closed.

"And if that isn't an option?" Carmen asked.

"Assisted living, once his wound heals. If he or you have the funds for that. Does he own his home?"

"No," Brooke said. "He has a little money and social security."

Kyle started to straighten the papers in his lap. "Medicare pays for a minimal number of days in a nursing home if a doctor warrants a need. You can appeal for more if the doctor wants to discharge before the allotted time, of course, and should . . . but you should know that it is likely that you'll be denied."

"What does that mean?" Brooke's head was spinning. All the information Kyle was pushing in was too much.

"When Medicare stops paying the bill, your father will be responsible."

"And how much is that?"

"Our rate is $430 a day."

"What the—" Carmen came halfway out of her chair.

Kyle lifted a hand. "We're not there yet, but I want you to understand what you're facing. Best case, your father regains all his faculties, is able to ambulate, use the bathroom, bathe, and not do anything destructive in the coming days and he can go home with the occasional home health nurse helping with his wound care until it heals."

Yeah . . . Brooke thought of the shell of a man in the bed upstairs right now and couldn't imagine that happening. Even if it did . . . the state of his home, his decision-making . . .

"More likely, your father will need more time. His activities of daily living need assistance. Diapers, bathing, dressing . . . These things can be taken care of in assisted living, but they won't accept him until the wound from surgery is completely healed. So, you're looking at a decent-size bill from us. We'll plead with the doctors to extend as long as we can, but still, I would expect a minimum bill of four weeks, expecting Medicare to stop paying after a month."

Brooke did some mental math.

"If your father owned a home, you could sell it to take care of these expenses."

Brooke looked at Carmen with a sigh. "My dad was married four times. It's kinda hard to have much of anything when you're constantly dividing your assets."

Kyle chuckled. "There are a lot of assisted living facilities in the area."

She closed her eyes again.

"However."

"What else?" she asked, afraid of the answer.

"I suggest you move your dad closer to you. If you choose the assisted living route, you'll still likely take him to his doctor's appointments, get him his essentials, visit. Yes, the facilities can coordinate that stuff, but it's easier on you if you're close by. The more you can do on occasion, the less expensive those facilities will run. It's hard to keep an eye on his care from far away. No reason to do that from Washington State."

She thought of the boxes in the condo.

The condo she might need to sell just to foot the bill.

"Thank you. I had no idea."

"No one really does until it happens," Kyle said before standing.

Brooke thanked him and she walked to the parking lot beside Carmen.

"Jesus."

"Yeah," Brooke agreed.

"Your dad doesn't want you wiping his ass."

As much as she loved him, she didn't want that either. "He could pull out of it."

They stopped in front of the brand-new car her father had frivolously bought that now meant an automatic deduction from his bank account. Even though Brooke hated the thing on principle, driving it made sense instead of renting something else.

"And what? Go back to living like he was at the condo? What's he gonna do next, buy a boat?" Carmen patted the top of the car.

Brooke yanked open the door, slid behind the wheel. Ten minutes later they were back at the condo.

Both of them moaned. The walls of the space closed in, the boxes loomed in corners, and the scent of her father never seemed far away.

"Screw this," Carmen said. "Pack a bag."

"What?"

"I have an idea."

"I can't . . ."

"A few days. Just trust me. We're driving."

"But my dad—"

"Is being taken care of. So shut up and pack a bag."

Carmen was right.

Still, Brooke hesitated. "Where are we going?"

"Just get in."

CHAPTER FOUR

It was nice to be in the passenger seat.

The music blared and the air conditioner ran on high since the outside temperature was in the nineties.

They headed south.

"I don't have my passport on me," Brooke said when it was apparent they weren't headed deeper into the desert.

"We're not going that far."

They'd crawled past most of the obnoxious traffic of the Inland Empire and had finally found the open highway.

Brooke looked at the map on her phone. "San Diego?"

"Have you been?" Carmen asked.

Brooke shook her head. "No. I've been to LA, Hollywood, Disneyland, and the place my dad calls home."

"Not even the beach?"

"Well, yeah, a couple of times, but I couldn't even tell you which ones. I was a teenager." Her visits to Southern California as a kid had been few and far between.

"You're in for a treat then. San Diego is totally different from anywhere else in California. Certainly from your dad's place."

"That wouldn't take much."

"It's not that bad," Carmen said.

Brooke glared at her friend. "It's too hot, too dry, and there's no water anywhere. Lakes, rivers . . . ocean. You haven't lived until the wind starts blowing and you can't open your eyes as you're walking into the grocery store."

"A few days in San Diego is the prescription you need then."

As the desert drifted into the rearview mirror and the city came into view, so did the coast and bay views from various places along the route.

They turned the air conditioner off and rolled down the windows.

The temperature had dropped twenty degrees even though the sun still hung bright in the sky. There was enough moisture in the air to kiss her skin, but not so much to suggest oppressive humidity.

Carmen booked a room at the Hyatt. The high-rise hotel offered views of the bay and glistening blue water that felt like home.

Brooke stood at the window staring down in absolute silence.

She'd missed this.

The water. The tranquility.

"You okay over there?" Carmen asked from the other side of the room.

"This is exactly what I needed."

"I know."

Brooke looked over her shoulder with a smile. "Let's walk."

Carmen grabbed her purse. "I'm ready."

Less than twenty minutes later, they were strolling along the waterfront just outside the hotel with cups of ice cream from Seaport Village. Tourists and locals meandered around them. "I can't believe how much cooler it is here," Brooke found herself saying for the half a dozen time since they'd arrived.

"It's the beach."

"I get that . . . but. I don't know. It doesn't seem to make that big of a difference inland up in Washington. Not as much as here."

"You're comparing apples to oranges."

"More like chicken to lettuce."

Carmen licked the ice cream off her spoon before talking again. "What kept your dad in Upland anyway?"

"Work. Women."

Carmen laughed. "He hasn't worked since the stroke, and when did his last marriage end?"

Brooke narrowed her eyes. "Oh, man . . . eight years ago, I think. He used to go out with friends."

"Before the stroke."

"Yeah."

"But not now."

"Not as much," Brooke said.

"Why stay?"

She shrugged. "It's what he knows."

Carmen pointed at her with her spoon. "It's not what you know."

"What are you saying?"

"Your dad put you in charge of his care, right?"

"Yeah." She had his advance health care directive before the stroke and durable power of attorney. It had been a godsend then and was proving even more useful now.

"Why not move your dad to Seattle?"

Brooke blew off the idea with an exaggerated breath. "He would hate Seattle as much as I hate Upland."

"So, you have to compromise your life to accommodate the remainder of his?"

Carmen had a point, but it wasn't that simple.

They walked away from the shopping crowds and found a bench. "I'm having a hard time wrapping my mind around the thought of him being in a home. Moving him to another state . . . I don't see it. Besides, there isn't a lot keeping me in Seattle either."

"Ouch," Carmen said with a recoil.

Brooke reached out, touched her knee. "Not you. You're my rock. You know that. Marshall and I had a lot of mutual friends. Me being gone makes it easier for them to figure out who to invite over without hurting someone else's feelings."

"You did not just say that. Who gives a crap about party invites?"

Brooke put down her half-eaten ice cream. "It's easier this way. The breakup. This distance is exactly what I need to put Marshall in my past. Maybe in a year I'll change my mind. Who knows what's going to happen in a year? My dad could get sick again."

"He could get better."

Brooke leaned her head on her friend's shoulder, looked out over the bay. "I used to be optimistic. Now I'm wondering if I need to sell the condo to have the money for a home for him."

"You still have to live somewhere."

"I know. But the market is really good right now. I could invest the money and rent a small place for me, and when my dad's money runs out, pull from the condo money. It won't last forever but . . ."

"Dads don't last forever."

Brooke shook her head. "I'll make it work. I just need to find a space that inspires me to be creative enough to do my job so I can afford to take care of us both."

"Well . . ." Carmen reached over, grabbed Brooke's ice cream cup, and stood. "We're here to get your mind off of all that crap for a couple of days and I suggest we start doing it. How about we find one of those booze cruises on the bay tonight?"

"A booze cruise?"

Carmen grabbed Brooke's hand, pulled her up. "Work with me here. I don't get out much."

~

"I can't believe you didn't take Scott up on his offer last night," Carmen started as they walked away from the hotel to explore the city the next morning.

"You mean the twelve-year-old?" The harbor cruise had been a great way to see the sunset and gather some background on San Diego. A light dinner and alcohol were provided . . . and plenty of single people were there looking for entertainment. Enter Scott. The man-child Carmen was referring to.

"He was not twelve."

"Pretty sure if you double-checked his ID, you'd find he'd swiped his big brother's to get on the boat."

"He's in the navy. I'm sure they'd frown on that."

"Even if he was twenty-one. I'm thirty-six. No. Just no."

Carmen moaned. "He was cute."

"Did it ever occur to you I don't want that? Any of that? I haven't wiped off my smeared mascara from Marshall yet, the last thing I want is to jump into anything else. Besides, I don't have time. And I don't live here."

"I don't think he was looking for forever."

"And I don't want for now. I don't want anything."

Carmen frowned.

"Don't look at me that way. I'm okay. I need to be me. I have to figure out my dad, my life . . . our lives. Then if something comes along . . . maybe."

"A Scott?"

Brooke rolled her eyes. "I think I can do better than *a Scott*."

They walked along Harbor Drive until they passed where they'd gotten on the boat the night before and turned into Waterfront Park. The long fountains and vast grassy areas were dotted with families and kids playing. A few children splashed in the water while parents snapped pictures that were sure to make it onto a social media page later in the day.

Funny, Brooke hadn't thought about her own pages in weeks.

It wasn't like there was anything interesting to post. Nothing brag-worthy.

She'd been downright depressed since she arrived in California, and for good reason.

Yet pausing and watching the kids playing in the park put a smile on her face.

Carmen nudged her, bringing the fact that she'd stopped walking to her attention. "You need a man who can give you one of those."

"Carmen!" Her name was a familiar warning. A friendly way of saying, "Drop it." The subject of babies didn't get brought up often, and when it did, Brooke changed it quickly.

"Fine. Let's go."

They walked away from the park, up a couple of blocks, and the crowds started to gather again.

"What is this?"

Brooke looked up and saw a huge sign spanning the street . . . Little Italy. On the streetlights were Italian flags. Restaurant patios and tables spilled onto the streets, taking up where cars once parked. Beautiful structures with proper fencing and fake greenery separated the dining patrons from the passing cars. Strings of outdoor lighting hung between the buildings, adding to the neighborhood feel of the area.

"This is crazy," Carmen said as she pulled her cell phone from her purse and started snapping pictures.

"You didn't know this was here?"

"I heard someone talking about it last night, but I didn't think it was so close to the hotel."

Brooke dodged a couple walking a big dog. "I missed it. That must have been when Scott was hitting on me."

Each restaurant was open to the street, hostesses standing at a podium smiling and inviting people passing by to look at the menu.

While the buildings didn't look anything like what you found in Italy, the atmosphere had a similar energetic feel.

Brooke found a smile on her face as she heard those working inside the establishments talking in rapid Italian as they ran around. She'd missed traveling when she'd taken care of her father the first time and knew she wouldn't be on a plane again anytime soon. Not to mention the breakup with Marshall, the travel influencer who could be in Italy right now for all she knew.

Brooke shook off the thought and welcomed where she was.

"This is fabulous," she said, soaking it all in.

"Are you hungry?" Carmen asked.

"Not at all."

"Want to get something to eat anyway?"

Brooke stopped walking, looked around. "Absolutely."

They perused their options and decided on D'Angelo's Trattoria, which had an authentic-looking menu and more ambiance than many of the places they'd passed by.

"Buongiorno," the hostess, a girl in her midtwenties with long dark hair and olive skin, greeted them.

"Hi. Table for two?" Brooke asked.

"Of course. Inside or out?"

Brooke pointed to the tables set for two on the patio connected to the restaurant. "Is this okay?"

"Perfect." The hostess smiled and walked them to their table, then handed them menus.

"Thank you."

"Prego."

As the woman walked away, Brooke leaned forward. "I love this town. I love this city. We're sitting outside and it's not too hot and it's not too cold."

"This bed is juuust right!" Carmen teased.

"I'm serious. It's like Seattle with better weather. Better than Seattle. The waterfront doesn't smell like fish guts."

"Ewhh."

"You know what I mean."

A waiter came to the table. "Hello, ladies. I'm Giovanni, I'll be serving you today. Can I get you something to drink? A Bloody Mary, maybe? A glass of wine?"

"How about a spritz? An Aperol spritz?" A staple when she had visited Italy.

"Good choice."

"Make it two," Carmen said.

He walked away and Brooke put her phone down. "He's Italian."

"I think they all are."

Brooke couldn't stop smiling. "I wonder if D'Angelo is a family name?" Her muse was sparked for the first time in weeks.

Someone arrived with water, set it on the table.

A few seconds of silence passed, and Brooke turned her attention to Carmen.

Who was staring.

"What?"

"I'm going to suggest something."

"Okay."

Carmen stopped smiling. "You have to promise me you won't instantly tell me it won't work or it's a bad idea. Promise me you'll think about it and instead of saying you can't, ask yourself how you can."

"You make it sound like I'm a horribly negative person."

Her friend offered a soft smile. "Not the woman I've known all these years. But lately, yeah. All this stuff with your dad and Marshall. I don't know, Brooke . . . your glass has been half-empty a lot lately."

Much as she wanted to deny Carmen's accusation, Brooke would be lying to herself.

"Okay. I promise."

Carmen looked around the room, at the people passing by the restaurant as they went on with their day. "Find a home for your dad down here. Sell the condo. Move to San Diego."

That's crazy.

39

Carmen must have seen the words on her face. "You promised."

"I did."

"It's the perfect compromise. Your dad is only a couple of hours away from where he's lived his whole life, not that it matters since he'll be in an assisted living home. You are in a city you have instantly fallen in love with. You can take care of him and not hate every day in a city you loathe."

The waiter returned with their drinks. "Have you decided on lunch?"

"We haven't even looked at the menu," Carmen told him.

"Flag me down when you're ready. No rush." He walked off to another table.

Brooke lifted her drink. "Your idea is tempting."

"My idea is brilliant."

"Gio!" the bartender yelled at their waiter and started in a rapid fire of Italian.

They went back and forth a couple of times, and for whatever reason, Brooke found herself smiling. "Crazy."

"Maybe we should figure out what we're going to eat."

An hour later they'd destroyed two appetizers and were on a second drink and had both ordered a main course.

Carmen was searching the internet for assisted living facilities in the general area, and Brooke left her to it in search of a bathroom.

One of the employees pointed her to the back of the restaurant.

There she found a vast space where she could see into the open kitchen, not like in a diner you'd see at any stop along an interstate, but like in a five-star restaurant that wasn't afraid of the patrons seeing the inner workings of where their food was being prepared.

Lunch was in full swing, and everyone in the kitchen was hopping.

And not surprisingly, like many of the employees in the front of the house, those back here were speaking Italian.

Loudly.

It made Brooke feel good about her choice in lunch spots. At least she knew her meal would be authentic.

She made her way to the restroom and then back out.

This time, as she passed by the kitchen, she heard a male voice yell out a name. "Francesca!"

Then, as if in slow motion, two things happened. A blur of a little girl, not more than eight years old, came darting around the corner at the same time a server turned with their hands filled with plates of steaming hot pasta.

Brooke saw the imminent collision, swooped down, and lifted the girl before she could knee-tackle the employee.

The waitress stopped short but didn't lose her balance. "Franny!"

"Sorry," the little girl said.

Big dark brown eyes looked up at Brooke as she set the girl on her feet. "You need to be careful. Those plates are hot."

"Francesca Mari!" The deep baritone of what could only be a ticked-off parent came from behind them.

They both looked up.

Brooke felt a little like the air in the room started to still . . . or maybe the man carried the heat from the kitchen with him when he'd walked out. Obviously, he was one of the cooks, from the uniform he wore. He was glaring at the little girl.

He said something to her in Italian, and she replied with something that made him frown even more.

When he grunted, Francesca turned to Brooke and tried to smile. "Thanks for keeping me from getting hurt."

Brooke tried not to laugh. "You're welcome."

The girl started to run again.

"Walk!" the father yelled.

They watched Francesca as she inched her steps to exaggerated slowness as if mocking her father.

Francesca turned back around.

Dad wasn't nearly as amused.

"I'm sorry," the man said.

"It's okay. I'm glad she wasn't hurt."

He looked beyond Brooke, at his daughter . . . a flicker of annoyance.

"She's adorable, by the way."

That, at least, brought a smile to the man's face. And the oxygen that was in the room had a hard time finding Brooke's lungs. Her guess was this man could use that smile and his chiseled jaw and dark skin to get just about anything he wanted from a woman. Toss in a little *amore* this and *amore* that . . .

What was she thinking? He was probably married.

Hello . . . he had a daughter.

Family restaurant with a little girl running around that the employees called Franny.

"Thank you. I appreciate your intervention."

His voice melted her insides like heat to chocolate.

Brooke stared at the man and found herself thinking about all the works of art scattered throughout Italy. No wonder so many men were etched in marble and stone. If all Italians looked like this man . . .

He cleared his throat.

She closed her eyes, felt heat in her cheeks. "I'll let you get back to work."

He nodded. "Probably a good idea."

Only his feet didn't move.

His smile softened when she dared another look in his eyes.

"Right. Uhm . . ."

Did he just laugh?

Brooke shook her head as she walked away. The heat on her back suggested the man watched her retreat.

She and Carmen spent two hours with their meal, and when the check came it had a zero written on it and the word *Grazie*.

They argued, but the waiter wouldn't hear it. Brooke had kept Franny from unknown injury, and that was worth a free meal for this restaurant.

With nothing to do but say thank you, that was exactly what they did.

"Are you ready to start looking for apartments?" Carmen asked.

"You're getting ahead of yourself, aren't you?"

"Am I?"

Brooke looked over her shoulder at the establishment they'd just left. *Was she?*

CHAPTER FIVE

"Today was better. Finally, things are looking up."

Luca glanced at his mother from the other side of the table. It wasn't often they shared a meal with receipts of the day between them, but business had been in a tailspin for what felt like forever. Between restrictions that were implemented off and on for years, and employee shortages, it was only recently that things were getting consistently normal.

"What's this?" Mari held a receipt in her hand.

Luca narrowed his gaze, saw his signature for the comped meal.

He thought of the kind eyes behind her smile.

Silence stretched for a moment too long, he caught it, cleared his throat. "Your granddaughter thought it best to run through the kitchen during the height of lunch. This patron intercepted and kept everyone from unnecessary trips to an urgent care."

"Hmm." His mother stared over the receipt as if reading his mind. "Was she pretty, this patron?"

Luca turned his attention back to the inventory sheet to avoid his mother's eyes. "I don't believe I said it was a woman."

"I'll take that as a yes."

"Mama. Stop."

She put the paper to the side. "What? A mother can't ask her handsome single son about a pretty girl?"

"Why don't you put that energy into schooling your granddaughter to not use the kitchen as a playground?"

Mari clicked her tongue as she did anytime she was dismissing someone's suggestion. "Poor child needs siblings. Her playmates are the employees. It's wrong."

Much as Luca wanted to disagree, he couldn't. But he wasn't about to give Franny a brother or a sister without the required mother to go with it. And that was too much effort.

Luca finished his notes on the inventory and pushed the paperwork aside. He reached for the bread and broke off a generous piece. "Maybe tomorrow you can take Franny to the park."

"Maybe."

Giovanni made his way to the back of the restaurant where they were sitting and tossed his apron on a chair. "We need to hire more waiters."

Luca moaned.

Mari clicked her tongue.

Chloe came in with Franny at her side.

How had his daughter gotten so big? "Shouldn't you be in bed?" he asked with a smile.

Franny took his grin as an invitation and ran to him and jumped in his lap.

"What did I say about running in the restaurant?"

"No one is here," she argued.

"She has a point," Gio said, reaching for the lobster ravioli Luca had prepared for the daily special. It was their mother's recipe, but she didn't spend as many hours behind the stove as he did. Not when Francesca needed supervision.

Sergio raised his voice from behind the bar. "I'm leaving."

"Are you hungry?" Mari asked.

"I ate earlier," he said with a wave of his hand. "Ciao, ciao."

A chorus of the same followed his goodbye.

Chloe walked behind him, locked the restaurant door. "I'm not here until after three tomorrow," she said as she approached the table.

"Which is perfect since I'm leaving at four. You'll have to wait tables," Gio informed her.

"I can wait tables," Francesca announced.

Her willingness to help had Luca hugging her tight. "In a few years, my sweet."

"Nonna says she waited tables when she was my age. Right, Nonna?"

All eyes moved to Mari. "It was a different time."

Gio was shoving food in his mouth and talking. "Labor laws would bury us, but if we don't hire some staff soon, we might have to dress Franny up and see what she can do."

That had Francesca giggling.

"It will work out," Luca found himself saying.

Franny's mouth opened wide for a lion-size yawn. Luca smiled and said, "Okay, kiss Nonna. Time for bed."

"But . . ."

He placed a finger on her nose, and she stopped her argument and slid off of his lap. Luca watched as his pride and joy moved around the table kissing everyone goodnight and returned to his side. He lifted her into his arms, even though she was getting way too big to do this much longer. "You've been eating Santorini's gelato," he teased.

"Only a little."

He walked to the back of the building and through the family door to the stairway. The floor directly above the restaurant was where his mother, Giovanni, and Chloe lived. He and Francesca had the one above that, although it was common that his daughter wanted to sleep with her aunt or grandmother, and Luca never stopped her.

She needed the women in her life, considering her mother wasn't a part of it.

"Papa?"

Franny's head rested on his shoulder as he walked into her bedroom. "Yes?"

"Can you take me to school tomorrow?" she asked when he set her down on her bed.

"I can, but Nonna will pick you up."

That seemed to make her happy by the smile on her face. She snuggled into the blankets and reached for the tattered stuffed llama she'd yet to give up when she slept.

"Go eat, Papa."

He kissed her forehead and tucked the blankets around her. "Sweet dreams."

Her eyes were already closing.

He backed out of the room, leaving the doors open on his way downstairs.

This was his life, every day, and he wouldn't change it for the world.

~

"How much do you want for this?"

Brooke looked over her shoulder at the man hollering from the other side of the driveway. It was eight in the morning, and the yard sale was busier than the sale rack at Walmart during the holidays. "Fifty."

The man narrowed his eyes, shook the power tool in his hand. "It's not worth that."

"You're right, it's worth a hundred, but I want it to go today." Power tools were the only thing of value her father had. And since she'd already danced on this stage once before, after his stroke, she knew how to price the items he'd decided to keep. And now that he no longer needed them, and she had no intention of using them herself . . . "Fifty-five for you."

"I'll give you sixty," another man said.

Brooke smiled. "My dad's in a nursing home. Highest bidder gets the tool."

The first man set it down and moved on. "All yours, dude."

By nine, all the tools were gone, and the bulk of the money she would make was in her pocket. Garden tools were the next to go. She planned on finding an apartment, and the extent of yard work would be a potted plant for him and maybe an herb garden for her. Rakes and shovels had no room in her life.

The minimum of furniture was staying in the condo up until it was sold.

Her father would only need a bed, a small sofa, TV, and side table for the space in the assisted living facility. She'd been combing through his things, without him, and choosing what he would keep and what was going to someone else forever.

The conversation about going into a home had been one of the hardest she'd ever had.

Her father's confusion was completely gone, but his physical self wasn't bouncing back like it had before.

"We have to think about what comes next," she'd started when it became apparent that he wasn't going to be able to care for himself once he was discharged from the nursing home. "Living alone isn't an option any longer."

Her father blinked several times before he released a long-suffering sigh. "I know. But you're here now."

She swallowed . . . hard. "I can't be your nurse."

He placed his hands over his protruding stomach. She could only imagine what he thought of in that moment. The wound that was slowly healing. The diaper he was wearing since getting to the bathroom in time was a struggle.

"We can hire a nurse."

Brooke hated to dash his hopes. "That's an expense we can't afford. Medicare doesn't pay for it."

"What if I get better?"

"What if you don't?" She sat forward, placed a hand over his arm. "Dad, listen, I can't live in Upland. Even if the condo was an option, I can't stay there. And as much as I love you, I don't see me cleaning your bottom."

"I'll wheel myself off a cliff before I . . . I let my daughter wipe my a-ass."

They were on the same page there. "I've looked into assisted living homes."

He narrowed his gaze, opened his mouth . . .

She cut him off before he uttered a word.

"It's your own apartment, Dad. Yes, there is help there, someone to keep you clean," she said as delicately as possible. "They do your laundry, keep the place tidy. Someone else is making your meals three times a day. You have a small space for your own food if you want it."

"O-old folks' home."

"Assisted living. And here is the bottom line. You can't afford to hire help, and I can't hire any help without selling the condo."

"Wh-where will you live?"

"Let's move to San Diego," she said with a smile. "It's close, but a compromise."

He shook his head.

"Dad. I'm doing everything I can here. I packed up and moved to California. You have to wiggle a little. You can't stay alone in the condo, and I cannot . . . I *won't* live there." Tears filled her eyes without invitation. "How fair is it for me to give up everything and you give up nothing?"

"I'm the one-one in the bed."

"And I'm trying to keep you as comfortable as I can. My work is suffering. My personal life is gone." She hated the emotion rolling down her cheeks.

"Assisted living."

"It's the best option. Please, Dad. I've crunched the numbers. Your savings will keep you there for a while, and the condo sale will make up the rest when it's needed."

He wasn't shaking his head anymore.

He covered her hand with his own. "You're not wiping my a-ass."

The decision had been made.

Now it was all about how to pay for it.

She needed the money from the condo to make it work, and eventually she'd spend time with a financial planner. If in fact her father didn't have any other issues and lived another twenty years, she needed a map on how she was going to provide for him.

His social security helped but didn't cover even half of what his bill would be. But he would have food and care with people available all day and night should he need it. And that was huge.

The compromise was San Diego.

He was going to a town outside of the city, and once he was there and the condo was in escrow, she'd find a small place and make it work.

Carmen was right.

Moving to San Diego was the best possible solution to the crappiest hand delivered to both her and her father.

Only once had her dad said that he didn't know anyone in San Diego.

Brooke looked him in the eye, not willing to cave. "Good friends will make the drive. Acquaintances won't. And when you're up for it, we can come back to visit. It's not a prison. It's senior living where you can come and go as you please, so long as your memory is intact."

Her father had smiled. "I don't r-remember my jokes."

"And I'm thankful for it," she teased. His jokes were awful. He thought they were hilarious.

At the end of the day, the hard decisions had been made, and now it was all about making it happen. She'd found her father's forever home and a real estate agent that insisted she'd get multiple offers on day one and likely be able to close escrow within thirty.

All she was waiting for was a discharge date for her dad and she'd hit the green light.

Then she'd look for her own place. Though she had considered looking sooner. Swinging rent, and the mortgage, and the down payment for her dad's place, and, and, and . . . It made her nauseous.

While the temperature rose, and the stragglers meandered in and out, Brooke sifted through the hordes of files her father hadn't bothered with in forty years. Birthday and Christmas cards, letters from his long-gone mother back when he'd moved from the East Coast to California. While one or two were interesting to read, they all said the same thing.

And the Dear John letters.

Her father, in addition to his failed marriages, had racked up quite a few pissed-off women in his time.

Why keep the letters?

After two or three, Brooke determined that her father wasn't a trusting man. Which she already knew. That lack of trust bred insecurity and jealousy, which was the downfall of every relationship.

And now he was alone. Yes, he had her, but it wasn't the same and Brooke knew that.

For a brief moment, she thought of Marshall. Realized that her thoughts hadn't traveled to him in over a week.

She missed the security of the relationship but didn't find herself pining for the man.

He hadn't reached out to her. Never truly tried to change her mind.

If he'd really loved her, wouldn't he have tried?

Brooke shook off the impending melancholy and glanced around at the bits and pieces of yard-sale leftovers.

She opened the trunk of her father's car, the one she'd decided to drive until everything was sold and they'd moved to San Diego. Then she'd stop payment on the damn thing and give it back to the dealership that sold it to her dad in the first place. She bagged up the clothing that didn't sell, the miscellaneous household items collected by an old man, and tossed the yard-sale sign in the trash.

Three trips to the Goodwill later and she was ready for a shower, dinner, and bed.

Her phone rang while she was chopping vegetables for her salad.

"Miss Turner?"

"This is her."

"This is Simone." The social worker and Brooke had spoken many times.

"Do you have a discharge order yet?"

"Sure do. A week from Thursday. The wound should be good enough for a simple dressing, and the assisted living facility has agreed to accept."

Brooke stopped cutting the food and rescheduled her week in her head. "Okay. Thank you. Let me know if something changes."

She hung up the phone, growing tired just thinking about the work ahead of her. A quick call to her real estate agent put a deadline on when she needed to get the condo ready to show. She could use the garage for the piles of crap that would take a long time to get through while the place was on the market. Four days to pack and clean. Then a trip to San Diego to finalize her dad's space at Autumn Senior Living. She'd drop off a few boxes on what would be several back-and-forth trips for the small things. After mapping out the new space for her father, she had decided it made no sense for her to rent a truck and lug any of his furniture into the new place. None of it would fit. He needed a twin bed and a tiny love seat. The condo furniture wouldn't work, and sadly, it was trashed anyway. It was more cost effective to shop and have it delivered before her father arrived. She'd use familiar lamps and pictures to make the place feel like home the best she could.

It's all she could do.

Brooke finished her dinner, cleaned the mess she'd made, and carried her second glass of wine to the living room.

It was strange to sit in a home she owned and yet feel like a stranger in it.

She and Marshall were always fluid, and home was wherever they landed. It worked, for a while. But she wasn't happy with Marshall. There was no safety. No security.

Brooke needed something different. She wasn't sure if San Diego was it, but it was the right place to start looking.

CHAPTER SIX

D'Angelo's was a little quieter compared to the time she'd been there with Carmen. Understandable, considering it was between lunch and dinner. In Brooke's experience, touristy places like Little Italy tended to stay busy most of the day, though.

Still, she had a seat in a booth with a couple of local rental magazines in front of her along with a newspaper.

She'd arrived in San Diego before noon, met with the director at the senior living facility, and wrote the big check to move her father in. Now she needed to concentrate on her move.

Her wish list was minimal. One bedroom would be ideal, but a loft or large studio would work. On-site parking . . . although once her dad's car was gone, would she need a car? She could Uber to her dad. No. If he got sick again, and he would, she'd need to get him to and from doctor's appointments. On-site parking was circled on her must-haves. Air conditioning?

Brooke glanced around the restaurant, saw all the open windows. A question mark on cooler air.

Dishwasher? Eh . . . it was only her.

Washer and dryer? Eh . . . schlepping her clothing to a laundromat wasn't new. Ideal, no, but not a big deal.

Pool and on-site hot tub? Sure, they'd be nice, but a balcony with a view would be better.

Checks and balances.

"Ricotta and spinach ravioli," the waitress said as she walked to the table, dish in hand.

"Oh, excuse me." Brooke pushed her magazines and notes aside and made room for her late lunch.

"No problem." She set the plate down. "Are you looking for a new apartment?"

"My first apartment, actually. Well, here."

The woman smiled with her eyes. "How exciting. You're going to love San Diego."

"I hope so. I've had a rough couple of months."

"I'm sorry."

Brooke wasn't sure why she said that to a stranger. "It's okay. Uhm, would you mind if I asked you a question?"

"Of course not."

"How hot does it get here? Do I need to have an air conditioner, or can I keep the windows open with a fan on?"

The waitress pointed to the floor. "Here, this close to the water, an open window and fan works for all but maybe two weeks of the year. Not in a restaurant, of course."

"That's what I thought."

"If you go inland, you'll want air."

Brooke sighed. "I want to see the water."

The sound of feet running caught their attention.

"Franny!"

Brooke laughed under her breath as the little girl slowed to a small trot through the empty tables of the restaurant.

"I see she still isn't listening," Brooke said.

"Ah, you've been here before?"

"A few weeks ago, with my friend. Francesca almost took out a waitress, and your cook graciously comped our meal. I felt it was only right that I return and pay for it this time."

"Ahhh, yes. I knew you looked familiar. I'm Chloe, and my niece, Francesca, has the run of the place. Now that we're busy again, she needs to find other places to play."

"Poor girl."

"Don't let her hear you say that. She'll play your sympathy for all it's worth. The baby in the family gets all. Trust me." Chloe looked at the pasta. "I'm keeping you from your meal. I'll leave you to it."

"I'm good. Thank you."

Chloe walked away and Brooke smiled.

The ravioli was even better than the last time. How you could beat lobster, she didn't know, but the way the cheese melted on her tongue was bliss.

How on earth did Chloe keep her slim frame with this kind of food available every day?

Brooke had asked herself that question the two times she'd been in Italy. Pasta, in European portions, was available like potatoes were in America, in one form or another every night. Bread, pasta . . . wine. Yet the women were slim, and the men fit. Brooke had chalked it up to all the walking one did while roaming the city. She'd stayed in Florence and Rome during her trips, Florence being her favorite. While Little Italy was not Firenze, it was the closest thing she would get to it on this side of "the pond." And in light of her father's health . . . the closest she'd get to it in years. Which was depressing if she were being honest with herself.

She'd take it. And maybe take the time to learn Italian so when she did return to the real thing, she'd have a better grasp of the world around her.

She liked the idea.

Intentions, life goals, and something to look forward to.

Another bite of cheese and pasta went past her lips, and she sighed with pleasure and closed her eyes.

"I see you're enjoying your meal."

Brooke's eyes opened to find an older woman standing a few feet from the table, a smile on her face.

"The ravioli is sinful. You should try it."

The woman put a hand to her chest and offered a slight bow of her head. "*Grazie*. My grandmother's recipe."

Brooke brought her napkin up to her mouth and swallowed her food completely. "This is your restaurant?"

"It is. Mari D'Angelo," she said in introduction.

"I'm Brooke Turner. I'm new here . . . well, soon to be new here. This is my second time in your restaurant and I'm in love."

The woman's smile was radiant. She had to be in her late fifties, maybe sixties. Her accent thick enough to suggest that English was her second language.

"You're moving to our Italy?"

"I'd like to. The rents are a bit steep, though."

The rushing of small feet preceded the appearance of Francesca. "Nonna, Nonna!"

"Slow down before your papa sees you," Mari warned the girl.

"Too late." A deep, sexy, Italian voice shivered up Brooke's spine as the quintessential Little Italy man came into view. Dressed in jeans and a casual shirt and not the white uniform of a cook, he had a strong jaw, with piercing eyes that looked through you.

Sexy. Way too damn sexy.

"We're going to the park," Franny announced to her grandmother.

Brooke found herself smiling. "Where you can run without risk of colliding with the waiters."

At her words, Francesca's father took the moment to look up. His gaze narrowed, then softened . . . slightly. "You."

He recognized her.

She was surprised. "Hello again."

Mari moved her gaze between them. "You know each other?"

Brooke shook her head. "No. Not really. When I was here before, Franny and I ran into each other."

Franny pinched her lips, glanced up. "We did?"

"That's not how I remember it." He took a moment and explained what had happened. Mari's smile settled on her face and her hands clasped in front of her as she watched her son speak.

"I see," Mari said when he was done talking. "Francesca is just as energetic as you were at her age."

As if proving her grandmother's point, the girl tugged on her father's hand. "C'mon. Let's go. Dinner will be soon."

Mari waved a hand at her son. "Go. I'm here for the first rush if you're late."

"We'll be back." His eyes traveled to Brooke. "Enjoy your meal . . ." His words trailed off as if in question.

"Brooke."

"Brooke," he repeated. "And thank you again."

"Please, it's not, wasn't . . . a problem."

He turned, said something to his mother in Italian, and walked away, Franny's hand in his.

"My son. A good man. Excellent father. Hard to do on your own. But he does it," Mari said after he was out of sight.

The hair on Brooke's neck did a little dance as Mari disclosed a little too much information for a patron in the restaurant. Or maybe that was the Italian way.

"I'm sorry, I've met your son twice now and have never gotten his name."

If Mari was smiling before, she was radiant now. "Luca. Strong name, *vero?*"

"Yes." Brooke glanced at her plate and Mari gasped.

She rattled something in Italian and then started apologizing profusely. "All this chatter and your food is cold."

Before Brooke could utter a word, Mari called out to the kitchen. By the time Brooke could take a second bite of her cold pasta, the matriarch of the D'Angelo family had another steaming hot plate in front of her and was whisking away the old one.

"Ah, better."

"You didn't have to—"

"I did. You eat, and perhaps we can talk over cappuccino when you're done."

It was nice to smile. "I'd like that."

~

The plate was empty, nearly licked clean, and Mari sat beside Brooke in the booth as if they were old friends.

"Let me see where you think you want to live," Mari said, pointing at the magazines Brooke had set aside.

"What I want and what I can afford are competing. But maybe you can tell me about neighborhoods, so I don't get stuck in an unsafe area."

"I'm biased to Little Italy. This restaurant belonged to my father before me and my late husband."

"I'm sorry. Your late husband, I mean," Brooke explained.

"It's been many years. My father went back to Italy to care for his parents when they were old and stayed. He has visited a few times since but is getting too old for the trip."

"He's still alive?"

"Eighty-one."

"That's lovely."

Mari smiled, looked back at the magazine. She picked up a pen and started crossing off some of Brooke's picks.

"No. No. Absolutely not."

Brooke looked over at what apartments she was crossing off the list. The cheaper ones outside of Little Italy were dropping like flies.

"No. Even Chloe would agree this neighborhood is a bit overrun these days."

Mari tapped her pen next to the picks just up the street.

The high-rise condo type locations in Little Italy with all the amenities and the price tag to go with it.

"You have question marks next to these. Why?" she asked.

"Budget," Brooke answered. "I have some unexpected and unknown financial . . . issues . . ." She didn't feel comfortable talking about her father's situation. It opened up too many questions that she truly didn't want to get into with a near stranger. Her hope of living close to the water was quickly becoming a passing dream. At least for a while. "Maybe there's a neighborhood a little farther inland you can suggest?"

Mari narrowed her eyes in thought, thumbed through the magazine. "Hmmm. You know. I may have a solution for you."

"I'm open to ideas."

She nodded her head. "Grab your purse. Come with me."

Brooke looked at her watch as she did, realized she was going to hit a ton of traffic on her way back to Upland, but pushed the thought aside. Narrowing her search with someone who knew the town was more important than a few lost hours sitting on California freeways.

Brooke trailed behind Mari as they wove their way through the back of the restaurant.

They moved through the employee-only sections where the muted colors of the establishment turned to bright white and clean surfaces easier to scrub. Mari said things in Italian to those who spoke to her en route to wherever she was leading Brooke.

Through a door, they were in a hallway leading to a stairway that looked less like a restaurant and more like a home.

"One of the things that my beloved parents enjoyed most about this property is the residence above. The first floor is the restaurant. The second floor is where I live with my children. Where I lived with my parents when I grew up and eventually with my husband." They walked by a door in the stairwell that Mari pointed to and kept climb-ing. "My Luca and Francesca live on the third floor." She pointed to another door.

Brooke began to see where this field trip was headed and started to get her hopes up.

On the fourth floor, Mari stopped. "This floor is a smaller apart-ment we've used for guests. Family when they visit, or my children when the elders come and can't climb as far up. I've considered renting it for a year now. People simply don't visit the way they once did."

Mari opened the unlocked door and walked in.

The large open room had a half-vaulted ceiling since it was on the top floor. The open beams were right out of the pages of an Italian travel guide and matched the decor in the restaurant below. The kitchen, off the living and compact dining area, was small but had a stovetop, an oven, and a refrigerator that would hold enough food for one person. Especially if you were a guest of the family who owned the restaurant downstairs. It made sense.

It was furnished in whites and off whites with splashes of yellow and olive greens.

It was beautiful.

Brooke walked in silence, poked her head into the cozy bedroom and the well-equipped bathroom, which had an old clawfoot tub with a shower and a long curtain.

There was a ton of natural light from the windows facing the street and airflow to the back as well.

"There is a terrace that you'd have direct access to but would be sharing with my family. A second door from the stairwell is how we get to the space. We have Sunday dinners there when the weather allows." Mari indicated a door on the far end of the kitchen. They walked through and out onto what wasn't a terrace so much as a rooftop patio. The view was spectacular. She could see the bay, the ships . . . feel the breeze on her skin.

There were lights strung up from one side to the other. A long family table took up a fair amount of room, and a seating area around a gas firepit completed the space.

Brooke closed her eyes and pulled in a breath. "I'm afraid to ask what this will cost."

Mari chuckled. "I wouldn't have brought you up here to disappoint you, m'dear. It is doing no one any good empty. It does not have an air conditioner. You should know that. That kitchen is pathetic, as you can see."

"It's perfect for me."

"You don't cook?" she asked.

"I don't really . . . it's not my strong point."

Mari shook her head. "I can teach you. Sunday dinners are long and loud."

"That won't bother me."

"It will take me a little time to get the furniture out for your things."

"No!" Brooke almost shouted. "I mean, can it come furnished? I'm a clean person. I'm happy to pay a hefty deposit and cleaning fee for anything that—"

"That would be perfect. Don't you have your own things?"

"Some, but nothing big. It's a long story." One she didn't want to share.

"Maybe over a glass of wine," Mari suggested.

"Or a bottle," Brooke countered.

The older woman smiled.

"I like you, Brooke."

Brooke's palms started to sweat. "How much, Mrs. D'Angelo?"

Mari didn't answer the question. Instead, she moved to the edge of the rooftop and picked at what looked like an herb garden. "Would you request a lease?"

"Well . . ." Brooke hesitated. "This is an experiment for you, right?"

"It is . . . but—"

"Then I wouldn't want to hold you to something you're not completely sure you want to do long term. Much as this would be ideal for me. Your graciousness in suggesting I rent this space is . . . well . . . if you could give me thirty days' notice if it wasn't working out."

Mari lifted her chin and smiled. "You're wise. Yes, that will work." She walked past Brooke and headed for the apartment.

"Mrs. D'Angelo?"

"Yes?"

"The price?"

Mari paused, sniffed the herb in her hand, and stood silent for a moment before telling Brooke a number.

It was the cost of a studio in a bad neighborhood.

"That's ridiculously low," Brooke argued.

Mari lifted a finger in the air. "No air conditioner." She lifted a second finger. "No elevator." A third. "A toddler's kitchen." A fourth. "Laundry is downstairs in the back of the restaurant, and the only time you can use it, even if you want to, is after hours. Of course, you're welcome to use my set at any time." Her thumb came up last. "My family is loud. Loveable, but loud."

Brooke didn't hesitate. "I'll take it."

A breath.

A pause.

"Good."

CHAPTER SEVEN

"You did what?"

"I rented the apartment on the top floor."

"The guest room," Luca corrected her.

"We need the money."

"We're fine."

"Pass the wine."

Luca stared at his mother as she casually asked for wine as if she'd just talked about finding a sweater for Franny.

"Mama."

"*Grazie,*" she said to Chloe, who handed her the wine but looked just as concerned about the conversation as any of them.

"This is our home," Gio said.

"It's still our home."

"With strangers inside it?" Luca insisted. He glanced at his daughter as she dug into her dinner like a starved child.

"You worry for nothing."

"Mama!" Chloe's voice rang in the room.

"You have nothing to worry about. I've vetted the tenant."

Luca almost choked on the word. "Tenant. Do you hear yourself?"

"What about Franny?" Gio asked.

"Exactly!" Luca pointed at his daughter.

Francesca stopped chewing her bread long enough to look up at the mention of her name.

"Adventure runs in her blood. Francesca will be fine."

Luca looked at his brother. "We can get out of it."

"Of course we can."

Mari's hand slapped the table. "I have never led this family astray. You will respect my decisions until I've proven I'm unable to make responsible decisions. These past few years have been difficult on all of us. We can use the money. And with a renter, we have a new set of business expenditures we didn't have before. We need them." She took a deep breath. "Now. I expect nothing less than the hospitality we extend to our family with our new tenant. They have rented the space fully furnished. So, if there is anything upstairs that you'd like to hold on to, I suggest you get it now. They are returning next week."

There were very few times in Luca's life that he wanted to defy his mother with his whole being.

This was one of them.

"Francesca needs stability," he argued.

"She'll have it."

"With a stranger walking in and out?" Gio shouted.

Luca appreciated his younger brother's support.

"A stranger today is a friend tomorrow."

"Or an enemy," Luca growled.

His mother turned to him. "When did you become so cynical?"

"When life proved I'm right." Breath hit his lungs hard. He shook off his thoughts. "Don't you think we at least deserved a moment of your time to discuss a decision that would affect all of us?"

Mari paused, lifted her glass of wine to her lips. "Some decisions in life are felt and spontaneous. And they are perfectly right. You'd do well to remember that. Your father proposed to me on such a moment. Picking flowers in a field." Her smile turned wistful, and her eyes glazed over in memory.

Luca hesitated to say more before she continued.

"He handed me that pathetic display of flowers and dropped to his knee. We were children." Mari caught Luca's gaze for a second. "In life, you'll have moments when you know you're doing the right thing. For me, this is one of those times. Let's eat."

The need to argue more was hot on his lips.

Dishes passed between them in silence. The only one who seemed unfazed was Franny, who was nearly done with her dinner, whereas the rest of them hadn't begun.

"Mama . . ."

Mari ignored Luca and said, "The new waiter seems to be catching on quickly, don't you think?"

And just like that, the conversation about the tenant was dismissed.

Or swept under the carpet, as the case was.

Later, after Franny was tucked into bed and all was quiet on the floors below, Luca walked up the stairwell to the top floor and into the guest room of their family home.

"You're late." Gio had already beat him to it.

Luca took the seat opposite his brother, his arms spread on the sides of the chair. "What the hell is she thinking?" His eyes traveled around the space that had always been their sanctuary. As children, they'd used it to escape the chaos of the restaurant and grown-ups. As teenagers, they'd entertained their friends. As adults, they'd invited family and friends for long stays without them getting underfoot.

"I knew I should have moved up here at the beginning of the year," Gio said on a hard sigh.

"No one could have seen this coming."

Gio shook his head, reached for the beer he had on the coffee table. "There's more in the fridge."

Luca waved him off.

"Maybe this is a good thing."

"Excuse me?" Luca said.

Gio shook his head. "I don't know. A sign. For me. Where am I supposed to entertain a woman, Luca? My mother's home? This has always been the space."

Luca hadn't even thought of that.

Gio's sexual wings had been snipped with his mother's actions.

"What are you thinking?" Luca asked, knowing exactly what his brother was going to say.

"I need to be on my own. It's time."

If there was something Luca understood more than anything, it was the desire to shift gears. But the one time he'd tried that, it backfired. Raising Franny with his mother and sister close at hand to give her what she needed from strong women was important. The last thing his daughter needed was a jaded father being the only influence in her life.

"What? No argument?"

Luca lifted himself from the chair and decided on that beer after all. "No argument. A request."

"What's that?"

"Help at the restaurant until we can find more staff." Luca cracked open the bottle, took a drink.

"Of course, Luca. I'm talking about getting my own place, not removing myself from this family." Gio spread his arms wide. "Even if I found a wife, this space wouldn't do for us for long. Not with the babies I want to have."

"Find the wife. Then move into my floor. Franny and I can take this one."

Gio laughed. "Have you forgotten the tenant? And this is one bedroom. Franny will be a moody teenage girl before you know it."

The thought made Luca nauseous. "You're right. Find the farmhouse in Tuscany and we'll all move in with you."

"You're joking, but when I make the trip, I might just stay."

Luca narrowed his eyes. "There are wineries right here. Temecula is thirty miles."

"And three times as expensive."

Gio had been threatening to go into the wine business since he was old enough to drink the stuff, which at their table was ten, despite what the American laws said. Watered down, of course. Eventually he educated himself and became a certified sommelier. He was working on his advanced certificate when the world shut down. The course he wanted to continue was in Italy, and that was where he was going to immerse himself. He'd put the trip off, but the time was coming and Luca knew his brother was ready to fly away.

"I will support whatever you decide, but truly hope you follow your dreams here. Keep a foot in Italy if you must. But keep your legs here."

Gio grinned. "I love you, too, brother."

Once again, they looked around the top-floor apartment and sighed.

"What the hell was Mama thinking?"

~

Brooke greeted her father at the door of the nursing home with a smile.

He'd lost thirty pounds and aged twenty years.

Despite the wheelchair, he was smiling.

"You ready to blow this scene?" she asked him with a chuckle.

"L-let's get the h-hell outta here." His stutter was a constant since the stroke and had worsened with this illness. When he wasn't stuttering, he was pausing, searching for the words he wanted to use.

The nurse had a clipboard with papers for Brooke to sign. "Since you're transporting him and not an ambulance, we need you to sign these waivers."

"No problem."

Ten minutes later, with the paperwork signed and her father tucked into the passenger seat of the Subaru she'd cursed since she'd found the thing . . . and the wheelchair shoved in the trunk, they were off.

"I'm hungry," her father said before they'd pulled out onto the main road.

"I'm not surprised."

"T-the food was . . . awful. And cold."

"It's a nursing home." As if that was an excuse. "What are you craving?"

"A burrito."

Brooke winced. She knew he was wearing a diaper. But it was a two-hour drive if they didn't hit traffic to San Diego. And a bathroom emergency was the only real concern she had. "You sure?"

Her dad grinned. "I'll be f-fine."

Without options, she pulled into the fast-food restaurant of his choosing, left her dad in the car with the windows down, and ran in to get him what he wanted. Once they were on the road, and her dad was moaning in pleasure at the taste of the food, her concern about how that food was going to process didn't seem to matter. "That good, huh?"

"The best."

Her father's culinary bar was pretty low. "If you say so."

"Is the food good where I'm g-going?" he asked.

"That's what I'm told." She pulled onto the freeway at a snail's pace. The traffic of the Inland Empire would not be missed once the condo sold and she never had to return ever again.

"But you haven't had it."

"No. There are a ton of rules about outside visitors. And since I have been in and out of a hospital with you, and then the nursing home, they didn't want me roaming around the place. They let me bring your personal belongings into the apartment and furnish it. That's it."

"Oh."

Brooke watched him out of the corner of her eye as he finished his food in thought.

She knew he was wrestling with the entire concept of moving into an assisted living home. He was not ready to let go of his independence even if it was being taken from him by Father Time.

"They have to keep you isolated for a few days. It's the rules, Dad. We've talked about this." Traffic eased up a little and she was able to hit the gas.

He sighed, but didn't comment.

"It won't be forever."

"You're selling the condo." It wasn't a question. This, too, they'd gone over, many times.

"It's the only way I can make all this work." Her voice rose and her patience was already running thin, and they'd barely been on the road for thirty minutes.

"I know you're doing all . . . everything. This is hard for me."

Brooke took a deep breath, reached over, and grasped her father's hand. "I know it is, Dad. None of this has been easy on you. I can't imagine. When you were in the ICU and on the ventilator, I didn't think you were going to make it."

"I was in the ICU?"

He'd asked the question before. "For over a week."

"I don't remember it."

"You wouldn't."

"I don't remember a lot of th-things." He looked out the window. "Maybe it will come back."

And maybe it won't.

"I'll be twenty minutes away. Once you're clear for visitors, we can watch the games together." She hated all things sports but watched them with him because he enjoyed them.

"I won't use that w-wheelchair for long," he insisted.

"I hope not."

He patted the door of the car. "You'll keep the car."

She shook her head. "We can't afford it."

"Yes, we can. I bought it."

Brooke swallowed. "You didn't put any money down on it, Dad. The payment is over five hundred a month plus insurance. You need that money from your social security for where you're living." And then a whole lot more from her pocket to make it work. "As soon as the condo sells, I'm taking this back to the dealership . . ."

"No."

"Dad?"

"What if I can drive again?"

She gripped the wheel and kept the cussing from exiting her lips. "Dad," she started calmly. "Even if you could drive, the hospital lost your wallet with your driver's license in it. The DMV will never reissue another license. We both know that."

God, she hated this argument.

She'd hated the car on sight, was disappointed that he'd taken brilliant care of it and yet the condo had fallen into disrepair. The fact that he had an ounce of energy to argue with her about it was insulting. Yet deep down she knew it was his last ounce of independence slipping away.

"I'll keep it for a little longer. But, Dad . . . we can't afford it. You have to trust me on this."

With his silence, she glanced over to see him staring out the window, his eyes glossed over with unshed tears. "This is hard, Brooke. I'm in a f-fucking diaper. I can't remember my prayers . . ." He started tapping his fingertips.

"I'm sure you've said enough Hail Marys to make God happy," she assured him.

"I know you're doing what you have to."

At least he said that. "I am."

When they pulled into the parking lot of his new home, Brooke wrangled the wheelchair out of the trunk.

One of the intake administrators was there, along with a front desk staff member who welcomed her father.

Joe turned on his charm, happy to smile at the younger, pretty women.

The main hall of the home was spacious with plenty of places for people to sit. Double doors spilled into a massive dining room that was currently empty. Glass doors opened into a central courtyard that housed a water fountain and gardens.

The current residents eagerly looked at the new resident and waved and called out a greeting.

Her father had always been social, and Brooke couldn't help but think he'd thrive in a place like this if he gave it half a chance.

A ride in the elevator got them to the second floor. She pointed out the route to his room as she wheeled him down the extensive hallway system.

Once inside, she closed the door behind them.

"Like I said, your couch wouldn't fit, so I bought this one."

Using his feet to move the chair, he moved farther into the small space and clasped his hands in his lap. "It's nice."

She'd hung his TV on the wall.

Family and friends were in framed photographs. Pictures of him dancing and snapshots of his working days were there as well. "I filled the closets with a lot of the clothes I found at the condo. I doubt you'll want to keep much. If you get bored, go through them and bag those you want to give away to make room. There are still some things at the condo. If you think of anything you want or need, you'll need to let me know in the next month."

He pushed himself into the bedroom, poked his head into the bathroom. "This is going to be fine."

She handed him a button to wear around his neck. "If you ever need help, all you have to do is press this and someone will come. They'll come right away and check on you."

Joe's eyes were moving slower, his movements stilled. "It's cold."

Brooke jumped up and moved to the wall unit to turn the heat on high. "They do your laundry and clean the room. They will even make sure you're taking your medication."

"I can take my own medication."

"Let's see how this month goes. And if you're improving, then great. Trust me, everything here is an extra cost. From them giving you a pill to making sure you shower. If you can do it on your own, great. But if you can't, I've got you covered. I don't want you worried about it."

He yawned. "Okay."

"They'll bring your meals to you for the first few days. Then you can go downstairs."

He forced a smile. "I'm going to be fine, Brooke."

God, she hoped so.

This needed to work.

He yawned again. "Are you driving back tonight?"

"No. I'm staying the night and will drive back tomorrow, pick up a load." And continue the cycle a couple times a week until she was completely moved in. Then once it was clear escrow was going to close, she'd do the last Goodwill haul and dump run and the condo would be a part of her past.

Thank God!

Her dad opened his arms. "Give me a hug and g-get out of here."

"I'll see you in a few days. If you need anything, call."

"It looks like you thought of e-everything, honey. I'll be fine."

She walked over, bent down to the level of the chair, and hugged him. "I love you, Daddy."

"Love you, too, b-baby. Thank you for this."

Brooke retraced her steps through the home, stopped at the reception desk, and let them know that she'd be in San Diego overnight should they need her.

She climbed behind the wheel of the car and looked up at the home. "I'm doing the right thing," she told herself.

She gripped the wheel, moved her head from side to side, and felt doubt creep in.

What other choice did she have? Someone was likely at his side right now helping him . . . cleaning him.

Brooke pulled out of the driveway with a knot in her throat.

CHAPTER EIGHT

Mrs. D'Angelo had shown Brooke her parking spot.

The reserved space was small and in the rear of the building sandwiched between a full-size SUV and a tiny Toyota that looked to be on its last legs.

Her first time in her new spot . . . her new home.

She had the key to the door to access her apartment from the back of the property. There also seemed to be a keypad for the automatic lock, but she wasn't given that code. Which was fine. She could of course get in from the restaurant as well, but until the family and staff really knew her, she didn't feel that was appropriate. And certainly not while she was moving boxes into her space.

Not that she had many.

Brooke stepped out of the car and moved around where there was more space to gather a box from the back seat.

"You can't park there!"

She stopped short of grabbing a box, stood up straight.

"Mrs. D'Angelo said this was my sp—" Her gaze captured the man talking and took a full stop.

Luca stood, his white chef uniform in place, one hand on a hip and the other midair as he noticed her.

It was as if they both recognized each other at the same time.

"Oh . . ."

"Your mother said—"

"You're the tenant."

He was not happy. Brooke didn't need a crystal ball to call that one.

She stiffened her spine despite her unease. "I am. I believe this is the spot where your mother told me to park."

Luca's arms dropped to his side. "It is."

"You're upset." The words came out of her mouth without permission from her brain. They were exactly what she was thinking, and her only excuse was that she was tired and had no bandwidth for bullshit after putting her father in the equivalent of an old folks' home.

Luca attempted a smile that he sucked at. "I'm surprised, although I shouldn't be. My mother is very . . ."

Brooke narrowed her eyes. "Very what?"

This time he smiled with a small laugh, and she felt he meant it. "Welcome. Brooke, was it?"

Was Luca good with names, or did he commit hers to memory as somehow his had been ingrained in hers? "Yes."

"Do you need help?"

The word *need* echoed in her brain.

She shook her head. "No. I'm fine. Thank you."

Brooke reached into the back seat and pulled a box out.

The strap of her purse slid from her shoulder, shifting her balance enough to make her catch herself.

She straightened to find Luca taking the box from her arms. "Please. My mother is many things. One of them is unforgiving if she learns I've been less than a gentleman."

Without letting go, she said, "Then we won't tell her."

"I insist."

Brooke had two choices. Play tug-of-war or let him give her one less trip up the stairs.

She met his dark, piercing eyes and let go. "Thank you."

She followed him inside with a suitcase dragging behind her. By the time they reached the top floor, she was out of breath.

"Having second thoughts?" Luca asked.

"Saves on the gym membership," she said.

A single nod and he opened the unlocked door and stepped inside. "Where would you like this?" he asked.

"Anywhere is fine."

Luca set the box in the center of the living room. "You're the first renter we've ever had." He crossed to the small kitchen space and lifted a key. "I placed a lock on the door. My mother has a key for emergency use only."

"You'll hardly know I'm here, Mr. D'Angelo," she assured him.

Some of the stiffness left his spine. "Mr. D'Angelo was my father. My name is Luca."

"I'm mindful that this is new for your family. And I'm not a twenty-year-old with her first apartment who wants to have parties. I'm new to San Diego and don't know anyone here yet. No worries there. That isn't me anyway."

Luca narrowed his eyes briefly. "It's less about noise, and more about my daughter's safety."

"From me?" *What was he getting at?*

He shook his head. "That came out wrong. Less about the parties, but who might be invited to them."

Or who Brooke might invite over to "entertain." She thought of Marshall, briefly, and rolled her eyes as she grasped the handle of her suitcase. "Oh, please. I've all but sworn off your entire gender. I'd switch teams if I could. Franny is safe with me, Luca."

"Thank you for your assurance."

She started toward the bedroom. "I only brought a few boxes. And I'm sure you have better things to do."

Someone saying "Hello" from the hallway caught their attention.

Brooke turned and Luca sighed. "Gio."

"Hello, brother. I thought I heard voices."

Luca's brother was faster with a smile. He waved a bottle of wine in his hand as he stepped into the apartment. "I came to welcome our new tenant."

"I'm Brooke."

"I'm Giovanni. The younger, better-looking brother." He stepped forward and extended his hand.

"The cocky brother," Luca corrected him.

"I came with wine. He probably came with a list of rules."

Brooke tilted her head to the side, glanced at Luca. Pretty accurate assumption coming from the baby brother.

"Is there a party going on up here?"

Through the open door walked Chloe, a face Brooke recognized.

They spotted each other and Chloe started to laugh. "I knew it. Mama wouldn't tell me, but I saw the two of you talking that day, and knew you were the one she rented to."

"Hello, Chloe."

Chloe turned to her brothers. "And you guys were worried. See, it's going to be fine."

"We weren't worried," Luca denied.

Brooke pinned him with a stare. "Excuse me?"

He lifted a hand as if to defend his words and then changed his mind and dropped it to his side.

"Good call," she told him.

Franny bounced into the room, Mari right behind her, albeit a bit slower. "I see no one is watching the restaurant," she said, unaccusingly.

"Look who is here," Chloe said as she moved to the side so Mari had full view of Brooke.

"Hello again, Mrs. D'Angelo," Brooke said.

Mari walked forward, smile stretching all over her face, and reached out with both hands. "You're going to love it here."

"Thank you."

Mari looked down. "Is this all you have?"

"I have a few more boxes in the car. It will take a few trips to get all my things here. Like I said, it isn't much."

Mari turned to her sons. "You heard her. Only a few boxes."

"I can—"

"Don't be ridiculous."

Luca chuckled as he walked by. "Told you," he said under his breath.

Gio handed the wine to Chloe as they left the room to grab the rest of her things.

"You're going to live here now?" Franny asked.

"I am."

The girl pursed her lips to the side as if measuring Brooke up.

"More girls in the house is a good thing," Chloe assured her niece.

"It is?"

"It is!" Mari said.

Good with that, Franny sat on the couch as Brooke was sure the child was used to doing.

"I will open the wine. Chloe, tell Tony to prepare the special so Brooke doesn't have to run out on her first night here. We'll toast our new friend, get her settled, and then leave her alone."

"You don't have to—"

"This is what we do, Brooke. I only know how to welcome you one way."

Chloe moved to the door. "Arguing is futile. She always wins."

"And more wine," Mari yelled as her daughter left the room.

Mari moved into the kitchen, more familiar with it than Brooke, and found a wine opener. "Where are the rest of your things?"

"Two hours north of here. I'll be back and forth a lot in the next few weeks."

The cork came free, and Mari opened a cupboard door where the table settings lived. She removed six wineglasses, a fair amount considering the small space they came from. "I had everything cleaned up here. Even the sheets on the bed. If there is something you expected to see and don't, let me know. I asked my family to remove their personal items."

The only difference Brooke saw was a few less family pictures on the walls. Then again, she'd barely arrived and the place was overrun with D'Angelos.

Luca and Gio walked in, paused. "Where to?"

"Bedroom, please."

They walked out and Gio left for the final trip.

Brooke looked over at Luca, wondering how they decided on who would grab the last box in the car. "Did he pick the short straw?"

Sure enough, Luca grinned. "Rock, paper, scissors."

Chloe returned, her hands full.

Brooke moved in to help. "This looks like more than wine."

"Tony will send a runner in fifteen minutes with your dinner."

There was a loaf of bread that Luca grabbed. A bottle of olive oil and another filled with balsamic vinegar. There was a brick of hard cheese and a jar of olives . . . and yes, another bottle of wine.

"This is crazy."

"Get used to it," Chloe said.

By the time Gio walked back in with the final box, the wine was poured, the bread was cut, and olive oil and vinegar were swirling in a small dipping bowl.

Mari handed Brooke a glass and took one for herself.

The others followed suit.

Franny was handed a glass of water.

"Welcome to our home. We hope you're as happy here as we are. *Alla salute.*"

"Thank you," Brooke said before sipping the wine.

"Now, let me formally introduce you to my family. Francesca, our princess who runs into the pretty ladies in the restaurant and eats too much gelato from next door."

"It's good gelato," Gio assured Brooke.

"Chloe, my youngest, who would be a vegetarian if not for her family heritage and keeps her figure by bending in positions that would put most people in the hospital."

Chloe lifted two fingers. "I teach twice a week. Self-proclaimed yogi."

Brooke grinned. "I could use a little namaste in my life."

"I can teach you."

"I'd like that."

Gio moaned. "Oh my God . . . two of them."

Chloe bumped her brother's side and shut him up.

"Giovanni," Mari continued. "My youngest son, and wine steward."

"Sommelier," he corrected.

"One day he will own his own winery and bless me with a dozen more grandchildren. If only he can find a wife."

Brooke laughed. "A dozen?"

"Someone has to work the fields."

"A dozen kids would scare off most women. You might want to keep that information close to the chest," she warned him.

"I keep telling him that," Chloe said.

"And then we have my oldest, Gianluca."

"Luca," he corrected her.

"Yes, yes . . . everyone here tries to shorten it to Gian. We don't like that, so Luca it is. Still, his given name is Gianluca after his father's grandfather. My Luca is a brilliant chef, a loving father, and a great provider for this family."

"A provider of rules we love to break," Gio chimed in.

"Like not throwing parties?" Brooke asked as she sipped her wine and looked him in the eye.

"Exactly. I see you've already got his number," Gio teased.

"I'm a quick study."

"And will fit in nicely," Mari added.

Catherine Bybee

Another voice joined the party. "Hey, Chloe . . . here's the food."

Chloe put the glass down and grabbed the food.

"Luca," the new guy said. "Tony says they're getting busy."

"Coming," Luca said, putting his glass down. He paused as he moved past Brooke. "Welcome again. And thank you for your assurance."

"You're welcome."

Mari hummed. "Good . . . all good. We'll leave you to yourself."

There was very little wine left in each glass as they set them on the counter.

"I can help clean this up," Chloe offered.

"It's okay. It will help me figure out where everything is."

"Nice meeting you, Brooke," Gio said as he walked out.

"Thanks for bringing up my stuff."

He offered a thumb in the air and walked out.

"Anything you need," Mari said.

"I'll ask," Brooke assured her.

Franny grabbed on to her grandmother's hand. When they left, only Chloe remained.

"Did my brother tell you not to throw a party?" she asked in a whisper.

Her expression must have given her away, because Chloe said something under her breath with a scowl.

"I think he was more concerned about if I was going to be walking men up the stairs past his daughter."

Chloe sucked in air. "Well, that's none of his business."

"Maybe so, but his daughter is his business. I get it." Even if she'd never really had that from her own father, it was nice to see a father take the role seriously.

"You're more understanding than I would be."

"Please, I'm not offended." *Maybe a little offended.* "You've all been more welcoming than I ever thought possible. C'mon, I haven't even

82

washed my hands and I've already had a party. Don't mention it to Luca. It's okay. Truly."

Chloe lifted both hands, dropped them. "Let me know when you'd like to join me for yoga. I have extra mats."

"I will."

"Ciao."

With the last D'Angelo gone, Brooke closed the door and blew out a breath as she leaned against it.

"My family is loud. Loveable, but loud."

She wasn't kidding!

CHAPTER NINE

"It's been three days. Did we scare her off?"

There was no *we* about it. If anyone did the scaring, it was him.

Luca saw the empty parking space between his car and the one his sister drove.

"She told me we'd barely know she was here."

"That isn't the same as not being here," Chloe argued.

By noon the day after they'd welcomed her, Brooke's car had disappeared, and she hadn't returned.

Chloe smacked his shoulder.

"Ouch. What was that for?"

"For telling her she couldn't have a man over."

Luca's jaw dropped. "I never said that."

"You said something like that."

"I did not." *I hinted, and passively judged, and put it in a group setting of parties . . .*

"She has the right to live her life in her own place."

Luca moved away from the window, looking down on the empty parking space.

His sister followed his gaze.

"She's a grown woman. I'm sure she's fine." Then why had he checked out the window several times a day to see if the silence from upstairs was supported by the lack of a car in the space below?

"An adult who could have a boyfriend and is afraid to have a life in her own home."

Luca shivered. "She doesn't have a boyfriend."

"How can you possibly know that?"

He sat on his couch, kicked his feet up onto his coffee table. "She told me."

"What?" Chloe practically yelled her question.

"Brooke said she'd given up men or sworn off us. . . something like that. And that I didn't have to worry about guys walking past our doors at night going to her room." He rubbed his eyes, more than a little tired since the restaurant was picking up with the season. It was nice to see the tourists return on schedule.

Chloe kicked his feet off the table and had him bolting upright.

"What is your issue?"

"Are you telling me our renter . . . a stranger to us, told you in, what, a few minutes, that she was a nun?"

"I doubt that. She did deny being a lesbian."

"Oh my God, Luca!" Chloe yelled. "What the hell did you say to draw any of this from her? No wonder she's disappeared and hasn't returned."

He squared his shoulders. "It was a very civil conversation."

"Really?"

"Yes."

"Did she ask if you had women over?"

He narrowed his eyes. "No. Of course not."

"Ah-huh . . . and did she ask if your lovers are men?"

"Chloe!"

His sister folded her arms over her chest and stared him down.

The longer she stayed silent, the more her words echoed in his ears.

Luca moved his head to one side . . .

The other . . .

"Son of a bitch." He jumped up and headed downstairs.

He found his mother in the restaurant office.

The early lunch staff was setting up and the doors had yet to open for the day.

The second his mother looked over the desk toward him, he froze.

Chloe pushed him from behind.

"Good morning."

The greeting was repetitive. They'd already seen each other when he'd taken Franny to school first thing that morning.

His mother sat back and folded her hands in her lap. "This should be good."

Luca recovered his voice. "Uhm, no. I was wondering if you had a copy of the rental agreement that Brooke signed."

A slight smile tugged at his mother's lips. "And why would you need that?"

He glanced at his sister.

Chloe widened her eyes but didn't say a thing.

"In case of an emergency."

"Is there an emergency?" Mari asked.

"No. Not right now."

His mother unfolded and sat tall. "Then you don't need it."

Chloe surged forward. "Actually, Mama, Luca's worried about her."

"I am?"

"I think she's probably fine. But you know men, they think we women are incapable of taking care of ourselves." Chloe was painting him as a womanizer. It was his turn to push his sister's shoulder until she had to adjust her feet to keep her balance.

"I never said that."

"Are you saying you're not worried?" Chloe asked.

"No. Like you said, Brooke is probably fine. But she did say she's new here and didn't know anyone. And we might have her phone number, but she doesn't necessarily have ours. A restaurant phone number in a cell phone wouldn't likely be called by a hospital." As Luca said those words out loud, he actually started to worry that maybe there was more to do with Brooke's disappearance than just her being scared off by the overwhelming force of their family.

Mari pushed away from the desk with a nod. "You make a good point." She pulled a file from the back of the file cabinet of the desk, opened it, and jotted down a phone number before handing it to him. "Let me know what you find out."

"Thank you."

Back upstairs, Chloe stared at him while he studied the phone number. "Well?"

"I'll call. I just can't have you staring at me while I do it."

Chloe rolled her eyes and turned around.

Luca dialed the number, walked into his bedroom, and closed the door.

Brooke answered on the third ring. "Hello?" Her voice sounded frazzled.

"Brooke?"

"Yes. Who is this?"

"It's Luca . . ."

She was silent.

"D'Angelo."

"Yes. D'Angelo." She blew out a breath as if she'd been holding it and he thought he heard her say "Thank God" under her breath.

"Are you okay?" Luca asked.

She cleared her throat, and this time when she talked, her voice sounded scratchy, as if she were on the verge of tears. "Yes. I'm fine. I saw the number and thought maybe . . . Never mind. Damn. Yes. I'm fine."

"You don't sound fine."

"You don't know me very well. This is my *fine* voice."

"I'd hate to hear your upset voice."

Luca heard her laugh. He liked that better than her fine voice.

"Why are you calling, Luca?"

It was his turn to clear his throat. "Well, Chloe was worried about you. I told her I'd give you a call and make sure you were okay."

"Chloe?"

"Yes. And my mother. I assured them that you were a strong, capable woman, but since you've been gone for a few days, and right after you moved in, they worried. It's an Italian thing," he lied. Well, it was an Italian thing, to worry. Or maybe it was a Catholic thing. Or was that guilt?

"*They* worried but *you* called. Interesting."

She was not buying it.

Luca ran a hand through his hair. "I volunteered. We wanted to make sure you had a contact number. A personal one. You know, in case of an emergency. We realize you don't have people here and . . . yeah. We worried."

"You can stop worrying, Luca. I'm okay. If I can keep my eyes open, I'll be back tonight."

He suddenly felt as if he was invading her privacy again. "This truly wasn't a call to dig into your personal life."

"It didn't sound as if it was." Her voice had softened. Her *fine* sounding much better to his ears.

"Do you have far to drive? Driving tired is a bad idea."

"Luca?"

"Yes?"

"I'm a big girl."

He shook his head, closed his eyes. "And I'm an ass. I'm sorry. You now have my personal number. Feel free to use it."

"Thank you. Tell your mother and Chloe I'll be home soon."

Luca smiled. "I'll do that. Do drive safely."

"Luca?" His name was a warning.

"Fine, drive like a crazy person then."

She laughed. "I'll do that."

He hung up the phone with a grin.

She was growing on him, this Brooke who he didn't want to like.

Luca turned to find Chloe staring at him through the doorway to his room.

"She's okay?"

"Yes. She wanted me to tell you she'd be back tonight or tomorrow."

"I'll let Mama know."

"Good. Now get out of here so I can have some peace before Franny gets home from school."

~

"I'm a p-prisoner."

"They're medical tests, Dad. Shit happens."

"You said three days."

Brooke spoke with her dad through the Bluetooth over the car speakers as she drove through traffic on her way back to San Diego. He had called to complain about something she couldn't do anything about. Which added another layer of crap to her already shitty day.

"It's barely been three days. And they have to get all your results back. This is a challenge for everyone. Try and be patient. I bet they have it by tomorrow." She wouldn't bet much, but she had to tell him something to appease him.

"I . . . I . . . Have you s-sold the condo?"

She knew where this was going. "I'm in escrow." Which wasn't going well, and they were likely going to fall out and start over with a backup offer, hence the bad day and the long three before it filled with inspections and repairs. All in an effort to get as much money as she could out of the place. She was exhausted and falling behind in her job. In order to concentrate and refocus, she needed to get out of Upland and turn her lens to her work. Losing her job was not an option.

"Can you stop it?" her dad asked.

"That isn't going to happen." She hit the brakes as traffic did what it did in Southern California. As the car slowed, her heart rate sped up. The conversation was making her blood pressure surge, she felt it with every beat of her heart. Her father's normal easygoing nature was hit or miss since the stroke, and obviously it was missing the mark today.

"I'm not, not liking it. Here."

The sun was setting, putting the glare directly on her face.

"Dad. I can't talk about this right now. I'm driving. Traffic is a bitch. If you're up in an hour, call me. Or I'll talk with you tomorrow. I bet they have your test results by then and you'll feel better."

For a moment the line was silent. Then she heard her dad yawn. "Fine."

Taillights turned red and the line went dead.

The music she'd been listening to came back onto the radio, and Brooke brought the car to a complete stop.

She felt tears swell and forced them back.

Forty minutes later she pulled into her parking space and released a deep breath.

Outside the car, the noise of Little Italy was bouncing off the street. It helped her find the smile that her father had managed to remove from her lips.

Unlike the time before, none of the D'Angelo men were watching, and she wrestled with her own boxes one at a time for six trips up and down the stairs.

By the time she was done, she was out of breath and happily fatigued after the long drive. And as much as she wanted to drop on the sofa, she had to go back out and find a grocery store.

Her phone didn't ring, thank God.

The corner grocery was small but had the essentials. She filled her cart and did her best to haul it all up the stairs in one go. But it took two.

No sooner had she closed the door behind her than she heard a knock.

By the time she opened it, the person who had knocked was gone, and a bag sat on her doorstep with a note stapled to it.

Brooke could tell without looking inside that it was something from the kitchen downstairs.

She nudged the door closed with her hip and took the bag to the small kitchen table while reading the note.

> *In case you're hungry.*
> *Welcome home.*
> *L*

The note stared at her . . . or was she staring at the note? Either way, Brooke stood there for what felt like an hour.

Luca must have been watching for her. Considering his initial welcome, or inquisition, this gesture gave her a sense that maybe he wasn't completely against her being there.

Smiling, Brooke quickly put away her groceries before washing her hands and removing a proper plate and utensils to eat her meal.

Two bites in of the cheesy shelled pasta delight with some kind of crumbly beef mixture and Brooke retrieved the unopened bottle of wine the D'Angelos had brought up the first night.

A simple pull of the cork and a pour and she felt as if she'd taken a slice of Italy and placed it in her living room.

The noise from the restaurant and the streets below drifted in through the open sliding door that led to the roof terrace. She closed her eyes at the simple pleasure of eating a meal she didn't have to cook herself while sitting in her own chosen space.

Two breaths later and she forced her eyes to open and acknowledged just how bone tired she was.

The pace was killing her. Like right after her father's stroke, she had a hard time finding any balance in her life, she was right back on the hamster wheel, and every opportunity to jump off the damn thing was met with an obstacle that only moved the momentum higher.

She just needed escrow to close.

Then the back-and-forth could stop and she could get on with her life.

Even if that meant arguing with her dad.

She moaned, thinking of the conversation she'd had with him. How much trouble was he going to be now?

Brooke pushed the food around her plate, losing interest, and sipped on the wine.

A couple of days of working and getting used to her own space and she'd feel better.

And a good night's sleep.

Or a week.

A week's worth of sleep.

As she leaned into the thought . . . her phone rang, and her dad's image popped up on the screen.

~

Her first stop was Walmart, where she acquired the smallest microwave oven she'd ever seen, one that would fit on the tiny kitchen counter in her father's space. Then she drove to Autumn Senior Living, and showed up at the front door.

The attendant was pleasant. "Good morning."

"Hi. I'm Joe Turner's daughter, Brooke."

"Yes, I remember. Were we expecting you today?"

Brooke shook her head as they stood on opposite sides of the door talking through the gap. "No. No. I got a call from my dad last night. He asked me to bring this. I was hoping I could take it up to him."

The girl shook her head but opened the door wider. "You can leave it at the desk, and we can get it to his room. He can't have visits while he is in quarantine or it sets back the time frame and involves another test."

Brooke followed her inside just far enough to set the microwave down. "Yeah, about that. Today is day four, they said three days. I know it's likely today something will happen, but my dad is going a bit crazy up there by himself. I need him to acclimate here."

"We're aware of that. The sample wasn't taken until yesterday. The results won't be in for two more days."

"What?"

"I'm sorry. The nurse . . . there was a scheduling issue. These things happen."

Much as Brooke wanted to bitch, standing in the lobby where a few residents milled around, two lumbering with walkers, one in a wheelchair, another walking at a slow but steady pace, she didn't want to make a scene. "Can you make sure my dad gets this right away? He complained that the food being delivered wasn't warm enough."

The girl nodded, assured her he'd get the microwave, and Brooke left the building.

When her phone rang as she pulled off the freeway and made her way home, she knew who was calling without looking at the number. "Hello, Dad."

"I got the m-microwave."

No "Hello" . . . no "How are you." Just right to the point.

"Good."

"They . . . you, didn't come up."

"I couldn't. The rules—"

"Fuck them."

Brooke gripped the steering wheel. "They're temporary."

"Brooke . . ."

93

She cut him off before he could start complaining. "Dad, why didn't you tell me that they didn't even swab you for the virus test until after you'd been there for a couple of days?"

"It doesn't . . . don't matter."

"It does matter, Dad. You came from one home to another, and they have to take extra precautions. The test takes three days for the results. You've been told that. Getting angry because the results aren't back right away and then yelling at me to do something isn't fair."

"Well." Her dad sighed. "I th-thought they got the results fast."

"Did they tell you that?"

"No."

Brooke pulled into her parking space, killed the engine. "Then you assumed." She removed her phone from her purse, switched the call from the car to her phone, and stepped out of the car. "I know this is hard, but I'm doing all I can."

"I don't like it."

She marched to the back door, her peripheral vision all but cut off. "What exactly do you think your options are?"

"Go back to the condo."

"It's sold," she lied.

"Live with you."

She stopped, sucked in a deep breath, and yanked the door open. "We've been over this." Brooke hit the stairs like a determined athlete. Anger fueling each step. "I don't have it in me to be your nurse."

"I don't . . . I'm better."

She paused on the second floor, moved the phone to her other ear, and kept climbing. "Are you still in the diaper?" Brooke almost never used the term *diaper*. She normally softened the reference to save her father the embarrassment.

"I don't need it."

"But you're still *in* it. And it's perfectly fine that you are, Dad. Give your body time to heal."

Her father was silent by the time she reached her door.

"Are you running?" he asked.

She unlocked the door and pushed her way inside. "My apartment is on the fourth floor and there isn't an elevator. You couldn't navigate the stairs even before you got sick. Living with me isn't going to happen."

Brooke pushed the door shut and walked right to the slider, opened it, and stepped onto the terrace.

"You did th-that on purpose."

"I did. I rented a place for one person, not two." Her head was pounding, and she wanted to cry. "I'm trying to make this all work. You have to do your part."

"You, you p-put me in an old . . . folks' home and forgot about me."

"It's been less than a week!" Brooke was practically yelling. "I can't forget about you if I wanted to. I've been picking up the pieces of your life and completely ignoring my own." She wanted to regret the words but felt them to her very core. She walked to the edge of the roof and had the greatest desire to throw her phone in childish rebellion for the discussion she was having with her father.

"I don't. I can . . . leave."

Brooke pulled the phone away from her ear and shook it in her hand and stomped her feet with sheer frustration.

She sucked in three short breaths and tried to reason with him. "And go where?"

"I'm not in prison."

"No," she assured him. "You're not in prison."

"Good."

Her father was quiet.

Too quiet.

"Da—"

He hung up.

Brooke stared at her phone in disbelief. "Fuuuuuck!"

She dropped into a squat and considered rolling into a ball and staying there . . . ohhhh, for about forever. Then she jumped up and all but ran back into her apartment, grabbed her purse and ran down the stairs, and hurried into her car, all while calling the assisted living home in hopes of stopping her father from doing something stupid.

CHAPTER TEN

Luca didn't have a moment to express his presence and Brooke was running away.

He'd seen her in the parking lot, by accident, and perhaps lingered on the terrace when he realized that she looked frazzled on the phone.

Some of the heat of her conversation was sensed while she was inside, but her words outside were heard clearly.

When Brooke had dropped to the ground, he found himself lunging forward, but she recovered before he could go to her and see if she was okay.

Now he followed.

At a distance . . .

Like a damn stalker.

He had dashed into his room, grabbed his car keys, and seen her pulling out of the lot.

The one-way streets surrounding the restaurant made it easier to follow.

Luca was a chef, not a proper prowler, and was sure that if Brooke wasn't so upset, she'd realize that someone was following her.

He could tell by the way she was waving her hands around in the car that she was talking to someone as she drove, her focus anywhere but her rearview mirror.

She jumped on the freeway and headed south. It was then he eased back a little, but always stayed in the same lane she was. It wasn't until she exited that Luca started to question what he was doing.

"Where are you going, Brooke?" He turned on the same street she did, kept way back when the threat of losing her wasn't possible. "Why am I following you?"

He was concerned. On the roof she'd looked ready to collapse and ready to explode at the same time, and it wasn't in Luca to watch a woman suffer and not try and help. That's not the way he was raised.

Although life had taught him that not all women deserved, or wanted, rescuing.

He was fairly certain that Brooke didn't want his help. He pictured her as the independent type that looked at you twice when you opened a door for her.

"You open doors and give your seat to a woman. If she doesn't like it, find another woman." His mother's words, not Luca's. *"It isn't because she can't, it's because you can."*

This was the mantra that ran through Luca's head as he buzzed around cars to keep Brooke in sight without giving away that he was following her.

I'm a moron.

Finally, she pulled into a parking lot.

But instead of driving up to the front, where most patrons of the shopping center would park, she found a space on the far end facing the busy roadway.

She rolled down the windows and cut the engine.

And sat staring across the street.

After watching her for ten minutes, Luca started looking around.

Across the four-lane road was an assisted living facility.

Brooke simply sat and watched.

For a half an hour, Luca watched her watching the front of the building. When someone would drive up, she'd sit forward. When they drove off, she relaxed.

Who lived there? Her mother? A grandparent? The words Luca had heard her practically yell, *"No, you're not in prison,"* played over and over in his head.

He wondered if whoever she was looking for had threatened to leave, and that was why she was stalking the home.

Glancing at his watch, Luca decided he needed to shift his plans for the day.

Gio picked up his call on the second ring. "Where are you?" he asked after a quick hello.

"You wouldn't believe me. I need a favor."

"What?"

"Pick up Franny from school. Take care of things. I'm not sure when I'll be home."

"Ohhh, tell me there's a girl. Please, God, you need to get laid."

"Gio!"

His brother's voice pitched higher. "That's it. There's a woman."

"It's not what you think."

"If there's a woman, it's what I think," Gio said.

Luca looked around his car. "I promise you'd be wrong. Just take over."

"Pick up my favorite niece, fill her with gelato, and leave her high on sugar for when you get home."

Luca cussed at him in Italian. "How about homework, a trip to the park, and a book before bed if I'm not home."

"Who is she?"

Luca didn't answer and assumed his request would be granted. "Thanks, brother." He hung up.

For an hour, Luca shifted from one side of the driver's seat to the other in debate.

He could only think of one time he'd been this indecisive before and that was in the sixth grade when he wanted to ask Becky Ahlstrom to dance but couldn't work up the nerve until the last song. When she said yes, he realized he'd missed out on the whole night because he was too chicken to go for what he wanted.

And here he was doing it again.

Well, okay . . . not the same thing. Walking over to Brooke's car and admitting that he'd seen her upset and then followed her to the parking lot and then sat there watching her for the last hour was more than a little strange.

Yet as every second ticked away, it was harder for him to explain why he was there.

"Fuck it."

Luca pushed out of his car and strode up to Brooke's with purpose. He walked to the passenger side and hesitated when he saw that she'd been crying. "Hey," he said, breaking her concentration.

She didn't exactly jump, but he could tell she was startled.

One look at him and she relaxed by a hair.

"What are you . . . Luca?"

Without asking, he reached for the passenger door, opened it, and slid inside.

He wanted to acknowledge her pain, the bright searing agony he saw in her expression. But instead, he closed the door and pushed the seat back to give his legs more room. "I figured since we're both going to sit here and watch the nursing home we might as well do it together."

"What?"

"That's what you're doing, right? Watching the home?"

"It's an assisted living facility and what the hell are you doing here?"

He wanted to vomit more than he wanted to admit what he had to. "This is going to sound more stalkerish than it actually is."

"I doubt it."

Luca kept his eyes focused on the home and not her. Keenly aware of her eyes on him as he spoke. "I saw you from the terrace. First looking down on you in the parking lot, then closer when you ran out." He lifted a hand. "You were on the phone yelling. I wanted to tell you I was there but then you were running away." He placed both hands in the air now. "I don't know . . . maybe it's too many women in my life, but you looked pretty upset."

His silence met with her silence.

The air in the car didn't move.

"You followed me," she said without emotion.

"I told you this would sound stalkerish."

She twisted in her seat, looked out the back window. "I've been sitting here for almost an hour."

"I thought it was only thirty minutes."

"An hour, Luca."

Damn it to hell . . . it sounded worse coming from her lips. "I know. I thought . . . maybe you needed to use the bathroom or were hungry. We could take turns watching the home. What are we watching for exactly?"

"My dad."

Okay, it was her father. "Good. Okay."

"Luca?"

"Yeah?"

"This is crazy."

He turned to look at her. "Crazier than sitting across the street watching an old folks' home for a man, who I have to assume belongs there, to somehow emerge and do what exactly?"

Brooke snapped her lips shut, nose flared as she sucked in a deep breath and slowly let it out. "It's a home, not a prison. He can leave if he wants to."

Luca nodded a few times, considered her words. "Does your dad have a car?"

"We're sitting in it."

"You're driving your dad's car?"

"That sounds like an accusation," she shot at him.

"It was a statement."

"It was a question . . . one with accusing tones."

Luca closed his eyes. "I don't have accusing tones."

Brooke blew out an exaggerated breath. "Oh, please . . . your tones have accusation all over them."

"They do not," he defended himself.

"Accusation. Condemnation. All kinds of 'ations.' You're as judgy as they come."

She hardly knew him to have come up with such an opinion. Her assessment meant nothing and yet . . . "That's not true."

"Really?"

"Yes," he said.

She twisted now, no longer looking across the street. All her focus and words . . . anger and emotion were squarely on him. And Luca felt as if he were in an interrogation room about to be cornered into a confession for a crime he didn't commit.

"I ask a question and you say the first words that come to your mind. If you hesitate, I'll know the words were judgy and this argument is over."

"Fine." Yup . . . the spotlight was on him and he was going down.

"You sure?"

NO! "Yes."

Brooke started. "Black."

"White."

"Pepsi," she said.

"Coke." His replay was instant. If this was the game, he was going to win.

"Ocean."

"Fish."

"First impression of me?"

Beautiful . . .

"One, two . . ."

"Beautiful." Luca squeezed his eyes shut. He did not mean to say that out loud.

The car was silent.

He opened his eyes.

Brooke was staring at him, disbelievingly.

She twisted in her seat and stared at the home.

"That wasn't what you expected me to say."

"It was a stupid game."

Suddenly, his concern about admitting his first impression of her felt paltry in how she received his feelings.

"You know you're beautiful." She had to know that. Jesus. One look in the mirror every morning and she must look back in admiration, like the queen saying, "Mirror, mirror, on the wall."

Her silence was killing him. "Brooke?"

She reached for the handle on the door. "I have to pee. My dad is in a wheelchair. Almost always wears a baseball cap. Huge Dodgers fan."

Before he could say a word, Brooke was out of the car and running away.

And as much as he wanted to run after her, he saw her exit as what it was . . . a personal retreat from his admission and the unwanted feelings it put on her. To avoid complete stalker status, Luca stayed in the car and watched the home for a man wearing blue in a wheelchair looking like he was making a prison break.

~

Brooke walked into the coffee shop and straight to the bathroom. One look in the mirror and she cringed. Bloodshot swollen eyes, blotchy skin . . . her hair was a mess.

Beautiful.

A screwed-up mess, that's what she was. Hot mess. Complete train wreck.

Not beautiful. Good lord, when was the last time she felt beautiful? It had been months.

The holidays. She and Marshall had gone to a small dinner party, and she'd dressed up for the first time in forever.

Now she wore a simple T-shirt, jeans, and plain tennis shoes. A staple outfit that didn't require thought or work. No coordinating shoes or sweaters. Boring. It said she didn't care what she looked like or what other people thought of her.

Not beautiful.

Luca was either blind or a better bullshitter than she gave him credit for.

A knock on the restroom door made her move.

Brooke splashed water on her face. A face free of makeup, thank God, or the mascara horror would have been epic. Another simple thing she didn't bother with, considering the constant up and down of emotions since her move to California.

She exited the bathroom and ignored the dirty looks from the people waiting for the restroom.

She marched back to the car, thankful that Luca had at least stopped the pity party she'd been deeply invested in while watching the home and wondering if her father was going to make an appearance.

Back in the car, she crossed her arms over her chest and refused to look Luca's way.

"You didn't grab a coffee?"

Brooke rolled her eyes.

"Every stakeout has coffee."

She shifted in her seat, stared at him. "What the hell are you doing here?"

"I told you, I—"

"And I'm not beautiful. I'm a damn mess." She pushed in closer, as if Luca couldn't see her. "Look at me. Puffy face. My eyes are so bloodshot if a cop pulled me over, he'd ask me what I've been smoking. I haven't had a decent night's sleep in months and look at this." She lifted her hair to reveal her forehead and pointed at a vein she knew was always there. "This pulsating barometer is a testament to my skyrocketing blood pressure that puts the cherry on top of just how unbeautiful I am right now."

Out of breath, she sat back, swiveled her head to focus on the home.

She heard Luca take a breath. "Okay then. Fine."

"Fine? What is *fine*?" What the hell did that mean? She looked at him now, spoiling for a fight. Something, anything, to cut out the misery that had become the hamster wheel of her life.

"You don't want me to call you beautiful, I won't call you beautiful." He looked as if he were holding back a smile.

"Good." She focused out the windshield.

"What about—"

"Besides, I'm your tenant," she cut him off.

"You're my mother's tenant."

"Family home. Family business."

"I was firmly against renting the apartment. My mother oversees your tenancy."

"Whatever." Brooke's stomach was starting to churn. "You don't think I'm beautiful, you just feel sorry for me."

Luca started to laugh.

The hair on Brooke's neck stood up. "What is so funny?"

"You're rather obsessed with my opinion of your beauty." Luca sat back now, completely comfortable in the car with one hand resting on the door through the open window.

He was relaxed, confident, and entirely too sexy, and she was pissed that she noticed.

"I like where I live and don't want to mess that up."

"Then don't."

A brief look his way, then back out the window.

He was staring at her.

"I won't."

"Good."

A few seconds passed.

"Stop staring at me."

He shifted but didn't stop looking at her.

"If you're as exhausted as your diatribe expressed, I can't help but wonder just how stunning you'll look after a few good night's sleeps and a little pampering."

She wanted to hate the image of decent sleep and a weekend at a spa without a care in the world but didn't. What she did despise was how far-fetched the reality of such a thing was.

Brooke raised a hand to the home across the street. "This is my reality. I can't even get my work done without the phone ringing and diverting my plans each and every damn day. Your pampering sleep-fest isn't going to happen. I won't look *stunning* anytime soon."

"Isn't there another family member or someone—"

"I'm it," she cut him off . . . again. The anger started to fade again, and the gut-wrenching sadness started to settle in. "My father was married four times. He sucked at personal relationships. And hey," she said in warning, "I'm not much better. Just off a breakup myself."

Luca paused. "Marriage?"

"No. He . . . *we* didn't believe in marriage."

"How bad was the breakup?" Luca asked.

Why was he asking? "I moved to a different state," she said as if that was explanation enough.

"How much of that was your dad?"

"It doesn't matter, Luca. I'm not the girl you follow because she's crying, because I'm a mess and seem to have made that a pastime. I'm not the girl you call beautiful or wonder what she'll look like when she puts on something pretty, okay? I'm the messed-up tenant that lives upstairs in the space you didn't want rented in the first place. And just leave it at that."

He was quiet for a few seconds. "Damn. I do appreciate your honesty and warning."

She felt like crying. "Glad we're on the same page."

Her stomach growled. And not a soft little rattle that said she needed a dainty something to ward off her hunger, but a noise that filled the car and suggested a half a side of beef might be in order.

"Ignore that."

"I'm good at many things, but ignoring a growling stomach isn't one of them," he said. "When did you eat last?"

She looked at her watch. It was almost three in the afternoon. The leftover dinner from the night before sounded divine. "Thank you for dinner. I should have said that before now."

Luca's eyes opened in surprise. "You haven't eaten since last night?"

Again, her hand indicated the home in front of them.

"You're going to end up with an ulcer," he warned her as he reached for the door. "There's a sandwich shop in the strip mall. Do you have a preference?"

"You don't have—"

"Brooke."

The look in his eyes said not to argue. Truth was, she didn't have any argument left in her. "I'm easy. Anything is fine." She reached for her purse, but Luca was already out of the car and jogging across the parking lot.

CHAPTER ELEVEN

They ate and watched the home Brooke's father was in.

Slowly, Luca noticed the fringes of nerves that Brooke seemed to have dangling from her fingertips start to fade. Food truly had a way of healing.

Luca took their quiet moments as an opportunity to digest all the tidbits of information she'd revealed, which left him with questions. Some he would dance around, and others he flat out asked.

"How long has your dad been in there?"

"Four days," she answered between bites. "I moved him in the first night I stayed in my apartment."

She'd looked tired that night, too, as he remembered it. He wasn't sure he'd actually seen her wide awake.

"Where was he before?" He took a bite of his sandwich and waited for her answer.

"A nursing home recovering from surgery." Brooke looked at her sandwich, then back out the window. "He had a stroke a couple of years ago. We managed to get him back to being independent." She faked a laugh. "At least I thought we had."

"We? Was that you and the ex?"

Brooke laughed for real this time. "Yeah . . . no. *We* as in the physical therapist, occupational therapist, speech therapist, rehab center. It was exhausting and took a long time. All Marshall did was bitch about me being gone." She took a bite and shook her head. "I should have known then."

"Known what?"

"That we wouldn't last." She kept shaking her head. "Anyway, I had to liquidate my dad's business and try and put some money in his account. You don't get married and divorced four times and have a whole heck of a lot later in life."

"I can imagine." One divorce and Luca had learned his lesson.

"After I nursed him to some kind of new normal, I finally returned home."

"Where was home?" Luca asked.

"Seattle."

"You commuted from Seattle?"

"No. I gave up my life to give my dad what he needed. I went home a couple of times, but basically stayed at my dad's place the whole time."

"That doesn't sound easy."

"Life is never easy." She twisted the cap off her bottle of water, took a drink. "I just couldn't make the trip back and forth like I'd planned. If I'm honest, I was happy for the break. But we talked on the phone. I knew Dad wasn't doing that great, but everyone was struggling these past few years, ya know?"

"I know," Luca said.

Brooke looked at her sandwich, then lowered her hands to her lap as if giving up on the effort to even eat. "A few months ago I got another call. He's sick and needs surgery. I get here and everything is a mess. The condo is in disrepair, things are broken, and it's pretty obvious that my dad wasn't taking care of himself for a while. I find this damn car in the garage. Who the hell sells a brand-new car to a man on a fixed income that can't even afford his own place to live? And what the hell was my dad thinking buying the thing in the first place? I was pissed, but since he was trying to die, I let it go. Bigger fish to fry and all that."

Luca watched her as she told her story, never once looking at him. Flashes of hurt, worry, and pain swept over her eyes as she spoke.

"It sounds like a lot."

"It was . . . is. He's back in a wheelchair, and this time he can't control his bodily functions. I can't keep the condo and hire home health care for him. It's too much. And I can't do it myself." Brooke glanced Luca's way briefly. "I won't do it."

"You're only one person."

She waved a hand at the home. "Tell him that. He's all pissed off today because the tests they make new residents take aren't back yet and he is still quarantined in his room. I got here first thing this morning to bring him a microwave because he was complaining about cold food being delivered to his room, and I find out that they didn't even test him until yesterday. He knows it takes three days, but he's still bitching. Then he threatens to leave."

As the story came full circle, Luca sighed. "So that's why we're sitting here."

"That's why *I'm* sitting here. I haven't figured out why you're here."

"I'm a sucker for a crying woman."

Brooke snorted. "You shouldn't admit that."

"True." He lifted the last of his sandwich to his lips. "Where is this condo that your dad didn't take care of?" He popped the food in his mouth.

"Upland. I hate it there. My friend Carmen came to help me and brought me to San Diego. Moving here was the compromise. I get a small place, sell the condo, and the assisted living home could literally be anywhere and it shouldn't matter. I'm close enough to do what I can for my dad. Sell the condo so I have some ability to afford it all and wait for the next phone call."

"I'm not following that part. What phone call?"

"*The* call. The one that always happens right about the time I think I'm on top of everything. The call that reminds me that I have no life." She pushed the sandwich away. "I'm just feeling sorry for myself. Ignore me."

Ignoring her wasn't an option. "Is the condo sold?"

"Yes . . . no. That phone call is hanging in the sidelines, too. I'm in escrow, but we think it's going to fall through."

"Why?"

"The inspection found issues. I've been there trying to fix them or hire someone to help fix them. No one seems to want the work."

"I understand that," Luca said.

"I have backup offers. It will sell, it's just going to take longer. And I want it behind me. I lied and told my dad it was already sold. I can't have him thinking it's an option to return there. It isn't."

"I'd do the same thing."

"You would?" She looked his way, sounded surprised.

"If your father's going to behave like a child, you can't give him all the adult information. Does your dad have a way to leave?"

She narrowed her eyes. "He has the strength to wheel himself out of there."

"And what? Roll to Upland? Does he have money or access to a credit card to hire a taxi?"

Brooke opened her mouth, then closed it. "Huh. No. I have all that."

Luca patted the dashboard. "You're driving his car, so he doesn't have that. What about friends? Anyone stupid enough to pick him up and take care of him somewhere else?"

She shook her head. "He has friends, but none have been around much since he's been sick. None stepped up to do much the last time, either."

Luca felt he made his point. "So how exactly is your dad going to run away?"

"My father isn't always known for making logical decisions. But I'm catching what you're saying."

"Chances are the heat of your father's frustration has passed by now. And I'm going to guess that the home will call you if he attempts to leave."

"They will."

"So how about we go home. You take that long bath and a two-day nap and let some of this stuff you can't control play out."

Brooke looked like she wanted to argue, so Luca continued and didn't let her speak. "Can you control the condo falling out of escrow?"

"No."

"Can you sit on your father and make him stay put?"

She shook her head. "No."

"Silence his calls, take the ones from the home . . . and as Chloe would say, breathe." As annoying as his baby sister was at times with all her yoga stuff, she'd be right in this situation. The only other suggestion Luca had was for Brooke to hand her phone to him and he'd be happy to field her calls for a day or two so the vein in her forehead could stop pulsating. Luca didn't think she'd go for that.

"Can I do that?" she whispered.

"Tell me why you can't."

Brooke was quiet for a good minute, then she finally said, "You're right. I can't control him."

She looked relieved just saying the words.

"What's your dad's name?"

"Joe Turner."

Luca made several mental notes as he waited for Brooke to make a decision on whether to stay or leave.

She sighed. "We should go home."

"Great idea."

Their eyes met and Luca felt his heart rate speed up. She offered a soft smile, and damn, she was beautiful.

"Thank you, Luca. I've been so tunnel-visioned I can't see anything."

It took effort to not reach for her hand. "We've all been there."

"You have?" she asked.

"Of course."

"I'd like to hear about that."

Luca wadded up the trash and tossed it in the to-go bag from the sandwich shop. "Another time." He looked at her half-eaten lunch. "Are you going to eat that?"

She winced. "I have some great leftovers at home that are calling my name."

"You didn't eat it all?"

"There was enough for three people. I don't know how you Italians stay so thin with all the pasta."

He lifted the bag for her to dump her trash. "I'll follow you." Mainly to ensure she actually went home and didn't change her mind.

"To make sure I go home," she said, catching him.

He could lie . . . "Exactly."

She sat forward, turned the key in the ignition. One last look at the home and she said, "Don't do anything stupid, Dad."

Luca smiled, got out of the car, and jogged to his.

She backed out of her space and waited. Her gaze caught his in the rearview mirror.

And the warmth in the pit of his stomach pulsed. "Oh, boy."

∼

Luca pulled into his space right beside Brooke, both of them exiting their cars at the same time. It was late enough that Gio should have picked up Franny, but early enough for him to help prep for the dinner rush. He glanced up and noticed a curtain moving inside his apartment. Someone was about to bombard him with questions, he felt that in his bones.

"I'm not used to this," Brooke said as they walked toward the back door together.

"Used to what?"

"Getting any kind of real help and advice with my life. If I seem ungrateful or say the wrong things, it's not because I'm not thankful."

He laughed as he held the door open for her. "Does that mean you're sorry for the judgy comment?"

She shook her head. "Let's not get carried away."

He laughed harder.

In the hall between the restaurant and the stairway to the residence, Brooke stopped on the first step. "Thanks again."

Luca nodded and she turned to walk away.

"How about something other than pasta tonight?" he found himself asking.

She stopped, turned. "You know, Luca, I *can* cook."

"You can?"

"Not like you, but I have managed." She took another two steps.

He stopped her.

"Chicken piccata? I'll send it up at six."

"You're too much."

"That's a yes," he said and turned away.

She continued to laugh as she walked up the stairs.

He diverted to the kitchen, poked his head inside. The wheels were turning, the staff busy but not hurried. "Do you need me?" he asked in Italian.

"Check in an hour," his second told him.

Luca's second stop was the office. Finding it empty, he did a quick pass through the restaurant, saw his sister taking an order.

Satisfied, he made his way upstairs.

Gio greeted him at the door, a stupid grin on his face.

"Brooke, really?"

Luca immediately looked around for Franny.

"She's in her room."

He sighed, walked in, and closed the door behind him. "It's not what you think."

"Yeah, sure it isn't."

Ignoring his brother, Luca walked past him and into his kitchen, grabbed a bottle of water from the fridge. "Your assumptions will make an ass out of you."

"She's beautiful and a little wounded. Exactly your type."

"A lot wounded and I'm not going there." Even if his body wanted to.

"Can I have that in writing?"

Luca didn't grace his brother's question with an answer. "Thanks for picking up Francesca."

Gio took the hint and started for the door. "I'm out tomorrow. Looking for my own place."

Luca glanced up. "Have you told Mama?"

"Not yet. When I find something."

Much as he didn't like the thought of his brother moving, he understood. "Let me know what I can do."

"I will."

Leaving him alone, Luca walked down the hall to check on his baby girl.

Her precious smile lit up when she noticed him, and she jumped up from her tiny desk, the one she did her homework on, to give him a hug.

"Hi, Papa. Uncle Gio gave me gelato."

As if the drips on her shirt didn't give her away. "I'm sure he did."

"I said only one scoop because you'd be mad if it was two."

Luca lifted his daughter up in his arms even though she was getting way too big to do this much longer. "Chocolate?"

"How can you tell? Do I have chocolate breath?"

He laughed and pointed to the corner of his own mouth with his tongue. "You left a bit."

Franny made an exaggerated move with her tongue to get the chocolate evidence off her face. When she did, her eyes rolled back, giving Luca even more reason to laugh.

"Do you cook tonight?" she asked him.

"Maybe. But not for a while. Do you want to hit the park?"

She wiggled out of his arms and ran to her closet. "Can we play Frisbee?"

"Whatever you want, *tesorina*."

Frisbee in hand, they left the apartment.

She thought it was all fun and games, but Luca wanted to burn off the ice cream long before bedtime.

Life was all about balance.

As he thought the word, he wondered when the last time Brooke went to the park and tossed a Frisbee around was.

Maybe someday he'd ask her.

CHAPTER TWELVE

The phone was blissfully silent. Although that didn't stop Brooke from looking at the screen every fifteen minutes or so throughout the rest of the day and into the evening.

Luca had dinner delivered as if she was on some kind of meal service.

She fired up her computer, logged in to her work email, and dug her heels in for a long night.

She made it until nine, when her eyes couldn't stay open any longer, and found herself facedown in bed in a dreamless sleep.

A loud noise jolted her out of bed. The first thing Brooke did was reach for her phone, certain that was the noise that pulled her from the best sleep she'd had in months. Only by the time she had it to her ear, she realized it wasn't ringing.

A car horn in the distance had her shaking the sleep from her eyes.

The sun was up . . . way up.

Brooke glanced at the clock by the bed and gasped. Nine thirty.

"Good God." She'd slept for twelve and a half hours and still felt like she could sleep more.

She rolled over, punched her pillow, and snuggled in.

Luca had been right. She needed to breathe.

And sleep.

Luca . . .

He'd followed her yesterday. Sat in her car and listened while she told him her life's story. Well, the last few years anyway.

No judgment.

No moment where he suggested she was being overly dramatic and looking for sympathy.

No. The man had listened, and once she was all out of words, he offered advice in the form of a question. None of the "You should," or "You'd be a fool if . . ."

Brooke found herself curling into a ball.

Her time with Marshall was so completely opposite.

If he didn't simply tell her she was an idiot for doing what she did, he'd ignore her work and complain about where he ranked in her life.

She was comparing apples to oranges. She'd been with Marshall for three years. She'd known Luca for a handful of days.

Brooke stared across the room where sunlight spilled in from the window.

Facts didn't stop her from comparing.

Luca won.

Jesus . . . how had she let herself fall for someone so selfish?

She shook away her thoughts and pushed the covers off the bed.

Once her feet hit the floor, she glanced at her phone.

No calls.

No messages.

She stretched her arms over her head and felt the muscles in her back rebel. As soon as she saw Chloe, Brooke was going to take her up on the yoga lessons. She felt as if she'd aged five years in a few short months. That road needed to end.

But first . . . coffee.

As her morning java brewed, Brooke opened the sliding glass door and let in the morning sun. It was still a bit cool, but the moist salt air was exactly what she needed. Looking around first to make sure she was alone, she padded out barefoot to the terrace, took in the view of the bay.

A brisk walk would help clear the cobwebs that had settled from sleeping in and hopefully pump her up for a full and productive day of work. And as much as she wanted to know if her father was having a better day, she decided to skip her routine phone call to take care of her own mental health. His stunt the day before had just about thrown her over the bridge. Taking some time off when she'd hired people to care for him wasn't uncalled for.

Ten minutes later, she was in her kitchen, hot coffee in hand with her laptop open, checking her email. She started clicking into work mail and stopped herself. Brooke finished her coffee as she found a pair of leggings and dressed for that walk. A set of earbuds and her phone tucked in a pocket and she was off.

It was time to find a path. A routine in her new space. Yeah, she still had to get rid of the condo and all the baggage that came with it, but there was no reason she couldn't begin her life in San Diego right now. Today.

She left the building out the back door without encountering any of the D'Angelos. There was some noise coming from the restaurant, but since they didn't open until eleven, it was relatively quiet.

The streets of Little Italy were hopping with activity, especially because the children had a midweek day off school, but Brooke moved beyond that toward the waterfront. She'd been to, and had frequented, the touristy spots already, and that wasn't the place to stretch her legs. Working in the opposite direction of people, she moved about the harbor on a sidewalk that appeared to stretch completely around.

Smaller recreational boats bobbed up and down as the water moved, mesmerizing her and making Brooke forget, if even for a few minutes, the concerns she'd had the day before. Aircraft carriers filled in the opposite side of the harbor off the island of Coronado. A place Brooke had yet to explore but was on her short list. The upbeat music in her ears kept any melancholy away as her brisk walk helped her map out ways of spending her free time once she found herself caught up.

Anytime her thoughts moved to her dad, she shoved them away.

Not today.

Today was about her.

It was time to focus on herself for a change.

After walking in one direction for a good half an hour, she turned back. She made note of a few places along the way she could take a lunch or her laptop and find a bench to get some work done. There were similar places she'd leave her apartment for in Seattle, but only when the weather cooperated.

Her phone rang, interrupting the music.

She saw the name on the screen and took a deep breath.

"Hello, Susan," she greeted her real estate agent.

"Hi, Brooke."

Susan's voice said all Brooke needed to hear. "It fell through, didn't it?"

Susan sighed. "We have backup offers."

Brooke moved toward the park on the waterfront and found the first available seat.

In front of her, the fountains ran and children played. "What happens now?"

Susan explained the events as they would unfold. Reminded Brooke that the repairs needed to be taken care of before the next inspection to avoid falling through again. While the call was not what Brooke wanted to hear, it wasn't complete doom and gloom.

This would set her back, but the market was stupid hot, and everything would be good . . . eventually.

The first step was to let the backup people know they could get the place if they were still looking and negotiate that deal. None of which Brooke had to be present for. She'd take her time and get back to Upland once a deal was in escrow. There was an electrical issue that needed repairs and then she'd repaint the walls affected. So, about half of them.

More trips to Goodwill.

More time sifting through her father's life and creating large amounts of trash each week. She was half tempted to toss everything sight unseen. But old files still beckoned from the depths of the garage. The last of it.

"I'll be in touch later today with an update," Susan told her before hanging up.

Brooke held her phone in her lap and stared absently across the park. This was just another roadblock. Nothing more.

She closed her eyes, took a long inhale, and blew it out slowly.

Her eyes fluttered open to find two small feet in front of hers.

Tilting her head, she saw Franny standing there holding a Frisbee. "Hi."

"Hello, what are you doing here?"

Franny lifted the Frisbee as if that was all she needed to do.

Brooke grinned and looked up in search of Luca. "Who are you here with?"

Her eyes found Luca's before Franny could respond.

"With my papa."

The man sauntered their way, a lazy smile on his face.

"He told me to come over and say hi."

That made Brooke laugh. "Did he now?"

"Yeah."

As Luca moved closer, Brooke kept up the conversation with his daughter. "Do you like playing Frisbee?"

She nodded several times. "I can catch it. But if Papa throws it too hard, it stings. I'm tough, so it's okay."

"I bet you are."

Luca moved within talking distance. "Hello."

"Good morning," she said.

"I thought that might have been you over here." He stopped a few feet away, rocked back on his heels.

"So, you sent your daughter to make sure?"

He winced. "That sounds bad when you put it like that."

Brooke matched his grin and found herself fidgeting under his silent gaze.

Franny looked between the two of them . . . twice.

"Grown-ups are weird."

Brooke blinked away her discomfort.

"What are you doing out here?" Luca asked.

She shrugged, lifted her phone in the air. "I was out for a walk. Then I got that call I told you about."

"The condo?"

She nodded.

"I'm sorry."

"It is what it is."

Franny shuffled her feet, impatient with the grown-up talk. "Can we play?"

Brooke stood, dusted off her butt from the park bench dirt. "I'll let you get back to it."

"Don't you want to play?" Franny asked. "It's a lot of fun."

Fun? That wasn't a word in her dictionary these days. "I don't want to impose."

Franny narrowed her eyes, looked at her dad. "What's *impose*?"

"It's when someone thinks they're interrupting," Luca explained. "You're not imposing," he said to Brooke. The look in his eyes said he liked the idea of her sticking around.

"Do you know how to throw a Frisbee?" Franny asked.

"It's been a long time."

Franny turned and, with a bit of dramatic flair, poised herself to toss the Frisbee. "It's all in the wrist," she said as she threw her entire body into it.

The Frisbee sailed through the air perpendicular to the ground and rolled a good ten yards once it hit the grass. She ran off after it, leaving Luca and Brooke alone.

"You don't have to stick around," he told her.

"Trying to get rid of me?" she asked, teasing.

He turned to her, waited for her eyes to meet his. "No, *bella*, that's not what I'm trying to do."

Brooke's Italian was limited to a dozen or so phrases and a few extra words, *bella* among them.

The endearment brought heat to her cheeks.

She decided a little bit of *fun* might be exactly what she needed. "I haven't done this since I was a teenager."

"It's like riding a bike."

"Why do people say that? The last time I tried riding a bike I nearly broke my head open."

"Wear a helmet," Luca suggested.

She laughed. "You're such a parent."

"Guilty as charged."

"C'mon," Franny yelled from across the park.

Luca put his hands in the air. "Throw it."

She did, and the disk made it a little more level with the ground, but it didn't go very far.

Luca picked it up and tossed it back, a steady arc that made it directly to his little girl.

"Throw it to Brooke," Luca coached.

Putting her entire body into it, Franny tossed it.

Brooke didn't need to worry about catching Franny's throws. So far all of them had hit the ground rolling.

Holding the piece of plastic in her hand, Brooke leveled it a couple of times before attempting to toss it back to Franny.

Her throw was completely off and hit the ground as well. "I can see how this is going to go," she announced.

A few more attempts and Luca stepped up beside her, placed the Frisbee in her hand, and walked behind her. "It's all in extending the arm and the wrist in one motion and letting go." His body pressed close to hers as he showed her the movement.

Not that she was paying attention.

The feel of his body molding against hers was right up there with turning on a light switch inside of her. His left-hand fingertips rested on her shoulder, the right hand held on to her as he guided her arm.

He smelled of an exotic blend of spice. Not cologne, or something fake . . . but spice. Maybe working in the kitchen all night long did that, or maybe it was simply the man.

"Brooke?" he called her name, breaking her out of her *spice man* thoughts.

She shook off the images in her head and made a couple of motions with her arm before Luca stepped back.

With him gone she could think.

Barely.

She tossed the Frisbee, following through, and the thing flew.

"You're a quick study," Luca announced.

"Sadly." The word came out of her mouth without invitation. And as much as she'd hoped Luca hadn't caught it, his grin said he did.

"Forget I said that."

He shook his head. "Not possible."

"Sh—"

Franny ran up, stopping the expletive midword.

"Are we playing, or what?"

Brooke's eyes found Luca's and they both smiled. "Oh, we're playing," he said.

She squeezed her eyes closed and couldn't help but smile. God, it was good to just blush, flirt, and be a girl.

Brooke rubbed her hands together. "Okay, Franny. Let's give your dad a run for his money."

The girl wrinkled her nose. "What does that mean?"

Brooke laughed. "Let's show him how well we can play."

Franny understood that and ran back to where she'd been standing.

"No more lessons?" Luca asked.

Brooke pointed away from her. "Get on your side of the park, *Machismo*."

She heard him laughing as he walked away.

~

Mari pulled in a long, deep breath.

The past few years had been some of the hardest she and the children had endured, outside of those that followed the death of her husband, Paolo D'Angelo.

Still, she was optimistic.

Her children were itching. All of them in their own way.

The one she worried the most for was her Luca.

She never liked Francesca's mother. A woman whose name seldom passed her lips.

She'd proven her true colors soon enough, and Luca was left picking up the pieces of his heart and taking on the challenge of bringing up a child alone. Though in truth, they were all better off that Antonia wasn't a part of their lives.

Francesca most of all.

But Luca needed more.

Each year he grew further apart from the world.

Yes, he took care of his daughter, his family.

But he didn't smile as much, or as wide when he did.

Never once did she find a little white lie in his answer to where he'd been or what he was doing when she asked.

Her firstborn needed someone to share his life with. And Francesca needed brothers and sisters.

"Amore mio," she whispered to the shadows in the room. "If you can help me out here, I'd appreciate it."

Mari brushed off her thoughts and worked her way outside.

A coffee with Rosa, a little gossip . . . that's what she needed.

Mari stepped out onto the busy street in front of the restaurant and felt a cold draft pass in front of her.

She turned.

Luca and Francesca were walking her way, hand in hand.

And on the other side of her precious granddaughter walked Brooke.

Mari stood still and watched as the air grew cool around her.

Francesca glanced up at Brooke and reached for her hand.

Mari held her breath.

Brooke accepted Franny's hand instantly, and her questioning gaze looked over at Luca.

Mari's son offered a brief smile, but worry sat squarely between his eyes.

Then, Francesca said something, and they both looked down and together they smiled and laughed.

Mari held a hand to her chest and sent up a prayer to whoever was listening.

CHAPTER THIRTEEN

A sharp knock on her door interrupted Brooke's concentration. "Come in," she called, thinking it must be close to dinnertime and the food fairy . . . aka Luca, was sending something up again.

She'd forced herself to stop thinking about him most of the afternoon to get some work done and had been somewhat successful. It helped that she was way behind and if she didn't finish the revisions on the soap campaign by the weekend, she'd have some serious problems at work.

Instead of a runner being at the door with a to-go bag, Chloe walked in with nothing more than a smile. "Hi."

"Oh, hello. This is a surprise."

"I know. I thought maybe I could pull you away for a happy hour drink. A little one-on-one time to get to know each other."

Brooke glanced at her computer, at the work in front of her. She should say no. "That would be great."

"Perfect."

A few minutes later they were walking down the stairs and out the back door.

They walked into Little Italy's main piazza, which was peppered with tables and people spilling out from restaurants. Some with to-go food containers, others with drinks for their meals.

"Did you want to find a seat out here?" Brooke asked, searching the square for an open table.

Chloe shook her head. "Not necessary."

They ascended the stairs of one of the busier bars on the street and stopped at the hostess.

Chloe and the woman spoke, in Italian, and hugged like old friends. Then they were escorted to the far end of an upstairs bar where they could actually hear each other and not have to hang off their barstools.

The place was crazy busy, a lot of young people enjoying happy hour.

"I take it you know the hostess."

"I know everyone in this town," Chloe said without apology.

"Is that a good thing?"

"It was fine until I hit puberty and started dating. Then everyone became a mama, a *nonna*, or just a meddling neighbor."

"Matchmakers everywhere?"

"Oh my God, yes. I'm twenty-five and you'd think my uterus is drying up from the way they talk."

If Chloe's was drying up, Brooke's was mummified.

The waitress arrived and greeted Chloe with a hug. "Salena, this is Brooke, she rents the apartment upstairs from us."

Salena was older than Chloe by a couple of years, but just as Italian and just as beautiful.

"Yes, your brother told me your mama had rented the place. Welcome," Salena offered to Brooke.

"Thank you."

"What are we drinking tonight? The sangria is fresh," she said.

Chloe put a hand in the air. "I'm sold." She turned to Brooke. "They have the best sangria on the block."

"You don't have to tell me twice."

"Two sangrias, coming right up."

As Salena walked away, Chloe leaned in. "Be sure and tell people you're a local. Most of the time you'll get a discount. Even in the retail stores. Eventually everyone will know who you are, but in the meantime . . ."

"Good to know."

"Perks of a small town in a big city."

That made Brooke laugh. "San Diego doesn't feel like a big city."

"It's not Rome."

"Have you been?"

"To Roma?" Chloe used the proper name for the city.

"Yes."

"Before my father passed." Chloe looked away, lost in a memory. "I've been to Tuscany more. Florence. Which is bigger than San Diego, yet more intimate . . . if that's possible."

Brooke sighed into the memories of her travels. "I agree."

"You've been there, too."

"I've been a lot of places. My ex was a travel blogger. Our first year together I think my feet were in America for maybe five months." It seemed so long ago.

"Sounds exciting. I love traveling."

The sangria arrived along with a small bowl of olives.

"I want to go to Bali," Chloe continued. "There is a yoga teachers' retreat there I plan on attending."

"What's stopping you?"

"The restaurant needed staff and it hasn't felt right to leave. But I'm anxious to do something different. Make my mark on this world."

Brooke lifted the wine to her lips. "I remember that time." She took a sip, nodded. "This is really good."

"You don't want to make your mark anymore?" Chloe asked.

"Half the time I just want to get through my day without needing a nap."

"You're too young to say that."

For the next ten minutes, Brooke offered Chloe the digest version of the situation with her father and how she was managing his life and juggling hers.

"You're an only child?" Chloe asked when Brooke was done explaining.

"No, not really. I have a half brother on my mother's side. And my dad did have a son with a different mother early on, but my dad wasn't great about taking responsibility, so they have no relationship. I don't even know him. Couldn't tell you if he's alive or dead."

"You're kidding."

"No." Brooke took a sip of her wine. "I have a stepsister. A sister whose mother was my father's fourth wife."

"Fourth?"

Brooke shook her head with a grin. "You asked."

"Oh my God."

"You know the really crazy thing?"

"There's more?"

Brooke nibbled on an olive. "I didn't even know my dad until I was a teenager. My mother moved us to Seattle, cut all ties. He didn't bother trying to fight to see me." Okay, this train of conversation needed to stop. All it ever brought was grief and sorrow. "Enough of that."

"Damn, Brooke. That sucks. I can't even imagine. And yet you're still doing so much for him."

"I'm all he has," she explained. "And he's been a decent father as an adult. He wasn't there for me growing up, but he's been around since."

Chloe reached out a hand, set it on top of Brooke's. "Family is the most important thing."

"Some families."

"What about your mother?"

Brooke lifted her glass, changed the subject. "Maybe we should grab an appetizer with these."

Chloe cringed. "Bad topic?"

"There isn't enough sangria in all of Little Italy to discuss my mother."

She leaned back. "The bruschetta here is good. Not as good as ours, but it will soak up the wine."

A second glass of sangria in hand and the restaurant had picked up, along with the noise level.

For the first time in weeks, Brooke felt truly relaxed. She hadn't even checked her phone. Just the thought had her reaching for her purse, and she stopped.

No.

Someone would call her if there was an issue.

With her head slightly buzzed from the wine, Brooke ventured into the topic of Luca.

"If it's not too much to ask . . . what's your brother's story?"

Chloe paused as a slow grin spread over her face. "Giovanni?"

Brooke snorted a laugh, picked up her glass. "No. Not Gio. Luca."

"You like my brother," Chloe said, point blank.

"I didn't say that."

"You're asking about him."

"He's charming. And has been very helpful. Franny is adorable . . . I can't help but wonder about her mother."

Chloe rolled her eyes. "Save your questions about Antonia for Luca. I won't say anything about her except that none of us cared for her. And since she's not here for Franny, I suppose that speaks for itself."

"I was wondering about that. So, she's still alive? Franny's mom?"

Antonia. Brooke made a mental note of the woman's name.

"Yes. And Luca has moved away from that time, but not moved on."

That shot up a big red flag in Brooke's head. "He still loves her."

"God, no. He just isn't willing to be the flirtatious man he was before he was a father. I was a teenager when my niece was born, but I remember the joy he had in life, the zest. Right after Francesca arrived, he was just as animated, and then all that ended. I couldn't even tell you why, so don't ask."

Brooke narrowed her eyes. "Luca has his stoic moments, but he seems to smile a lot to me."

"*Around* you," Chloe corrected.

"He's a player," Brooke concluded.

Chloe tilted her head back, busted out in laughter. "Gio is a player. *Bella* this and *bella* that. I don't think Luca has called a woman beautiful since he was twenty-one."

Brooke sucked in a breath and held it.

"Francesca. He tells my niece she's beautiful. And he compliments my mother and me. Family is the most important thing to him."

And my family is as dysfunctional as they come.

Chloe tilted the last of her wine back and set the empty glass on the table. "Let's settle up here and go home for the main course."

"How do you stay thin with all the pasta?"

She laughed. "Yoga."

Chloe waved at Salena for the bill.

"I've been meaning to ask you about that. Can I join you?"

"I have a class on Tuesday and Thursday, but I practice every day on the terrace. Around seven."

"In the morning?"

"Yes. I have extra mats. Come out if you're awake. You'll like it."

~

The kitchen was popping. Orders were flying in, and Luca was demanding the staff to perform.

And they were smiling.

Happy to be busy.

The past few years had been sketchy. Lots of downtime and half the staff . . . hell, quarter staff. That wasn't the case tonight.

They'd made it.

The restaurant had made it, Luca thought.

"Luca?"

He heard his sister calling his name.

He looked up, saw her standing at the door to the kitchen. It was her night off and she was dressed for an evening out.

"*Sí.*"

"Brooke and I are in the grotto." Chloe waved a paper in her hand. "Unless you have a better idea," she said, handing her requests for dinner to him.

Luca took the paper without looking at it. "Brooke?"

Chloe smiled and walked away.

Oh shit.

His sister and Brooke.

Brooke and his sister.

Luca looked at the order, considered the request, and then threw it away.

They wanted a shared pasta plate and a shared main.

And what kind of *shared* information were they exchanging?

Luca dished up a few orders while preparing what he planned on serving his sister and Brooke.

When it was done, he cleaned his hands and picked up the plates. He told his second he'd be a few minutes and to take over.

He walked past the main dining room and into the grotto. A private space that locals knew about, and those who bothered to look up details about the restaurant's features. Private parties and special events . . . and yes, family meals were often taken in that space so long as paying customers weren't dominating the room.

Two small parties were there, and Brooke and his sister. They were laughing, a bottle of wine between them.

He met Brooke's eyes before he made it to the table.

She had beautiful eyes. Revealing and honest. Right now, they told him she'd been drinking and, if he wasn't too far out of the game, she was happy to see him.

Luca had to admit, that feeling was mutual.

"Buonasera."

"You didn't have to bring it yourself." Chloe was speaking, but Luca didn't look at her.

"I did." He set the plates down with a smile. "It looks as if you both have been enjoying the evening."

"We've had a great time," Chloe said for the two of them. "Did you know that Brooke has been to Rome and Florence?"

Luca glanced at his sister, then back to Brooke. "I did not."

"No wonder she loves it here so much."

"And I thought it was the company," Luca said, smiling.

The heat in Brooke's cheeks blossomed as she met his stare.

A brief moment of quiet passed before Chloe cleared her throat. "A shared plate doesn't mean twice as much food, Luca."

He forced his eyes away from Brooke to look at his sister. "You don't have to eat it all."

"Italian cooks . . . 'You don't have to eat it all' and then when you don't, 'What was wrong with the food? Are you sick?' Beware, Brooke, this is a trap."

"In Italy they don't serve American portions," Brooke said.

"We can't get away with that here," Luca said under his breath.

"D'Angelo?" a patron called from the other side of the grotto, pulling Luca's attention away.

He looked directly at Brooke. "If you'll excuse me."

As Luca turned, he heard his sister snicker.

CHAPTER FOURTEEN

"Hi, Dad." Brooke relented and called her father after two days, but not before she'd learned that he was now able to roam about the facility. As much as a wheelchair would allow him to roam, that is.

"You finally . . . finally called."

Instead of addressing his comment, she added her own. "I'm fine, thanks for asking. I heard you're out of isolation."

"You sound mad."

Brooke closed her eyes and smiled before she spoke again in an effort to sound happier. With the phone on speaker, she clasped her hands in her lap to keep from biting her nails. "I don't want to argue with you. The last time we spoke was very upsetting."

Her dad snorted. "You-you're t-telling me."

Deep breath in . . . long breath out . . .

"Have you made any friends?" she asked.

Another snort. "Everyone here is old."

"The price you pay for not dying young," she said, joking.

Then, after a second, she heard her father laugh. It didn't last long, but it was better than a disgruntled snort or snide comment.

"I tried."

It was her turn to chuckle. "Sex, drugs, and rock and roll. And that damn motorcycle."

Now her dad laughed hard.

Brooke felt a genuine grin. "Should I bring up the four wives?"

"No," he said, plain as day.

"Okay. I'll stop while I'm ahead."

She heard her father yawn. "Th-the food isn't bad. Needs salt."

"You can add it. It's safe to say many people there have issues with their blood pressure."

"They're old," he accused again.

"And you're thirty?"

"Ha."

Brooke sat in a chair by her open slider, enjoying the breeze while they talked. "Think of it this way, Dad. You're the young one there, you have the pick of all the women. You can find wife number five."

"Bite your tongue."

"Just make sure she has money, okay?"

"Ha. Not a bad . . . bad idea."

She knew he was joking.

"When will I see you?" he asked.

"I just turned in my revisions for the campaign I was working on and I have a call with my boss later today. They want me to work with a team on my next project." She wasn't terribly happy with that.

"Oh? Do you do that?"

"Not normally. But I've been delayed a lot. I think it's their way of making sure the work gets done on time."

"Oh. My fault."

Brooke nodded her head but kept her words in. "Reason, not fault. Life happens. Anyway. I do need to focus on work. If it's okay with you, I'll be there on Tuesday."

"You can come and take me to lunch."

"I know. Let me get ahead at work, and I'll do that. Deal?"

Her dad finally relented with another yawn. "Deal."

Brooke sighed in relief.

They spoke for a few more minutes. She asked how he felt physically. Was he sleeping? How was the care?

He answered but didn't bother with questions of his own.

At the end of the call, she was happy she'd picked up the phone. They were in a better place . . . for now.

Brooke fiddled with the phone, turning it on end, over and over while she thought about the conversation.

A noise from the other end of the terrace drew her attention to what was in front of her.

Luca walked her way, his expression filled with guilt. "Was that your father?"

"Eavesdropping, Luca?"

He lifted a finger in the air, pointed behind him. "I was out here before I heard you on the phone. I'd have to walk by you to go back downstairs . . ."

She didn't give him a pass. "Eavesdropping."

He deflated. "Yes. I'm sorry. I tried to stop myself, but then I was too interested in hearing the conversation. I'm a horrible man."

Her insides started to warm. "An apology, a confession, and then throwing yourself on the sacrificial sword. Well played."

"Saint Luca," he said, standing taller, smiling wider.

"I doubt that."

"Well . . ." He wore a sheepish grin. "Your father?"

"Yes. That was my dad."

"You are very patient with him." Luca leaned against the wall outside, folded his arms across his chest.

"I have my moments. Trust me. Reasoning with an elder who has lost their independence is a monumental task when they're not on board. I need him on board."

"And your work?"

"You heard that part, too?"

"I heard the whole thing, *bella*. Is your work giving you trouble?"

His endearment didn't go unnoticed, but she didn't bring attention to it. Instead, she answered his question. "I haven't worked on a team project since I was fresh out of college. Even when my dad had the stroke, I was assigned people to work with me, not the other way around." It was a giant step in the wrong direction. But delays in her projects were a reflection on the company, and they needed to cover their asses.

"You seem resigned to it."

"I am. I deserve it. My focus has been everywhere but work. One more reason for me to cut my losses with the condo and get it behind me as fast as possible."

"Did you get another offer?"

He remembered.

"I did. We opened escrow yesterday. Monday I'm going up there to meet the air conditioner guy, the electrician, finish the painting, and haul the rest of my dad's crap to the dump. Anything left over comes back with me. If it doesn't fit in the car, I don't need it."

"That sounds like a big list."

"I've given myself a deadline."

"How long will you be there?"

"Only Monday. I have to be here on Tuesday to see my dad. So, I'll get up early and likely drive home by midnight."

Luca narrowed his eyes. "I don't like that idea."

"I wasn't asking you," she said with a half smile.

Luca pushed away from the wall with a huff. "We have our Sunday dinner."

Brooke smiled. "I remember. You won't bother me."

He shook his head. "You misunderstand. *We* have dinner on Sunday. This family. This household. You're part of that. We want you to join us."

Brooke literally took a full stop and had a hard time finding words. "I don't know what to say."

"Dinner is at seven thirty," he said with a wink.

~

"You've never done this before?" Chloe asked as they rolled out their mats the next morning for yoga.

"A couple of times in college, but I didn't really get it."

Brooke followed Chloe's example and sat, cross-legged, on the mat.

"There is a lot to yoga. More than the poses and the exercise of it all."

"That's what I keep hearing. After the last couple of years, I think I could use a bit more of what I think yoga can offer."

"I started for the exercise," Chloe admitted. "For the yoga butt."

Brooke laughed.

"My second year in college I broke up with this guy . . ."

"It's always a guy."

Chloe nodded. "Always. Once the hangover was gone, I sat on the mat and tapped into my breath. Really tapped in. The following year I took a week and gained my certification. But I'm still new."

"How can you say that?"

"There is so much to learn and explore. You'll see. We'll start slow."

For the next thirty minutes, Chloe worked with Brooke on less than a dozen poses, but each one was made more challenging with Chloe standing beside Brooke, making sure she was doing them correctly. The whole time Chloe reminded her to breathe.

When they were done, lying flat on their backs looking up at the sky, Brooke felt muscles she'd forgotten she had.

"I needed that," Brooke said.

"I'm glad."

"You're a great instructor."

"Thanks."

"What's Bali going to teach you?"

They both stared at the sky as they spoke.

"I don't know. I just know I need to go."

"A life quest," Brooke said.

"As opposed to a bucket list?"

"Bucket list is what you do before you die. Like hurry up and check a box. The problem with checking a box is you don't always enjoy what you're doing. Life quest is the feeling of exploring and discovery that admittedly is like a bucket list, but without death looming. Sounds silly."

Chloe laughed. "It sounds like something a yogi would say."

"One practice does not make me a yogi."

"Every journey starts with one step."

Brooke turned her head now and rolled her eyes at Chloe.

They both started laughing.

After gathering up their mats and grabbing a drink of water, Chloe brought up Sunday night. "You're joining us for our family dinner."

"I hope that's okay. Luca said you guys wanted me there."

"Ah, huh . . ."

Brooke stood tall. "Is that not right?"

"Oh, no. We want you there."

"What does that mean?"

"Nothing." Chloe turned to walk away.

"You're a bad liar, Chloe."

She turned, walked backward. "I know. Be sure and remind yourself how you're not interested in my brother while he is flirting with you over dinner."

Just thinking about that brought heat to Brooke's cheeks.

"How much flirting can happen? It's a family dinner."

Chloe laughed as she walked away.

~

Brooke tried on three outfits and then when the coastal clouds started to billow in, she decided on outfit number four.

Casual family dinner.

One where she wasn't asked to bring a thing. But because she didn't know how to do anything empty-handed, Brooke placed a vase of fresh flowers on the table they were going to be eating on.

The D'Angelos had heat lamps surrounding the area, which Gio had turned on before Chloe and Mari showed up with the place settings.

Family dinner meant she wasn't a guest, so Brooke took their presence as an invitation to help.

"What can I do?" Brooke announced herself with a question.

"Don't you look lovely," Mari said.

Chloe looked Brooke up and down and giggled. She knew, without a doubt, what the woman was thinking.

Brooke had put on makeup, something she hadn't done since she moved in. There was a curl to her hair, and she wore earrings. It was Sunday dinner. She knew not to show up in sweats and a ponytail.

Chloe was put together.

But then, Chloe was always put together.

Mari had lipstick on, her hair pulled back.

Brooke wasn't overdressed.

Still, Chloe chuckled.

"I'll gather the rest of the dishes," Chloe announced and walked away.

"I'm so happy you'll brave my family." Mari set plates around the table.

Brooke followed her with silverware. "You've all been incredibly welcoming. I can't tell you how appreciative I am."

"The most important course is here," Gio announced as he waltzed onto the terrace. He held up a caddy with three bottles of wine.

Would they really need that many?

He stopped and looked at Brooke. "Who is this?"

Mari chided Gio in Italian, at least that's what it sounded like to Brooke. "Ignore my youngest son."

"A woman makes an effort, she wants to be noticed. Right, Brooke?"

She rolled her eyes. "Your sister told me you're the biggest flirt in Little Italy."

Gio placed his free hand over his heart. "I'm wounded."

"His sister is right," Mari scolded.

"My family is against me." But he was smiling as he set the wine on the table.

"Not against you. Just pick one already and fill this table with grandbabies."

Gio crossed to his mother, kissed her cheek. "In time, Mama. In time."

Francesca burst onto the terrace at a run, her everyday pace, this time calling out, "Zio Gio! Zio Gio!"

Gio turned and swooped her up into his arms and spoke to her in Italian.

She giggled at whatever he said.

Mari turned to Brooke. "You should know that at Sunday dinners Franny is not allowed to speak in English. It is our way to ensure she is fluent."

"That's brilliant."

"It's how all of my children learned."

"You're a wise woman."

Franny said something that sounded like a question.

Gio translated. "She asked if you speak Italian."

Brooke shook her head. "No."

Franny wiggled out of Gio's arms. "I can teach you."

Mari clicked her tongue and Franny instantly said the sentence again in Italian.

"I'd like that."

"You're very polite," Mari said.

"No, truly. It's a disadvantage only speaking one language."

The matriarch of the family beamed. "Francesca will tax you, but she will learn more by helping you."

Franny turned to the doorway and started rattling in Italian.

Brooke felt heat on her neck before she turned to see the cause.

Luca stood a few yards away, his hands laden with plates of food.

Gio moved to his side and took one from him.

Luca's gaze swept her frame with an appreciative smile.

"Smells amazing," Brooke said, trying to break the silence.

"There's more . . ."

"I'll get it, brother," Gio said. He paused at Luca's side, said something only the two of them could hear, and with a laugh, walked away.

"Papa, Papa . . ." Franny kept talking until he finally turned to her.

"Is that right?"

She nodded.

"My daughter is going to teach you Italian."

Chloe showed back up with wineglasses, Gio on her heels with more food.

Soon the table was swept up with activity.

Wine was poured.

Sparkling water was poured.

Luca sat at one end of the table and Mari at the other.

Brooke was encouraged to sit to Luca's right, and Chloe sat on her other side.

Gio and Franny sat beside each other.

Once everyone was seated, they paused.

Chloe leaned over. "We're Catholic for one meal a week," she whispered.

"We're Catholic every meal, we say grace at least once a week," Mari corrected.

For a quiet moment, Mari sent up thanks for their meal, for their family, and their new friend. When she was done, the noise commenced.

Dishes were passed around in a lively fashion.

Franny spoke to her grandmother in Italian, and Chloe announced that she and Brooke had started practicing yoga together. "You guys should join us."

"You'll never see me doing Happy Baby," Gio said.

Brooke laughed. "If you went to a class, you'd see all the ladies doing Downward Dog," she teased.

Gio stuffed a piece of bread in his mouth, spoke around it. "Too dangerous. My dog would get way too happy."

She and Chloe laughed.

Franny said something, again in Italian, that Brooke didn't understand, and Luca slapped the side of his brother's arm.

"We can't have a dog. Uncle Gio was joking," Luca told his daughter.

Brooke caught on and tried to hold in her laugh.

"Behave," Mari scolded her son.

Gio didn't look at all offended as he washed the bread down with his wine.

With her plate filled, Brooke looked at the mounds of food. Salad, cheeses, pasta, some kind of chicken that smelled of lemon and was sprinkled with capers. It was all just so damn fantastic.

She felt Luca's gaze.

Gio and Franny were talking back and forth, Chloe and Mari engaged in a conversation.

Brooke placed a hand on her wineglass and lifted it toward Luca. *Thank you,* she mouthed in silent acknowledgment of his effort. But more, for inviting her to be there.

He lifted his glass with a smile and they both sipped.

When they were done, he leaned close and encouraged her to lean in.

With his lips close to her ear, he said, "Can I compliment your beauty now?"

The cool night air instantly heated, and for a moment, it was just the two of them at the crowded family dinner.

CHAPTER FIFTEEN

Brooke walked quietly down the stairs, past the apartments of everyone else in the building, and onto the ground floor.

It was early.

The sun barely up early.

Her hair was in a ponytail, she wore shorts and a tank with a sweater tossed on to ward off the morning chill in San Diego that wouldn't be there when she made it to Upland.

She let herself out the back door and stopped short when she looked across the parking lot.

Luca stood behind his SUV with two cups in his hands and a smile.

"Good morning, *bella*."

"What are you doing?" Not only up, but awake and showered from the looks of it. His hair still a bit damp.

"Taking you to Upland." He walked to her, grabbed the bag from her hand, and handed her what smelled like coffee.

"Excuse me?"

"Your list for today sounded as if it would take three to get through. I would only worry that you'd attempt to drive after doing it all, and since I'm not a fan of unwanted stress, I decided to help."

"Excuse me?" Didn't he have better things to do? And since when did a man she hardly knew volunteer to do the dirty work?

"You don't want my help?" he asked, looking like a wounded puppy.

"I didn't say that."

Luca winked, moved to the passenger door of his car. "I'll drive. My car has more room for the *crap*, as you called it, that you need to bring back."

She hesitated at the door. "Are you sure, Luca? It's going to be a filthy day. I'm tackling the garage and the oldest of the old files. Painting . . ."

"An honest day's work."

Brooke jumped into the passenger seat. "I'm not a fool. But I warned you."

"You have done that."

The streets in San Diego were quiet this early in the morning. "Make your way to the 15 and we won't get off until we reach the 10."

"You got it."

She snuggled into her seat, sipped the coffee. "I can give you money for gas."

Luca glanced over at her, then back out the windshield.

"I'll take that as a no."

"Friends don't offer help with a price tag."

She thought of Marshall. "Some don't offer to help at all."

"We call those acquaintances."

"Ha! Or exes."

Luca looked over his shoulder, changed lanes. "The boyfriend."

"*Ex*-boyfriend, thank you."

"He didn't help you?"

Brooke cautioned herself about opening up about an ex. "You don't really want to hear about Marshall."

"Actually, I do."

Was he serious?

"Why?"

Luca shrugged. "I want to know about the man who held your heart."

"Who said he held my heart?"

"You didn't love him?"

Wow, talk about right to the personal questions. "Did you love Antonia?"

Luca did a quick look her way, then back out the windshield. "Who told you about Antonia?"

"Chloe. But only that she was Francesca's mother. She didn't give a single detail."

He grinned. "But you asked."

"Guilty."

"Hmm . . ."

They were quiet for a moment.

Brooke sipped her coffee.

Luca reached for his.

"Tell you what," Brooke said. "We answer question for question, Marshall for Antonia. If it gets uncomfortable, we change the subject."

She wasn't sure Luca was going to agree.

"It's a long drive. We could just listen to the radio," Brooke suggested as she reached for the sound system.

"Fine."

She sat back. Yeah, he wasn't fine. She'd give him the first question. "You go first."

"Did you love him?"

Brooke had thought about that a lot since they broke it off. Was it love? Infatuation? Settling? "I convinced myself I did. I cared for him. He didn't throw the word *love* around often and neither did I. I just figured we were the kind of couple that didn't talk like that. You know?"

"No, *cara*, I don't. Unless the feeling wasn't there."

Yeah, that was the conclusion she'd come up with in his absence. "What about you? Did you love Antonia?"

"Yes."

The answer was quick and direct.

No hesitation whatsoever.

And it hurt Brooke to hear. But the next question was the real risk. "Do you still love her?"

"No."

Just as quick and decisive.

He sighed. "I'm not so cold. I love that she gave me my daughter. I will always be grateful for that. And if she were a mother as well, truly a mother, I might bring myself to care."

"How long has she been gone?"

He grinned. "That's three questions to one of mine."

"Okay. Shoot. Your turn."

"How long were you with him?" *Him* had a name, but Luca wasn't using it. Brooke found that intriguing.

"Three years."

"Why? If you didn't love him, why stay?"

"We were in a committed relationship."

"You weren't married."

"No."

"How committed could it have been?"

She narrowed her gaze. "Now who is jumping ahead with the questions?"

He paused.

"How long has Antonia been—" Brooke didn't finish her question before Luca interrupted.

"Francesca was three."

"She just left? Abandoned you? Her daughter?" Sadly, Brooke understood how that felt growing up. But she didn't remember her father since her parents had split before she was two.

"She wanted a different life. Divorcing me and abandoning Francesca was her way of achieving that." Luca's jaw twitched as he spoke, tight emotion crossing his face.

"That sucks. I can't imagine walking away from a child. If things were bad between the two of you, that's one thing . . . but your kid? No. I've been on the other end of that, there is simply no excuse."

Luca's lips lifted, slightly. His eyes drifted her way. "Yet you take care of the man who abandoned you."

Brooke rubbed some of the sleep that lingered in the corners of her eyes. "A fight that Marshall and I had a lot. He didn't agree and therefore didn't support my efforts."

"Not even when your father had his stroke?"

"No." Brooke twisted a finger around a lock of her hair and stared out the window.

"I'm sorry. A partner should support your decisions."

"After three years, I figured that out." *I'm a slow-ass learner.*

"I suppose if a child was involved, you'd have had a harder time leaving him. You can be thankful that wasn't the case."

His words were a punch to the gut. Brooke closed her eyes and tried to pull back any and all emotion. She let her hair go, drank her coffee. How many times had she thought the very same thing?

And with those thoughts . . . guilt.

"Bella?"

Brooke reached for the radio. "Let's listen to some music."

CHAPTER SIXTEEN

They'd been getting somewhere. As uncomfortable as it was having Antonia brought up in conversation, it was nice to have that out in the open. Luca liked to think Brooke felt the same way about her past.

And then she had shut down.

They listened to music, talked about his family . . . Chloe and Giovanni. Franny and how excited she was to be Brooke's Italian teacher.

By the time they pulled into the driveway of the duplex-style condominium, the tension of the early conversation was gone, and Brooke was back to quirky remarks and teasing.

"Fair warning, the place smells like old man and fresh paint. The combination is disturbing. No matter how much I've scrubbed, I can't seem to get the smell of my father out of the place."

He laughed. "I can handle it."

She twisted the key in the lock and opened the door.

Tile floors greeted him with the smell of lemon-scented cleaner, paint . . . and yes, an underlying odor that he couldn't identify.

"See, it smells like my dad."

"I haven't met your dad."

"When you do, you'll agree," Brooke announced.

He stepped farther in, closed the door behind him. "My father smelled like basil, oregano, and garlic. With a hint of rosemary."

Brooke glanced over her shoulder. "He smelled like you."

"Is that what I smell like, *cara*?"

She started to blush and turned away. "Okay, then. Let's open the doors and let some fresh air in before it gets too hot. My dad was a machinist, not a cook, his pores were filled with oil and dust."

Luca watched Brooke buzz around the space as he poked his head into the rooms.

It was a two-bedroom condo with a small kitchen and attached garage. It was void of furniture apart from a desk that should have been put out of its misery in the eighties, an overstuffed chair, and a small dining set with four chairs, which looked newer but were stained and probably a reason for the offending smell. The floors were tile and most of the walls had a fresh coat of paint.

"The electrician should be here between nine and noon. And the air conditioner people said around ten. Let's hope they show up."

And if they didn't, Luca would see if there was something he could do to fix the problems. He knew his way around a home, a kitchen, and everything in them. Not an expert, but he'd done a fair amount of tinkering in his years.

"Put me to work," he told her.

She started walking down the long hall. "The master bedroom closets need paint."

The "Dad" smell she spoke of grew stronger as he followed her.

She showed him where the supplies were, and he took over.

"I'll be in the garage if you need me."

Luca watched the soft sway of her hips as she walked away.

The woman really did have a nice . . .

He shook the thought from his head and focused on the work he was given.

Two hours later, the closets were finished, and the back room was heating up.

Brooke sat in the middle of the garage in an old folding chair, her back bent over a file cabinet with a garbage can to the side.

"No electrician yet?"

"Hey." She looked up, dirt smudged on her cheek. "Not yet. The air people called and said they're on their way."

He looked around the garage, glanced up. "Is everything in here going all right?"

"Yeah. I have three piles." She pointed. "Goodwill, dump, and keep."

"The garbage pile is getting big."

"I know. Once the workers get here, I was going to run by the home improvement store. There's always a guy there with a truck that says he'll haul trash. I might just have him take it all. The useful Goodwill stuff he can either sell or dump."

"I'll go by now, see if I can find the guy. Do you think you'll get through all this by what, five? Six?"

"Let's say five."

"You got it."

Brooke tossed the paper in her hand in the trash can, sat back, and smiled at him.

"What?" he asked.

"Nothing."

"No, no, *bella* . . . that look meant something."

She sighed. "Thank you for being here."

Luca stepped forward and reached out and touched her face. His thumb removed the dirt from her cheek. "You're even beautiful with soot on your skin."

He removed his hand . . . slowly.

"Let's see if you're saying that by the end of the day."

~

"Oh my God, Carmen. He was standing at his car first thing this morning. Like 'Hop in, *bella*, let's get shit done today.' Who does that?"

153

Brooke had picked up the phone as soon as Luca was off in search of a dump guy.

"We're talking about the single, hot, Italian dad, right?"

Brooke rolled her eyes. "Yes. Luca."

"Oy, oy, oy."

"Stop it. I need advice. And I need it before he gets back."

Carmen stopped teasing. "You don't need advice. You need to relax. He sounds like one of the good ones. Let it happen."

"Let it happen," she mocked. "I don't 'let' things happen. Shit happens to me and it's never good."

"You didn't used to be such a pessimist."

"Once upon a time the glass was half-full. Not these days."

"Okay, Debbie Downer. You want my advice . . . here it is. Keep doing whatever it is you're doing."

"I'm not *doing* anything. Zero effort."

"Really?" Carmen didn't sound convinced. "Makeup . . . a nice dress?"

Brooke hesitated. "Maybe . . . a little last night, but that was it."

Carmen chuckled.

"Carmen!"

"Sorry. Okay . . . any red flags?"

Brooke thought about that. "He loved his ex-wife."

"That's a red flag?"

"I guess not."

"Is he good to his mom?"

Brooke looked back on the dinner the night before. "To the whole family. He takes being the oldest brother quite seriously."

"And his daughter?"

All Brooke could do was smile. "Great dad. We should all be so lucky."

"He's Italian, does he smoke?"

"No."

"A lot of Italians smoke," Carmen pointed out.

"In Italy. The San Diego variety are less in that wheelhouse."

"That's good." Carmen sighed. "I don't know what to tell you, Brooke. How does he kiss?"

"He hasn't kissed me," Brooke nearly yelled.

"Now then . . . we have a problem."

"There hasn't been . . . I don't even know if—"

"Stop right there. He did not drive your sorry ass all the way to Upland to do grunt work all day if he wasn't interested in kissing you, *bellllaaa*. More than that, you want him to."

Brooke closed her eyes, and even in her own head she couldn't convince herself that Carmen was wrong.

"Let it happen. You deserve some happiness, Brooke."

The van with the air conditioning repair guy pulled into the driveway.

"I gotta go."

"I want a kissing update the next time we talk," Carmen teased.

"Love you," Brooke said with a laugh.

"Back at ya, boo."

She hung up.

Her best friend was such a dork.

~

Brooke's father didn't throw anything away.

A conclusion Luca came to as he watched Brooke comb through countless files that the man had collected over the decades.

Luca returned from contacting a trash hauler and scheduling a pickup to find both the electrician and the air conditioning repairman working.

The pile in the center of the garage grew as he removed dusty boxes from the rafters and opened them to find even more paperwork.

"I'm half tempted to throw it all away, sight unseen," Brooke threatened sometime after noon.

"I don't blame you."

No sooner had she said that than the air guy asked them to follow him to the control panel for the thermostat.

"I was looking for a plug and thought you might want to see this," he said as he pointed at the bottom of a hall closet.

Brooke glanced inside. "I emptied it out."

"Not all of it, lady. Look at the bottom."

She dropped to her knees and gasped.

Luca leaned down beside her as she reached into a dark space and pulled out a jar of coins.

Not just a jar, but a restaurant-size peanut jar that was an effort to lift.

"What the hell, Dad." She scooted the jar out, reached back in.

"There's more?" Luca asked.

The air guy laughed and walked away.

Brooke handed Luca the next jar and reached in again. "You would think"—she grabbed another—"that my dad would have told me about these."

"Maybe he forgot."

She reached back in, and by the time she was done, they counted fifteen jars in various sizes. All filled with coins of every denomination.

Brooke looked at the money. "I guess I can't throw things away without looking at them first."

"This is insane."

She wiggled to sit up from her cramped position on the floor.

Luca reached out to give her a hand.

He didn't let go right away, and she looked up.

He rubbed his thumb on her palm.

"I found the problem with the air conditioner," the repair guy interrupted them.

Brooke broke free and walked away.

By three, the hired workers were gone, the problems fixed. And even though the inside of the condo was cool, they were out in the garage working up a sweat.

Luca had piled the junk in the driveway and waited for the man he hired to come and take it all away.

The only things left in the house were those that required two people to get out. Even though Brooke said she could do it, it was against Luca's fiber to let her when he knew a man was coming soon. Some might consider that sexist, but he thought of it as chivalrous. He knew she could, he just didn't want her to.

Back in the garage, he lifted a dusty box onto the now empty workbench and opened it. "More papers," he announced.

Brooke groaned. "Just start sifting through them. At this point the only thing I'm interested in is a possible funeral plot, death benefit, or forgotten letter from a rich aunt I never knew about." She laughed. "Everything else gets thrown away."

She was exhausted, he could see it in her eyes. "Why don't you take a break?"

"I will when we're done. We're almost there."

He pulled out the first yellowed folder and opened it. Old bank statements. "Who is Gilroy?"

"My grandfather. He's been dead for over twenty years. Throw it away."

In the trash it went.

Gilroy dominated the top of the box. "All this has his social security number on them."

"He's dead."

"True." In the trash . . .

Luca dug more, found an old black-and-white picture. "Do you know who these people are?"

Brooke glanced at it, shook her head. "Trash."

A pile of old holiday cards was the next to find the garbage bin.

He found a letter, pulled it from the opened envelope. It was addressed to Brooke's father. Luca flipped through the pages to the end, read the name of the sender out loud. "Do you know who Elaine is?"

Brooke's chin shot up. "My mother."

Luca handed the letter to Brooke and watched her for a moment.

Her eyes scanned it until she backed up and sat in the only chair in the garage.

He wanted to ask what the letter said, but instead he picked up another letter. This one was also addressed to Mr. Turner, only it started out . . .

Dear Dad,

Luca flipped to the back, saw Brooke's name in flamboyant letters like teenage girls did.

He turned it back around and read the first few lines.

> *Hi . . . remember me? How was your Christmas? New Year's? My birthday was great, thank you so much for asking. Wait . . . you didn't ask. In fact, I haven't heard a thing from you. I thought you promised that after we met you were going to stick around. I guess my last letter when I asked your advice on what to do with Mom's new boyfriend hitting on me made you nervous. Maybe you thought I'd ask to move in with you. I know your wife doesn't like me. I don't need to go to a whole new state and not be welcome. But you could have at least sent a letter.*
>
> *I figured it out. The thing with Bill. I moved in with my girlfriend and her parents. I only have six months before I finish high school. I'm not going to let Mom fuck that up.*
>
> *Here is my new address, if you care.*

I'm not asking you for money. I just need a dad.
Please write back.
Brooke

Luca didn't mean to read the whole thing.

His heart broke in his chest for the young lady writing that letter.

He looked up at the woman, still reading the pages of the letter her mother sent to her dad.

In the box, more letters in Brooke's teenage hand were addressed to her father.

Read them.
Read them all!

He didn't.

No matter what his mind screamed.

Instead, he looked at the woman behind the pen who now sat staring beyond the open garage door in thought.

"Cara?"

She looked up, her eyes glazed. "I'm okay."

"There's more."

Her eyes widened and she jumped up.

Luca handed her the letter he'd just read. "I read this one. It feels like a violation now. I'm sorry."

And he was, because the letter had been personal, and not something he should have stumbled upon.

Without a choice, Luca stood by and watched as she read her own words to her father and her eyes swelled with tears.

His palms itched to reach for her.

Only when her hand fell to her side, her chin dropped to her chest, and a sob tore from her throat did he give in to the urge and pull her into his arms.

She let him.

In fact, she wrapped around him as if he were a life preserver and the only thing keeping her afloat.

God, this woman.

This strong, valiant, beautiful woman was holding so much together for someone who had left her and caused her to write a letter like that. Did he ever come to her rescue? Did he bring her in and make it better? What happened after that letter? So many questions. Why had she done all this for the man, *was* doing all this for him?

Brooke cried into his shoulder. Her fingers dug into his back, and her frame pressed into his.

All while Luca whispered to her in Italian. Telling her he was there and that she could cry and it was okay. That he would catch her.

When her tears emptied, and her body released the last of the pain, she sniffled against his chest and pulled away.

Luca pressed a palm against her cheek. "Are you okay?"

She bit her lip, nodded, then changed her mind and shook her head. "I just need to get this chapter done. Get my dad on autopilot so I can process all of this."

He moved away, even though he could continue to hold her into next year. "Let's push through then."

Brooke reached for the box he had been going through.

"Do you want to keep all of that?" he asked.

"Yeah. For now."

He could only imagine the pain in those letters. There was comfort in knowing that she was only a few feet away, upstairs, should she need his shoulder again.

Brooke stood tall, and within minutes they were back at the work in front of them. Twenty minutes before the five o'clock deadline, the work was finished. His car was filled with the remainder of Brooke's belongings and the papers, letters, and files she deemed important enough to keep.

They both stared at the pile of trash.

"Sad that one's life is reduced to a pile of rubble," she said.

"Don't forget the money."

She smiled. "Oh my God, the change."

Luca placed a hand over her shoulder and pulled her into his side. "You're an amazing woman, Brooke."

"Who needs a shower."

They both did.

He brought his fingers to her chin, moved her face to look at him. "*Bellissima, tesoro.* Even with dirt on your face and a twig in your hair."

Her hand shot up to her head, and she moved closer.

When she didn't run away, he did what he'd been dying to do from the first time he'd seen her walk up the stairs of his family home.

His lips reached for hers.

She leaned in.

He pulled her close.

Yes. This. Exactly this. Luca opened her lips like a fine wine and sipped her slowly to savor the taste.

Fingernails pressed into his arms, and his hand moved behind her head to tilt it back.

Her tongue teased his.

Mutual. This was all so mutual. Any possible doubt about how mutual this was shot away with how her body pressed against his.

His hand met with the ponytail she wore. He wanted to pull it free and feel all of it in his fingers. Instead, he rubbed her neck, opened his lips, and caught her top lip between his teeth before returning to the kiss.

Their breath mixed and grew heavy and thick. How would she feel in his arms like this, after a long, hot shower? Their bodies wet and lax, lathered in soap . . . How would she look waking next to him in his bed, her hair on his pillow, her lashes fluttering open to gaze only at him?

He wanted to find out.

This woman whose hand slid down his hip enough to touch a part of his ass that only a lover would touch.

He wanted her.

And she, he knew, wanted him.

Luca eased their kiss. The garage was not the place for this to happen.

Her eyes slowly opened and looked up at him. "Whoa."

"Bad?" he asked, knowing it wasn't.

She laughed. Any tension that might have been, broke. "Awful. We might need to do that again to see if it gets any better."

Luca grasped the back of her head. "Challenge accepted."

CHAPTER SEVENTEEN

It was done.

The condo was empty.

The problems had been fixed, and everything should pass inspection.

The only thing that could possibly be needed was one last cleaning day, which Brooke had already decided to hire out.

She watched the place fade away in the side mirror as Luca pulled back from the curb, and hoped she'd never see the place again.

Sad as that sounded.

"You okay?"

"I'm good." And she was. "Hard-ass day."

Luca reached across the center console, and Brooke took the invitation and placed her hand in his.

"Thank you."

"You've already said that."

"I still feel it."

It was just after seven. They jumped on the freeway only to find traffic.

"This drive home will explain all my crankiness by the time we get there," she told him when they reached the first red taillights on the 10 freeway.

"When were you cranky?" he asked.

She squeezed his hand. "The night I moved in. I all but bit your head off for offering to help move boxes upstairs."

"Oh, yeah. You were cranky."

Brooke fake gasped. "Ah! You could sugarcoat that a little."

"Spunky. Feisty. Someone I hated to admit that I wanted to get to know better."

"Hated?"

Traffic completely stopped in front of them.

As in *zero* miles per hour.

Luca turned to her.

"I did not want to rent the apartment."

"Right." She tried to pull her hand away.

He held on.

"Because doing so felt like a failure."

Brooke paused.

"When my father died, Francesca was an infant. I knew my marriage wasn't good. My father knew, but he pretended not to know. I promised to take care of our family. To be there in his absence."

"That had to be hard."

Luca paused. "Renting a part of our family home was a failure to that promise. It wasn't you."

His fingers twitched, and then squeezed.

"That seems deeply personal. Why did you choose to tell me that?" she asked.

Traffic started to move.

"God, *cara*, after all I've seen today, how can you ask that?"

"I don't understand the comparison."

Luca brought their joined hands to his lips and kissed the back of her hand. "And that, my dear, is what makes you so very beautiful."

~

They didn't pull into the drive until nearly midnight.

Everything was quiet.

The restaurant long since closed and the staff gone home.

What should have been a two-hour drive turned into four because of three separate accidents and a detour that took them off the freeway.

Luca thought for sure Brooke would fall asleep, but she didn't.

They talked about everything.

Family. The state of the country. Politics.

He talked about Franny and the absolute joy she brought to his life.

It was when they were pulling into the drive, both of them ravenous after skipping dinner thinking they'd be home in time for a late meal, that they were talking of Francesca's desire to have a puppy.

"Every kid needs a pet at some point."

"I gave her a hamster. It died in a month."

"Ouch." They decided to leave the belongings in the car until morning and went straight to the restaurant kitchen.

"Hamsters are sensitive to heat. She placed the cage next to the window, couple of days later the thing was belly-up."

"She must have been devastated."

Luca opened one of the kitchen's refrigerators and removed several bins of cut-up vegetables. "You toss us a salad. I'll whip something up."

"You're going to cook? I thought we'd just throw something in a microwave."

He removed a chicken breast. "We've eaten nothing but garbage all day."

"I'm sure there is nothing in this kitchen that you could classify as garbage."

"True, very true." Still, Luca sliced the chicken thin so it would cook a little quicker and did his thing.

Out of the corner of his eye, he watched Brooke poke around and find what she needed to make their salad. "Maybe when Franny is a little older, a dog will be okay. They at least have the good sense to move out of the sun."

"The hamster would have if not for the cage. Luckily I found the poor thing before my daughter."

"Yuck."

"I felt rotten. The whole ordeal showed me that we weren't ready for another responsibility. I depend on my family to help with Franny. I can't ask for more. A dog would be a lot more. Besides, Giovanni will be moving soon and that's one less pair of hands around here."

"Did I know that about Gio?"

"No, actually. I'd appreciate if you kept that quiet. I don't think he's told anyone else yet."

Luca seared the chicken, turned down the heat, and put the tomatoes, lemon, and spices into the pan to let it simmer.

"I would imagine living with your mom at his age isn't conducive to having a personal life."

"Exactly."

Brooke put the lids on the containers and started moving them back to the fridge. "I suppose it's only a matter of time before Chloe wants a place of her own for the same reasons."

"Yeah, no. That's not going to happen."

Brooke giggled. "Why? Because she's a girl."

"Exactly."

Brooke's giggle turned into a full-blown laugh. "So, she lives with Mom until she gets married?"

"Yes."

"And Francesca lives with you until she gets married?"

"Of course." Although the thought of his daughter and dating—let alone marriage—made him nauseous.

"That's sexist."

"I like to think of it as tradition."

"A sexist tradition."

"It's Italian. It's family. It's expected. I know they might have other ideas, but . . . it's an option."

Brooke leaned against the counter, slid a piece of pepperoni she'd sliced for the salad into her mouth. "I'm glad you found the word *option*. Although I'm fairly certain you'd fight with Chloe or Francesca if they wanted to exercise that choice."

Luca walked over to Brooke, reached around her to grab a piece of pepperoni for himself, and leaned against her when he did. "I like to keep the women in my life nearby," he said, his lips close to hers.

"Is that right?"

He touched his lips to hers, briefly, then pulled back and put the food in his mouth. "And safe."

"And what keeps me safe from you?" Brooke asked.

He looked her up and down. Messy from a full day of work, tired from the long drive, and beautiful from head to toe. "Nothing, I hope."

~

"The rules here are stupid."

Brooke sat in the courtyard of the assisted living home with her father, who had to find something to bitch about.

"A lot of things in life are stupid. Suck it up." She wasn't about to sugarcoat anything.

"You're t-testy."

"I finished getting the rest of your stuff out of the condo yesterday. Would it have hurt you to throw anything away, Dad?"

He shrugged without apology.

"Your dead father's tax returns from the fifties. Seriously?"

"I was going . . . going to."

"And every greeting card ever sent for every holiday . . . ever!"

"People don't do that any-anymore. It's email and a text."

Brooke nodded. "I did keep a box of pictures. Maybe you can tell me who the people are."

He didn't appear interested.

"When do I see the doctor again? I'm taking too many pills."

"I'm working on finding new doctors for you down here." Actually, she'd put that on the sideline. His current doctors had given her a six-month supply of his prescription medication to give her time to get him situated with new providers.

"You look better," she told him. "Eating three healthy meals a day is working for you."

"Food isn't bad," he relented.

"Finally . . . something positive from you."

"I'm trying."

"So am I, Dad. Trust me. Some days are harder than others." And after finding the letters she'd written to him so many years ago, letters begging for his attention and love only to get so little in return, and only when it was easy and convenient for him . . . today was really freaking hard to sit there and listen to him complain about anything.

The thirty-minute visit was over in no time.

He complained.

She was thankful to have an excuse to leave.

The next time she came, she'd have to take him out for a haircut. And lunch, he told her.

Brooke agreed and hugged him goodbye.

In the car, she gave herself a moment.

When she opened her eyes, she looked around.

She really needed to get rid of her father's car.

She needed the condo money first.

Her dad needed a new doctor.

And Brooke needed a month in the Bahamas.

~

Luca noticed Brooke as she tried to slide past the open door to the restaurant and up the stairs to her apartment.

But he'd been watching for her.

He ducked around the help in the kitchen, dusting his hands on his apron as he followed her into the stairway.

"Cara?"

He liked that she turned at the sound of his voice, at his pet name for her, and smiled.

"Hey."

A few steps up and he was beside her. "How did it go?"

She sighed. "Frustrating. But okay."

He pushed back a lock of her hair that had fallen out of place and tucked it behind her ear. "Did you tell him about the letters?"

"No."

"Will you?"

"I don't know. That's all in the past. A lot happened between then and now."

He rested his hand on her arm. "But it still affects you."

"A little."

Her smile did a number on his stomach.

"Don't you have better things to be doing right now than standing here with me?" she asked.

Luca leaned closer. "No," he said. "Not at all." When she didn't back away, he pressed his lips to hers.

Slow, even pressure until she opened and moved forward.

Her response was exactly what he wanted.

Assurance that the day before hadn't been a fluke, that she was still willing and anxious to be in his arms.

Her fingers slid up his chest, and Luca caught his breath.

He eased his lips from hers, watched as she sucked in her lower lip. "Hmmm."

"I should probably get back to work," he told her.

"I have an online meeting in an hour."

He kissed her forehead and moved away. "You know where I am if you need me."

She smiled and walked up the stairs.

Luca made his way back into the kitchen and found his brother smiling at him. "Not what I think, huh?"

Luca started to deny him with a hand in the air, then dropped it to his side. "Maybe a little."

Gio patted his shoulder before gripping it hard. "At least I like this one. We all do."

"A step in the right direction."

"A giant step," Gio concluded.

~

A knock on Brooke's door pulled her out of her work at four o'clock.

She smiled as she opened it, thinking it was going to be Luca.

Her eyes tracked down to find Franny smiling up at her. "Hi."

"Hello," Brooke replied.

"We can start your Italian lessons today," Franny announced, walking past Brooke as if invited and heading straight to the living room.

Brooke looked beyond the open front door to her apartment to see who was with her. "Does anyone know you're up here?"

"I told Nonna."

Brooke decided to keep her door open should someone come searching for her.

"I need to finish something on my computer first," Brooke told her.

Franny plopped next to the coffee table, pushed the knickknacks aside, and started to dig into the pink backpack she'd brought with her. "That's okay. I have homework, too."

The girl was stinking adorable. "You do your homework, I'll do mine, and when we're done, we can work on Italian."

Franny frowned. "Sometimes I need help with my homework."

"What grade are you in?"

"Second."

"I passed the second grade. I should be able to help you."

Franny giggled. "You're silly."

Brooke started finishing up her work, one eye on Franny. The girl stuck her tongue out of the corner of her mouth when she was concentrating on something.

When she looked up, Brooke would drop her eyes to her laptop and pretend she wasn't staring.

How could anyone walk away from this little girl?

She supposed she was asking the same question in her head about herself, all those years ago.

If Franny was hers, she would fight tooth and nail to be with her every day.

Brooke's email pinged and demanded her attention.

A few minutes later, Franny unscrambled from her seat, walked over to Brooke, and handed her a paper. "Is this right?"

There were eight math problems for Brooke to review.

"Wow. You're really good at this."

Franny beamed. "Papa says I can count the money when I get older."

"A girl should know how to count money."

"I'm going to have lots of money when I grow up."

"Is that right?"

"Yup. I'm going to be famous."

Brooke smiled. "Famous for what?"

"I don't know yet."

Brooke tried not to laugh and nodded toward the coffee table. "Do you have more homework?"

"I have to read out loud to an adult."

"Let's do it." She pushed her computer aside and walked with Franny to the sofa.

They sat, and Franny snuggled so close to Brooke she was practically in her lap.

She opened her book to page one and started reading. The book was a little more advanced than Brooke thought she'd see, but not having children of her own didn't make her a good judge to know if Franny was average, advanced, or what. Not that it mattered. The girl was charming the pants off Brooke with every turn of the page.

Occasionally, she would stumble over a word, and Brooke encouraged her to sound it out. The word would come, and they were off to the next page.

Franny finished the book with an articulated "The end!"

"Well done." Brooke squeezed her shoulders close for a sideways hug.

Behind them, someone cleared their throat.

They both turned around to find Luca standing just inside the door.

"Hi, Papa. I'm all done with my homework."

Luca was smiling, his eyes on Brooke. "Is that right?"

"Yeah. Miss Brooke helped me."

"Did she?" He pushed off the doorframe he was leaning on and walked into the room.

Franny jumped off the sofa to hug him.

He lifted her in his arms.

In his eyes, Brooke saw Luca's love for his daughter and felt her heart melt just a little.

"Did you *ask* Miss Brooke to help you?"

Franny nodded several times. "She wanted to help." She looked over at Brooke. "Right?"

"Absolutely. I needed to brush up on my second-grade math."

"Now I'm going to teach her Italian."

"Do you have time for that?" Luca asked.

Brooke looked at him like he was crazy. "Are you kidding? I've been waiting all day for this." She stood and walked over to the two of them. "I have an idea, Franny. Do you have any books in Italian?"

"Nonna does."

"Why don't you go get them, and you can read them to me and tell me what the words mean."

Franny wiggled from her father's arms. "Okay."

And she was out the door.

Luca ran a hand through his hair. "I'm sorry, *cara*. She told my mother she was going upstairs to do her homework. My mother thought that meant her own bedroom."

"It's okay. She's an absolute joy."

"Still, I know you have work to do."

"I was almost done for the day. Trust me, it's okay."

Luca reached for her as he seemed to be getting used to doing, and Brooke let herself be pulled into his orbit once again. He'd come straight from the kitchen and smelled of spice and him. "You're good with her."

Brooke shrugged. "I like kids."

He tilted her chin and grazed her lips with his own. "Thank you," he whispered over them.

She kissed him this time . . . a little longer. "You're welcome."

He was trying to keep his distance . . . with his body anyway. But his lips were attached, and his hand grasped her arm for dear life. He drew away. "Your kisses are becoming my oxygen."

"That doesn't hurt to hear."

His dark eyes liquefied with a moan.

Footsteps had them moving apart.

Franny walked through the door, looked at the two of them. "Hi."

Brooke recovered first. "Did you find the books?"

"Yes." Franny walked to the couch and sat.

Luca and Brooke exchanged glances.

As Brooke took her space beside Franny, Luca excused himself. "I see I'm not needed."

"Nope," Franny concluded without apology.

Brooke tried not to laugh.

"Dinner is at five thirty," he said.

"I'll make sure she's home by then," Brooke announced.

Luca backed out of the apartment, and his daughter opened a colorful Italian book designed for a toddler.

CHAPTER EIGHTEEN

Mari had been friends with Rosa since they were both pregnant. Rosa with Dante, Mari with Giovanni. A few years later, Chloe arrived, and once the kids grew older, the mothers saw a possible match.

For years, they imagined their children growing up and falling in love, but alas, that wasn't meant to be. Dante moved away almost immediately after graduating from high school to explore Europe, fell in love with sailing the Mediterranean, and was now chartering pleasure cruises for tourists off the Amalfi Coast.

When Mari and Rosa came together to have coffee, or wine—or pizza they secretly ordered from Filipes—they always spoke of their children. And other people's children if theirs weren't providing any gossip.

Today, the focus was on Luca.

"What do you know about this woman living in your home?" Rosa asked almost as soon as they had coffee in front of them.

"Brooke is a lovely girl. Well mannered. A delight with Francesca."

"I hear she and Luca are getting close."

Mari's eyes widened. "Where have you heard that?" Though she'd sensed that was the case, she'd seen nothing herself.

"Dante told me."

"How would Dante know?"

"Giovanni speaks with Dante all the time. According to my son, your Luca is not opposed to kissing Brooke in the stairs of your home."

Mari lowered her coffee to her lap. "Why am I hearing this from you and not my own children?"

"They probably don't want to excite you," Rosa teased.

"Why not? We could all use a little excitement in our lives."

Rosa clicked her tongue. "As if the last few years haven't been exciting enough."

"You know what I mean. Antonia was such a tragedy. Luca deserves someone loyal and caring like Brooke."

"You rented to her with this in mind," Rosa concluded.

"We know what's best for our children."

Rosa sat forward, lowered her voice. "Then how do we put Chloe and Dante in the same place once again?"

Mari raised her cup in her friend's direction. "You need to drag your son home."

"He's been home many times, and each visit I think just maybe . . ."

Mari thought so, too. Their kids got along well, fought like brother and sister, but smiled at each other in a way that suggested perhaps there was more. Then again, they knew their mothers wanted to see a union. "One child at a time. Luca first. Francesca needs brothers and sisters. There were too many years between him and Gio and Chloe." Not that she and her late husband hadn't tried.

"I want grandbabies," Rosa moaned.

"Nothing with Anna yet?"

"You would think my daughter was a nun."

And the conversation switched.

But in the back of Mari's mind, she congratulated herself on renting the apartment to the right woman.

Now all she needed to do was give her son and Brooke some time alone.

Hmmm . . .

~

Every Saturday, Little Italy hosted a farmer's market that closed one of the streets and brought hundreds of people into their small section of San Diego.

Brooke and Chloe set out early, before the masses of people arrived to gather the best picks of flowers and produce, not to mention some amazing street food.

Brooke was happy to see familiar faces and excited to be able to put names to them. Equally, it was nice to be remembered.

It wasn't until the third person they passed asked about Luca, and was looking at Brooke instead of Chloe, that she turned to her friend and asked what was up. "Why is everyone asking me about your brother?"

Chloe laughed. "Small town."

"What does that mean?"

"Everyone knows you and my brother are a thing."

Brooke lowered her sunglasses. "What?" She and Chloe hadn't even talked about it.

"All the mamas are talking. All the women who have been trying to get Luca to look at them since he's been single are whining. You're the talk of the town."

"Who said we were anything?"

"Do you, or do you not, know how my brother kisses? Not that I really want to know how he kisses . . . but . . ."

Brooke opened her mouth, closed it . . . opened it again. "Who saw us?"

"It might have been Giovanni. But it could have been one of the kitchen staff. Hard to say."

"*Buongiorno*, ladies." It was Santorini from the gelato store. "How are you today?"

"It's a beautiful day," Chloe said.

"And how is L—"

"Luca is fine," Brooke cut him off.

"Wonderful. Tell him to bring Francesca by today. I have her favorite," he said directly to Brooke.

Suddenly it felt as if everyone was looking her way.

Paranoid, she knew . . . but still. "This is nuts."

"Don't worry, it won't last long. Soon there will be something else for everyone to gossip about. For now, that's the two of you."

"Does Luca know people are talking?"

"Probably."

Chloe placed her hand through the crook of Brooke's arm. "We all like you, Brooke. And Luca hasn't smiled this much in a long time. You're good for him."

"Hi, Brooke." Maria from the grocery store. "How's Luc—"

"He's fine," both Brooke and Chloe chimed in with a laugh.

Back home, Brooke left Chloe at her door and walked one flight up to Luca's place and knocked.

"Come in."

Brooke opened the door slowly and poked her head in. "Hello."

"*Cara*, you don't have to knock."

"Yes, I do." She walked all the way in, looked around for Franny.

"She's in her bedroom." Luca crossed from where it looked like he'd been sitting on the sofa and greeted her with a short kiss. "Happy Saturday."

He reached for the bags in her hands. "Do you want me to carry these upstairs for you?"

She let him take them and pointed to his kitchen counter. "Actually, some of that is for you."

"Oh?"

Brooke smiled and reached into one of the bags and pulled out a cluster of orange beets. "These are from Anderson Farms. I forget the woman's name."

"Lynnette."

"Right. She knew you and asked that I give these to you. Said she had more if you wanted them for a dish you make."

Luca took them, brought them to his nose. "Mmm. I might have to swing by there."

Brooke reached back in. "Basil from Rosa's garden."

He sniffed the bundle.

Next, she handed him a bouquet of peonies.

"Who gave me these?" he asked.

Brooke had no idea what the guy's name was. "The second flower guy as you head up the block. He said, and I quote, 'Hand Luca these and tell him I have a special bouquet he can pick up to give you on your next date.'"

"Must be Hyun. He's been at the market for years."

Brooke stared at the flowers, then Luca. "Does it even faze you that all these people handed me things to give to you? And that's not all. Santorini wanted Franny to know he has her favorite ice cream, and at least a half a dozen other people wanted me to tell you hello."

Luca handed back the flowers with a smile. "I suppose that means we've made the gossip mill."

"You *suppose* . . . ?"

He tilted his head to the side. "Does that bother you?"

"To have people I don't know talking about me? It's not something I'm used to."

Luca placed a hand to the side of her face, leaned in, and kissed her. When he pulled back, he looked her in the eye. "They are talking to find out if the rumors are true. Once they know they are, they will stop talking altogether."

"Are they true?"

"Aren't they?" he asked, a question in his eye.

She shuffled her feet. "Yes . . . no. I don't know. A few stolen kisses. A whole lot of flirting. We haven't even been on a proper date."

He was laughing. "What are you doing tonight?"

"You're working." Saturday was busy for the restaurant, and since she'd been there, Luca always worked Friday and Saturday.

"Not anymore."

"Luca, I didn't say that to beg a date out of you."

"You're not begging anything out of me. I have a woman on my arm I want to show off. And she needs the rumors to end. Tonight, we'll go out. Be ready by seven."

"And who will take care of things here? What about Franny?"

Luca gathered the bags she had come in with and walked her to his door. "You let me take care of that. You be ready."

~

Luca made the promise, now he needed to scramble.

Once Brooke's apartment door closed, he went downstairs to his mother's.

He found Chloe and his mother in their kitchen putting away the market finds. He greeted them in Italian, complimented them both before he started to ask for favors.

Only he didn't have to.

"I want to borrow my niece tonight," Chloe said. "That new animated film is out, and I need an excuse to see it. We haven't had a sleepover for a while, either."

Luca narrowed his eyes.

"And you're working too much," his mother added. "When was the last time you took a Saturday night off?"

"Have you been talking to Brooke?"

His mother glanced over her shoulder as she put flowers into a vase. "Why would you ask that?"

Luca walked first to his mother, kissed her cheek. "I love you." Then to his sister . . . the same thing. "I need to run a quick errand. Keep an eye out for Franny?" he asked.

"You never need to ask," his mother told him.

He had his cell phone to his ear as he walked out the back door and up the street in search of Hyun. "Thomas, it's Luca . . . I need a last-minute reservation."

~

Brooke opened the door, promptly at seven, to a threshold filled with flowers. Behind them stood Luca, a smile as broad as the sky. One look at her and that smile turned sultry, and the flowers dipped low. *"Bella!"*

"Are those for me?"

A combination of peonies and roses screamed that Luca had taken Hyun up on his offer.

"Beautiful flowers that don't come close to how stunning you are."

Brooke had spent the afternoon pampering herself. A blowout and a mani-pedi put her in the right frame of mind for a date. She wore a cap sleeve dress in dark blue and had a sweater to go over it as the night progressed.

From the look in Luca's eyes, it worked.

He wore a button-up shirt, slacks, nice shoes. He'd groomed some of the roughness off his face and left enough to keep the sexy edge she'd grown to like. "You clean up well yourself."

She reached out for the flowers. "Should I put those in water before we go?"

"Right." He handed them to her and followed her inside.

"You really didn't have to take Hyun up on his flower offer."

"Would you have been disappointed if I didn't?"

Brooke's immediate reaction was to shake her head, but "Yes" came out of her mouth.

"Your honesty is refreshing."

She did not have an empty vase but did find a glass pitcher that made a good substitute.

Once she was satisfied the flowers wouldn't die while they were out, she dried her hands on a kitchen towel and turned to Luca. "Ready?"

He reached for her hand.

They walked down the stairs side by side. Instead of heading out the back, where the cars were parked, Luca directed her through the door to the restaurant.

It was packed. Typical for a Saturday night. "Do you need to check on something?"

He shook his head but moved toward the bar. "No, *mia cara*, this is to help those tongues stop wagging."

"How exactly—"

"Luca?"

Giovanni stood a few yards away and waved him over.

Luca raised a hand, turned to her, and leaned close to her ear. "Give me a moment?"

She smiled, noticed a server, a hostess, and the bartender watching them. "Okay."

Luca winked as he walked away.

The eyes that were on her darted in other directions when she glanced up.

"Can I get you something, Brooke?" Sergio asked.

She shook her head. "I don't think so. We're headed out."

"Oh."

Luca was already walking back her way. He stopped in front of her, smiling. "Ready?"

"Yes."

He leaned down, kissed her briefly for all to see. "That should do it," he whispered.

"You're crazy."

Luca reached for her hand and walked her out of the restaurant.

CHAPTER NINETEEN

Coasterra was an upscale Mexican-style restaurant on Harbor Island that overlooked the San Diego Bay and had magnificent views of the city.

Luca had managed a table on the water's edge without anyone sitting in front of them.

The food was reminiscent of the time Brooke had gone on a girls' trip to Tulum. Fresh fish and a variety of vegetables cooked with Mexican spices. They had jalapeño margaritas and were finishing their meal off with a shared sorbet and coffee.

"Did you always want to be a chef?"

"I was destined to be a chef. I learned to cook before most learned to read. My father would bring me into the kitchen every week. When I started school, my math lessons were in the kitchen, then eventually in the office."

"You were groomed to take over the restaurant."

He shrugged. "I'm the oldest."

"You could have said no."

"Don't look so glum. I didn't want to. I like tradition and family. Having a foundation for my daughter. How many people have that these days? In this country? How many family businesses die in one generation? My grandfather built this, passed it to my parents, and it will be passed on to me and my brother and sister."

"Do you see Giovanni and Chloe being an active part of D'Angelo's forever?"

"Forever is a long time. Gio thrives in wine. His place is on a vineyard. Maybe he returns to Tuscany . . . perhaps he finds land an hour north and builds his name in Temecula. But he always has a place here. And Chloe . . ."

"Chloe has other ideas."

Luca reached out and grasped Brooke's hand. "My sister is wise to know she wants something different."

Brooke squeezed his fingers in hers, felt the safety of his touch. "Do you bring Francesca into the kitchen with you?"

His smile wavered. "No."

That surprised her. "Why not?"

"I'm waiting for her to ask." Luca looked out over the bay.

"To give her a choice." Brooke's heart melted just a little bit more for the man sitting across from her.

Luca gave a single nod.

"I may not feel a burden for what I've taken on. There is no guarantee my daughter won't."

"You're a good man, Luca."

He brought their joined hands to his lips, kissed her fingers. "Are you finished?"

She looked at her empty coffee cup with a nod.

They walked along the outside of the restaurant with other couples enjoying the bright lights of the city reflecting off the water and the romantic aura in the air.

"I really do love this city," Brooke told him. "Where else can you walk around in a sweater in late spring and not feel cold?"

"Do you miss Seattle?"

"Not at all," she said without hesitation. "I miss Carmen. But we talk all the time. There's a couple of other friends I used to hang out with. But their families keep them busy, and when you don't have kids of your own, they tend to fade off. Carmen is the only one that didn't change our friendship after she had Ben."

They stopped to look at the lights of the city.

Luca placed an arm around her shoulders. "Do you want children?" he asked.

Brooke knew he'd ask the question at some point. "I do."

He pulled her close and kissed the side of her head.

She hated that she felt the need to ruin a beautiful night with reality, but it wasn't fair to him if she didn't start with the honesty he deserved.

"I think I should tell you something." She felt her body stiffen.

"Okay."

She took a deep breath.

Couldn't find the words.

"Whatever it is, *bella*, it's all right."

Deep breath in.

Slow breath out.

"I don't know if I can have kids."

Luca was silent.

"Two months before my father had his stroke, I had a miscarriage."

Luca tightened his hold on her. "Oh, *cara*."

"The hurt was so deep in my soul." She pressed her fist to her heart. "I can't describe it. And then . . ." The next part was worse . . . somehow.

He turned her toward him, placed both hands on the sides of her face. "It doesn't matter."

"But it does. Marshall proved in those moments that he didn't want to be a father. I've stayed on birth control just in case. And once I realized things were never going to work with him, I was thankful." She lowered her eyes. "I feel like such an awful person for even thinking that."

Luca's fingertips raised her chin to meet his eyes. "Look at me, *amore*. You are not an awful person. You're human."

The care in his eyes ripped her open. "What if that was it? What if that was my only chance of having a child? What then?"

"Did the doctors say that?"

She shook her head. "I hardly remember anything they said."

His arms wrapped around her and held on. "Things happen for a reason. I believe that. Even the hard things that want to destroy us."

Brooke held on. "I just think you should know. Before things get to be . . . more, between us."

His chest shook with a small laugh.

In that moment, insecurity rose and bit her in the ass.

She inched away from him. The last thing Brooke needed was a casual fling that everyone in Little Italy would talk about once it was over.

"*Cara?*"

She looked him dead in the eye. "If this is casual for you, I need to know right now. I'm not asking for tomorrows. I'm not asking for commitment. I just need to know if you're going into this thinking only of right now."

Luca kept one hand on her arm and placed the other on the railing they were standing beside.

"You're like French bread," he told her.

"What?"

"A hard shell on the outside with soft, delicious goodness inside. No, *cara*. If you were casual, my family would know nothing about you and me. There would be no neighborhood gossip to squelch. I, too, am not ready to make promises, but I am willing to explore what we've started."

She tried to smile and found it difficult.

Until Luca reached for her.

His hand touched her face, another at her side. "We are in the same place, Brooke."

She wanted to believe that so much.

And when he leaned down and kissed her . . . the fear that sat at the surface of all her thoughts drifted away, and hope took its place.

When Luca pulled back, he said, "Let's go home."

On the short drive back to Little Italy, Luca held her hand. He talked of how much the city had grown and how busy it was now compared to a few short years before.

They pulled into the parking lot and walked through the back door.

The restaurant was still open, but from the noise inside, the night had calmed, and the evening was winding down.

Brooke watched to see if Luca had a desire to check on things.

He gave the door leading into D'Angelo's a glance but headed up the stairs.

As they passed his floor and headed to hers, Brooke's heart started to tap a little faster.

She took out her keys. "Locking it is a habit."

"A single, beautiful woman can't be too careful."

"Has this door ever been locked?" she asked as she stood inside the threshold.

Luca shook his head. "Not since I was born."

With a laugh, she stepped inside and put her purse on the kitchen counter. When she didn't hear him behind her, she turned.

He stood at the doorway like a vampire waiting for an invitation.

"What are you doing?"

He looked to the left . . . the right. "If I come in, *tesoro*, I won't want to leave."

Oh my God . . . who invented this gentleman and then broke the mold?

Brooke lifted a foot and removed one of her shoes, then the other. "Did it occur to you that I might not want you to leave?"

One corner of Luca's mouth lifted as he stepped into her apartment and the door behind him shut.

Brooke smiled. "Can I get you—"

The question was cut off as Luca reached her in three steps and pulled her into his arms.

Unlike anytime he'd kissed her before, this time he meant it. His lips were on hers and open, his tongue searching and asking hers to respond.

When she did, he sighed into the kiss. "Beautiful and passionate," he whispered. He reached around her hip and pulled her flush with his.

Brooke leaned her head to the side as he trailed his lips down her neck and back up.

The warmth in her belly spread south and encouraged her to press even closer. She turned her head and met his lips once again, combing her fingers through his hair to pull him in. Brooke lifted her knee to the side of his leg, felt his hand wrap around her thigh.

The hard length of his erection, through his clothing, pressed against her in all the right ways.

"Bella," he whispered over her lips.

She opened her eyes and found him staring at her through a hooded gaze.

He said something to her in Italian, something she didn't understand, but when he lifted her up, his hands covering the globes of her ass, she wrapped her legs around his waist and held on as he walked them to her bedroom.

"I can walk," she said, half teasing as she nibbled his ear.

"I'm not letting you go."

Brooke knew Luca spoke of now, but the words felt more like a promise than anything she'd ever heard before.

Beside her bed, she untangled her legs from his waist and slid her hands down his chest.

He watched her as she released one button after the other until his shirt was tossed to the floor.

She fanned her fingers over his skin, felt the prickle of the hair on his chest. "You've been hiding all this goodness under your clothing," she teased. And it was yummy. Muscles she could always tell he had now rippled under her touch.

Luca reached for the zipper of her dress. "And what have you been hiding, *tesoro*?"

"Mine is softer," she warned him. While she wasn't embarrassed of her body, she certainly wouldn't go down in history as being athletic.

"I certainly hope so," he said.

As one side of her dress slid from her body, Luca kissed her shoulder before taking a moment to look at her. "My God, *bella*. You're such a gift." His hands circled her waist as his eyes came back to hers.

"You sure know all the right things to say." She'd never been referred to as a gift.

"I will always treat you like the treasure you are." He sealed that promise with a kiss, this time his hands taking full advantage of her nearly naked state. His palms came up to cup the sides of her breasts as they pressed against his chest.

Her nipples responded and rubbed against the lace of her bra. His thumbs teased through the fabric.

Brooke squirmed and ran a hand down his hip and around the front of his pants.

Luca paused with her touch, his breath strangled.

"You're overdressed," she told him.

He reached for the button on his pants, and she helped them off his hips.

Brooke touched him through the thin layer of his briefs. His erection strained to be released.

Her fingers no sooner circled around him than Luca was leaning her down onto the bed and crawling up beside her.

With one knee placed between her thighs, he presented just enough friction to bring her hips off the bed with the want of more. "You're killing me, Luca."

"Now you know what it's been like watching you all this time." He kissed her neck and trailed to the top of her breast. "I've wanted to taste this . . ." He pushed her bra down, exposed the tight nub of one nipple. He licked and nibbled.

Brooke found it impossible to keep her eyes open as new sensations rolled over her.

". . . and this." He moved to the other side.

She ran her fingernails through his hair and held him close.

He lifted her slightly and unhooked her bra, tossed it to the side.

He returned to long, lingering kisses that drove her absolutely mad.

Every touch, every sweep of his tongue, made her body tighter with need.

Brooke pressed against his knee, dug her fingers into his back, his butt. "Luca," she called with a cry.

"Tell me what you want, *bella*."

"Anything. Something. You . . . more."

His hand slid down her stomach and under the lace of her panties. One finger slipped between the folds of her sex and then a second. "This?"

Her hips surged. "Th-that's a good start."

A little dance of fingers playing in and out, circling her clit. Nothing hurried about Luca's moves, just a well-choreographed waltz that brought her close to the edge time and time again. She'd find her breath hitch, and an orgasm within reach, and he'd pull away. The third time she placed her hand over his. "Please don't stop."

"Anything you say, love."

Luca kissed her hard and took her to the edge again, and when she went over, she called his name as her release crashed through her.

"Better?" he asked close to her ear.

"So much better." Brooke smiled up at him, reached for his cock. "Tell me you have a condom."

He grinned and pulled away from her briefly to retrieve his pants from the floor.

A condom was removed from his wallet, and Luca shed his briefs.

She took the condom from his hand before he had a chance to open it. "My turn," she said and pushed him onto his back.

Luca lay back and placed his hands behind his head with a grin.

Brooke removed the wrapper and waved the plastic in the air. "I learned this in college," she said before placing the condom between her lips and her teeth.

Luca narrowed his eyes and Brooke bent over his cock and slowly rolled the condom in place with her mouth.

One of those hands so casually tossed behind his head now sat at the back of her head as she did all she could to take him in. His hips surged, two, three times, and then Luca pulled her away. "I will not last like that," he warned.

She lowered her lips to him again, up for the challenge.

Only he lifted her away. "No, love . . . climb on."

Smiling, she did. Slowly taking him in and feeling every inch of him filling her.

He was not a small man, but he'd prepared her body for his and once she opened for him, he started to move. "God, Luca . . ."

He pulled her down, kissed her hard, and thrust into her over and over.

They rolled together, changed angles, and Luca found yet another spot on her body that drove her off the cliff.

Brooke was swimming in pixie dust and rainbows, her body pulsating with aftercurrents as Luca told her his orgasm was close.

She squeezed every internal muscle she had to aid him in his pleasure and was rewarded with her name on his lips as he shuddered his release.

CHAPTER TWENTY

Luca slipped out of Brooke's bed before five in the morning.

She'd been awake enough to know he was leaving and satisfied enough to ask him to come back soon.

He tiptoed down the stairs to his apartment, double-checked that Francesca wasn't there, and fell into his own bed. He could have used a couple more hours sleep but found himself staring at the ceiling and thinking of the woman who had been in his arms for hours.

Brooke was, without a doubt, the best thing to happen to him in a very long time. It wasn't just the sex, although the night before had been everything he'd hoped and more. She was caring and sensitive. Deep in her convictions and how she loved.

Her father, who, from what Luca could tell, didn't deserve the devotion she bestowed upon him, still was given all the care Luca himself would give to his own family.

Although Luca wouldn't wish anything bad upon her, he was happy that her past relationship had crashed and burned.

What an idiot this Marshall must have been to let Brooke slip away.

That idiocy was Luca's gain.

If he ever met the man, Luca would probably thank him, crazy as that sounded.

Luca rolled onto his side and looked at the empty pillow beside him.

He would bring her there, as soon as she'd let him, to give him the image he wanted in his head of her in his space, calling his name.

He closed his eyes.

This was all good.

Everything about it.

All he had to do was enjoy and see where and how the two of them fell into place.

~

"You look very . . . relaxed," Chloe observed out loud when she and Brooke met on the terrace for a yoga session.

Brooke smiled at Chloe, who was grinning like a cat with a yellow feather hanging out of its mouth. "I'm a little sore, truth be told. Your brother is—"

Chloe closed her eyes and put her hands over her ears. "No. Stop. I don't want to hear this."

They started laughing.

Chloe tilted her head. "I'm really happy for you both. I know my brother is a wonderful and loving man. He just needed the right woman."

"Let's not jump ahead too far. We just started this . . . relationship."

"I have a good feeling about it."

Brooke sat on her new yoga mat and stretched her legs out in front of her. "I'm a bit older than you, and with that, a few more failed starts under my belt. Sometimes, the more you get to know someone, the less you like them. Or the attraction fades . . . or someone else comes along that makes the sparks fly higher. You name it, I've been on the other end of that line more than I care to admit."

"Luca is loyal to a fault. We were all happy when Antonia walked away. He wouldn't have done it, no matter how unhappy he was."

"For Franny."

Chloe nodded. "My niece is his world."

"As she should be."

"Have you dated someone with kids before?" she asked.

Brooke shook her head. "No."

"It will be a learning curve for both of you. He hasn't dated, not that any of us knows about anyway, since the ex."

Brooke thought of the comment Luca had made the night before, about how if she were casual, his family would know nothing about her. It made her wonder if he'd been a saint since his divorce, or just very good at keeping his private life private.

She moved to her feet. "Unless you want details of how amazing your brother is in bed, we might want to get moving here or I'm going to start singing a song you don't want to hear."

Chloe shook her head and fake screamed. "I'm happy for you, but ewhh."

~

Sunday's family dinner was met with a little preamble Luca wasn't expecting from Brooke.

She showed up at his door an hour before their meal, an apron in her hand.

"What's this?" he asked, looking over his shoulder to see if Franny had heard the door.

Not seeing her, he leaned in and kissed Brooke and pulled her inside.

"Teach me."

He looked at her. The apron. "What?"

"You're making dinner, right?"

"If I don't, my mother will insist she does."

Brooke moved straight to his kitchen. "Then teach me so I can help. You shouldn't have to do it all."

Could his heart warm for her any more?

"I might not be able to make pasta from scratch, but I can chop and mix and taste . . . I'm an excellent taster."

"You're sure?" he asked.

She waved the apron before wrapping it around her waist.

Luca couldn't help but wonder what she would look like with only the apron on.

He shook the fantasy from his head and walked into his kitchen. When he passed her, he placed a hand around her waist in a touch that only two people who had been intimate would know.

"I think this might also be a good time for us to talk about Franny."

Luca opened his refrigerator. "What about her?"

Brooke lowered her voice. "If you haven't dated much, we might be a shake-up in her life."

He'd given that a lot of thought as well. More than once over the years his daughter had asked if she was going to get a new mama. Broke his heart every time she said it.

"I'll go with whatever you want to do here, Luca. And regardless of how you and I play out, I want you to know that she will not be a casualty of us."

"I'm not sure I'm following you."

Brooke glanced across the apartment to the hallway to the bedrooms, then back at him.

"Let's say we're good. And Franny knows we're dating, and she gets attached." Brooke pointed a finger to her chest. "And then you change your mind about us. Or . . . I don't know, something happens, and we decide this isn't going to work."

"You already have us breaking up." He didn't like the sound of this.

Brooke placed a hand on his arm. "Hear me out, okay? I've been on the other end of my mother's failed relationships where I hung my heart on one of the good guys she should have held on to. When it was over, they were gone, and I was left thinking all men were assholes. I'd have been better off if she'd kept her casual flings out of our family home."

"I already told you you're not casual, *cara*."

Brooke placed her other hand on his face, her expression softened. "I know. And I believe that's what you feel . . . right now, today. I'm feeling the same way."

He paused. "I feel a 'but' coming."

"But . . . ," she started. "If . . . *if* that changes, I need you to know, right now and from this moment on . . . that if Franny is involved and invested, I will be whatever she needs. Because she's not asking for this . . . for us." Brooke pointed between the two of them. "And if we don't make it, it's not fair that she is part of the fallout."

Brooke's hand on his arm had clenched into a fist. Her eyes were pinpoints and staring at his.

Her message, the one that said she'd put Franny first, punched him in the gut.

"Brooke . . ."

"I needed to get this out before dinner. Before there is any chance for us to show affection in front of your daughter. I won't be offended if you want to hold off on that for her sake. You're the dad here. You're in charge. I just need you to know where I stand."

This woman. *This woman!* "Do you have any idea what—"

"Franny!" Brooke said as an announcement, looking over his shoulder.

Luca dropped his arm from where he'd been holding Brooke's hip and turned to see his daughter walking behind the kitchen island.

"Hi, Brooke. What are you doing here?"

Brooke took a step back, a little out of Luca's reach. "I came to help your dad with dinner."

Franny wiggled her nose. "Papa doesn't need help."

Brooke shrugged. "I know that." She lowered her voice and pretended Luca couldn't hear her. "I offered to help so I would find out what he puts in the ravioli so maybe I can make it on my own sometime."

Franny jumped up onto one of the barstools. "I wanna help."

Luca stopped staring at Brooke and watched his daughter. "Excuse me?"

"I wanna help. If you're going to show Brooke, you can show me."

Luca felt the air entering his lungs a little too fast.

Brooke glanced at him, her lower lip between her teeth.

"Okay, ladies. Put your hair back and your aprons on. Nobody wants hair in their pasta."

"Do you have an extra hair tie?" Brooke asked his daughter.

Franny bounced off the barstool and reached out a hand. "In my room."

The two of them walked away. . . Brooke glanced over her shoulder, a concerned smile on her face.

In the few minutes they were gone, Luca gathered his composure and made a plan.

Together his daughter and Brooke returned to the kitchen. Brooke's hair was up in a messy bun, and Franny had a braid down her back.

"We're ready," Brooke announced.

He looked at the two of them.

"So am I."

~

Luca brushed Brooke's hair over the pillow and smiled down at her.

She was flushed and out of breath.

"You know, Luca . . . when you said you needed my help this morning, this isn't exactly what I thought you had in mind."

Their legs were still tangled from their lovemaking, their hearts still racing. He'd called her after taking Franny to school and asked her to come down.

"I needed the image of you in my bed," he confessed.

"Do you practice saying all the right things?"

"It sounds like a line, but I assure you, it isn't."

Brooke stretched under him. "This beats yoga."

"Don't tell my sister that."

"Chloe doesn't want to hear any of it, trust me. After Gio's comments at dinner last night, it's safe to say your whole family knows what's going on."

"Giovanni needs to mind his own business." His brother had joked about how relaxed they both looked. Brooke had blushed and his mother had smacked Gio's shoulder to shush him up.

"Your brother teasing us means he approves. I'm not offended," Brooke said.

"My family adores you."

He felt Brooke run her foot up his leg. "Do you ever get the feeling your mother planned this?"

"Planned us?"

"Yeah. The way she was watching us last night made me wonder if she would have rented the apartment to just anyone."

"We'll eventually find out. I wouldn't put it past her."

Brooke lifted her lips to his for a brief kiss. "As much as I'd love to stay here all day, I have to get some work done."

Luca rolled to the side and watched her climb out of his bed.

The image of her slim waist and heart-shaped butt would last in his mind for some time. "Let me know if you ever want to skip your yoga session."

Brooke slipped into the clothes Luca had quickly rid her of once she entered his room.

"*Skipping yoga* is a great code name," Brooke teased.

He put on a pair of shorts and walked her to his door.

"I pick Franny up at two thirty if you need a break."

"You sure?" Brooke asked.

"I'm sure." He kissed her and watched as she started up the stairs. From below he heard a noise and saw his sister. "Well, well."

"Nothing to see here, Chloe, move along," Brooke called out.

Luca laughed and closed the door before heading to his shower.

~

At one, Brooke sat in front of her computer for a Zoom meeting with the design team on the Downes account.

Portia Corrigan, her boss, had requested a last-minute call, and none of them had a clue what it was about.

Kayleigh, the youngest of the team at just twenty-two and fresh out of college, looked like she jumped out of bed with makeup on and a frozen smile on her face. Mayson was a little older and someone Brooke had bounced ideas off of before. He was twenty-eight and had moved away from Seattle two months into the pandemic and now lived in Boise. Nayla was a seasoned new hire from New York who had experience with fashion design and, from what Brooke could tell, had the most to add.

Even on a Zoom call, Nayla looked as if she were about to walk the runway herself. Kayleigh hadn't seemed to shed the private school uniform, whereas Mayson and Brooke took working from home to mean a T-shirt and no attention to personal primping.

"Thank you all for logging in," Portia started. "I won't keep you long."

"Whatever you need," Kayleigh said.

Brooke held back a sarcastic smile.

"I've been combing over the ideas and work coming in, and individually things work, but collectively I think we're missing what Bret Downes is looking for. He said as much when I showed him the progress."

"That's not good," Brooke replied.

"No. It's not. But we have a way to fix that."

"How?"

"I want everyone to clear their schedule for the next two weeks and get to Dallas. I've booked four rooms at the Marriott. Nayla, I put you in an executive suite since you're on point for this one. You'll have intensive daily sessions. Meet with Bret and visit his manufacturing plant. Try on his clothing, be a part of the photo shoots. I want you all to eat, live, and breathe this designer's brand so that when you come away, we not only have exactly what he wants, we deliver what he doesn't even know he needs."

It wasn't the first time Brooke had been asked, or better yet, told, that she needed to drop everything for a client. It was, however, the only time since she had been with the company that she wasn't in the executive suite running the show.

"When do you want us there?" Brooke asked.

"Wednesday. I will meet you at one to introduce you to Bret and set everything off on the right footing."

"Can I add something here?" Nayla asked.

"Always," Portia commented.

"I know pajama bottoms and stained T-shirts were the uniform of choice during the lockdowns, but this is the fashion industry. Designers don't trust people that don't dress the part."

Brooke glanced at her shirt.

There wasn't a stain.

"Hey, I'm wearing pants," Mayson joked.

Brooke laughed. "Point taken, Nayla."

"We'll see you on Wednesday. If anyone has trouble booking a ticket, let me know as soon as possible," Portia told them.

They each logged off the call, and Brooke leaned back against her chair.

She didn't even know if she had two weeks' worth of executive clothing to impress a fashion designer.

She picked up her phone and called Mayson directly.

"Hey, Brooke."

"Were you really wearing pants?" she asked.

"No. I'm in my underwear."

She pushed away from her desk and moved to her bedroom. "My clothes won't impress a designer," she whined.

"Nayla is just flexing her power."

Brooke fingered through the hangers, pulled a shirt, and tossed it on her bed. "No. She's right. I doubt anything I wear will make a statement, but if I only have on jeans and T-shirts, this could go sour."

"It's Dallas, there's plenty of shopping to be had when we're there if you run out of clothes."

He had a point.

She sat on the edge of her bed. "What am I going to do about my dad?"

"I thought he was settled in a home."

"He is. But . . ." What happens if there is an emergency?

"It's only two weeks."

"Right. Text me your flight information. Maybe we can catch a ride from the airport together."

"Sounds good."

They hung up and Brooke continued to remove clothing from her closet.

A shopping trip in Dallas was going to happen.

Sometime later, a knock on her door preceded Luca's voice. *"Cara?"*

"Back here," she called from her room.

She sat on her suitcase and was attempting to zip it up.

Luca took one look at her and his smile fell. "What's going on?"

"My boss"—she managed the last few inches of the bag and moved to her feet—"is making all of us go to Texas."

"Today?"

"No. Wednesday. But my flight leaves tomorrow night. This designer wants all of us in one place. It's the right move, honestly."

"How long will you be gone?"

"Two weeks."

Luca did not look happy.

"I know . . . the timing sucks."

He placed a hand to her face, smiled. "It will go by fast."

She paused. "I do have a favor to ask."

"Whatever you need."

"It's more of a 'in case' favor. If my dad needs something while I'm gone, can you—"

"Absolutely."

"Thank you."

Luca glanced at his watch. "Can you still come with me to pick up Franny?"

Brooke grabbed her phone and sunglasses off the dresser. "I'm ready."

~

Luca stood outside the back door of the restaurant kissing Brooke good-bye. "I should be the one taking you to the airport."

"There's hungry people in this town, and Chloe can't do what you do."

He kissed her again. "I'm going to miss you."

"Good," she said with a grin.

"Call me when you land."

"I will."

He walked her to Chloe's car, where his sister was already inside with the engine running.

Luca placed her bag in the trunk and opened the door for her.

Another kiss and they were backing out and driving away.

When he turned to the restaurant, he saw his mother standing in the doorway watching him.

"Brooke will make a great addition to this family," she told him.

"You're jumping ahead," he said.

"Am I? You like her."

"I like her a lot, but that doesn't mean I'm ready to marry her."

Mari placed a hand on his shoulder. "Don't let her get away," she warned him.

"This is a business trip, Mama. Nothing more."

"I know. The D'Angelo men know what they want and run toward it. Don't stumble and fall along the way. That's all I'm saying."

Luca kissed his mother's cheek. "Your advice is noted."

He worked his way back to the kitchen and forgot time.

CHAPTER TWENTY-ONE

"Papa?"

"Yes, *tesorina*?" Luca sat on Franny's bed with her as she did her daily reading before going to sleep. He treasured these moments, knowing they wouldn't last forever.

"Are you going to marry Brooke?"

Luca felt his back stiffen. "Who told you that?"

"She's your girlfriend, right?"

"And who told you that?" He was going to have to talk to his family.

Franny glanced up at him. "I saw you kissing."

"Oh."

"And Regina at school said her mama was talking with Rosa and they all said Brooke might be my mama soon."

"Well, Regina, her mama, and Rosa haven't talked to me."

"I don't understand."

Well, damn. "I kissed Brooke because we like each other."

"Regina says kissing is where babies come from. Is Brooke going to have a baby?"

"Oh God." Where were his mother and sister when he needed them? Luca was not prepared for this conversation. "It takes more than kissing for Brooke to have a baby." Of course, they'd done that, too.

Franny sat up in bed, tucked her legs under her, and waited patiently for an explanation.

"Which I'll tell you about when you're a little older." Because he had no idea what to tell her now.

"I am older."

"Soon, *tesorina*. Soon."

Franny lowered her eyes in a pout that often got her her way.

Not this time.

"If you made Brooke my mama, do you think she'd leave?"

Luca narrowed his eyes. "Brooke had to leave town for work. She'll be back."

Franny shook her head. "I mean forever. Like my mama did?"

He gathered his daughter in his arms and held her close. "I won't make anyone your mama who will leave us, *tesorina*."

"Promise?"

Luca made a promise he knew he couldn't one hundred percent control. "I promise."

He tucked his little treasure in for the night and left her room. In his kitchen, he poured a glass of wine and glanced at his phone.

A text had come in from Brooke.

On the ground but stuck on the tarmac due to lightning. I'll call when I'm off the plane.

He immediately texted back. Be safe, cara. I need your help.

Three little dots said she was texting back.

Luca sipped his wine and waited.

With what?

Franny asked where babies came from.

An open mouth emoji followed. You poor man. What did you tell her?

Luca smiled. Nothing. I chickened out and said I would tell her when she's older.

I'm trying hard not to laugh right now. She is a bit young.

Another sip of wine. She saw us kissing.
The dots went on and on. When did she see us?

No idea. I'll tell you all about it when you can talk.

Thirty minutes later, Brooke was finally able to call, and when she did, she was walking through the airport.

"What an ordeal," Brooke said once he picked up. "There's a crazy storm here. We circled the airport for a good thirty minutes, then had to stay on the plane for almost an hour after it landed."

"I'm sorry."

"I'll take this over having a birds-and-bees talk with my kid."

"I'm sure you would have handled it better than me."

"Is this because she saw us?"

Luca left his empty glass on the counter and moved to his bedroom, kept his voice low. "I think so. And gossip. Her little friend heard the mamas talking, so Franny had questions."

"About babies?"

"About you. About us."

"Oh. I'm sorry."

"Why?"

"It puts you in an awkward situation, doesn't it? It's one thing to have the town weighing in on our dating, but Franny?"

"Don't forget my mother."

"Oh no. What did she say?"

He thought of his mama's comments and decided to keep them to himself. "It doesn't matter."

"Sure it does. It puts pressure on you. Everyone needs to chill. Not Franny. But the mamas putting thoughts in her head. I'm sorry I'm not there to help you with all this."

He sighed. "I'm glad you care enough to want to be. But I got it. I'm used to the gossip in this neighborhood."

"Talking with adults involved is one thing. Completely different when it comes to kids . . . if you ask me."

Brooke wasn't wrong.

"I'm at baggage claim. I need to put the phone down to get my luggage."

"Okay, *cara*."

"Luca?"

"Yes?"

"I miss you already."

He smiled as he disconnected the call.

Brooke was right.

Everyone needed to chill and let them be what they were going to be in their time.

~

Bret Downes came from serious money.

There was nothing small scale about the campaign they were putting together. The man already thought he was up there with Versace, Prada, and Gucci.

He wasn't.

Nayla fell right into the size-zero runway model vibe and thought his impressions of high fashion, bold makeup, and flashy urban backgrounds were the way to go.

Mayson, with his move to Boise, saw the limitations of Downes's reach if they only marketed to the upper Manhattan crowd.

Kayleigh did a whole lot of agreeing with what everyone else was saying. The girl either didn't have an opinion, was afraid to voice it, or both.

Portia's gaze fell on Brooke.

And Brooke was watching Downes and his reactions to the ideas being passed around.

"Here is the problem that I see," Brooke started. "Our job is to give you a campaign that you love. Design ads and media pages and billboards that will put your name on the fashion map. But what I think you want from us, and what will actually get you on that map, are two different things right now. A few years ago, I'd have agreed with Nayla. Give New York a run. But the world has been slow in opening back up, I'm not sure focusing only on the urban socialite is the way to approach this. I say we dip a toe in that water, so in a couple years, when New Year's Eve bashes are back in full fashion, you're a name people will consider."

Downes was listening.

"How do you suggest we do that?" Nayla asked.

"It starts with the models."

Mayson knew where she was going.

Portia did, too. It was something she'd talked about before and often found the door closed in her face.

"Bret, look at the women in this room. Would you say any of us are overweight?"

He looked at each of them, then back to Brooke. "No. You're all . . ."

"I'm not looking for compliments. But none of us would be put in your clothes and walk the runway. Why? Because no one here is a size two or less. If you've paid attention at all in recent years, you'd see that the industry is moving away from designing and modeling women in outfits that only twelve-year-olds can wear. If you want a campaign that will get you noticed, and sell your clothing, you must be inclusive. That starts with the models. Age, size . . . body type. Give us the freedom to explore this path, and let's see what we can come up with."

Downes was silent as he leaned back in his chair, his pen tapping against his knee.

Brooke half expected him to stand up and leave right then, dismissing her ideas completely.

"Portia?" he asked.

"This team will give you what you want, Bret. Brooke's suggestion might just give you what you need to come back to us next year for more."

Downes tossed his pen on the table in front of him and stood. "All right. Let's see what you come up with in the next two weeks. If it starts to look like I'm catering to Walmart and Target, I'll find another firm."

He shook Portia's hand before walking out the door.

Once it was shut behind him, Portia turned to the rest of them.

"Two weeks. I want to see everything before you show it to Downes. Nayla, make sure there is enough of the flash that he wants. Brooke, keep it real so the man sells something. Mayson, make sure it turns the heads of everyone looking . . . and Kayleigh . . ." The girl sat taller. "I did not hire you onto this team to nod and agree with everyone. If you have an opinion, voice it. Be prepared to hear it sucks and work to make it better. Understood?"

Kayleigh's smile fell. "Yes."

"I fly out in the morning. I'll be back for the final in two weeks. Let's do this."

Portia walked out the door, and Brooke released a breath.

"I hope you know what the hell you're doing," Nayla voiced the second Portia was gone.

Mayson sat back and laughed. "Brooke's been pitching this for years."

"We have an opportunity here to influence a designer to let out a stitch here, change a fabric there, and stop making women believe they have to starve themselves for fashion."

"Most of his designs are already in production."

"Production of sizes greater than a two. We'll be fine."

Nayla looked at her watch. "Meet in my room in an hour."

Kayleigh followed her out.

Brooke and Mayson bumped fists when they were alone. "Showtime."

~

The shrill of the phone yanked Luca out of a deep sleep.

His hand reached for it and he fumbled to answer. "Yeah?" he said, placing it to his ear.

"Luca?"

It was a woman. His mind went to the only woman he would expect a call from in the middle of the night. "Brooke?" Only it didn't sound like her.

The line was silent.

"Hello?" Luca reached over, turned on the bedside light.

"It's Antonia, my darling. I need your help."

CHAPTER TWENTY-TWO

She was thinner, if that was possible. Her hair longer . . . but her eyes were the same ones he looked into every day with their daughter.

They stood just inside the front door of the restaurant.

Antonia had called from outside, her car parked down the street.

He had no desire to have her in his home, but having her outside on the phone with him in the middle of the night would be worse.

"You look good, Luca. It's like you don't age."

He had no desire to exchange pleasantries.

"What are you doing here?"

She didn't answer. Instead, she turned a full circle and stepped deeper inside. "This place doesn't change. Better, if I'm honest. I see the outside seating on the street."

"Antonia." Her name was his way of getting her to talk.

"Give me a moment, Luca. This is hard for me."

"It's the middle of the night."

"Barely one in the morning. I'm surprised the restaurant isn't still buzzing with activity."

She clearly didn't remember that by one they were always closed unless a private party was involved.

"How is Mama? Are Chloe and Giovanni still here?"

Luca's jaw ached with the question that didn't come out of her mouth.

"Your daughter is fine, thank you for asking."

Antonia brought a hand to her mouth, her smile falling. She took a few short breaths and looked him straight in the eye. "I've made a terrible mistake. I need to undo it before it's too late."

"What is it? An overextended credit card, a car payment you can't make?" The woman knew how to create bills. Paying them was never her strong suit.

"Our daughter, Luca. With Francesca. I made a mistake walking away. I thought it was best. Probably was, since I had some growing up to do. But I can't go another day not knowing her."

Luca felt cells in his body freezing.

The ones that stood in warning.

As much as he hated Antonia for walking out of Franny's life, he knew, in his gut, it was for the best. She would only disappoint their daughter in ways Luca could not save her from.

And why now? "This couldn't wait until the morning?"

"If I came in the morning, people would see me. And I wanted to give you the courtesy of seeing me first."

"You want me to thank you? You disappear from Franny's life for—"

"Please don't tell me you call her Franny. You know how much I hated that."

Luca glared. "*Franny's* life. Divorce me, walk away from what was us . . . but your daughter?"

Antonia looked around. "Can we sit for this conversation? I've been driving for hours."

"So you've been within driving distance this whole time?"

Her face lost all expression. "Not all of it, no. Above Napa this last year."

He closed his eyes, stopped the slew of questions that wanted to spill out. "I don't want to have this conversation at all."

She sat at the closest table without invitation.

"This isn't how this should go, Luca. I am sorry. I am. We both know I wasn't ready to be a mother."

"And you think you are now?"

She swept her hair over one shoulder, and it was then that Luca noticed the thick layer of makeup on her face. Lipstick in place, eyebrows perfectly painted. She had always been polished, but it was obvious she came in here looking her best. And in his experience, women did this for a reason.

"I know I am now."

"How?"

She looked up at him, her expression blank.

"I've grown up."

Luca ran both hands through his hair. "Where are you staying?"

"Excuse me?"

"What hotel?"

"I just arrived in town. I came straight here."

Jesus Ch—

"You're *not* staying here."

She had the nerve to look shocked. "San Diego is expensive, Luca. I don't have the funds for a hotel."

This wasn't his problem.

"I can stay on the couch."

"No!"

"In the family room upstairs."

Brooke. Jesus . . . Brooke.

"That isn't an option."

Antonia widened her eyes and looked up. "I can call Rosa. She always has a spare room."

Luca cringed. Outside of being one of his mother's oldest friends, the woman was the biggest gossip in Little Italy.

Left with little choice, Luca walked behind the bar and turned on a light.

He found the number he was looking for and dialed it.

"Good evening. Marriott Marquis . . . how can I help you?"

Luca glared at his ex-wife. "I need a room."

Ten minutes later, Luca was locking the restaurant door after Antonia had walked out.

He thrust a fist against the doorframe and cussed at the universe.

"I don't know about you . . . but I need a drink."

Luca turned around to see his brother standing in the doorway of the kitchen wearing lounge pants and a worried grin.

"How much of that did you hear?"

"Enough to need a drink." Gio walked behind the bar, grabbed a bottle and two glasses.

"Damn it to hell."

"She's back to be a mom."

"Do you believe that?"

"No." Gio poured a generous portion of something amber into a glass and handed it to Luca. He drank it without question and put the empty back on the bar.

Giovanni refilled.

"What are you going to do?"

"I have no fucking idea."

~

"This isn't going to work." Nayla stood in front of the storyboards bitching.

They had the weekend to bring the ideas together and get the last-minute models and the setting onto a stage to show Bret how to move forward. Once they had that approval, they would face the next hurdle.

"Why?"

Nayla looked at the images of the models. "They're average."

"They're beautiful," Kayleigh pointed out.

"But average."

"I think your problem is they're not scowling." Mayson pointed his pencil at Nayla.

The phone in Brooke's back pocket rang.

She glanced at it, saw her father's face.

She dismissed the call. He knew she was out of town and to call back only if there was an emergency.

"Mayson might be right," Brooke said. "You're used to high fashion and a lack of expression."

"How can you say that?" Nayla was truly offended.

"Because she's right," Kayleigh said. The girl had found her backbone and was using it. "Those ads look plastic."

"Those ads cost hundreds of thousands of dollars."

"And only appeal to people who *make* hundreds of thousands of dollars," Mayson pointed out.

"That's what our client wants."

Much as Brooke hated to admit it, Nayla was right.

Brooke's phone rang again.

Her father's face.

"I have to get this."

Nayla rolled her eyes. "Am I the only one here who takes their job seriously?"

"Hey, back off," Mayson growled.

Brooke walked away from the group. "Hi, Dad . . . is everything okay?"

"I need a haircut."

"What?"

"I need a haircut. You said we could do it this w-week."

Brooke squeezed her eyes shut. "Dad, I told you I needed to go out of town, remember?"

"Oh, yeah."

"I'm in Texas. Your haircut has to wait."

"But—"

"Dad, I'll call the home. They have someone there who can do that for you."

"Not this week. Nobody wants to work anymore."

"Dad . . ." Brooke looked up to see Nayla staring at her. "I'll call and see what I can do. Is everything else okay?"

"It's fine."

"Good. I have to go."

Brooke disconnected the call and turned to face her team.

Nayla scowled. "Can we get back to work here?"

~

"I literally have less than five minutes to talk."

Luca heard Brooke's frantic voice over the phone and knew this was not the time to drop his news.

"Is everything okay?"

"I told you that Nayla was on point for this project. But I pitched an idea that we're running with. If it tanks, I'm ninety-five percent sure I'll be looking for another job."

"That's a lot of pressure."

"Tell me about it. And then, in the middle of a meeting, my dad calls for a haircut."

"A what?"

"You heard me. A haircut. Seriously, Luca. I told him I was going out of town and to call for an emergency only. He calls because he needs to look good for the ladies during bingo." Brooke sounded as if she was walking.

"Where are you?"

"On my way to my room to change. God forbid you meet the client in casual clothing. I like dressing up. There's a place for it. But Texas is hot." She paused. "Is everything okay there? How is Franny? Tell her I'm studying."

"Are you?"

"No. But lie for me, okay? I'll cram on the airplane coming home. Shit." The sound from the phone grew distant.

"What happened?"

"I dropped my key. I'm sorry, Luca. It's not normally this chaotic."

He sighed, had so much to tell her but knew this wasn't the time.

"Is everything okay?"

"It's fine, *cara*. I have a chef out. I'll be working a lot the next few days."

"Text when you can. I'll get the messages and respond."

He smiled. "I will."

They said their goodbyes and Luca disconnected the phone.

Franny walked around the corner from her room, ready for school. "Was that Brooke?" she asked.

"It was, and she wanted you to know she is studying."

Franny smiled. "Good. Because I have a pop quiz."

Luca paused. "A what?"

"Pop quiz. It's a surprise test teachers do sometimes. And I have one for Brooke."

"I'm sure she'll do fine."

Franny hiked her backpack over her shoulder a little higher. "Let's go."

Luca found himself staring at his daughter and worried about sharing her with a mother she didn't remember. "Let's go," he repeated.

~

"What do you want? What do you really want?" Luca sat across from Antonia in one of the many tables in the courtyard of the Marriott. They moved away from the pool, and anyone that could overhear them.

She had suggested they talk up in her room. He refused.

He didn't trust her and wanted to make sure there was no misunderstanding in his feelings.

"I have no ulterior motive, Luca. I want to know my daughter."

"For how long? A week? A month?"

Antonia sat forward. "I don't expect you to understand. I have lost years already. My own fault, I know. That's going to change."

"How do you plan on doing that?" Luca rubbed his thumb and forefinger together in circular motions. The questions coming out of his mouth had been thought of the night before with Gio. Antonia never planned anything, unless it was a way to get what she wanted without working for it.

Even now, looking at her, he could see the shadow of an ulterior motive. She was perfectly polished. Her nails painted, those eyelash extension things women liked. Luca couldn't tell you a designer label to save his life, but her clothes didn't look worn or outdated.

The car she drove was not the one she'd left town with years ago.

"It starts with me seeing my little girl. Spending time with her."

"What does that look like to you?" he asked.

"I don't understand the question."

"What is your plan, Antonia? Your life plan? How do you plan on being a part of Franny's life? You gave up custody when you walked away. You handed me divorce papers and said we could fight, or I could give you what you wanted, and you'd leave." He pointed to his chest. "I held up my end of the bargain. You got your lump sum, your freedom, and never looked back."

"A mistake I will live with for the rest of my life. I'm her mother, Luca. I have rights and you know it."

His jaw tightened. "Be careful."

Antonia softened. "We split amicably, and we can do this the same way. I don't want to fight you."

All he could think about was fighting her.

The phone in his pocket buzzed. He pulled it out and looked at the screen.

Brooke's name popped up. He forced the call to voice mail.

He considered the woman in his life. Look at the effort she was putting in for the parent that was absent nearly all of her childhood. Did she despise her mother for keeping her away from her father in her childhood? Is that even what happened? How would Franny feel as an adult if he forced Antonia to go away?

He wiped his hand down his face, scratched at the stubble on his jaw.

"What is your plan, Antonia? Where are you going to live? Do you have a job, or did you invest the money I gave you and don't need to work, what?"

She blinked several times; her half smile never fell. "I have some provisions. I need a little time to figure the rest out."

"Time? How much time?"

"You sound so angry, Luca."

"I am angry. But more, I'm worried for my daughter. She's learned to live without you. To have you come back into her world just to leave again could scar her for life."

Antonia recoiled. "I'm not a monster."

She was to him.

Antonia looked away. "I haven't been well, Luca."

He paused. "What do you mean?"

She closed her eyes. "I promised myself I wasn't going to tell you about this. I don't want sympathy to rule you here."

He hated how sincere she sounded. "Tell me."

"I've been ill."

He hesitated. "What kind of illness?" She didn't appear sick to him.

"It started with fatigue. The doctors ran blood tests, haven't completely ruled out cancer, but haven't found anything definitive yet."

"You're tired."

She narrowed her eyes. "They looked for autoimmune issues, and things I couldn't even pronounce. I had managed my money well. Better than before I met you." She smiled briefly as if the statement was a compliment. "But the money dissipated quickly as the medical bills piled up. And then I simply kept having problems. The experience has changed me, Luca. Made me realize that I may not live forever."

For the first time since he laid eyes on her, he started to feel something other than anger.

Luca looked around the courtyard. "I'll pay for the hotel for a week."

She nodded once, then said, "Wouldn't it be better for me to stay in the upstairs apartment?"

"You can't. It's rented. My family wouldn't want you there anyway."

"I could change their minds with time."

He doubted that.

But this was Franny's mother, and didn't he owe her something for that? The time she asked for, at the very least.

"A week, Antonia. And you'll need to figure something else out."

"And Francesca?"

He scooted his chair back. "I need to speak with my family. Find the best way to do this." As much as he hated it, he didn't see a way around it.

"Thank you."

With a nod, he stood and walked away.

CHAPTER TWENTY-THREE

Luca paced his mother's living room with Chloe, Gio, and his mother staring at him. "Antonia is back. She showed up last night, called me from outside the restaurant and wanted to talk."

"What?" Chloe asked.

"She told me she wants to see Franny."

His mother cussed in Italian, something she rarely did, and they all looked her way.

"I put her up at a hotel. She wanted to stay here—"

"Absolutely not," Mari said.

"I know, Mama. I told her that."

"Does she think she can just walk back in like she's been gone for the weekend?" Chloe asked.

"Sounded like it to me," Gio said. He looked at the women. "I overheard Luca and her last night talking."

Luca knew his family's reaction would mirror his, but he also needed them to understand the limits of what they could do to keep her away. And should they?

"She's been sick, apparently," he told them. Luca looked at Gio. "I went to speak to her today, she told me she hasn't been well."

"Sick? What kind of sick?" his mother asked.

"They're looking at everything from cancer to chronic illnesses. She didn't offer many details and I didn't ask. She says it changed her. Made her want to be a mother."

"Did she look sick?" Chloe asked.

"No," Gio answered. "Not from what I saw."

Luca shook his head. "I can't say she looked bad. But I didn't try and stare."

Mari clicked her tongue.

"I know, I'm skeptical, too."

"Now she wants to be a mama?" Mari asked.

"I don't believe I'd stand much of a chance at keeping her out of Franny's life if she truly wants to be a part of it."

"Oh, Luca," Chloe said.

"It needs to be on my terms. Supervised. I'll need all your help with that."

"Of course, brother."

"Is she really going to stick around?" Chloe asked.

"I don't know."

"What are you going to say to Franny?" his brother asked.

Luca pressed his thumb and forefinger to the bridge of his nose. His head had been pounding since the phone rang the night before. "That her mother wants to see her."

"Let us know what we can do," Gio said.

Luca nodded, glanced at his watch. It was time to pick up Franny from school. "I need more time to figure out how I'm going to tell Franny about her mother."

"I don't like it," his mother said with a scowl.

"Neither do I, Mama. Neither do I."

~

Brooke sat in her hotel room surrounded by clothes.

Not hers, but the designer's.

She lifted one of the dresses up and tried to see where in San Diego she'd find a woman wearing it. It was meant for a woman without curves, little waist to show off, almost a pencil-cut length. The fabric didn't give. It belonged in an office or under a designer coat in cool weather.

Nayla had purposely given Brooke all the clothing meant for slender frames and almost dared her to come up with models and ad ideas that didn't fit the high-fashion mold of New York.

It was frustrating.

At least Mayson had her back, and they were working together to achieve the vision Brooke had given to Downes.

What Brooke needed was a fresh set of eyes, ones that didn't see six-foot-three runway models staring down a camera.

She picked up her phone, found Chloe's number for a video call.

Chloe picked up on the third ring. "This is a surprise."

Brooke smiled, happy to see a familiar face. "I hope it's okay. I'm working on a problem I think you might be able to help with. Is now a good time?"

"I have a few minutes before I'm expected downstairs."

"I need your opinion on a few items of clothing. Mainly, where you could see yourself, or someone else, wearing it in San Diego."

"I can do that," Chloe said with a laugh.

Brooke turned the phone around and showed her the dress.

"Oh . . . uhm."

"I know."

Chloe hummed, took a breath. "Wait. I could see that up in La Jolla, or Del Mar. The golf functions at Torrey Pines at an evening event."

Brooke hadn't thought north of San Diego. The places Chloe described were a bit more upscale. A lot of old money.

"Okay, what about this?" Brooke held up a blazer with hard lines and big buttons.

"Actually, I like that. I would totally wear it with jeans and a T-shirt. No bra."

"No bra? Why?"

"Because it's edgy. Like daring someone to look close."

Brooke smiled. "I like it."

The last thing she showed Chloe was a dress that looked more like a sack than something anyone would wear.

"I got nothing," Chloe said, laughing.

"Me either."

"But if you can get me that blazer, I'd totally take it."

"I'll see what I can do." Brooke dropped the sack dress on her bed. "How is everything there?" She hadn't heard much from Luca outside of a few text messages. Mainly good mornings and good nights.

Chloe rolled her eyes. "As good as can be, considering. We're all pretty anxious."

Brooke narrowed her eyes. "About what?"

"Antonia. Luca's going to talk to Franny tonight."

Hearing Luca's ex-wife's name had Brooke stopping cold. "What?"

Chloe shook her head. "Wait . . . you don't know?"

"Don't know what?"

"Luca hasn't told you?"

"Luca hasn't told me what? What about Antonia?"

Chloe pulled the phone away from her face. "Damn it. I thought for sure Luca would have said something to you by now."

The skin on Brooke's arm started to crawl. "Tell me what, Chloe?"

"Antonia is back."

Brooke turned, felt the bed on the back of her knees, and sat. The woman Luca had loved, who had given him his daughter, has returned and he couldn't be bothered to tell her. "How long has she been there?"

"A couple of days. I'm sure Luca has a reason for not—"

Brooke forced a smile to her face. "I'm sure he does." A knot formed in the back of her throat. "Listen, I've got to go. Thank you for your help."

"No problem. Brooke, are you okay?"

No. She wanted to crawl into a corner and hide. "I'm fine. Crazy busy."

"If you need any more help, let me know."

"I will. Thanks."

Brooke dropped her phone on the bed and squeezed her eyes shut.

~

The hardest day of Luca's life was the one where he had to tell his little girl that her mother was gone. When Franny asked when she was coming home, Luca had told her he wasn't sure.

Every day Franny asked about her mother.

Eventually those days spread out and turned into weeks, then a month would go by. And then one day she simply stopped.

He sat with her at their dinner table, just the two of them. With family around them all of the time, it was a rarity that they enjoyed a meal only father and daughter, so Franny was eating it up.

As always, Franny had a lot of things to talk about.

Her teacher, the other kids, the playground problems. The schoolwork itself was never a part of the conversation.

Once dinner was nearly done, Luca forced her attention on what he had to share.

"I have some exciting news."

Franny's chin lifted and her attention narrowed in. "I get to have a puppy?"

Oh, how he wished that was the case.

Luca took a deep breath. "Your mama is in town."

Franny's smile slowly fell, her eyes blinked several times. "What?"

"Your mother, Franny. She's in San Diego and wants to see you."

He watched his daughter deflate in the chair. The fork in her hand fell to the table, and her lower lip quivered. "Where has she been?"

Luca opened his arms and Franny moved into them, her head instantly on his shoulder.

"I don't really know, *tesorina*. But she is excited to see you. Do you want to see her?"

He felt her head nod against his chest. Her tiny voice broke as she asked her next question. "Why did she leave, Papa?"

"I don't have all these answers. Maybe someday I will. You don't have to do anything you don't want to." Dear God, don't let him eat those words.

Franny pulled away, her eyes damp with tears.

It killed him to witness.

"I don't remember what she looks like."

Luca forced a smile to his face. "Well, you have her eyes. She has long dark hair, and is tall, like you will be when you're older. Your mother is very beautiful, like you."

"I'm scared, Papa."

"It's okay. I'll be right there the whole time."

"When will I see her?"

He'd give her time to think about it, change her mind. If Franny hesitated at all, he'd make Antonia fight to see her.

"Tomorrow after school."

She snuggled close. "I love you, Papa."

"I love you, too."

By the time Luca snuggled Franny into bed and lulled her to sleep, it was after nine. He checked his phone to see if Brooke had sent him any messages.

It was already after eleven where she was, and chances were she was already in bed.

Instead of a phone call, he sent her a text.

I hope you had a good day.

He looked at his words, thought about how to tell her about Antonia. The last thing he wanted to do was add any stress to Brooke's week. He knew how important this job was for her. And what could she do for him or Franny anyway other than worry? Once she was home, he knew she'd have advice. Practical advice that he really wanted to hear. Considering he'd already made decisions based on what he thought Brooke would do, he felt she was whispering in his ear. But damn, he wanted to hear her voice and share all of this with her.

If you have time, and things aren't too crazy, call me.

Luca pressed send and put his phone aside.

~

Brooke woke to Luca's text at six in the morning. There was an early team meeting before bringing Downes in.

When she wasn't actively working, she was thinking about Luca and what was going on at home.

It was stressing her out.

She hated the childish insecurity that hovered around every thought and every hour that he wasn't actively trying to get ahold of her.

And how was Franny? The girl must be so confused. The more Brooke thought about it, the more it pulled her out of her work, and that wasn't something she could afford right now.

Brooke walked out of her room and over to Nayla's for the Zoom call with Portia. En route, she texted Luca. Pivotal meetings this morning. I'll call this afternoon.

It was the best she could do. She wanted to add "I miss you." Or "I'm thinking of you." But felt they were half bullshit. She did miss him but was ticked he hadn't told her about Antonia more than she missed him. Yes, she was thinking about him . . . about how hurt she was that he was keeping secret something so huge in his life. While both statements were true, they were charged with a whole lot of bullshit.

Forcing a smile, Brooke walked into the morning meeting with the confidence she needed to convince the client that they were the right company to move forward with.

Portia was online within minutes, and the split screen displayed everything they'd put together to make the client happy.

"We have a taste of the high-fashion world Downes desires without making it out of reach for others."

"That's a golf course?" Portia asked.

Brooke nodded. "Which is upper middle class, but still reachable."

"What is this?"

"Downes's line has enough edge to have a club feel. High-style 'I want to be seen' clothing," Nayla said.

Brooke glanced at Mayson, who rolled his eyes. The idea had been Brooke's and was coupled with Kayleigh's image of the club scene. All of which came from Chloe's thought of the braless blazer. Once that pearl had been placed in their heads, they all brainstormed, and even though Nayla was stuck on red carpets and Hollywood, they decided *golf* clubs was a better direction. And the women in those clubs weren't all a size two or less.

Nayla put in her images of runway-ready models. Which they all agreed was the way to play it should Downes decide that the other ideas were not to his liking.

It took a few minutes, but Portia started to nod. "I like it."

Brooke offered Mayson an under-the-table fist bump.

Portia sat forward. "What's the next step?"

~

"Two *ravioli al granchio*. One *gnocchi neri*." Luca called out the order as it came into his hands and moved to complete it even before his last word was uttered. The lunch rush was the busiest of the week. As a rule, he worked nights, but he wanted to keep the evening free for his daughter.

Chloe stood on the waiter's side between the kitchen and the restaurant. "I need a bruschetta," she told him.

Normally she'd put it with a written order, but occasionally it was verbal when it was for a table of VIPs or friends.

Luca acknowledged her with a nod, called it out to his team.

"How are you doing?" she asked when there seemed to be a lull.

"The busier I am, the better," he admitted.

"How is Franny taking it?"

"She's nervous."

"We all are," Chloe told him.

He appreciated that his sister felt the same way.

"And Brooke? Is she okay?"

The bruschetta was handed to him, and he placed it in the window.

"I haven't told her."

Chloe reached for the plate and stopped midstream. "Luca."

"I know. I should have—"

"Brooke and I spoke yesterday. I told her about Antonia. Jesus, what is wrong with you two?"

He stopped in his tracks and stared at his sister. "You what?"

"I assumed you had told her. I mentioned it. Why didn't you say something to her? Is it a secret?"

Suddenly the seafood ravioli and squid ink gnocchi didn't matter. "Chloe!"

His sister lowered her voice and leaned in. "Antonia has already been around town. She's looking for a place to stay. Do you want Brooke to find out about her from the town gossip? Or is there something else going on inside your head?"

"What are you suggesting?"

"I'm suggesting you get your butt on the phone and call your girlfriend."

Another order came in, and Luca called it out to his staff. "It's going to have to wait."

Chloe groaned, took her appetizer, and walked away.

Thirty minutes later there was enough of a lull in the kitchen for Luca to step out and called Brooke.

Thankfully, she picked up the phone.

"Hi, stranger."

"It's been hectic," he started. "How are you?"

"Busy. I'm on a break right now, so I have a few minutes to talk."

Luca stood outside the back door of the restaurant, away from the ears of his staff. "Chloe told me you spoke."

It took a second for Brooke to respond. "Yeah. It's crazy how she could find a minute to tell me what's going on and you couldn't."

That made him look bad. "I honestly didn't want to distract you from your work. I know how important this job is."

"Considering how huge this is, I'd think . . . never mind." Her words were sharp, anger laced her voice.

He squeezed his eyes shut. "I should have said something."

"When men keep things from women, there's a reason. I shouldn't be offended. We're new. You don't owe me anything."

"*Cara*, don't say that. I may not owe you anything, but I want to be here for you, and you for me."

"I want to believe that."

"You can."

"We'll see. How is Franny?"

"Seeing her mother this afternoon at the hotel."

"Antonia is staying in a hotel?" Brooke asked.

"Yes. She wanted to stay here, but I said no. Put her in a hotel instead."

"Wait, what? You're paying for her hotel?"

He ran a hand through his hair. This was not going like he wanted it to. "Yes. It's complicated."

He heard Brooke's nervous laugh over the line. "More complicated by the second."

"None of this is making me look good, is it?"

"No."

"She means nothing to me, Brooke."

"You're lying to yourself. If she meant nothing to you, she wouldn't be in a hotel that you're paying for. Here's the thing . . . I'm going to put my feelings aside here for now. This is about Franny and how she's handling all this. I have one piece of advice, if you want to hear it."

"I'm listening."

"Don't say anything good or bad about Antonia in front of Franny. Don't make one promise you can't keep when it comes to her mom. She'll hold it against you."

"Thank you, *cara*."

"You can thank me by not keeping shit from me."

"You're right. I'm sorry."

"And, Luca?"

"Yes."

"If your feelings change about anything, tell me."

"My feelings aren't going to change."

Brooke laughed. "People's feelings change every day. I gotta go."

"I'll call you tonight."

"Okay." She didn't sound convinced. "Bye."

"Ciao."

Luca disconnected the call. "Fuck!"

"That does not sound good," Sergio said from the back door.

"Women."

Sergio started laughing and continued to laugh as he walked away.

CHAPTER TWENTY-FOUR

Franny squeezed Luca's hand in a death grip as they stood outside the hotel looking up at it.

"Are you ready?" he asked her.

She shook her head, her face void of color. She wore a dress, one she picked out for one of those school performances where all the classmates stood onstage and sang for their parents. It was rose pink with ruffled sleeves and completely girlie. She picked out sparkly white sneakers after having a slight meltdown that the dressy white shoes she hated to wear didn't fit any longer.

It took Luca showing her online images of girls wearing dresses with cute tennis shoes to convince Franny the outfit worked. All of it came together when everyone in the restaurant complimented her as they walked out.

Luca guided her through the hotel lobby and out into the courtyard. He scanned the tables, his eyes landing on his ex-wife.

She wore dark sunglasses and was on a cell phone.

When she caught sight of them, she raised her hand and got off her call.

Franny tugged on his arm until he leaned over. "Is that her?"

"Yes."

They crossed the courtyard slowly. As they did, Franny moved closer and closer to Luca's side.

"Oh, my . . . would you look at you. How grown-up you are."

Franny placed a timid hand in the air. "Hi."

Antonia knelt down, opened her arms. "Don't you have a hug for your mama?" It was then that Luca noticed the high heels and the skirt she wore.

Franny pushed closer to Luca's leg.

"Why don't we give Franny some time here, Antonia."

The smile on her face wavered as she stood without the hug. She removed her sunglasses and looked between the two of them. "Of course. Sit, sit. I ordered some snacks. I hope you're hungry."

Franny smiled. "You're pretty."

"Oh, baby, that's so sweet of you to say. You are, too."

"I told you that you looked like your mother," Luca said.

"I can't get over how big you are."

"Nonna says she's going to buy a shoe store because I go through so many pairs."

Antonia laughed. "And funny." She looked at Luca. "She's so witty."

A waiter showed up at the table with french fries, fried chicken pieces, and an order of mini tacos.

"What do you want to drink, precious?" Antonia asked Franny.

"Just water."

"They have milkshakes and soda . . ."

Franny looked up at Luca for permission.

He wasn't about to say no.

"Whatever you want, *tesorina*."

Franny shook her head. "I don't want a tummy ache."

Luca looked at the waiter. "Water is fine."

"How very grown-up of you."

He watched his ex . . . "You don't really drink sodas very often, do you, Franny?"

She shook her head. "That machine is gross."

"It is."

Antonia sat forward. "Well, eat, at least."

Franny sat up a little more in her chair and reached for the fries.

"How do you like school?"

"I like it. Brooke says I'm really good at math."

Antonia smiled. "Is Brooke your teacher?"

Franny shook her head, a french fry in her mouth. "She's Papa's girlfriend."

"Oh?" Antonia looked directly at Luca. "I didn't know your father had a girlfriend."

"She's pretty, too. She likes going to the park and playing Frisbee. Do you like going to the park?"

"I *love* going to the park."

Luca pictured Antonia in the park with her high heels and tight skirt. *Yeah, no.*

The waiter returned with the waters and quickly disappeared.

"Why did you go away?"

Antonia opened her mouth, closed it.

She glanced at Luca before grabbing her sunglasses and putting them back over her eyes.

He couldn't help but think she was hiding from the question.

"Well . . . your father and I got a divorce and . . ."

Luca narrowed his eyes at her, a warning to keep any blame off him. He'd shut this whole party down if Antonia thought she could pin this on him.

". . . and I thought it was best."

Franny nibbled on the end of a chicken nugget. "I have a friend at school, his parents got divorced and his mama didn't go away."

Luca sat back, kept his mouth shut. The innocent and pure questions from his daughter were interrogation enough.

"I had my reasons."

Franny put the chicken down and looked at her.

What Antonia didn't know was that her daughter was better at waiting for an answer than any adult he knew.

"What reasons?"

Luca felt, more than saw, the glare coming from behind Antonia's sunglasses. "Well, sweetheart, I don't think today is the time to go over this. I'm sorry I left, but I'm home now and hope I can make it up to you."

Franny had something to say, but she was holding it back.

Antonia leaned over and brought out a colorful gift bag from her side. "I bought you something."

"It's not my birthday."

"I know, honey. I was there. But I missed your birthday, so . . ." She pushed the present closer.

Franny reached for the gift, pulled the paper from the top, and unearthed a Barbie doll.

She smiled. "Thank you."

"You're welcome, honey."

Luca stared at his ex-wife. He supposed if he were in her shoes, he'd be buying Franny gifts as well, but it hurt to watch. She was trying to buy her daughter's love.

The question was . . . would it work?

~

"To us!" Mayson raised a glass, and Brooke and the others followed.

"We did it." Kayleigh seemed surprised.

Brooke looked between the four of them feeling justified and happy, but more than that, just thankful it was over. At least the two weeks away from home.

She'd had three phone calls from her father. All for things like the haircut he felt he desperately needed, to a toilet seat raiser that would make his life easier, to a legitimate need for an eyedrop medication that she then had to spend two hours on the phone to fill.

"Now the work really begins," Nayla told them.

"Could you be more of a killjoy?" Mayson asked.

"You know I'm right."

"We're here to celebrate getting the client, Nayla. We are all aware we're back to work on Monday." Brooke couldn't wait to put Nayla in her rearview mirror. With the four of them working together on the job, they should have all the design needs for the client within the month. Then poof, Nayla and Brooke never had to work together again.

If Portia insisted, Brooke would agree only if she were the one in charge. Nayla was good at her job, but the woman didn't bend well. And she'd forgotten there is no *I* in *team*.

"When are you headed home?" Mayson asked Brooke.

"I changed my flight to tonight since we finished early."

He turned to Kayleigh. "What about you? Any chance we can grab a ride to the airport tomorrow?"

Brooke glanced at Nayla, who looked away. "Are you sticking around?" Brooke asked.

"I am. I haven't been out of Manhattan much. I thought I'd rent a car and take the weekend to see what's around here."

Brooke was surprised to hear that, considering Nayla seemed to eat, sleep, and breathe this job.

"Have fun."

"Find a cowboy," Mayson added.

His way of saying Nayla needed to get laid.

Brooke glanced at her watch. "I have to break this up. I will see you all on next Tuesday's Zoom meeting." She stood and pushed her chair back.

"Safe flight," Mayson said.

"You too." Brooke looked at Kayleigh and Nayla. "It was a long couple of weeks, but it paid off."

"Good luck with your dad," Kayleigh said.

"Thanks."

"See ya Tuesday," Nayla added.

Brooke said her goodbyes and left the hotel bar.

She'd already packed and only had to do a final check in the room before walking out with her luggage.

During the ride to the airport and wait through security, Brooke considered letting Luca know she was coming home early.

Only she really didn't want to. She wanted to get into her apartment and decompress without the long conversation they needed to have. Her flight would land after eleven, and hopefully she could sneak in without being noticed.

Brooke had spoken with Luca twice since she'd confronted him. She kept the conversation on Franny and how she was handling everything. What Brooke really wanted to know was if Luca was still paying the woman's bills and why.

But more than that, she wanted to not care. Because caring was hurting a part of her she'd only recently felt come back. And now that the hard rush of work was behind her, she'd have nothing but time to contemplate the situation.

Or get busy.

Escrow was closing that week. She needed to get rid of her father's car and get one of her own. She still hadn't explored San Diego to any extent.

Her dad needed a haircut and doctors.

She needed to find an ob-gyn and get refills for her birth control pills.

At least she hoped there was a need for that.

She'd stay busy. Then maybe if Luca's feelings changed, she could plow through the time and get over him fast.

The error in dating someone who lived in the same building became super apparent.

A little luck came her way in the form of an upgrade on her flight. She had a window seat in first and access to unlimited wine.

She took advantage, and by the time they landed she was beyond tipsy.

An Uber ride home, and she was doing all she could to drag her bag up the stairs as quietly as possible. She made it five steps beyond Luca's apartment when she heard the squeaking hinges of his door.

"Shit," she said a little louder than intended.

"Brooke?"

Her shoulders slumped. "Yeah."

"I thought you were coming home tomorrow."

She heard him walking up behind her.

"I changed my flight."

"Why didn't you call me?" He was beside her, the bag in her hand now in his.

Brooke took him in . . . all of him, ruffled hair, five o'clock shadow. Damn, why did he have to look so good?

"I didn't want to bother anyone."

He narrowed his eyes. "You're never a bother, *cara*."

She swayed toward him an inch, then pulled back. "I might have drunk a lot on the plane."

Luca grinned. "That's what I'm seeing in your eyes."

"Alcohol is my truth serum. It's best I go right to bed."

Luca's smile fell.

Shit . . . had she said that out loud?

Damn!

"Interesting."

Luca took her bag up the stairs and stopped at her door.

Brooke dug for her key, finally found it, and let them in.

Luca took her bag to her bedroom, and she walked to the kitchen window and opened it.

She braced her hands on both sides of the sink and sucked in the salt air. It was good to be home. Even with the uncertainty of it all, she was happy to be back in San Diego.

She felt Luca's arms before she even heard him behind her.

Brooke stiffened.

"Talk to me, *bella*," he whispered in her ear.

She shook her head. "I'm not going to say nice things."

"Then say awful things. But talk to me."

With her eyes out the window, she opened up. "I didn't think you and I were casual. I thought maybe we were going somewhere."

His hands squeezed her waist. "Brooke—"

"Secrets are what casual people do. And if that secret has something to do with an ex, it feels more like an indiscretion."

"There is nothing between Antonia and me, Brooke." Luca moved to her side, placed a hand on her chin, and directed her gaze to his. "Her appearance was a complete surprise."

"I understand that. But you kept it from me."

"I didn't—"

"No. What if I told you that while I was in Texas, Marshall called me and showed up—he wanted to talk?"

Whatever Luca was about to say drifted away like smoke. She saw the gears in his head turning.

"Did he?"

She didn't answer him. "See? You need to know. And right now, you want to know if I'm telling you this to make a point or if he did. And if he did, what did we talk about? Why are you just hearing about this now? Did I keep it from you as some sort of revenge? Or did something happen between the two of us?"

Luca stayed silent.

She put a hand to his chest. "If two people are starting something that isn't casual, they don't keep secrets . . . ever. Because when you do, trust is lost. And *trust* is everything."

Luca covered her hand with his, his head lowered.

"I've had a really long, exhausting day." And if he stood there much longer, she'd likely melt into him, and all her bravado would fade with a single kiss.

Luca gathered both her hands in his, kissed them. "I'll make this up to you."

"And I'll give you a chance to do that. But tonight, I want to sleep."

He kissed her hands again, placed his palm on the side of her face, and then walked away.

Brooke blew out a breath before turning to her pantry.

One more glass of wine wouldn't hurt.

CHAPTER TWENTY-FIVE

It hurt.

One eye opened and the thorns of a thousand roses stabbed the back of her brain.

The clock on the bedside table told her it was after nine in the morning.

So much for getting a jump start on all the things she needed to do.

She closed her one eye and willed her head to stop pounding.

Her phone buzzed beside her.

A text message, likely the noise that had woken her in the first place. She reached for her phone, found a message from Chloe.

I heard you're home. Yoga?

The thought of lifting her ass in the air in a Downward Dog made her stomach lurch.

I'm dying.

Chloe's reply was a question mark.

Brooke sent a wine emoji.

Her phone rang.

"I'm seriously dying. You can have my shoes," Brooke said.

Chloe laughed. "Gio has the best cure for wine hangovers. I'll be up in ten minutes."

"I love you."

Chloe kept laughing and hung up.

If she didn't move, she might see the next hour of the day.

A knock on the door preceded Chloe's voice. "Brooke?"

"Back here."

Chloe was quietly chuckling as she walked in the room. She pointed her thumb behind her. "There's still a half a bottle back there."

"I had a running start from the plane."

Chloe sat on the side of the bed, placed the glass of whatever Gio's cure was on the table.

Brooke forced herself into a sitting position.

"Did the job go bad?"

She shook her head. "We nailed the job."

"Why then?"

"Antonia."

Chloe opened her lips. "Oh."

Brooke looked at the glass on the bedside table, noticed the brown color of the liquid inside, wrinkled her nose at it.

"It works. Trust me. I learned early. It's two gulps and just breathe." Chloe handed it to her.

Brooke placed her nose to it.

"No. Just drink it."

What was the worst that could happen? She'd toss anything in her stomach up? She thought that was going to happen anyway.

"Cheers."

One gulp.

Two gulps.

She tasted wine and pepper and something else she couldn't identify.

"That's awful."

"Breathe."

Brooke closed her eyes and did as instructed. After four deep breaths she opened them.

At least she didn't think it was coming up.

"I'm okay."

"We've all been there."

Brooke shook her head slowly. "Why do we do this to ourselves?"

"Because men have a hard time connecting their actions to their brains sometimes. Luca told me you're upset."

"I'm glad he figured that out. I'm more hurt, Chloe. I really like your brother. I want him to be different."

Chloe placed her hand on Brooke's leg. "He feels shitty."

"Good."

She smiled.

"I want to be the modern, confident woman here, but damn it's hard."

"Sometimes a woman simply wants the man in her life to only have room for her. I don't think you're asking too much of Luca to keep it honest about Antonia."

Brooke placed her hand over Chloe's. "Thanks."

There was a knock on the front door.

She and Chloe exchanged glances.

"Want me to get that?"

"Yeah. I need to get rid of what died in my mouth."

Chloe left the bedroom and Brooke moved into the bathroom.

When she was done, she walked into the living room to find Chloe standing over a bouquet of spring flowers.

A huge bouquet.

"I'd say that Luca is trying."

Brooke's heart started to thaw. She reached for the card.

You are the only woman in my life.
L

"He had them delivered?"

Chloe nodded.

Brooke moved toward the kitchen. "My friend Carmen would say to hold off forgiveness until jewelry was involved."

"I like how your friend thinks."

In the kitchen, Brooke poured herself a glass of water.

"How is Franny taking all of this?"

"It's hard to tell. She seems afraid to talk about it to any of us."

Brooke sipped the water cautiously. "Man, do I remember that."

"What do you mean?"

"I met my dad when I was a teenager."

"You're kidding."

She shook her head. "My dad walked away before I was two and didn't look back. Sound familiar?"

"Oh my God."

"When I did meet him, I remember being under the microscope. My mother watched everything I said or did regarding him. She wasn't exactly supportive of me being excited to get to know him. Which I get now, but for me . . . I wanted a dad. I can only think that Franny feels the same way. No matter who Antonia is, or if she's even worthy of Franny, she is her mother. Franny knows that. But she'll be afraid to show any excitement to Luca or any of you."

Chloe sat on the sofa, her expression blank. "You're the only person who can relate to her."

Brooke took her water to the living room. "But I'm not without my own bias. I hate Antonia on principle. I'd bitch-slap you all the way to Sunday if you tried to do it to your kid."

Chloe shook her head. "Never gonna happen. If I ever have kids, they'll be smothered in my love."

Brooke felt that to her core. "Me too."

"None of us understood how she could walk away. But when she did, it seemed inevitable."

"Why?"

Chloe hesitated. "I think you need to ask Luca."

Brooke shook her head. "No. You started this conversation, and I don't want to wait for the next time Luca wants to open up. What's *her* story? Not *their* story . . . I'll ask him about that."

Chloe swiped her hand over her forehead. "I need coffee."

Brooke motioned toward the kitchen. "Help yourself."

Chloe made her way to the kitchen and moved around like she knew the space. Of course she knew it, since she'd likely placed everything where it was long before Brooke showed up.

"Antonia was a niece of our grandfather's friend. She wanted to visit the States. My grandfather connected her with Mama—"

Brooke stopped her. "Please tell me she didn't live in this apartment."

Chloe shook her head, continued moving around the kitchen to make a pot of coffee. "No. She lived with Rosa, actually. My mother's longest friend."

"Thank God."

"She came to the States. Toward the end of her visit, she and Luca were dating. Obviously, you know they eventually married, and Francesca was born."

Brooke hesitated in her immediate assumption. "Accidents happen, so I won't jump on that one."

"No. Actually, Franny was born ten months after they were married. Everyone counted. Trust me."

"That's a relief."

"It was for all of us. But it didn't stop the fact that after Franny and a few years . . . Antonia got her citizenship and she moved on."

Brooke cringed. "Damn."

"It's what most of us think."

Brooke sat with the new information, let it roll around in her head. "How did Luca pull away from that?"

Chloe shrugged. "He had Franny. He took the role of father seriously and never looked back. To be fair, he takes on the role of oldest son, my father's replacement . . . all of it seriously. Luca needs to be needed."

Brooke sat a little taller. "What are you trying to tell me?"

"I think I said it. Luca is a good man with a big heart. We all thought she shut that down. Then you came around and put a smile back on his face." Chloe paused. "Don't let her win. She doesn't deserve him."

Brooke felt the lump in her throat that had been there ever since she'd heard of Antonia's return. "I'm not the mother of his child."

Chloe sucked in a breath, blew it out slowly. "That's debatable."

~

"I have paid for the room through tomorrow." A week longer than he said he was going to. "After that it's on you or you need to leave," Luca told Antonia once he was able to get her on the phone.

"We can't discuss this?"

"The only discussion is if you'd like to pay for the bill yourself. And considering you eat at the hotel daily and charge it to your room, you might want to do that." Though he knew she wouldn't.

"Francesca likes coming to the pool." Franny had gone there once to go swimming. Antonia wore a bikini that hardly covered a thing and didn't so much as dip her toe in the water. Luca had worn swim trunks just in case, but when it became apparent that Antonia wanted to engage him in conversation and not their daughter, Luca called Chloe to come by and supervise the visit.

He left for an hour and when he came back, Chloe and Franny were soaking wet and exhausted from playing in the pool, and Antonia was frustrated.

"So rent an apartment with a pool."

"Be reasonable, Luca."

He thought of Brooke. "I am. You're seeing Franny at the park after school today. That's what this is all about. Not me paying for your room and board."

"Now I don't think I can do that today. I'm going to have to find a place to stay, aren't I?"

"Excuse me?" Luca stopped in front of the window in his living room, shaking his head.

"You could have given me more notice. I don't want to miss an opportunity to see Francesca, but you leave me little choice."

This was rich. He felt her manipulative fingers weaving in like they had so many times in the past. "Your choice."

Her voice softened. "Luca?"

"Ciao."

"Luca!"

He hung up.

His phone immediately rang. Antonia's name popped up.

And a knock sounded on his door.

"Come in."

Brooke peeked inside and Luca set his ringing phone on the kitchen counter. "Good morning."

She was a breath of fresh air. Although her eyes looked a little heavy from a lack of restful sleep. "Good morning."

"I wanted to stop by and say thank you for the flowers. They're beautiful."

"My pathetic attempt to remind you I care and I'm sorry for making you think otherwise." He walked over to her, unsure if he was welcome to take her into his arms.

"It's certainly a start."

She was smiling, and that was better than the night before. "I have more than flowers in my romance toolbox."

"You don't have to buy my affection."

"Who said anything about buying? I make a fantastic macaroni necklace."

Now she was laughing.

"Oh, *bella*, it's so good to see you smile."

He reached for her.

She let him.

"I'm glad you're home," he said quietly.

"I am, too."

He leaned closer. "Can I welcome you properly now?"

She lifted her lips to his with a nod.

Thank God.

So sweet, so soft . . . like spring rain and butterflies. He let their kiss linger, savoring every second, every tiny noise she made.

When he did pull away, she whispered, "Hello."

"Mmmm."

"I can't stay," she said with a sigh. "I have to take my dad for a haircut. He called me three times while I was in Texas."

"*Cara*, why didn't you ask for my help? I could have done that for you."

"You haven't even met my father."

"That doesn't matter."

She stepped back. "It's only hair. He could wait."

Luca ran his hands down her shoulders, her arms, and grasped her hands. "Will you be back by the time Franny is out of school? We are going to the park."

"I'd love to come."

He thought of his ex-wife. "Full disclosure. Antonia was supposed to meet us there, but she has to find a place to stay since her welcome at the hotel is over."

Brooke winced. "She's flaking on Franny?"

"Yes. And going to blame me, from the sound of it."

"That's ridiculous."

"It is."

"Well, thank you for telling me. I'll still be there."

Luca kissed her again, this time briefly. "I'll see you this afternoon."

"Have a nice day."

He smiled. "I will now."

Brooke walked away, and much of the anxiety that had been hovering in his head for days started to fade.

His phone buzzed on the counter. He glanced at it, thinking it was Antonia whining. When he saw a text from Chloe, he picked it up and read it.

Flowers die. Jewelry doesn't.

He dismissed her comment, put the phone aside.

Three steps toward his room he stopped, turned back to the kitchen, and looked at the text again.

"Huh."

~

"Look at you!"

Brooke's father was walking out the doors of the assisted living home with a walker and not in the wheelchair.

"Getting stronger every d-day."

"That's fabulous." And it was. He was smiling, and even though he had hippie hair at this point and the stuff growing out of his nose could be braided, he looked like he'd put on ten of the thirty pounds he'd lost in the hospital. "You look good."

"I look . . . look like a bum."

She opened the car door, helped him with his seatbelt. "Let's take care of that for you."

After tucking the walker in the trunk, she slid behind the wheel and drove out of the parking lot. "There's a barber shop not too far away I thought we'd try out."

"And lunch."

"Yes, Dad. And lunch."

The barbershop was run by two Korean women who were fast and efficient.

Her father complained because he couldn't understand everything they said.

Brooke rolled her eyes, shook her head, but kept her mouth shut and paid for it all.

Lunch was a little easier going. They found a Mexican restaurant where her father could get a quesadilla with way too much cheese. It was then that he asked about her life.

"How was Texas?"

"We made the client happy and got the job."

"That's goo-good."

"It is. I pitched a campaign featuring normal women in fashionable clothing and it worked."

"What do you . . . what do you mean 'normal'?"

"Normal weight. Not a size zero."

"Heavy?"

She shook her head, then nodded. "Some, I guess. Normal."

"Huh."

"Don't be judgy, Dad."

"I didn't say . . . say anything."

"Your nonverbal language says a lot. If you ever want to know why you burned through so many wives, I have a clue."

"Hey!" But he was smiling. "Maybe I can visit your place. See it?"

Brooke glanced at the walker. "Four flights of stairs. But I can certainly take you to the restaurant for lunch or dinner. I'd like you to meet someone."

Joe gave her a sideways glance. "Oh?"

"His name is Luca."

Her father smiled, though the right side of his face never cooperated as much as the left since the stroke.

"He's a chef."

Her father smiled bigger. "I like to eat."

She patted his hand. "I know you do, Dad. I know you do."

CHAPTER TWENTY-SIX

"She's not coming?"

Luca saw, heard, and felt his daughter's disappointment when he told her Antonia wasn't showing up at the park.

"Something important came up."

Franny walked slower once he delivered the news. "Did she leave?"

Luca cringed, placed a hand on her shoulder. "No, *tesorina*. Not that I know of. She just couldn't make it today."

Side by side, they walked toward the park. He'd had the opportunity to spend a lot more time with his daughter the last few years, and he tried to keep it up as much as he could. He knew these hours were limited. It was only a matter of time before she wouldn't want to hang out with him.

"How was your spelling test?"

She shrugged.

"That bad?"

"I dunno."

Franny was shutting down in front of his eyes. He knew why, and there wasn't a damn thing he could do about it.

The park was filled with a lot of familiar faces. Although Franny wasn't searching the crowd for a friend. She was watching her feet, deep in a pout.

Luca, on the other hand, saw a face he hoped would bring a smile back to his daughter's.

He nudged her shoulder. "Look who's here."

Franny's chin shot up. "Mama?"

That cut through him like a poison arrow.

He pointed.

Franny's face brightened, and her excitement was even greater. "Brooke!" She broke into a run, then wrapped her arms around Brooke's waist in a hug. "You're back!"

"I told you two weeks."

Franny hugged her harder.

Brooke looked over at him, concern on her face.

Luca shook his head.

"I heard you had some pretty big excitement while I was gone."

Franny pulled away, smiled. "My mama came back."

Brooke knelt to Franny's level, kept a smile on her face. "I know. That's crazy. How does that feel?"

"Strange. Good . . ." Franny looked over her shoulder at Luca, then back to Brooke. "But weird."

"That's a lot of emotions. Are you talking to anyone about it?"

"What do you mean?"

"Like a best friend? Someone you can tell all the strange parts to and the good parts and the weird parts?"

Franny shook her head. "I told Regina, but she doesn't understand."

Luca listened to what Brooke was saying and considered her words more than his daughter did.

"Then we need to find someone you can talk to."

"Like who?"

Brooke shrugged. "I bet we can find someone. And in the meantime, you can always talk to me."

"Really?"

"Yup, really! I met my dad for the first time when I was just a few years older than you."

Franny's mouth dropped open. "No way."

"Yes way. I remember it being great one minute and confusing the next. I'd get angry and sad and happy. I still get that way when it comes to my father."

"Really?"

"Sometimes."

Franny lowered her head . . . paused. "I'm sad she didn't come today."

Brooke looked at Luca. "We can tell."

Franny glanced over her shoulder. "I'm sorry, Papa."

"For what?"

Tears started to pool in her eyes. Her lips quivered. "I-I don't know."

Luca took two steps and opened his arms and Franny fell into them. Her little body shook as she cried.

He held her tight and looked at Brooke.

The compassion in Brooke's eyes was so deep, he could see the hurt for his daughter.

He held her for a few minutes until the sobs turned to whimpers, then sniffles.

Sitting back on his heels, he looked at Franny. "Feel better?"

She nodded.

"It's been a hard couple of weeks."

"Papa?"

"Yes?"

Franny's eyes shifted from side to side, a question weighing on her. "Can I call her Antonia and not Mama?"

The air in Luca's lungs was sucked out with the question.

He glanced at Brooke, who offered a subtle nod.

"Absolutely, *tesorina*. If that's what you want to do."

The three of them walked over to a bench, where Franny tossed her backpack. "Wanna play Frisbee?"

Luca reached inside the pocket of the windbreaker he wore. "Yes, but before we do, I have something for both of you."

Brooke and Franny looked over at him.

He removed two small boxes, one in silver and the other gold. Handed the gold one to Brooke and the silver to Franny. "I saw these and thought of the two special girls in my life."

Brooke tilted her head with a smile. "Macaroni?"

He winked. "Open it."

Luca watched Brooke's expression when she saw the gold heart dangling from a chain.

"Luca, it's beautiful."

She removed it from the box.

"Mine is like yours," Franny said.

It was, only smaller and in silver. "Thank you, Papa."

"You're getting so grown-up, you should have pretty things."

Brooke set the box down and fiddled with the clasp.

"Here, let me." He took it from her.

She turned around and lifted her hair out of the way.

Once it was in place, she modeled it for him. "Thank you."

He leaned over, kissed her. "You're welcome."

"My turn," Franny said.

Luca put the necklace on his daughter and accepted her kiss on his cheek.

He sat back and looked at them both.

"Bellissima."

"Who is ready to play some Frisbee?" Brooke asked.

Franny jumped up. "I am!"

~

Mari sat with Rosa at one of the outside tables at the restaurant drinking cappuccino.

"I'm glad you could meet on such short notice."

"You make it sound so formal," Mari said to her friend.

Rosa sighed. "Antonia called me, twice now . . . asking to stay in my spare room."

Mari's smile fell. "You want my blessing."

Rosa waved a hand in the air. "You tell me no. Then no. But she is Franny's mama, and I didn't want to put her on the street without talking to you first."

"She won't be on the street."

Rosa shrugged. "I don't know. Most people are loyal to Luca and you. She doesn't have much money and hasn't been well."

"As she keeps telling everyone." Mari wasn't convinced. "What is her game? She has to work eventually . . . or find another man to support her. I think she returned to snare my Luca again. Thank God for Brooke."

"Perhaps I let her stay with me long enough to learn her plan? If she is in my home, I can see her coming and going . . . maybe discover what she is thinking. And again . . . she was your daughter-in-law . . . for what that's worth."

Mari hesitated.

"And if Francesca visits her mama, she'll be in my home. A familiar face where I can watch and be available."

That wasn't something Mari had considered.

Rosa sipped her coffee. "But if you don't like it, I say no."

"No, no. You make good points."

"And if Antonia has truly changed, we have all given her a chance."

Mari cradled her cup with both hands. "And if she hasn't . . . we see what she is doing before she does it."

"Sí, sí."

"Thank you for coming to me first, Rosa. You're a dear friend."

"Always."

They drank their coffee, and beyond the restaurant patio, Mari noticed her son's head above the other people walking on the sidewalk.

The crowd parted enough to see Brooke at his side, the two of them holding hands and Franny skipping alongside.

Her heart warmed. "Now that is the family I want to see happen."

Rosa turned in her chair. "It appears it already has."

"Send up your prayers, my friend."

Franny saw the two of them and ran their way. "Nonna, Nonna . . . look what Papa gave me."

Franny was holding the pendant on the end of a chain.

"Your papa is so thoughtful."

"Isn't it pretty?"

"Very."

Franny shoved it in Rosa's face. "See? He gave one to Brooke, too. Only hers is gold."

Mari glanced at Rosa, the two of them shared a smile.

Luca and Brooke approached, and Mari found herself staring at the heart necklace hanging from Brooke's neck.

"*Buonasera,*" Mari said to both of them. "Good to have you home."

"I can't tell you how nice it is to be back."

Mari stood and kissed Brooke on both cheeks. She purposely looked at the necklace and then to her son. "Your father taught you well."

Brooke's face took on a crimson glow.

"You remember my friend Rosa?"

"Of course. Lovely to see you again."

Franny turned away. "I'm going upstairs. Bye, Rosa."

Rosa blew her a kiss as she ran off.

"I should check on the kitchen," Luca said.

"Hold on," Mari said, stopping him and Brooke from walking away. "Antonia asked to stay with Rosa. And kindly asked my opinion on the subject."

Luca looked first to Brooke, who reached out and grasped his hand.

"If she is going to stick around, it might be best for Franny to visit her in a familiar place," Mari said.

"Not a bad thought," Brooke said.

Luca sighed, looked at Rosa. "Thank you for consulting with us. If you want her there, it will not offend me. If you don't . . . it will not offend me."

Rosa placed a palm to her chest. "*Grazie*, Luca."

He turned to Brooke, kissed her lips briefly, touched her cheek, and walked away.

Mari's heart melted. "Oh, my."

"Isn't young love beautiful?" Rosa sighed.

~

"That jacket looks amazing on you!"

Chloe was working as the hostess, wearing the blazer Brooke had managed to bring home from Texas . . . a gift from the designer.

Brooke sat with Franny at a table toward the back of the restaurant, where they ate dinner and Brooke helped Franny with her homework. When Chloe had a moment, she sat with them. As did Gio, though they were both running, as they often did on busy nights.

Brooke looked over toward the kitchen and every once in a while would catch Luca craning his neck to look at the two of them. It was a rare occasion that Brooke saw Mari in the kitchen with her son.

The two of them spoke in Italian and laughed while they juggled the orders and kept things rolling.

"Do I want to know what this would retail for?"

Brooke shook her head. "No. Just enjoy it. If you knew what it cost, you'd never wear it."

Chloe pulled at its edges. "I'm going to sleep in it."

Franny wiggled her nose. "That wouldn't be comfortable."

"She's kidding," Brooke whispered.

"No, I'm not."

Brooke and Chloe laughed.

Gio sauntered over, his expression guarded. "Incoming." He leaned his head toward the front of the restaurant.

Brooke looked up and noticed a long-legged Italian woman wearing a tight skirt and confidence walk up to the bar. She immediately started talking to Sergio and walked behind the counter to place a kiss to both cheeks.

She was stunning.

"Is that—"

"Yes," Chloe cut her off.

Brooke looked down at her comfortable jeans, light sweater . . . and her hair pulled into a ponytail, and tried to swallow her insecurity.

She failed, but she did try.

Franny was still working, her pencil down in her homework, and hadn't noticed her mother walk in the door.

Chloe said something to Gio in Italian, and he walked away and back to the kitchen.

Forcing a smile, Brooke nudged Franny. "Franny, look who came to see you."

Franny followed Brooke's gaze; an instant smile came to the little girl's face.

Brooke nodded. "Go say hi."

With a smile, Franny scrambled out of the booth and ran through the restaurant toward her mother.

One of the waitresses chided her for running.

Not that it halted even one step.

Brooke watched as Franny stopped short of Antonia and had to tap the woman's arm to get her attention.

Antonia smiled at Franny, continued talking to Sergio, then after a few moments turned to her daughter.

"I really hate that woman," Chloe said.

"Try not to show it, for Franny's sake."

"I am."

Franny grabbed Antonia's hand and pulled her toward Brooke.

"Oh, boy."

Someone from the restaurant staff called Chloe.

"Go," Brooke encouraged her. "I can handle it."

"Send up smoke signals if you need help."

"I will."

Chloe walked away and Brooke braced herself.

The closer Antonia got, the more her confidence oozed.

Franny bounced into the booth. "Brooke, this is my . . . Antonia."

If Antonia realized that Franny had refrained from calling her "mother," she didn't respond.

The woman was too busy watching Brooke.

Antonia's condescending smile said more than the first words out of her mouth. "So, you're Brooke."

Brooke stepped from the booth and reached out a hand. "Hello, Antonia. I see where Franny gets her beautiful eyes."

The compliment caught the woman off guard.

"Uhm . . . thank you. Francesca looks so much like I did at her age. I do think she'll have her father's height."

Not that Antonia was short. The woman was a good three inches taller than Brooke.

Or maybe that was the high heels.

Sergio walked up behind them with a glass of wine in his hand. "Your favorite, if I remember."

Antonia took the wine and gushed in Italian. They went back and forth, locked in conversation, forgetting that Brooke was there and didn't understand them.

Brooke smiled anyway as she sat back down.

Franny leaned over. "I don't understand everything they're saying either."

"I bet you know more than me."

Franny giggled. "Well, duh. I'll teach you. I forgot. I have a test for you."

"I have to study first. I've been super busy with work."

She wagged a finger in Brooke's direction with a smile.

They turned toward the silence to see that Sergio was walking away and Antonia had locked a stare on the both of them.

Franny nudged Brooke over. "You can sit with us."

Antonia glanced toward Brooke.

Brooke made room for the other woman with a smile. "We're doing homework."

"Oh . . . what subject?"

Brooke wanted to respond with "Second grade." But didn't.

"Reading comprehension."

Franny pushed her paper aside. "Why didn't you come to the park today?"

Antonia lifted her chin. "I had to move out of the hotel."

Brooke stared at Antonia as if to warn her about bringing Luca into that reason.

"I'll be staying with Rosa."

"Auntie Rosa?"

Antonia tilted her head to the side. "She's not really your *zia*, is she?"

Brooke stopped her. "Sometimes family are the people that you choose and not the people that you're born to. Rosa is a sister to Mari, and therefore an aunt to Franny—"

"Francesca," Antonia corrected.

Brooke didn't comment, kept a slight smile to her lips.

The knot in her belly was tight, but she knew she was getting her points across to the other woman without saying one unkind word.

"Antonia!"

They both looked up.

Instantly, the tension ended as Franny's mom moved to her feet and hugged the woman who'd just walked up to the table.

The two spoke in Italian, obviously old friends.

Brooke was pretty sure she rolled her eyes.

Franny put her hand on Antonia's arm.

"Mama?"

No response.

"Mama?"

The two women kept talking.

"Antonia?" Franny's voice reached another level.

Brooke was pretty sure three tables around them heard her.

Antonia frowned. "Francesca. Don't call me that. I'm your mother."

Brooke patted Franny's hand.

"Papa says it's rude to speak in Italian when people around you don't understand what you're saying."

Brooke glanced at the eight-year-old girl and was pretty sure she'd grown up in that very moment.

The woman with Antonia instantly apologized.

Brooke smiled and Antonia glared.

Luca stepped around the corner, two plates in his hands.

"Ciao, ladies," he said, passing his ex-wife and her friend.

He set the plates on the table, leaned down, and kissed Brooke. "For my girls."

"Is this lobster?" Franny asked.

"It is. To celebrate Brooke's return."

She couldn't help but smile. Luca's romance toolbox was pretty stacked.

"You're sweet."

He winked. "You okay?" he asked in a whisper.

She nodded.

Luca stood and turned toward Antonia. "Were we expecting you?"

"No, my darling. I thought I'd make it up to our daughter and visit since I couldn't make it to the park today."

He hesitated, glanced at Brooke.

She shook her head as if to tell him to ignore her comment.

Not in front of Franny. Alone, fine, he could correct Antonia on her "my darling" bullshit, but with Franny there . . . no. Let it go. The girl had enough to deal with right now.

"Eat while it's hot, my loves." He turned to Antonia. "Can I get you anything?"

She smiled. "Whatever they're having is fine."

Luca shook his head. "It's not on the menu tonight. If I'd known you were coming, I could have made more. Perhaps the cannelloni we have on special tonight?"

The slight was smooth . . . and a direct hit.

And likely the truth.

Brooke felt herself falling for the man by the second.

"Oh, dear . . . you know I don't care for all that cream and cheese. A salad is fine."

He smiled. "Your choice."

"Wonderful seeing you again, Antonia. Let's have lunch soon," her friend said.

"I'm so sorry . . . how rude of me." Antonia made introductions, which Brooke promptly forgot.

The woman walked away, and Antonia sat back down.

Luca took a seat beside Brooke, nudged her arm. "Eat, *cara*."

Without much more encouragement, Brooke took a bite and moaned. "Oh my God."

"Papa is the best." Franny scooped a whole ravioli into her mouth and talked around it.

"You'll be just as good if you keep practicing," Luca told his daughter.

Franny lit up. "You think so?"

"It's in the family genes."

"You're teaching her to cook?" Antonia asked.

Luca lifted his hands in the air. "We own a restaurant."

"I like cooking with Papa. Brooke and I made pasta for the first time." Franny sighed. "It looked like Play-Doh, but it tasted great."

Brooke lifted another forkful of lobster ravioli to her mouth. "Next time we add orange dye. It will really look like Play-Doh."

Franny laughed.

Antonia looked at the two of them. "Cute."

Luca patted Brooke's thigh. "I should get back."

"Go. We're good."

He glanced at Antonia. "I'll send someone out with your salad."

She nodded with a smile.

Just the three of them again, Franny ate with abandon and Brooke slowed down, aware that Antonia watched her every move.

"How is the wine?"

Antonia lifted her glass. "Sergio was always so good to me. I remember when he met his wife." She sipped her wine, and her eyes landed on Brooke's neck.

Slowly they drifted to Franny's. "That's a lovely necklace, Francesca. Where did you get it?"

"Papa gave it to me."

She paused, sat back.

Brooke locked eyes with her.

Antonia looked away. "You know, I'm really not feeling very well. I think perhaps I should go lie down."

Franny looked up from her plate. "Are you okay?"

"I'll be fine. It's been a long day." She edged closer to the end of the booth.

"You don't have to go," Brooke said.

Antonia lifted a hand to her temple. "Truly, I have a terrible headache."

"When will I see you?" Franny asked.

"I'll speak with your father and arrange a time. Enjoy your dinner."

Before Brooke could placate her with a "Nice to meet you" or "Let's do it again soon," she was gone.

Antonia stopped by the bar on her way out, laughed at something Sergio said, and was out the door.

Brooke blew out a breath, rolled her head from one side to the other.

As round one went, she didn't think she did too bad.

"Are you going to eat all of yours?"

Franny was finished.

Brooke scooped half of her dish onto Franny's plate. "Go for it, kid."

"No one calls me kid."

"I'm not Italian. I'm going to call you kid."

Franny nudged her shoulder.

Brooke nudged her back.

The weight of someone's stare caught her attention.

Brooke looked toward the kitchen, saw Luca watching them. His smile said all she needed to hear.

CHAPTER TWENTY-SEVEN

Luca rolled over, pulled Brooke tight against his frame. "Don't leave."

"Franny will wake up and see us."

"She knows you're my girlfriend."

Brooke glanced over her shoulder, and her satisfied eyes looked at his. "That doesn't mean she thinks we're sleeping in the same bed."

He brushed her hair aside. "Technically, we're not sleeping."

"Luca."

"No. Please, *cara*. I want you here. All night. By my side. Tomorrow I will let you sleep alone in your bed."

Brooke curled into the pillow. The only thing she wore was a smile and the necklace he'd given her.

"You're hard to say no to."

He hummed and brought her closer. "I'll remember that and use it to my advantage."

Brooke pulled his arm around her and held it tight. "Franny was a real trouper today."

"So were you."

"I'm an adult. I can handle it. We need to be on the lookout for behavior changes. Problems in school . . . stuff like that."

The fact Brooke said *we* and not *you* wasn't lost on him. "And what do we do about it if there are changes?"

"We get her into counseling. It might be a good idea anyway. Having a parent abandon you is one thing, having them come back is another. It's a lot to process."

"Do you have any idea how comforting it is to have someone here with me during this?"

"You have your family."

"I do. But it isn't the same. There's a weight that has lifted knowing you care and that you're here."

"That's what relationships are supposed to be, right?"

He kissed the side of her head. "That doesn't mean it's ever happened in my life."

Brooke rolled onto her back, looked up at him with a soft smile. "Me either."

Luca traced the necklace on her chest and wondered if she knew she was stealing his heart one day at a time. He looked up to find her eyes had drifted closed.

"Goodnight, *amore*," he whispered.

She hummed but didn't respond as sleep took over.

~

"Escrow is closed." Brooke waved a copy of the final closing statement with the amount of money that was being deposited into her account within the hour.

She stopped by the office of the restaurant to share her news with Luca and found him there with Mari.

"That's wonderful, Brooke. We should celebrate," Mari said.

"I'm going to celebrate by buying a car." She leaned on the side of the desk.

"What's wrong with the one you have?"

"It's my dad's. Not only can he not afford it, he'll never drive it again." Her brief euphoria faded. "I need to take it back to the dealership where he bought it."

"When do we need to do that?" Luca asked.

Brooke grinned. "I wasn't asking for you to give up a day."

He pinned her with a stare. "You can help me, but I can't help you? That isn't how this is going to work, *mia cara.*"

This whole partnership thing was growing on her.

"It would probably be a good idea to find a new car before ditching the old one. I don't need new. Reliable, something I can put a wheelchair in the back of if my dad needs to use one again. Good crash rating if I'm driving Franny around at all."

Mari turned to her son with a smile, said something in Italian, and patted his hand. Brooke understood the words *family* and *love* and that was about it.

"Mama!"

Brooke laughed.

Mari looked at her. "I told him I approve of you."

Yeah, that's not exactly what she said, but likely the gist of it.

"If you want to return your dad's car before you find the next, you can always use mine. Good used cars are hard to find."

He had a point. "You sure?"

Luca did the stare thing again.

"Okay, fine. Thank you."

Mari patted her chest; the gesture was becoming a thing. "Brooke . . . next Sunday, I'd like to invite your father for our dinner. If you're okay with it."

"He'd really like that. He can't make it up those stairs, though."

Mari shrugged. "We'll use the grotto."

"My father has no filter."

"You don't have to make excuses for family."

Brooke exchanged glances with Luca. "You up for that?"

He laughed. "You just went head-to-head with my ex-wife. I can handle your father."

"Point taken. I'll invite him."

"Wednesday for the car?" he asked.

It sounded like they had their week planned. Brooke glanced at the time. "I can pick up Franny from school."

Luca huffed. "I approved Antonia to do that today."

"I don't like it," Mari said.

"Franny asked me. She'll tell me if she's uncomfortable."

Brooke unfolded from her perch. "I'll get some work done then, get ahead before Wednesday." She took a step toward the door.

Luca stopped her. *"Cara?"*

She turned.

He crooked a finger in her direction, and she walked back over to him.

He stood, kissed her, and smiled. "Congratulations on closing escrow. I know that was weighing on you."

Her heart warmed in her chest. "Thank you."

She walked away and as she did, Mari started speaking in Italian, laughter in her voice.

Brooke really needed to take some serious lessons if she was going to be a part of this family.

~

The door to Brooke's apartment was open, almost as if her place was simply an extension of the home. She did that to keep an ear out for Franny, hoping to catch her and see how the brief trip from school to home with Antonia went.

She listened to music on her computer and had two screens going. The work for the Downes project moved along without too many hiccups. The team had a couple more weeks to complete the bulk of the work and be available for revisions over the next month. All in all, Brooke's part of the job would be over, and she'd be ready for a new assignment . . . maybe more.

Noise from the hallway caught her attention.

She turned the music down, heard Franny talking.

Right as Brooke stood, she heard Antonia.

The door to Luca's apartment opened, then closed.

Brooke considered interrupting. Then thought that maybe Franny wanted to show her mother her room, or her toys . . . her life.

Sitting back down, Brooke kept an ear for Antonia's exit.

When it came, it was followed by something unexpected . . .

Footsteps walking *up* the stairs.

Adult footsteps.

Brooke felt Antonia's presence before she turned around.

"Hello," Antonia said, announcing herself.

Brooke turned, acted surprised. "Oh, hello. Can I help you?"

Antonia walked in without invitation and closed the door behind her. "Actually, yes."

Once again Luca's ex-wife wore heels and a skirt, a blouse that covered her shoulders but not her breasts. Well, it covered them, just not as well as it did her shoulders.

"Hopefully we can keep it brief. I'm working."

Antonia looked beyond her. "What is it you do?"

"That's not what you came in here to talk about."

"No. It isn't. I'd like to know why you're trying to poison my daughter against me?"

"I'm sorry?"

"She's calling me by my first name and said you told her to do so."

Brooke felt a fight coming. "That isn't how that conversation went."

". . . and that you don't approve of her spending the night with me."

Brooke didn't know where that one came from at all. "I think perhaps there has been some miscommunication."

Antonia lifted her chin. "You know . . . Luca and I were getting along extremely well before you returned from your little Texas vacation. I was surprised to even learn about you."

"What is this? An attempt to make me jealous?"

Antonia looked her up and down, rolled her eyes. "Please. I know Luca better than you ever will. You are not worthy of trying to make jealous. Now, getting between my daughter and me . . . that is another issue."

"I would never do that."

"That's not how I see things. Especially with one of Luca's temporary lovers."

"Wow, okay." Brooke stood, walked past Antonia, and opened the door. "I'm glad we had this chat. I have work to do."

Antonia walked away, her head high.

Brooke kept an eye on her until after she'd passed Luca's door.

"Round two . . ."

~

Later that night, once Franny was in bed, Brooke sat on the terrace with Luca drinking wine and enjoying the night air. She told him about the entire exchange . . . word for word.

"This is unacceptable, *cara*." Luca was pissed.

"We are in agreement there."

"I'll call her out tomorrow."

Brooke held a hand in the air. "Hold up. This all feels desperate to me. She wants to make me jealous. She has an edge there. She is your ex-wife. The mother of your daughter, something I am not. She's absolutely stunning and probably puts any swimsuit model to shame."

Luca placed a hand on her knee. "And ugly on the inside, Brooke. She doesn't hold a candle to you . . . or a match."

Brooke looked at him . . . paused.

She made a waving motion with her hand. "Okay, keep it going . . ."

They both laughed.

"My point is, she has the tools to make me jealous. Why does she want to? Does she think she can get you back?"

"That won't happen."

"Your family would disown you." Keep Franny and kick Luca to the curb.

"True."

Brooke sipped her wine and vocalized what she'd thought about all day. "All of this feels desperate, which makes me wonder if her pursuit of being a mother is part of some unknown plan. Is she using Franny to get what she wants? And if that's the case, you're going to have to hold me back because I'm going to kick her ass."

"I don't know if she can be that cruel."

"You know her better than I do."

"I'll talk to her."

Brooke shook her head. "I say we ignore it. Let her guess whether we're talking to each other about every detail. She's looking for attention, and giving her any is feeding into it."

Luca moaned.

"I bet she does something else soon. Something to come between us. She doesn't strike me as a patient woman."

He laughed. "She's not."

"As long as she doesn't involve Franny."

"She might not. We can hope."

He patted her thigh. "Are you ready for your dad's visit?"

It was Brooke's turn to groan. "My dad will put Antonia's melodrama to shame."

"Are you really nervous we won't like him, *cara*?"

"No. Everyone adores my father. It's me he rubs wrong."

Luca reached for her hand, intertwined her fingers in his. "I can't adore a man who abandoned his daughter."

"It was a long time ago, Luca. Better off in the rearview mirror."

His eyes took on the glow of the moonlight. "I may like him, but I'll never adore him."

"That's fair."

~

"Where's my car?"

It was Sunday. Brooke and Luca had returned the car to the dealership earlier in the week, and after a lot of back-and-forth, and a threat of legal action for taking advantage of an elderly person on a fixed income, they accepted the car.

Brooke walked away, stopped the payment, canceled the insurance, and considered it all good.

Now she was driving Luca's SUV and picking her dad up for a slightly earlier than normal for the D'Angelos, and later for her father, Sunday meal.

Her father had put on a nice pair of pants, and from his report, he wasn't having as much trouble getting to the bathroom in time. Which gave her some confidence that they would get through a meal without incident.

"I told you I was going to return it."

"Oh." He didn't look happy.

She helped him into the SUV, put the walker in back, and climbed behind the wheel.

"Is this yours then?"

"No. It's Luca's. I'm borrowing it for now."

She pulled out of the parking lot and onto the road.

"I am getting better."

"I see that."

"I might be able to, to, to d-drive."

Not this again.

Brooke thought about how she would talk to Franny. "We'll cross that bridge when we come to it. For now, I can't spend your money on a car that I'm driving. It makes it look like I'm stealing from you."

"You're not."

"I know that. But a judge might see it differently. It's called being responsible with money, Dad. I know it's a foreign concept for you."

"Hey!" But he was smiling.

She winked at him.

"I talked to J-Jay."

Jay was a friend from Upland.

"That's great. How is he?"

"He said he will, uhm . . . v-visit."

"That's great, Dad. I told you, it's not a prison."

Her father looked out the window. "I know."

CHAPTER TWENTY-EIGHT

Luca had the staff on alert.

When Brooke and her father arrived, one of the waiters told him she was there, and he rushed to the back door to meet them.

He saw her standing beside the passenger door, walker in one hand, the other on her father's shoulder.

"I don't need this," Joe said to Brooke.

"Humor me. I can't have you falling tonight."

Luca grinned as they argued and walked toward the back door.

Brooke glanced at him, already looking frazzled. He saw a shoulder rub in her future.

"Why are we w-walking in-in here?"

Luca stepped toward them. "I know it looks like the service entrance, Mr. Turner, but it's the family entrance."

Joe looked up, saw him, let go of the walker, and stood taller. "You are Luca."

"I am."

Joe reached out a hand.

While he did shake it, Luca remembered that the man's stroke had affected his right side. Still, Joe looked him straight in the eye, and he had to admire that.

"You're the one, one . . . sleeping with my daughter."

"Dad!" Brooke yelled, but started laughing.

"What? Am I wr-wrong?"

"Okay, Dad. Listen, yes, that's funny. But none of that in front of Franny. She's a kid."

Joe waved Brooke away. "I know. I had a st-stroke. I haven't lost it com-completely."

Brooke blew out a breath. She looked at Luca. "I warned you."

"You're not wrong, Mr. Turner, but I promise my intentions are good."

Joe looked at him.

Then Brooke.

Made a point of looking down.

"I don't see a r-ring."

"Oh my God!"

Luca laughed.

"Don't take advice from a man with four divorces under his belt."

Joe shrugged. "She's not wr-wrong."

Luca was still laughing. "I hope you're hungry."

"It smells good."

Luca walked slowly beside them as they made their way through the staff portion of the restaurant and toward the grotto.

Franny ran their way, dodging a waiter.

Luca stared at her.

She blinked those big brown eyes of hers, and he shook his head. God help him when she asked him for a car.

She stopped in front of Joe. "Hi."

"Dad, this is—"

"I know wh-who this is." He smiled. "You're Franny."

Franny looked between father and daughter. "You look like Brooke."

"I couldn't de-deny her."

"Dad!" Brooke's voice held a warning. And if that wasn't enough, she flicked him with a finger.

"Hey. Elder abuse."

Luca swiped a hand over his face and down his jaw. This was going to be a very interesting night.

"C'mon. Everyone is waiting." Franny walked ahead of them.

Brooke whispered something to her father that Luca couldn't hear.

Luca glanced at her, mouthed *It's okay.*

They stepped into the grotto and his mother moved in. "Mr. Turner. Finally, we meet you. I'm Mari D'Angelo. Mother of this clan."

Joe smiled. Looked around the room. "A pl-pleasure. I don't speak as well . . . as good." Joe shook his head. "I had a stroke."

Luca's mother smiled. "We know. Take your time. We have all night. And many more, I'm sure."

Joe moved the walker aside and used the backs of the chairs to walk beside Mari.

"Dad."

"I'm fine."

Luca moved next to Brooke, who watched her father like he'd watched Franny taking her first steps.

"He's stubborn."

"Hmmm. I know where you get it now."

Brooke stopped. "Wait."

"Kidding."

"No, you're not."

Luca shrugged.

She flicked him with the same "elder abuse" she'd delivered to her father.

"My daughter, Chloe, and son Giovanni."

Mari pulled out a chair. "Here. Sit next to me so we can talk."

"Zio Gio e Zia Chloe," Franny said.

"That's Uncle Gio and Aunt Chloe, Dad. Franny practices her Italian at Sunday night dinners."

Luca winked at his daughter. "We can make an exception tonight."

"Okay." Franny bounced into a chair opposite the one pulled out for Joe.

The entire grotto was cleared for their family dinner, not something they normally did, but considering the occasion, Luca and his mother agreed.

Brooke was tense, shoulders up to her ears, her attention hyperfocused on her father.

Luca's mother made him comfortable and asked what he wanted to drink.

He went along with the wine on the table . . . all the while Brooke watched like a nervous mama.

"*Cara*, can you help me with the plates from the kitchen?"

"What?" Brooke looked at him. Then her dad. "Oh, okay."

They walked out of the grotto together, and he stopped her once they were out of sight of the family.

"Breathe."

She hesitated, then did what he said.

And again.

"It's going to be okay. Whatever happens." Luca leaned down and kissed her.

∼

"This is killing you, isn't it?" Chloe leaned over and whispered the question in Brooke's ear.

They'd eaten dinner and all night her father had come dangerously close to saying all the wrong things.

"I'm dying."

Luca chuckled beside her, hearing their conversation.

"He's adorable."

Brooke nudged Luca. "I told you."

Both Gio and Mari were taking their time talking with Joe, realizing that it took him a while to respond and letting the conversation slow down.

Franny's voice rose from the other end of the table. "If Papa and Brooke get married, you'll be my *nonno*."

"That's right. A-as soon as y-your daddy makes an honest wo-wo—"

"Dad!" Brooke said in warning.

Mari grinned.

"Oh," Joe said.

"I'm going to kill him," Brooke said under her breath.

"I'm not Italian. You can call me G-Grandpa."

Okay . . . some of the edges were wearing off of her.

Brooke nudged Luca. "Don't let him get in your head."

"About what?"

Chloe laughed.

Brooke rolled her eyes. "Seriously, the man's been married four times. He rushes everything in his life. He has mentioned or implied marriage no less than four times tonight."

Luca shrugged. "If I was having dinner with Francesca's boyfriend, I'd do the same."

Brooke looked at Chloe.

Chloe nodded. "Well said, brother."

Her father pulled their attention. "Luca?"

"Yes, sir?"

"Show me where the bathroom is."

Franny jumped up. "I can show you."

Joe shook his head. "No. That was code for . . . I want to t-talk to your dad."

Franny giggled.

Luca pushed his chair back.

Brooke did everything she could to sit still.

The two of them slowly made their way out of the grotto, and Gio started laughing. "Your dad is a riot."

"Delightful," Mari said.

They were amused, and she was stressed out.

Brooke reached for her wine.

~

Luca attempted not to hover as he and Joe slowly made their way toward the restaurant bathroom.

"I-I like you," Joe admitted only a few feet from the grotto.

"The feeling is mutual."

"The l-last guy was a real sh-shit."

Luca smiled. "That worked to my advantage."

Joe stopped walking, smiled up at him, and then continued the slow crawl to the restroom. "I know she . . . that Brooke thinks getting married is, is stupid. That's my fault. And her mother's. But she deserves a good . . ." He shook his head. "A real man to step up."

They stopped in the hallway to the restrooms, and Luca turned to him. "Brooke told me you're Catholic."

Joe nodded once.

"So are we. Am I. If your daughter and I are on the long road, we're doing it with my last name, not yours."

Joe lifted his chin, his half smile reaching his eyes. "Glad we had this little ch-chat."

Luca opened the door to the bathroom so Joe could walk in.

~

It took a while, but her father and Luca returned. Instead of sitting, her father smiled and looked around the room. "This has been . . . wonderful. But I need to get home."

Brooke scooted her chair back.

"I'm driving," Luca said beside her.

"I can . . ."

Luca shook his head. "We'll take him together."

She nodded while everyone stood.

Mari hugged her father. "Such a pleasure, Joe. You've raised a lovely daughter we love having with us."

Joe shrugged. "I-I can't take credit for that."

Mari narrowed her eyes.

"I didn't raise her." Her dad looked over at Brooke. "I don't know why she . . . why she puts up with me sometimes."

Brooke felt Luca's arm on her shoulder.

"Joe, it's been an unforgettable night," Gio said and shook his hand.

Chloe moved around the table for a hug and a goodbye.

Franny hugged him with abandon. "I'm going to call you Grandpa Joe."

"Okay, kid. I wasn't a great dad . . . but I'll try and . . . and be a good grandpa." Her father yawned.

"Let's get you home," Brooke said.

Twenty-five minutes later, Brooke walked her father into the assisted living home. The attendant at the front desk had to open the locked doors to greet them.

She hugged her father, told him she'd see him the following week, and walked back out to Luca in the running car.

She got in the passenger seat and slid into a lump. "God, that was painful."

"It wasn't that bad."

She'd been waiting for nearly an hour to ask her next question. "Really? What did he want to talk to you about when you went to the bathroom?"

"Nothing. Dad stuff."

"What does that mean?"

Luca turned onto the deserted street. It was after ten and the roads were empty.

"Nothing he didn't say in front of you. It's fine, *cara*."

Luca pulled into a deserted parking lot.

"What are you doing?"

He reached for her. "Come here."

She leaned over and he kissed her. Everything about how he touched her made her forget the stress of the day.

Brooke tried to move closer, felt his tongue swipe against her lips.

All the stress of the night pooled into this kiss, this moment.

She heard Luca turn off the engine as he attempted to pull her closer. The center console of the SUV made the moment almost impossible.

"Luca?"

His lips moved to her ear, kissed and nibbled the side. "Yes?"

"The back seat might be more comfortable."

He drew away, and before either of them could say a word, they unbuckled their seatbelts and jumped out of the front and into the back.

Luca was on her in a breath. His hand pushed away her shirt, his lips found the soft part of her breast and sucked in a nipple.

Brooke moaned, reached for his belt.

In his car . . . are we really going to do this in his . . .

Luca's hand slid over her jeans and cupped her sex.

Yes, apparently, they were doing this in his car.

Brooke could not get out of her clothes, or at least the important parts, fast enough.

With her panties on the floor, and his pants around his ankles, Brooke climbed on top of Luca and felt him press against the most welcoming parts of her body.

"So good."

They started to move, and the windows in the car fogged over.

CHAPTER TWENTY-NINE

Two days later, Antonia showed up at Luca's door shortly after he'd walked Franny to school.

"What are you doing here?"

Wearing slacks, high heels, and a blouse unbuttoned enough to show the tops of her breasts, she was only slightly dressed down from any other time he'd seen her since she'd arrived.

"Must you be so toxic, Luca? I'm here to discuss our daughter." Antonia spoke in Italian, setting the language for the conversation.

He opened the door and let her in. "You could have called."

"And be put off? Or asked to meet you in the restaurant where others are listening? It's as if you're afraid I'm going to attack you if we're alone together. We were lovers, Luca. You can't be afraid of being alone with me."

"I choose not to be alone with you to avoid giving you the impression I *want* to be alone with you. And because I have someone I care about in my life. Her feelings are important to me."

Antonia moved deeper into his apartment. One he had shared with her. Her hand reached out and followed the table along the back of the sofa. "That was me once."

"You left."

"The doctors said I had postpartum depression."

"Franny was almost three. And your American citizenship was finalized six months before you disappeared."

Her eyes shot up to look at him. "You don't truly think that of me."

Luca leaned against the wall, crossed his arms over his chest. "It doesn't matter what I think, Antonia. It was a long time ago."

She started toward him.

He stopped her with a stare. A gift he knew he was good at.

"I loved you, Luca. Still love you, if I'm honest with myself."

He shook his head. "I'm not sure you're capable of loving anyone but yourself."

"You don't think that." She smiled. "Remember the night we snuck into the harbor and made love on McAllister's boat? Our love was radiant that night."

Luca breathed in the memory and let it fade away. "We shared some good times. In the past."

"Try and remember them, my darling. Then perhaps you'll accept that I am back in your life."

Luca shook his head.

"We have a daughter. We will always have that."

He pushed away from the wall and walked to his kitchen. "What is it you wanted to talk to me about?"

"Brooke."

"She is not on the table for discussion."

"How stable is it for Francesca to accept Brooke as a constant in your life, only to have that gone if you two have a fight? The woman is so insecure she's spreading lies about the things I've spoken to her about."

"What things?"

"I'm sure she's told you."

This entire conversation was coming out of nowhere. Instead of telling her she was crazy, he gave her the opportunity to prove it.

"Remind me."

"We had a private chat about a week ago when I brought Francesca home from school. She cornered me in the hall. She must have told you."

"No," he lied.

Fake concern crossed Antonia's face. "That's telling, isn't it? She told me I was a bad mother. That if I wasn't going to stay, I should just leave now."

Nothing about this rang true, but Luca kept his thoughts to himself and let Antonia dig herself deeper.

"Franny is excited to get to know you."

Antonia released a long-suffering breath. "Oh, I know, my darling. And I am so sorry I haven't been here. But to have your little girlfriend say such nasty things to me, I can only wonder what poison she's saying to our daughter."

"Brooke only has Franny's best interests at heart."

"How can you really know that?"

"Because she's proven it with her actions ever since we met." He let those words settle in and take hold.

"That was meant to hurt me."

"If that's what the truth does. Where have you been, Antonia? What kept you away from our daughter all of these years?"

"I don't want to discuss—"

"I honestly don't care what you want. We deserve to know. Franny is in a constant state of worry that you'll disappear again. Maybe if we knew that something in you has changed, if I knew something has changed, I could give her some hope that you mean what you say and you're going to be around for the rest of her life."

"I will."

Luca narrowed his eyes. "Where have you been?"

She looked away. "I went to the mountains, at first."

"Mountains? What mountains?"

"Colorado."

He remembered her saying something about her love of skiing. Something he had never done.

"I spent the winter staring into a fire and wondering if I had made the wrong choice. And since I couldn't say yes or no to the question, I stayed away. I thought it was the right thing to do. For Francesca. For you."

Luca really wanted to believe her.

"I stayed a season, moved around. As the years stacked up, it was harder and harder to come back."

"Then you got sick," he concluded. "Only you haven't so much as sneezed since you've been here."

She shrugged. "I sleep a lot. Ask Rosa. But yes, being home and spending time with Francesca has given me more energy than I had a month ago. I wish I had been more stable when I had our daughter. Being away from my family and not having the ability to move around wasn't easy for me."

Yes, he remembered her complaining about the ties to the restaurant and her desire to fly all over the world.

"And now that you've seen it, spent your money, you're back."

She rolled her eyes. "I've grown up. I'm ready to settle down."

"You mean get a job, your own place?" Antonia was allergic to work. Just asking the question was making her squirm.

"I'm thinking about going back to school."

Luca crossed his arms over his chest. This ought to be good. "For what?"

She looked at the ceiling as if she was coming up with the idea right then and there. "Interior design."

He could actually see her doing that if she put her mind to it. "Good plan."

"I thought so," she said, smiling. "We were good together."

"In the past." Luca took a step back. Put more space between them.

The softness of her voice faded, and cattiness moved in. "I have concerns about Brooke."

"She has concerns about you."

"Be careful, Luca. She's an older woman who is likely wondering if she'll have a family of her own. Clearly you can see she is attaching herself to you, all of you, to fulfill that need. And perhaps we shouldn't let Francesca get too attached to Brooke's father. Grandpa Joe, really, Luca? You're not married to the woman. How manipulative is that, using a little girl to plant the seed of matrimony?"

"I'm not asking for your advice on my love life. And up until last month, you had no idea who Franny was attached to and who she wasn't. So instead of spending your time thinking about what is happening inside these walls every day, why don't you sign up for those classes that will help you earn a living?"

Antonia sighed. "I should go."

Luca nodded, walked toward the door, and opened it.

"Well, hello," Brooke's voice came from a half a flight of stairs above them.

Luca stepped back.

Antonia smiled.

~

"Rumors are flying." Chloe helped Brooke get into the right position for a Side Angle Pose.

Yoga on the terrace was kicking her butt yet making her feel good at the same time.

"Oh yeah?"

"Salena asked if Antonia and Luca were getting back together."

"Where did she get that idea?"

"Horse's mouth." Chloe changed her pose. "Reverse Warrior," she told Brooke.

Brooke moved into position. "Doesn't she realize the rumors will get back to Luca and she'll have to eat crow?"

"Who knows. Anyone who sees the two of you together knows Luca has it bad."

Brooke couldn't stop smiling. "I have it pretty bad, too."

Chloe laughed. "You've got a certain glow about you."

"It's all the sex."

"Blah . . ." She kept laughing.

"You knew I was going to say that," Brooke said.

"Warrior Two." Chloe shifted.

Brooke followed, took a breath. "Who is your ob-gyn? I need to make an appointment."

Chloe shot Brooke a concerned look. "Is everything okay?"

"Routine. I'm on my last month of pills, need to get a doctor to prescribe more."

"Dr. Archer. She's local. Tell her you know me, they'll get you in quick."

They moved position again. "Text me her number."

As Chloe had predicted, Brooke was able to make an appointment to see Dr. Archer in two weeks, the quickest appointment in history, and was now filling out intake forms.

Every time the question was asked about pregnancies and births, she felt her heart ache.

But it was when she had to pull out a calendar to look up her last period that Brooke paused.

She went to the bathroom and pulled out her pack of pills. Had she forgotten to take the placebo pills and went right into the week of real ones?

Wait . . . no. She'd spotted in Texas.

Brooke shook her head, returned her pills to her vanity, and walked away.

~

Luca sat with Brooke outside on the terrace after the restaurant had closed and everyone had gone to bed.

"Antonia wants Franny to spend the night."

"What does Franny want?"

"To make everyone happy."

"What do you think?" Brooke asked.

"I don't know, *cara*. If Antonia hadn't left after we divorced, I'd have to share Franny. I'd be used to it by now."

Brooke squeezed his hand. "She'd be just down the street. And Rosa is there."

Luca cringed. "You're encouraging it?"

She cleared her throat. "Your Honor, the reason my ex-wife isn't fit to have our daughter overnight is because she lied to me and my girl-friend in an effort to get me back." Brooke widened her eyes. "I don't think that's going to fly in court."

"They haven't spent more than two hours with each other, and only with someone else around."

"I hate to say it, but that needs to change. Unless Franny isn't com-fortable. Or Antonia does something other than spread rumors that no one is believing."

"Why are you so reasonable?"

"Because I've taken my personal feelings out of the equation. Do I like it? No. Do I think this is just another way for her to get to you . . . yes. Probably. But if it isn't and she only wants to know Franny, we have to give her a chance to do that. Or to fail. We're between the proverbial rock and a hard place here. Give her the rope. She either hangs from it or uses it to swing to another branch. But you give her the rope. Because making her fight for it only hurts Franny and your relationship with her in the long run. At this point, Antonia has done nothing to suggest she's an unfit mother since she's been back. No court would keep her away from her daughter."

"I hate that you're right."

"Me too."

"Did your mother make your father fight for you?"

Brooke looked at him like he was crazy. "Please. She could only hope he would come around and take me for any amount of time. Then I wouldn't be there casting my 'judgmental eyes' on her when she came in drunk or with another guy."

"Oh, *cara*."

Brooke shook her head.

"My dad came back into the picture hot and heavy. Kind of like Antonia. Only in the form of a weeklong vacation, then he returned to Upland with the wife that didn't like me, and I was up in Seattle. And he ignored me. I begged that man to pay attention to me, to help me get away from my dysfunctional mother. He didn't step up."

Luca pictured the care Brooke gave to her father. "How did you get to where you are now?"

"I was desperate for a father, Luca. I didn't have your strong family surrounding me like Franny has. I didn't have the stable and supportive father that you are to your daughter. My father might not have been the lifeboat floating away from the *Titanic*, but he was at least a piece of wood I could float on. And when the next wife moved on, I was there. We picked up an adult father-daughter relationship, and that's what I got. I always said it was better than nothing. We have our bumps, but I do love him. And he loves me. But if there is one thing Antonia and my father have in common, it's that they love themselves more than they could ever love anyone else. It's proven by their actions. And in my experience with my dad, those actions go on repeat."

"That's why you're adamant about giving Antonia rope to hang herself."

"I am."

"And if that rope hurts my daughter?"

Brooke paused. "Do you think Antonia means to harm Franny?"

"No." He didn't see that. "Not on purpose. What do you think?"

Brooke looked away, as if lost in thought. "Antonia is going to hurt Franny no matter if she stays, goes . . . does something in between. I'm just trying to figure out a way to minimize the damage. I don't think your ex-wife is going to surprise us by doing the right thing. I know her kind."

Luca sighed, curled closer. "I let Franny spend the night."

"Yup. And be ready to go get her when she calls."

He leaned forward. "Let's go to bed."

"You go. I'm going to sleep upstairs tonight."

He narrowed his eyes. "Why?"

"I'm on edge. Moody."

"Is it me?"

"No. Not at all. I just want to sleep in my own space."

Something behind her smile looked sad. Luca wondered if it was the memories of her childhood, or the reality of her relationship with her father.

He kissed her.

"Go. I'm going to stay out here a little longer."

"Are you okay?"

Her hand touched the side of his face. "I'm fine."

Luca hated that word with a fiery passion.

~

He didn't know what was harder. The fact that Franny was away, or the fact that she didn't call.

Luca was buying her a cell phone. That's all there was to it. Maybe Antonia was keeping her from a phone.

As the hours ticked by, and the dinner rush passed, no call came.

Chloe and Brooke were both watching him, looking for clues that Franny needed something.

He kept shaking his head from the kitchen.

And nothing.

Gio was out, on a date, and even he called in to see if there was any news.

It was his mother that had been the only fly on the wall later that night when they were gathered in the office.

"Rosa said they came home from dinner, watched a Disney film, and now Franny is asleep on the couch."

"This is . . ."

"Unexpected," Brooke finished for him.

"Stressful," Chloe said.

They all agreed.

"I'm going to bed," Brooke announced.

"I'll be up in a bit," Luca told her.

She shook her head, looked around the room. "This might be TMI, but I started my cycle and all I want is a hot water bottle and a Motrin."

Luca found himself smiling, despite the misery on her face. He'd always considered a woman sharing her most intimate moments the point that defined their relationship. "I can drizzle some chocolate over a cannoli and bring it to you."

Brooke's eyes lit up.

He smiled.

She smiled.

His mother patted her chest and sighed.

Chloe rolled her eyes. "Oh my God, you two are making me sick."

CHAPTER THIRTY

"What can I do for you today?" Dr. Archer was in her midforties from the looks of her. Kind eyes and easy smile.

"I made the appointment looking for a routine checkup. I'm new to San Diego and need new doctors. But . . ."

Dr. Archer leaned against the counter and waited patiently.

"I had an unusual period, and it was in the middle of my pill cycle."

"Unusual how?" Dr. Archer looked at Brooke's paperwork as she spoke.

"Well, that I had one while I was taking the hormones, but it was heavy. Super uncomfortable."

"Do you think you were pregnant?"

She swallowed. "No. I don't . . . I don't really know. My last cycle was light."

Dr. Archer tapped the paperwork. "You've had a previous miscarriage? When was that?"

"Two and a half years now."

"And did you conceive while on the pill?"

Brooke nodded.

"Did your doctor change your prescription?"

"Yes. But my partner and I use condoms, too."

"Same partner?" she asked.

"No."

"Do you ever forget the condoms?"

Brooke thought about the fogged-up windows of Luca's SUV. "A couple of times."

Dr. Archer put the paperwork aside. "Let's rule out if you've had another miscarriage and go from there."

Just hearing that made Brooke wish she'd brought Luca with her. "Okay."

Brooke lay back, and Dr. Archer performed a physical exam. "When did you stop bleeding?"

"Three days ago."

"I don't see any evidence that suggests a missed pregnancy." She continued with a normal exam and had Brooke sit up. "I'm going to run some blood work and we'll get a urinalysis. Did you do an at-home pregnancy test?"

"No."

"Like I said, I don't see anything, but the blood work will tell us if you were pregnant. I'll have those results tomorrow. If that comes back negative, I want you to return for an ultrasound. Make sure we're not missing anything."

"Okay."

"Now, about your contraceptives. When was the last time you took a break from birth control pills?"

Brooke looked at the ceiling. "Not since I went on them in college."

"Not even after your miscarriage?"

She shook her head. "My boyfriend was not ready to be a father."

"If you're bleeding midcycle, something isn't working. Let's assume everything with you checks out. You're young, no other risk factors. My gut tells me you're probably fine. I'm not sure the pill is the right choice for you. I suggest you take a break from the hormones, three months. Give your system a chance to cycle. I'll run some more tests and then we discuss an alternative birth control."

Brooke swallowed hard. "That's risky."

Dr. Archer smiled. "Discuss it with your partner. He's going to need to understand the risk and be condom-ready in the meantime. I can put you on a different pill, but I don't think they're working. We will find something that does. But let's not make every month a stressful worry of 'what if,' okay?"

"Okay."

"Go ahead and get dressed. I'll have someone come in and draw blood. I'll call you tomorrow with the results and schedule you for an ultrasound."

"Okay."

Dr. Archer left the room, and Brooke put her clothes back on.

Ten minutes passed and no one came in.

She poked her head out the door to see if maybe they'd forgotten she was in there . . . or maybe she needed to find the nurse, and she heard a familiar voice.

Brooke instantly recoiled.

"You've gained three pounds. That's good."

"No, it's not. The last time I didn't gain weight until I was close to five months."

Brooke sucked in a breath.

"Every pregnancy is different. You had morning sickness the last time, this time you don't. Maybe you're having a boy."

Brooke closed the door as the people behind the voices walked by.

Holy shit.

A few minutes later, the nurse walked in. "I'm sorry to keep you waiting."

"It's okay." Brooke rolled up her sleeve for the blood draw.

When the nurse was done, she opened the door.

Brooke hesitated. "I noticed my boyfriend's ex-wife come in. It would be really awkward for her to see me here. Maybe I can stay here until she leaves, or you can make sure she and I aren't in the lobby at the same time."

The nurse winced. "Absolutely. What's her name?"

"Antonia D'Angelo. Although I'm not sure she still uses that last name."

The nurse smiled with her eyes. "I'll be right back."

A few moments later, she swung the door open. "Coast is clear. The doctor is with her now."

"Thank you."

Brooke slid out of the office and scurried out of the building.

"Holy shit!"

~

Brooke returned home from her doctor's appointment and went directly to the office and found Luca working.

"Hey."

"*Bella.*"

"Can I pull you away?"

He tilted his head. "Is everything okay?"

She nodded, shook her head. "More or less. Let's take a walk."

"That's never good." He pushed away from the desk.

"We're fine. I have news."

The moment they were out of the office, Brooke took his hand in hers.

He kissed the back of it, told his shift manager he was leaving for a while.

They walked out onto the street, smiled at their neighbors, waved at their friends.

"What's going on?" Luca asked.

"Not here."

"Oh, it's a secret."

They walked toward the waterfront park, and Brooke kept them going until they were down by the bay.

"Are we far enough away?" Luca teased when they stopped against a railing separating them from the sea.

She looked left, then right. Didn't recognize anyone. "Yes."

"You're adorable." He kissed her forehead. "Okay, *cara*, what's your news?"

Brooke took a deep breath. "I had to go to the doctor today."

Luca's smile fell. "What's wrong?"

"Nothing. I'm fine."

"What kind of doctor?"

"An obstetrician."

Luca took in a sharp breath. *"Cara!"* He looked in her eyes, then at her waist. "You're pregnant?" He was smiling. "Please tell me you're pregnant."

Brooke was at a complete loss for words. "Oh, God." She shook her head. "No. Wow."

His shoulders fell.

"Luca, holy cow. No, honey."

"Why were you there then?"

Brooke squeezed his hand. "I was there for a routine visit, but there's a slight chance I might have been."

He looked horrified. "Brooke, why didn't you tell me?"

"The *doctor* thinks I might have been."

Brooke walked them over to a bench where they could both sit down.

"My cycle is really off and heavy and since I'd gotten pregnant on the pill before, she wants to make sure it didn't happen again. I honestly never truly thought I was. I didn't take a home test or anything of that nature. I would never keep anything like that from you."

"But you went to the doctor."

"I was already scheduled for a routine visit. I'll know for sure tomorrow if I was pregnant."

Luca placed a hand on her face. *"Mia cara."*

"Either way I have more tests. And in the meantime, she wants me to go off the pill for a few months."

"Flush them down the toilet."

"You're not worried?"

"About being a father? About bringing a life into this world with the most wonderful woman in the world? No."

Brooke found herself holding her chest and wanting to cry.

"What's the matter, *tesoro*?"

"I didn't expect this." A single tear fell down her cheek.

"Get used to it."

She leaned forward, and he moved in for a kiss. She loved this man. Never felt that more than in this moment.

"Now," he said when he pulled away. "No more doctor appointments without telling me. Next time I'm going with you."

"I thought that when I was sitting in there."

He kissed her again.

"We're going to have to be very careful. Buy the Costco box of condoms."

Luca shrugged. "Eh."

"Luca!"

"You don't want to have a baby?"

"Yes. I do. At some point."

"Okay then."

"What is that supposed to mean?"

He grinned. "Nothing."

This man . . . this man! He couldn't have responded better to the whole *what if*.

"Now . . . for the really big news."

Luca looked at her as if she were crazy. "What?"

"Guess who *is* pregnant?"

He was silent.

"Antonia."

"What?" His jaw dropped.

"Yeah. I overheard her at the doctor's office. Was she sick with Franny?"

He still looked shocked. "Very sick. Couldn't keep anything down for three months."

"She was upset because she isn't sick and is putting weight on." Although Brooke wouldn't know it to look at her.

Luca shook his head. "She tried hard to get me to go to her room when she first got here. While you were in Texas. I always met her in public."

"That won't stop her from trying to say otherwise."

"Easily proved when the baby is born."

"It makes sense now, doesn't it? She's not looking for a sugar daddy because pretty soon it's going to be obvious she's pregnant. Where do you go when you need something reliable?"

"You go home."

"And here she is. And the lies and rumors she's been trying to spread and the attempts to get between us all have a deadline for her."

"The part about her being sick . . ."

"Sick with a nine-month cure," Brooke told him.

"Why didn't I see her lies before?"

"She's a damn good liar, Luca. Cut yourself a break."

He groaned. "I have Franny."

"And she's the world. It wasn't all bad."

Luca collected her hands in his. "Anything else to blow my mind today?"

Brooke laughed. "No. That's all I got. I'll try again tomorrow."

His nose brushed against hers, and he looked deep in her eyes. "I want you to have my children," he whispered.

"Luca."

"When the time is right."

"You better not say that in front of your mother or she'll lock us in a bedroom and not let us out until the stick has two pink lines."

He wiggled his eyebrows. "That is a collaboration I can approve."

"You're killing me here."

He pulled her off the bench and they turned toward home.

Luca gathered her in his arms from behind, placed his hands on her belly.

She brushed him away, laughing. "Stop it."

"No." He reached for her.

Brooke dodged him.

He returned and swung her in his arms. "Thank you for this woman!" he shouted toward the sky.

A couple walking by pointed at them.

"He's off his meds," Brooke shouted.

They were still laughing and playful when they walked back into the restaurant.

They stopped short when the woman they'd been discussing stared back at them.

She tried not to look disturbed and failed. "I see you two are acting like teenagers."

Brooke laughed, looked at Luca. "We have the rest of our lives to act old."

Antonia gave up any pretense of being amused. "I came to discuss our daughter."

Luca indicated a booth in the back. "We can all go over there." He kept Brooke's hand in his.

"Alone."

"Whatever you have to say about Franny can be said in front of Brooke. We don't keep secrets from each other."

"That isn't always true, now, is it?"

"Antonia, let it go. Brooke and I are solid from the foundation up. Now, can we move this conversation from the middle of the restaurant and let the patrons eat in peace?"

"Fine."

They sat as waiters walked by. "Did you want something to drink?" Brooke asked Antonia as if showing her that it was Brooke's place to extend hospitality.

The other woman looked taken aback.

Brooke turned to Luca. "I could use a glass of rosé. And food, I forgot to eat today."

Luca laughed at her. "You've had a lot on your mind."

He waved at a waiter, spoke in Italian.

Brooke loved listening to him talk in his native tongue.

"Antonia, would you like something?" Luca asked.

Antonia responded in Italian—she didn't sound nearly as musical as Luca—and the waiter left.

"I need to learn to roll my *R*s better," Brooke said to Luca before glancing at Antonia. "Franny's been teaching me. She reads me children's books. It's about as precious as it gets," Brooke told Antonia.

"So she's said."

Mari walked around the corner with a cautious smile. "What a surprise."

Antonia greeted her speaking so fast Brooke only caught a few words.

"It's good to see you all getting along," Mari said. "Best for Francesca, *vero*?"

The more welcoming everyone was, the more Antonia squirmed.

"Couldn't agree more, Mama," Luca said.

The waiter arrived, and surprisingly put glasses of wine before each of them. Brooke had a rosé while Luca and Antonia both drank red.

Any other time the two of them having a similar drink or a passing smile would have brought up a boatload of insecurity.

Only it didn't.

"I'll leave you alone," Mari said before walking away.

Antonia lifted her glass. "Our favorite," she said.

"You should try the 2019. It's even better. Giovanni changes my favorite every year."

Antonia basked in what she felt was the upper hand.

But Luca's *hand* was on Brooke's thigh saying, *It's only wine.*

Besides, Luca wasn't wrong about the 2019, it was better. However, it was the middle of the day and as much as day drinking was a thing, red wine would put her to sleep by five.

That didn't stop Antonia.

As the first sip went down, all Brooke could think about was her unborn child. A sip here or a sip there is fine . . . but why take the risk?

"What did you want to discuss about Franny?" Luca started.

Another sip and Antonia put the glass down. "School is out for the summer tomorrow."

"It is."

"I'd like to have her spend more time with me."

Brooke felt, more than saw, Luca tense beside her. "She'd probably like that," Brooke said.

"I'll leave that up to Franny," Luca said.

"Weekends to start."

Brooke and Luca both looked at Antonia.

"What do you mean by 'start'?"

Antonia put the wine to her lips, drank more.

Brooke felt her empty stomach rebel.

"To start."

"I'm not following you," Luca said.

The waiter arrived, put food on the table, and walked away.

"This looks delicious," Antonia said.

As the seconds ticked by, Luca grew more tense at Brooke's side.

"You were saying?"

Antonia picked up her fork and knife, cut into the caprese salad. "I was very depressed when I left." She took a bite of the salad, chased it with wine.

Brooke cut into her food and hung on for the woman to continue.

"Terrible postpartum depression. Clinical depression, if I'm completely honest. More than one doctor told us that, isn't that right, Luca?"

"What is your point?"

Another drink of wine.

"I wasn't in my right mind."

Brooke grasped Luca's hand and squeezed.

"Are you in your right mind now?" Brooke asked.

Antonia dropped her fork. "What kind of question is that? Of course I am."

"You are sitting here with your ex-husband and his significant other talking about your daughter. On the outside, that can look stressful," Brooke said.

"My mind is quite sound, Brooke. Luca's *significant other* does not need to imply that I'm crazy. What does 'significant other' mean anyway?" Another drink from her glass.

"We're talking about giving Franny a sister or brother. That's what it means," Luca said, deadpan.

Antonia lost her momentum.

The silence had Brooke reaching for her glass of wine and realizing Antonia's was nearly empty.

"How progressive of you."

Brooke let the silence eat at the woman.

Luca played with his wineglass.

"I want to spend more time with Francesca. I don't want to have to go to a court to prove I'm capable of doing so."

"No one is denying you."

"Right."

More wine.

"Did you expect opposition?" Luca asked.

"Yes."

"Again. This is up to Franny. If you put pressure on her, then you'll get resistance."

"Sometimes children don't always know what's good for them."

Brooke couldn't stop herself. "You know . . . maybe the wine isn't a good idea for this conversation." She pushed her glass aside and reached for what was left in Antonia's.

Antonia said something in Italian and volleyed for the glass.

It was Luca's turn to hold Brooke down. "I think this discussion is good where it's at. I'll talk with Franny, see what she wants. We can go from there."

Antonia smiled as if she had won and glared at Brooke as she finished what was in her glass.

CHAPTER THIRTY-ONE

Luca, Brooke, and Franny were calling it family night.

Their family night.

Midweek when Luca wasn't needed in the kitchen and the three of them could have a private meal, one they prepared together that looked like Play-Doh but tasted amazing.

This first one was celebrating Franny's graduation from second grade.

Luca looked to his right and then his left.

Life was perfect.

Brooke's doctor had said she hadn't suffered another miscarriage, which gave them both peace. Brooke had been taken off the pills and Luca wanted to convince her to ditch the condoms as well.

He thought about how he needed to physically restrain Brooke from spilling Antonia's wine on her and smiled. His Brooke was going to be a wonderful mother when the time came. Already was when it came to Franny.

"Go fish," Brooke said, her cards in her hands.

Luca picked up a card, discarded another. "Your mother stopped by today," he said, bringing up the topic for Franny.

"Six of hearts," Franny said, pointing to Brooke.

Brooke moaned, forked over her card.

"She wants to spend more time with you."

"Jack of spades." Franny pointed to him.

"Go fish."

She moaned.

"Are you okay with that?" Brooke asked.

Franny shrugged. "I guess."

It was Luca's turn. He moved his cards around. "You don't want to?"

"All she does is look at her phone. And she treats me like a baby sometimes."

"It's up to you."

Franny shrugged. "I don't want to make her sad."

Brooke reached out a hand. "She's a grown-up. If this is too much, too soon, we slow it down. I'm not saying you shouldn't give her a chance to catch up, but you don't have to rush."

"Thanks, Brooke."

Luca had his answer and dropped the subject.

"Oh, I forgot something . . ." He got up from the table and walked into his bedroom.

"Hey, we're playing a game here," he heard Brooke complain.

He returned with a plain paper bag and handed it to Franny. "I meant to give this to you earlier."

"It's not my birthday."

"I know. But it's summer and you are spending more time away from these walls."

Her jaw dropped as if she knew exactly what was in the bag.

She tore into it with abandon and screamed.

Go fish was forgotten.

"A cell phone!" She jumped from her chair and threw herself into his arms. "Thank you, Papa."

"No Facebook."

"I'm eight."

Luca did the math. She was halfway to dating.

"Can I have TikTok?"

Brooke and Luca said "No" at the same time.

"This is so you can call me anytime. Night or day. I'll be there."

The cards were forgotten, and Franny was deep into the workings of her phone.

"Tonight, this is fine, but family time means the phone is put away. Never during a meal."

"Okay, Papa. Thank you. I can't wait to tell Regina."

Brooke reached over the table and took his hand.

They both watched Franny poke and tap around the phone. "Everyone's number is in here."

Luca smiled. "Yup." Even her mother's, much as it pained him to do so.

Franny jumped out of her chair and scrambled into the living room.

Brooke stared at him. "You did that for *you*."

"Yup."

"Because of Antonia."

"Guilty."

Brooke blew out a breath.

Paused.

"Did you put her on Friend Finder?"

Luca lifted the coffee cup to his lips. "Yup."

Brooke lifted her cup to her lips.

Both of them watched Franny from across the room.

~

"Guess who is coming home this winter?" Rosa asked Mari during their weekly coffee.

"Dante?" Because who else could it be, really?

Rosa's smile spread ear to ear. "My heart is full."

"For good? Is he staying?"

"No, but he says he wants to diversify his income stream. Whatever that's supposed to mean."

"I'm happy for you."

"I asked Antonia to find different accommodations by the fall."

Mari lifted both hands in the air. "That's fair. She's not paying you anything and isn't family."

Rosa rolled her eyes. "You'd think I was kicking her to the street. Screaming and yelling. I never saw her like that."

"The woman is allergic to work," Mari pointed out.

"Then she brought a man home."

Mari leaned forward. "What? Who?"

"Some man . . . I think he was in the navy. I shut that down. Not in my house. What was she thinking?"

"Sad . . . really. She knows she can't have my Luca."

Rosa sighed. "I told her she'd be better off going back to her parents, back to Italy, where she could have a place to start over."

"Hard on Franny, but maybe best for Antonia. Her struggle reminds me to give Chloe room to educate herself and find work outside of what I have built. I never want to see my daughter struggle as Antonia is."

"Please, Chloe has worked since she was Franny's age. Antonia hasn't worked a day."

Mari found a smile. "Speaking of Chloe . . . when will Dante be coming home?"

~

Luca sat across from Antonia in the piazza up the street from his home with a calendar on the table.

"Four nights a month? That's all you're suggesting?"

"I asked Franny what she wanted, this is what she said. Maybe once you have your own place and she isn't sleeping on a sofa, that will change."

311

"Are you sure this isn't your *significant other* talking?"

Luca was getting sick of that title. "Leave Brooke out of this."

Antonia dismissed the calendar, sat back. "I'm starting to think that the only way I'm going to have any relationship with my daughter is to get in front of a judge. I came to this country with nothing, and you promised to take care of me."

Luca shook his head. "You divorced me."

"You didn't fight. You offered a paltry amount of money and shooed me away."

Luca watched as Antonia's world crumbled around her. The unreasonable behavior was what he remembered from her first pregnancy. Only this time it seemed amplified. "Your memories of our past are twisted, Antonia. You might need to seek some help with that."

She switched from English to Italian. "I'm tired of you and your *significant other* implying I'm crazy."

"Those are your words." If she wanted to speak in Italian, he'd reply in the same. "Take me to court. Bring a third party into the discussion. Be prepared for a long battle. Not only will I not give in so easily, but the courts themselves are backed up over a year."

"It will be worth it."

Luca didn't let her words get to him because he didn't see her following through.

"By the time we ever see a judge you'll have your hands full."

Her eyes narrowed. "What is that supposed to mean?"

He lowered his voice, kept speaking in Italian. "I was there the first time you were pregnant, Antonia. I remember the mood swings. The impossible ability to talk sense to you. The way your fingers swelled."

She looked down at her hands and quickly pulled them off the table.

"The court may well grant you more time with our daughter. They may even suggest I pay you some kind of monthly amount for that effort. But they will not tell me I need to support a child that is not mine."

Antonia was breathing hard now and not saying a word.

"And the day you think you're going to exploit Franny to babysit your child I will pull it all back to court and make you fight again."

She was seething.

"Now. One overnight a week is what Franny wants. She's happy to spend time during the day, movies, trips to the zoo . . . whatever, so long as it is within the city limits."

Every muscle visible on Antonia's body sat in a tight coil ready to spring. "I'll see Francesca on Tuesday."

Luca smiled, offered a single nod. "Okay."

~

Brooke and Luca walked Franny to her mother's on Tuesday. It was only two blocks away, and yes, at nearly nine years old she could have gone by herself, but they wanted to see Antonia and make sure she was ready for the night.

According to Rosa, she'd had a big meltdown after her confrontation with Luca.

It was then that Luca shared what they knew about Antonia's pregnancy with the rest of the family, except for Franny. Luca had called Antonia and asked how she wanted to handle that news. When she said she would be the one to tell their daughter, Luca let that stand.

Once Franny knew, the world would know.

Or at least their chunk of it in Little Italy.

As they approached Rosa's house, Luca reminded his daughter of the rules. "Call if you need us. Anytime, day or night. Come home if you're uncomfortable. Call to tell us you're on your way, and if it's after dark, wait for us to come and get you."

"I know, Papa."

"And if one of us doesn't answer, just keep calling until someone picks up."

"I know, Brooke."

"I think we're annoying her."

"When I start third grade, I'm walking to school without you."

"Excuse me?" Luca asked.

That was about the sassiest thing Brooke had heard come out of Franny's mouth. "I'm not a baby."

"It's not about you," Brooke said and pointed at a stranger walking by. "It's about him." She pointed to a homeless man on the corner. "Or him."

"That's Charlie, he's harmless."

Brooke rolled her eyes.

"It's about the person who isn't harmless, Franny."

They passed Charlie, and Franny waved at him.

Brooke's point was moot.

They arrived at Rosa's and Franny turned to them. She hugged and kissed Luca first, then Brooke. "I'll be good. I won't eat candy late. And I'll call if I need to come home. I'll be fine!"

Brooke took Luca's hand.

Franny opened the front door. "Mama Antonia? I'm here."

They heard the woman's voice before they saw her. "Don't call me that. I'm just Mama."

It was Franny's turn to roll her eyes.

Antonia moved to the doorway.

For the first time since Brooke had met the woman, she wore jeans and an untucked T-shirt. Her hair was pulled back, and she wore minimal makeup. "Oh. The whole family is here, huh?"

Franny walked past her mother and into the house. "Hi, Rosa."

Brooke tugged at Luca's hand. "We'll see you tomorrow," she told Antonia.

Instead of saying anything, the woman walked in and closed the door.

"She's going to be fine," Brooke told him.

Luca grumbled.

"C'mon. I'll buy you ice cream."

He looked down at her with a smile.

CHAPTER THIRTY-TWO

The wretched shriek of the telephone ripped Luca from his sleep.

Franny!

His hand shot out for the phone, his body came upright.

Brooke scrambled at his side.

He attempted to answer the call, only it wasn't his phone that was ringing.

"Hello?"

Luca turned on a light. It was after midnight.

"This is her."

He placed a hand on Brooke's shoulder. She had her cell phone to her ear.

"Is it Franny?"

She shook her head. "My dad."

Oh no.

Brooke slid out from under the covers. "What hospital?"

Luca followed her to the kitchen, turning on lights.

She picked up a pen and was looking around.

He found a piece of mail and turned it over for her to write on.

She jotted down the name of a hospital. "Okay. I'm on my way."

Brooke lowered the phone, placed a hand on her chest.

Luca slid beside her. "What happened, *amore*?"

"They don't know. He's on his way to the hospital with chest pain. It might be a heart attack."

He rubbed her arms until she looked at him. "Get dressed. Let's go."

"Okay." She nodded. "Okay."

They hustled, dressed quickly, and were walking down the stairs. "Get the car started, I'm telling the others where we are."

Brooke's eyes took on a deer-in-the-headlights look. "Okay."

She made her way downstairs, and Luca let himself into his family's apartment.

He heard Gio moving around in his room and headed there first. "What's going on?"

"It's Brooke's dad. They think he's having a heart attack. We're on our way there now."

"Oh, Luca." Gio turned off his TV and walked to him. "What hospital?"

Luca told him and left him to tell the others.

Brooke was painfully silent on the way.

Luca pushed the traffic laws and made it to the hospital in twenty-five minutes.

They made their way through the surprisingly large number of people in the emergency room lobby to the reception desk. "Joe Turner was just brought in," Brooke said.

The lady behind the glass looked at her computer. "This is your father?"

"Yes."

"And you are?" She looked at Luca.

Brooke pushed in. "My husband."

"Okay . . . give me a minute."

Brooke turned to Luca. "You've been promoted. Hospitals aren't quick to let people back."

"It's okay, *amore*." He liked the title anyway.

"Come around to the double doors."

Brooke held Luca's hand in a death grip as they were led out of the lobby and into the heart of the ER.

The noisy and bustling emergency room. "It's only Tuesday," he said to the woman walking them in.

She laughed. "Yeah, we're slow."

Brooke moved close. "At least we get to come back. When he had his stroke, that wouldn't have happened."

They were brought to Joe's room. There were two people at his bedside, and he was hooked up to an IV, a monitor, and oxygen.

"Hi, Daddy," Brooke said when he looked up.

Luca stopped at the door to give everyone room.

"Hi, baby."

She walked over and took his hand briefly. "What's going on?" she asked the staff.

"He was complaining of chest pain and shortness of breath. His blood pressure is high, but his EKG isn't showing an acute MI. Heart attack. We're running some tests to see what's going on."

"Okay."

"He did respond to the nitroglycerine. He's bought himself a few hours in the ER. I'm Dr. Mahoney. We'll know more in a little bit."

Luca saw Brooke visibly relax as the doctor left the room.

"How are you feeling now, Mr. Turner?" the nurse asked.

"Sh-shitty."

"Dad!" Brooke looked at the nurse apologetically.

"How about on a scale of one to ten, how bad is the pain in your chest now?"

"Same."

The nurse looked at Brooke and started asking questions about her father's medical history.

Luca sat back and watched as she recited nearly everything, down to his prostate exam. None of it written down, all of it in her head . . . and a lot of it.

Once the nurse left the room, Brooke pulled up a chair beside her dad.

"Here we are again."

Joe smiled briefly, then his gaze traveled to Luca. "Nice to have company this time."

"It sure is."

For the next few minutes they gave Joe crap about his hospital fashion choices and perfect middle-of-the-night timing. All of it to get a smile out of the man, which it did.

He looked tired and uncomfortable . . . and older than he had only weeks before when he'd visited for their family dinner.

One of the ER staff poked their head in the room. "There's family outside. We can't have more people coming back."

Luca tapped the side of the gurney. "I'll go fill them in."

He walked through the ER and out the doors. Past the lobby he found his mother, brother, and sister outside.

"How is he?" his mama asked first.

"They're running tests. The doctor is not convinced it's a heart attack."

"Oh, thank God."

"How is Brooke?" Chloe asked.

"She is amazing. She has this whole hospital thing down."

Gio patted his shoulder. "We're here if you need anything."

"They won't let you back."

"We know," Mari said. "We have food."

"Mama, it's one in the morning."

She frowned. "Not for you, *amore mio*, for the staff."

Luca shook his head. His mother's answer to everything was food.

He followed his brother to the car and removed two catering trays he recognized from the restaurant kitchen. They were warm.

The receptionist took one look at them as they walked up with the food, heard it was for the staff, and let them both back without question.

They were directed to leave it in a break room and were thanked by the passing staff.

Before walking out, Giovanni poked his head in the room where Joe was resting. "Hi, Joe, nice to see you're keeping everyone on their toes."

"Doing m-my job."

Brooke stood and kissed Gio's cheek. "You guys didn't need to come."

"Of course we did."

Dr. Mahoney came around the corner. "Thanks for the food. That's really nice of you."

"Our pleasure," Luca told him.

The doctor walked on by.

"You brought food?"

"We're Italian. Food is life."

Gio placed his thumb in the air. "We're right outside."

Luca slapped a palm on his brother's shoulder, gave it a squeeze. "Thank you."

Thirty minutes passed before they saw the doctor again.

"The good news is, you're not going to the cath lab tonight."

"What does that mean?" Luca asked.

"He's not currently having a heart attack. But with his history and his blood pressure, which is having a hard time coming down, I've asked a cardiologist to see him. We need to keep him overnight, if not a couple of days."

"I hope your f-food is better than the l-last joint." Joe yawned as the words left his mouth.

Dr. Mahoney shook his head. "Yeah, it's not."

Luca laughed at the same time the phone in his pocket buzzed.

He pulled it out, thinking it was his family outside checking on them.

Franny's smiling face stared at him, and he froze.

It was almost two in the morning.

He couldn't answer the call fast enough. "Franny?"

"I want to come home, Papa."

"Baby, what's wrong?"

Brooke moved to his side.

Luca tilted the phone so Brooke could hear the conversation.

"Zia Rosa and Antonia got into a big fight. Rosa left and I don't want to be here. Come get me, Papa." Franny was crying.

Brooke turned away. "We've got to go. Something is wrong with Franny."

"Go, honey," Joe said.

"We'll take care of your dad," the doctor said, concern on his face.

Luca was already walking out the door, Brooke on his heels. "We're on our way, *tesorina*. But we're not home. Brooke's papa had to go to the hospital."

Franny cried harder. "Hurry, Papa. I don't want to be here."

They rushed out the doors of the ER and found the others taking up space on a bench outside.

Giovanni jumped up when he saw them. "What is it?"

"It's Franny." Luca spoke into the phone to his crying little girl. "I'm going to hand the phone to Brooke. We're on our way."

Brooke took the phone and spoke in a calm voice. "Hey, sweetheart. What's going on?"

Luca didn't stop, headed straight to his car.

Gio jogged to catch up.

Mari and Chloe close behind.

"Franny's crying and wants to come home," Luca said.

Mari reached in her purse. "I'll call Rosa."

"Apparently she left."

"What?"

"Should we stay here for Joe?" Chloe asked.

Luca shook his head. "They're admitting him. No point in sleeping in the parking lot."

"We'll meet you at home."

"Luca?" His mother stopped him. "Drive carefully. You're no use to anyone dead."

He kissed his mother as he and Brooke jumped into his car.

"Okay. That's fine. We're on our way."

Brooke put the phone in her lap.

"She hung up?" Luca asked as he pulled out of the parking lot.

"The phone was on five percent and she forgot the charger in her room. She was afraid it was going to die."

"Did she say what happened?"

Luckily no one was on the road at two in the morning on a Wednesday.

"Just that Rosa and Antonia had a big fight. Antonia was drinking and Franny didn't want to wake her mom up to take her home."

He gripped the steering wheel. "No more Mr. Nice Guy."

"I agree."

Luca stopped at a red light, no one was there, and he moved on.

"She'll have to hire a lawyer."

"I'll find one for us tomorrow," Brooke told him.

He turned onto the freeway and hit the gas.

Brooke placed a hand on his leg.

Luca glanced at her, saw the worry in her eyes. "I love you."

Her hand squeezed and she looked at him. "I love you, too. She's going to be fine. She's just scared."

Luca saw the speedometer hit ninety and eased up on the gas.

Brooke kept glancing at the phone as if willing it to ring.

It didn't.

What normally would take them twenty-five minutes to drive, took them eighteen.

Luca skidded to a halt in front of Rosa's house and jumped out of the car. He took the steps two at a time and didn't bother knocking.

He opened the door, calling his daughter's name. "Franny?"

Rosa's home was a mess. A table knocked over, a lamp on the floor broken. Dishes everywhere.

"Franny?" He moved through the house, found Antonia across a bed sleeping. "Wake up!" he yelled.

He heard Brooke's voice behind him. "What the hell happened? Franny?"

Antonia stirred.

She was drunk. "What are you doing here?"

"Where's our daughter?"

"She's sleeping."

"Franny?" Brooke's voice grew frantic.

Luca turned to see her put the phone to her ear.

He waited.

"It went to voice mail."

He ran a hand through his hair. "She must have walked home."

Brooke was back on the phone. "Friend Finder."

Luca moved to her side and looked down as the app came into view. A blip showed Franny one block away.

Because of the one-way street, they would have to go around, so instead they both started on foot.

"Franny?" Luca called as they got closer to the dot.

"Franny?" Brooke's voice sang over his. She stopped, turned in a circle. "It says she's right here."

It was an empty street. All the establishments closed. Not even a stray dog wandering around.

Brooke ran to the other side of the street, looked around the parked cars. "Franny?"

Luca's heart raced.

"Did the phone die right here?" he asked.

Brooke put it back up to her ear again.

They heard the ringtone from Franny's phone.

Following the noise, they found her pink backpack forgotten on the side of a building.

Luca lost his shit.

~

Brooke rushed in front of Luca when he turned back toward Antonia's house.

"Stop, stop."

"I'm going to kill her."

"Baby, stop. Think about Franny. Let's go home. Maybe she ran and dropped this. If she's not there, we have to call the police. C'mon, Luca, stay with me."

Brooke had never been more scared in her life, but the look on Luca's face was even worse.

Feral. He was serious about removing air from Antonia's lungs and Brooke knew it.

She pulled him toward home. "Franny?" Brooke called again.

Hearing his daughter's name snapped him out of the rage he was in.

He started to run.

"Franny?"

They hit the back door at a sprint, punched in the code to open it, and yelled all the way up the stairs.

Brooke started praying to anyone listening that Franny was in her bed.

Luca ran through the door first, his cry told Brooke she wasn't there.

She heard footsteps running up the stairs.

"What the hell is going on?" Giovanni yelled.

"Franny's missing."

Just hearing Luca say that made it start to set in and brought a deep cold into Brooke's soul.

Brooke turned to Gio. "Get the police here before he does something stupid."

Luca turned toward the wall, punched both hands into the plaster, leaving a mark.

Brooke went to him. "Come here, honey." She wrapped her arms around him.

He resisted at first and then grabbed her tight.

Chloe and Mari both walked in. Brooke saw Gio tell them the news.

Mari screamed.

Gio was on the phone.

"Have you checked our apartment?" Chloe asked.

"No." The answer was met with all of them rushing down a flight of stairs and calling Franny's name as they searched all the rooms.

"I'll check the restaurant," Chloe said, breaking away from them.

Gio continued to talk to the 911 operator as they searched.

"Franny!" Luca cried in desperation.

That's when they heard it.

A tiny voice.

"Papa?"

They all turned to see Franny standing just outside, in the hall.

Luca rushed to his baby and was on his knees, gathering her in his arms. He spoke to her in Italian.

Brooke felt tears rolling down her face.

When Luca finally leaned back, he pushed Franny's hair out of her eyes. "What happened?"

"I got scared. I know you said not to walk by myself but I . . . I'm sorry, Papa."

"It's okay."

"I heard a noise and hid. I was going to call, but the noise was closer, so I ran."

"You didn't come to your room?" Brooke asked.

She shook her head. "I hid upstairs."

"Why?"

"I thought Mama Antonia was going to come after me and take me away."

"What do you mean?" Mari asked.

Chloe walked back in the room, her hand over her heart when she saw her niece.

Franny started crying again. "She said she was going to take me to Italy and I couldn't say no. She got mad at Rosa. They were yelling and I don't want to go to Italy, Papa. I want to stay here with you and Brooke, Nonna and Gio and Chloe."

Brooke clenched her fists. How fast could a woman fuck up her kid?

Gio stood with the phone in his hand. "Do we want the police?"

She looked at him and decided for all of them. "Yes. Have them meet us at Rosa's. We need some documentation of unfit parenting so this never happens again."

CHAPTER THIRTY-THREE

Two weeks later Brooke, Luca, and Franny stood outside San Diego International, not out of some desire to see a loved one off . . . but to make damn sure Antonia got on the plane.

And for Franny.

The night that took years off everyone's lives hadn't ended until nearly dawn.

A police report was taken, and Antonia knew at that point she wouldn't be left alone with her daughter without a court order.

With the welcome mat at Rosa's pulled up and left with little options . . . Antonia was going home to her parents.

Alone.

Well . . . almost.

The story was she'd been in a relationship with a wealthy man above Napa, he'd set her up in an apartment, and from the sound of it, at least to Brooke's ears, the man was either married, or had no intention of making Antonia anything more in his life. And then she became pregnant.

He kicked her out almost immediately. Antonia had sobbed when she explained what had happened.

"Why not stick around and make him own up to his responsibilities?" Brooke had asked.

Antonia's reply was that he'd said he would keep her in court and make her life hell. Something about the explanation didn't ring true to Brooke.

Luca had suggested, privately, that perhaps the baby wasn't his and the man knew it. And if that was the case, the child likely belonged to someone who didn't have the bank account to pursue.

Not that Antonia owned up to any of that.

And none of it mattered. She had returned to San Diego in hopes of winning Luca back and being a mother to Franny.

When she realized that wasn't going to happen, she felt desperate, and that desperation had made her do horrible things. Unforgiveable things. And now she was leaving.

"I know you won't believe me, but I am sorry," she said to Luca.

Luca didn't accept her apology, or comment.

"Have a safe flight. And let Franny know you're okay when you get there," Brooke encouraged her.

Antonia knelt to Franny's level. "I'm leaving because it is better for you that I go. But I will write you letters . . ."

"Don't make promises you won't keep," Brooke said.

Antonia looked up at her, then back to Franny.

"I will write letters. And we can text and call. And maybe if you visit your *nonna*'s papa, you can visit me as well."

Franny nodded.

Antonia opened her arms. "Can I have a hug?"

Franny moved into her mother's arms, hugged her hard, and sniffled back the tears.

Antonia told Franny she loved her in Italian, and Franny did the same in return.

Standing tall, Antonia put her wide-rimmed sunglasses over her eyes and told them goodbye.

They watched her until she mixed into the crowd at the airport, dragging a single suitcase behind her.

Franny reached up and grasped Brooke's and Luca's hands in hers.

"You okay, sweetie?"

She sighed. "I want gelato."

"Yes, me too," Brooke said with too much enthusiasm.

Luca turned a sideways glance Brooke's way. "You've been eating a lot of gelato these days. Is there something you need to tell me?"

She knew what he was getting at. "No."

"Maybe Mama Brooke just likes ice cream," Franny said.

Brooke did a double take.

"*Mama* Brooke, huh?" Luca asked.

"Yeah. Once you get married, I can just call you Mama. When you have a baby, it will be confusing to call you Brooke when my sister or brother calls you Mama." Franny pulled them both toward the parking lot.

Brooke couldn't help but smile. Franny had zero filter. It was one of the reasons she got along so well with Brooke's father.

"Your dad and I don't have to be married for you to call me Mama."

Franny chewed on that for a minute. "Yeah, but then I call you Mama and people ask if you're married to my papa and I say no and then it's just weird."

Brooke cringed.

"Yeah, that's just weird," Luca agreed.

"Then hurry up, Papa."

Brooke was trying hard not to laugh.

They went straight from the airport to Santorini's Gelatoria next door to D'Angelo's.

Gio, Chloe, and Mari were hovering around, waiting to hear about Antonia's departure and how Franny handled it.

Luca and Franny went inside to get the ice cream while Brooke talked to the family.

"She's one resilient girl. Like with any good breakup, all she wanted was ice cream."

"I'm glad Antonia's gone," Chloe said.

"Me too. Maybe they will have a decent adult relationship, but Antonia has the mothering skills of a rabbit."

"Rabbits don't mother?" Chloe asked.

"Not really. A useless fact I have in my head. They come by once a day to feed their babies for like two weeks and then they're gone."

Gio winced. "That's awful."

"Cara?"

Brooke turned to find Luca handing her an ice cream cone.

"Thank you." She took a swipe with her tongue. "Good call, Franny."

Luca handed Franny his cone. "Hold this a second."

"Where did you learn about the bunnies?" Gio asked, dragging her attention away from Luca.

"I was looking for code words for my own mother."

"Brooke, that's terrible," Mari said, laughing.

"I think she's onto something here. We can call you-know-who Fluffy and we'll all know who we're talking about."

Brooke laughed, saw Luca reach down to the ground.

"Did you drop some—"

She came to a full stop when she saw Luca on one knee, a box in his hand open with a diamond solitaire sitting in black velvet.

"Cara, amore mio . . ."

Brooke's jaw dropped. They were in the center of the sidewalk, outside the restaurant on a busy summer day.

People all around them stopped and stared.

"I have never loved anyone the way I love you. You are my rock when I am weak. My sanity when the world around us is crashing in.

You make me laugh and warm my heart. You're a mother to my daughter, and a daughter to my mother. Please, my love . . . let me make you my wife. Marry me, Brooke."

She started nodding before he finished talking.

The gelato slid from her fingers and hit the ground.

Cheers went up in the crowd that had gathered, and Luca stood.

He removed the ring from the box and slid it on her finger. "I love you," she said only to him, right before he kissed her.

Clapping.

People were clapping.

Santorini's voice sang over the cheers. "My gelato brings hearts together."

Luca ended their kiss, looked her in the eye. "I love you."

"Mama?"

Brooke looked down at Franny . . . ice cream dripping over her hands.

Franny looked back at her and said, "I love you, too."

"Oh, baby." She kissed Franny's cheek.

Chloe took the gelato from Franny's hands and tossed it in the trash.

"Santorini, a fresh one for Franny. Everyone else, champagne. We celebrate!" Mari announced.

The crowd dispersed as they walked inside.

Mari called out to the room that her son just got engaged and a round of champagne was on the house.

"Now I don't have to move," Gio told them.

"Move? No one is moving," Mari said.

"Not anymore. Brooke moves in with Luca, I move upstairs. Now I can stay."

Mari put both hands in the air. "When were you leaving? You weren't going to tell your mama?"

Gio hugged his mother. "No, I was waiting for this guy to do this thing, and now I'm good."

Chloe hugged Luca, then squealed when she hugged Brooke.

Franny ran inside with a fresh ice cream, Santorini at her side.

Staff came out from the kitchen to offer their congratulations.

EPILOGUE

Any excuse to eat, drink, and celebrate life.

Brooke had quickly learned that becoming a D'Angelo meant she'd be entertaining constantly, not that she minded.

Less than three weeks after Luca put the ring on her finger, the restaurant was closed for a formal engagement party.

Carmen and her family flew down from Seattle.

Mayson made it from Idaho.

They'd sprung her dad from assisted living for the day, and even though he was supposed to be taking it easy, he was eating up the attention as father of the future bride.

"He looks a lot better than the last time I saw him," Carmen said, pointing to Joe, a glass of champagne in her hand.

"I'm pretty sure he's on the hunt for wife number five," Brooke half teased.

"Please tell me you're joking."

They both watched him laughing alongside Maria, the grocery store owner who was also a widow. "I wouldn't put it past him," Brooke moaned.

"What are you ladies huddled over here talking about?" Luca slid beside Brooke and dropped a kiss to her lips briefly.

Every time she looked at him, she found a smile on her face. This was really happening. He was going to marry her.

She couldn't be happier.

"Brooke thinks Joe is trying to upstage you guys by finding a future ex-wife."

Luca narrowed his eyes in Joe's direction.

"Maria can cook, but she'll make him work the stockroom."

They laughed and dismissed the idea.

Mayson approached with a small plate in his hand loaded with a sampling of D'Angelo's finest appetizers. "Marrying an Italian is genius, Brooke," he said, stuffing his face.

"Save room for the main course."

He waved his plate in a small circle. "Don't worry about me. I can put it away."

"I'm glad you like it," Luca said.

Mayson hummed and put the plate on the table to his side. "No Portia today?"

Brooke shook her head. "She'll get a wedding invite."

"And when will that be?" he asked.

Brooke glanced up at Luca. "We're talking December."

Luca scowled.

"What's wrong with a Christmas wedding?" Carmen asked.

"It's too far away."

Carmen nudged Brooke's shoulder. "Oh my God, listen to this one."

Brooke rolled her eyes. "He thinks I'll be pregnant by then and doesn't want anyone talking."

As if to prove her point, Luca pulled her closer and nuzzled her neck. "I don't see a reason to wait."

"It takes time to plan a wedding," Carmen pointed out.

"Not when you own a restaurant and have a florist, a baker, and a priest on speed dial."

Mayson simply laughed.

Brooke turned to stare at her fiancé. "What about your grandfather? And Dante? Chloe and Gio said he wants to be here and he's coming in December."

Mayson looked at Carmen, spoke only to her. "Do you think they do this all the time?"

"Argue about the date?" Carmen asked.

"Yeah."

She nodded. "I'm positive. Want to place a bet on who is going to get their way?"

"My money is on Luca."

Luca stood taller.

Carmen narrowed her eyes in thought.

"Don't you dare bet against me," Brooke warned with a smile.

"Not against you."

Luca nudged Brooke's shoulder. "I like your friends."

"Traitors."

Franny ran up with her friend Regina. "Papa? Mama?"

The title wasn't getting old. Every time Brooke heard it, her heart filled with love. "Yes, sweetie?"

"I told Regina she could come to the wedding. She can, right?"

The little girl standing beside Franny smiled up at them with hopeful eyes.

"Of course."

Franny turned to her friend. "See, I told you."

Before anyone could say anything more, the girls ran off.

Santorini walked by with a plate of food, and Mayson tracked it like a wolf to prey. "Oh, that looks good."

He followed the path to more carbs as Chloe and Gio veered toward the happy couple.

"Your son is adorable," Chloe said to Carmen as she approached.

They all looked across the room to find Leroy talking with Mari, Ben at his side.

"Remember that in an hour when it's past his bedtime."

Gio turned to Luca. "I spoke with Dante today. He said he could make it anytime, you just yell, he'll jump on a plane."

Brooke gasped, pushed at Luca. "What are you telling people?"

He lifted his hands in the air, feigning innocence. "What?"

Carmen started to walk away. "I think I need to find Mayson and lay that bet."

Brooke was starting to think it was a losing battle, this waiting until December idea.

"It will be good to see Dante again. It's been too long," Chloe said, her voice soft.

Gio glanced her way. "He hasn't changed, Chloe."

"I know."

"What does that mean?" Brooke asked.

Luca leaned closer. "Someday Gio will settle down and plant his roots deep. Dante is like water in the stream, just like his father. Always moving. Not good for our Chloe."

Brooke looked closer at Chloe. "Then why is 'our Chloe' blushing?"

"Because Dante is gorgeous. You'll see."

Brooke laughed, leaned closer to Luca. "I have all the Italian man I need right here."

Gio said something in Italian and pulled his sister away, giving Luca and Brooke a moment alone.

Luca ducked them into an empty corner of the restaurant and into his arms. After a kiss that shouldn't have taken place in public, he released her lips and looked in her eyes. "You've made me the happiest man on the planet."

"I can't believe this is happening."

"I say that every day."

Brooke melted into his gaze. "My whole world had to fall apart in order for us to meet and land here. Now I have a partner and someone who truly loves me."

"With all my heart, *amore*."

"Thank you, Luca."

"For what?"

"Giving me the fairy tale."

"You can have it sooner if you let me."

She was so close to giving in. "Tell you what. If I get pregnant before December, we do it your way. If I don't . . ."

There was a very devilish gleam in Luca's eye. "Challenge accepted."

ACKNOWLEDGMENTS

Every book requires a village to write, this one even more than most based on the content within its pages.

Thank you, Holly Ingraham, for helping me see past the parts that were personal and perhaps didn't need to be told, and fine-tuning everything else. Working with you is always a pleasure.

Maria Gomez and Amazon Montlake for believing in my work and giving me the freedom to write the stories I need to tell.

Jane Dystel, for every email, phone call, and kick in the pants. You're more than an agent and always will be.

Angelique, my sister from stepmom number three . . . Thank you for being there the day I found "those letters." The ones written in my own hand so many years ago that brought me right back to my teenage days, when I was so desperate to be heard and loved. For standing beside me and letting me cry on your shoulder and let out all the emotion I didn't realize I was holding in. I love you, sis.

Ellen, for helping clean the filth, sift through the trash, count the change, and sell the condo. Love you, lady.

To my dad, who I doubt will ever read this book. Some might read this and wonder many things about you . . . and about me. The past few years have been a constant struggle. And yes, there have been times I've sat and wondered why . . . why am I doing all I am doing, and how did I ever get to this place? But the bottom line is always very simple.

I love you. You have always been good with your grandsons, and that's what has mattered to me most of all. You and I do not see eye to eye on many things, but we have somehow come to a place where we can laugh at our differences or at least say our piece and move on.

Except for that stupid car.

Seriously? WTH?

But in the end . . . I do love you. And am here for you.

Now to Tim.

I honestly cannot think of the last few years and not see you. You were, without a doubt, the most unexpected light in all of this crazy. You held my hand when I cried so many times, I lost count. You stayed on the phone with me for seven hours as I crawled my way through traffic until two in the morning when I finally pulled into my driveway in San Diego. You have given me a mantra that I try to repeat often: "In the worst-case scenarios, the worst case almost never happens." Your friendship with me cost you your friendship with my father, and for that I am truly sorry. I can't thank you enough for the countless hours of unselfish time you dedicated to me and my father. Not only when liquidating the shop but moving him out of the condo. You even put up Christmas lights. Never once did you ask anything in return. You go around telling everyone you hate people . . . but I'm here to tell you, people love you. My family is blessed to know you. With every inch of my being . . . thank you.

And one more tiny word to the reader . . .

My dad was married five times, not four.

See . . . this *is* a work of fiction.

Catherine

BOOK DISCUSSION QUESTIONS

1. Do you think the title fits the story? If not, what would you have named the book?

2. What do you think the main themes of the book are? How do friends and family factor into those themes?

3. Early on, we see protagonist Brooke break up with live-in boyfriend Marshall. Have you ever had to break up with a long-term love? What was the catalyst?

4. The book takes place in a post-pandemic reality. What do you think the author got right and what do you think has changed (or will change)?

5. Brooke's relationship with her father is complicated by a thorny past, yet she continues to support him. Do you agree with her choice to take care of him? Why or why not?

6. Dating someone with children can be difficult. How do you think Luca and Brooke handled their relationship around Franny? Are there things you would have done differently?

7. What was your favorite aspect of the story? What emotions did it evoke?

8. Have you read other books by this author? Which one was your favorite?

9. If you could ask the author anything about the story, what would it be?

ABOUT THE AUTHOR

Photo © 2015 Julianne Gentry

New York Times, *Wall Street Journal*, and *USA Today* bestselling author Catherine Bybee has written thirty-eight books that have collectively sold more than ten million copies and have been translated into more than twenty languages. Raised in Washington State, Bybee moved to Southern California in the hope of becoming a movie star. After growing bored with waiting tables, she returned to school and became a registered nurse, spending most of her career in urban emergency rooms. She now writes full time and has penned the Not Quite series, the Weekday Brides series, the Most Likely To series, and the First Wives series.